THE ACCIDENTAL IMMIGRANTS

THE
ACCIDENTAL
IMMIGRANTS

Jo McMillan

Bluemoose

Copyright © Jo McMillan 2025

First published in 2025 by
Bluemoose Books Ltd
25 Sackville Street
Hebden Bridge
West Yorkshire
HX7 7DJ

www.bluemoosebooks.com

British Library Cataloguing-in-Publication data
A catalogue record for this book is available from the British Library

Paperback ISBN 978-1-915693-17-4

Printed and bound in the UK by Short Run Press

*For all the people who lose their lives
trying to reach a safer shore.*

1.

What is your FULL name?

Have you ever used any other name?

What is your name?

Questions like that should be easy to answer, but what was she to say? She was tired and hungry and locked up. She was an immigrant, a detainee. She was a criminal. An illegal. Weren't those the names they'd give her?

Have you ever used any other name?

The answer to that was yes or no. But things are never that simple. People's lives aren't simple. It would take a story to answer that question, but would they let her tell it?

2.

Date of birth
23 . 4. 84

Place of birth
LONDON

Marital status
UNMARRIED

Name of ~~spouse~~ PARTNER
ARLO BROWN

Date of birth of ~~spouse~~ PARTNER
20 . 10 . 86

Place of birth of ~~spouse~~ PARTNER
HASTINGS

Date of ~~marriage~~ PARTNERSHIP
21 . 6 . 2010

Nationality
ST. MIRAN

What ~~is~~ ARE your main language S?
GREEK AND ENGLISH

Do you speak any other language?
FRENCH. SOME ALBANIAN

BRIEFLY explain why you left your country.

PLEASE SEE OVER →

3

Bombs are falling all the time somewhere in the world. But this one was different because this bomb fell on them. It was a stunning, five-hundred-pound burst of TNT that cracked open the midsummer sky, lit up the east and made, for one eternal moment, a second sun. And from that brief dawn at dusk, though they didn't know it yet, Tess and Arlo were leaving.

It was 21 June, their anniversary, and they were marking it on the scaled-down keep of Dover Castle on the hill above Mirapolis. The Ionian Sea was laid out flat and black and fingered pink with the last of the longest day. Tess nodded in the direction of the water. 'Lucky them in the Old Country... A longest day that's longer than ours...'

The Old Country was 2,500 kilometres away, over the north-west tower, across a sea and a continent and an ocean channel.

Arlo said, 'Though lost now to darkness.'

England was two hours behind St Mira and the sun hadn't yet set.

'And colder,' he said. 'And cloudier. And a different kind of light.' It was one of the reasons Arlo had left. He'd given up on a cramped wet island at one end of Europe to make a new life on an empty bright island at the other. He raised his glass. 'Happy us,' he said.

Tess took a sip. It was the same wine they were given every year as a gift by their neighbour, Vera, who got it from a woman in Euphoria Valley, who wore gold slippers to tread her own grapes and made wine that was honeyed and bodied and long. 'To mark your wedding,' Vera always said when she presented them with the bottle – though they weren't officially married. There was no legal document from the Mirapolis Records Office signed and sealed with the image of St Mira. They just both had the intention, never said but understood, that they were in it for better for worse, for richer for poorer, in sickness and in health, as long as we both shall live.

I do.

I do too.

Tess and Arlo had come back to Dover Castle to mark every anniversary, even the first, because they'd known it was the first year of many. From the start, they'd always been together.

Tess sank into the sling of her deckchair. 'My Arlo...' She threw out an arm and knew his hand would catch it. 'I feel so safe here in this castle,' though really she meant in this hand of his, in the stillness of his fingers. Her gaze traced the crenellations, the make-believe fortress put up by the British a hundred-and-fifty years ago, as they scouted for off-shore oil and declared in English to the Italian fleet to keep their distance, the oil's ours.

Tess breathed deep, swallowing air that was sticky with the sweat of figs and ripe with thyme. It was quiet now. The cicadas that had been clicking their ribs in the olive trees had stopped. The first bats were out. It was just before civil twilight. Tess tipped her face to the sky. She knew that when the last of the sun had gone, five giant planets that had spun through space as if they weighed nothing would keep an appointment right here: the tiny lights of Mercury, Venus, Saturn, Mars and Jupiter would appear an inch above the horizon, threaded along the ecliptic. She knew that the Boom Star, born in an explosion eighteen-hundred years ago would shine over them, because light once made, travelled without regard until people got to see it.

'Thank you for keeping the date,' she said to Arlo, who had been here dependably in the orbit of her life for twelve whole years now. And her life before him had been lived by somebody else, so twelve years counted as eternity.

*

Twelve years ago today, Tess thought she'd heard the Dover Castle bell, and then decided she hadn't because she didn't want visitors. This was her home and she was busy. She had this and

5

that to do: books to read, thoughts to think, and why would they want to come here anyway?

But then the bell sounded again – that hollow toll Tess knew from the valleys, from the necks of goats that were exempt from gravity and shone white against the sheer sides of mountains.

Could she ignore it?

True, Dover Castle was her home, but it was also her place of work. And alongside maintaining the enclosure known as Kentish Town, and mowing the English lawn, and tending the handful of English graves, as per her contract with The National Trust and the St Miran Monuments Board, she was supposed, if appropriate, to grant access.

Would it be appropriate?

No. It would be a child who'd rung the bell because that's what bells were for. Or one of those dull but inexhaustible academics, who'd be writing a monograph on the English psyche and the comforts of simulacra, and want to talk for hours.

Hello!' A shout that carried from the gate to the keep.

Yes, it was one of those, with big lungs.

'Hello?'

But also doubt. So maybe not one of those.

Tess stood on a chair for a sideways glimpse of the gate. She recognised the face, even at this distance. 'Oh, *hello...*' said aloud, it was so surprising. Though, in fact, she now said everything aloud, she'd lived by herself for so long.

He'd only ever said that one word to Tess, and only in response. She'd greeted him with an open face and a comic little wave, which was meant to be friendly, but taken, she suspected, as a gesture of loneliness and need. And he'd said 'hello' as if he meant 'goodbye' – in a bit of a hurry, no time to talk.

Tess knew exactly how many times he'd said that word to her. It was as often as she'd been to the English film nights at StUKCO, where he ran the projector, lined up plastic cups of squash, and flitted in and out of the shadows. Five months, five films, five hellos, which made seven times, including today's.

'He-*llo...*' sung this time. It was tuneful. Soulful, even.

'Tess?'

How did he know her name?

Tess took the Gate Key from its hook. It was heavy, rusty, and left by the English in 1912 when they quit the island because the oil had run out. She opened her door to blinding light and the pent-up heat of a June afternoon. Tess put a hand to her forehead as if fending off a blow from the sun. She watched him, a diminished man dazzling in the distance. Maybe it was the light; maybe it was the future coming to visit, as it sometimes does. But briefly, Tess stepped outside this moment and was remembering it from the haze of years away.

Then a blink, and she was reaching for the too-small gardening clogs that came as part of the job. She scuffed her way to the gate. It gave her time to focus on him: a lithe, brown, skittish object. There was something animal about him, as if alarmed to be out of the cover of woods, wild but essentially harmless. As she drew nearer, he grew into the man she'd seen before – though he looked different from his StUKCO nights. No hat, for one. She'd only ever seen him with a fisherman's cap. It had marked him out as new to St Mira.

'Hello,' he said.

Which made it nine.

'I'm Arlo.'

Tess already knew that he was Arlo Brown, a tutor at the St Miran-UK Cultural Office, a nice man, a curious fellow, still finding his feet, a good teacher, trying hard with Greek, single and possibly gay – depending on who you asked. Because after the third film night, she'd made enquiries.

Arlo had brought a flower. He held it like a microphone. Was he about to make an announcement?

'A rose,' he said.

It was a red one.

'Is now a good time?'

It depended what for.

7

The rose, it turned out, was for the cemetery. Tess led Arlo across the grass, through the cool of the sprinklers that were always on. She caught the tail-end of Karelias cigarettes and the scent of citronella. Arlo had stuffed his trousers into his socks and buttoned up his shirt. 'The insects seem to like me.' His eyes were fixed on the ground as if careful where to tread.

Tess thought most things would be drawn to Arlo. 'You're much liked.' She knew he'd know about the sleights of the passive because he taught English, he worked with words. They walked on, placing cautious feet, staying within the boundaries of the striped English lawn. She said, 'Sweetness is detectable a long way off.'

'It must be sugar in the blood.'

Arlo hadn't been on St Mira long. He'd still taste of England, of shared Twixes and last Rolos.

They reached St Mary's in Castro. It was a rough stone chapel with three-by-two pews and a ship's bell that had called Victorian men to Sunday prayer. 'Here they are, then,' she said. 'The dead men.' The graves were old and worn by the weather, dark moss and lichen filling the shape of their names. The men were born in small Kentish towns and had died of odd diseases before the age of thirty.

And then there was this one, the granite polished, the engraving sharp:

Albert Vertete
Born sadly Newham London 1945
Blown on stormy seas to his destiny
Died contentedly here 2002

Arlo placed the rose at the base of the headstone. 'It's Albert's birthday. His widow asked me to do the honours.'

'Vera? You know *Vera*?'

'She lives directly below me. *You* know her?'

Tess knew Vera from the Records Office. When she'd first arrived in Mirapolis, Tess was forever in and out of the place, piecing together the St Miran side of her family. Vera would say: 'I will follow my nose, I will follow my heart.' They were, she believed, the only two reliable parts of the body. And she'd go into the archives and bit by bit, unearth the certificates of the births, marriages and deaths of every Matzarakis on the island.

Arlo reached down and rearranged the rose, making it neater, lining it up. 'And all this time I've been avoiding you, Tess, because I thought you were here for the sauce.' He meant the Smethwick Condiments Company. They sent buyers out for St Miran olives, which they cured for a year in malt vinegar. It was the secret ingredient in their traditional brown sauce. Arlo also avoided the squaddies from Amyna – the few with a pass to leave the base. Plus the handful of globe-trotting money men, who moved borderless wealth at the Frourio. And as far as Arlo knew, no-one else ever made it here.

He knelt now and ran his fingers through Albert's gravel. Vera had told him to 'pick a stone, any stone,' as if it were a card trick. He had to follow his instincts, she'd said. Don't think. Just pick the one that speaks to you. Vera said the stone would tell her something, and she would tell it to Arlo.

He flicked aside the unripe olives and cherry stones dropped by the birds and retrieved a pebble that was brown and perfectly round. He turned it in two fingers and examined it close, trying to read the signs. 'Does it say anything to you?'

It said to Tess that Vera had set this meeting up. The rose was a ruse to come here and talk to her – possibly even give to her, if things went well. Tess took the stone. It was light, almost aerated. She wondered about saying something cosmic, such as: it's the colour of the planet Mercury, the messenger of the ancient gods. But actually it was just like a Malteser. 'Sweet English things?' she said.

Later, they went onto the roof to watch the sun go down. They sat in deckchairs, their bodies flung backwards, their knees close. They drank wine that Tess had bought months before

9

from the bottom shelf of The Cheap Shop, which is what she drank when she was alone, which was always.

The wine didn't have a label. The owner of The Cheap Shop claimed a cousin had a vineyard, which Tess didn't believe. This was grape juice diluted with something from a backyard still. A small glass, she knew, made everything easy, such as instant sleep, such as things to say to guests you hadn't expected and didn't think would stay.

'So, it was goodbye England...' Tess waved farewell to the wall. 'Were you pulled or pushed?'

'Can it be both? It felt like both. Isn't that Newton or someone?' Here in Mirapolis, he had a permanent teaching job, and it came with a flat in the centre of town and free travel home at Christmas. Back in England, Arlo had taught Skills for Life in a Portakabin not far from Stamford Bridge, on home-match days vying with Chelsea to be heard. It was a long trek on the underground, a short-term contract paid by the hour, and paperwork done at home for free. He'd taught reading and writing to students from around the globe, though mostly from the World's End estate. Millions of British people were functionally illiterate. Think of the forms not filled in, he said. Of the books not read. Of the books not written.

And then the council had made savings, and Skills for Life was dead. Kensington and Chelsea sent him into exile, he said. But he had no regrets. He loved these mountains. He loved this stillness. The island was hard to reach, and it had no beaches, so tourists stayed away. Exile on St Mira was like exile on St Helena but without having so far to go. 'And that's life, isn't it? Unplanned. Unexpected. Complicated. People are complicated. Or *I* am anyway.' Then he had second thoughts. 'Though not *that* complicated. At least not to *me*. And not to you, if you get to know me.' Then he played with his glass, running a fingertip round the rim. Was he trying to make it sing? Or to make the last thing he'd said not the last thing he was saying?

Tess knew about complications, but now wasn't the time to reveal them. So she told Arlo something easy, a detail that could be met with wistfulness, an understanding, gratitude for the intimacy: 'I came to St Mira to scatter my grandfather's ashes. He wanted to be blown on familiar winds.' Stan had been born on the island, though he'd lived in Streatham all his adult life.

Arlo breathed deep as if picking up traces of him. Or was it *her* scent he was inhaling? He said, 'And then you just stayed. You never went back.'

Not a question. How did he know? 'And then I went to the Records Office.' Tess wanted to find out about the Matzarakises of St Mira. And while she waited for Vera to dig out the files, she'd got the job at Dover Castle.

'And no family back in the UK.'

Had he been talking to Vera? Tess finished off her wine. She cupped the empty glass. She'd told family stories before, and people blushed and said how sorry. But it was hard to hear, and if admitted too soon, it came out as confession, as an unburdening not asked for, and you were unlikely to see them again.

So Tess kept to safe things, to Stan – told Arlo how the teenage Konstantinos had left St Mira at the end of the war and got on a boat to England. And somewhere between Folkestone and Charing Cross, he'd turned from Konstantinos Matzarakis into Stanley Matthews. 'You can't go far wrong with that,' the man on the train had said. Tess's grandfather had arrived in England a stranger to the country and a national legend.

Arlo looked at her. Tess watched a question form. What was coming next? Maybe about her parents? How keen was he to know? How keen was he full stop?

'What happened to your mother?'

Could she tell him? That Isadora had lived on a houseboat and taught PE at a Battersea comp and snagged on a shopping trolley dumped in the river on her early-morning swim of the Thames?

No.

Arlo said, 'Or your father?'

Tess turned towards the sea. For all she knew, he was out there now. Nikos Petrou. Fisherman. Isadora had been greeting the dawn in the ruins of Delos as he rowed past. She'd waved to him. Or maybe he to her. But they'd waved anyway.

Tess didn't know what had happened next, how long they were together: an hour or two, or days, or weeks. She didn't know where she'd been conceived: then and there on the floor of the House of Dolphins, later in his boat, or in his fisherman's cottage. But Tess chose to believe they were together for a while because her mother had put 'Petrou' on her birth certificate. Perhaps Isadora had hoped that someday, Nikos would tire of Greece and want to live in Battersea instead.

Or maybe Isadora had decided Tess would be 'Petrou' as a note to self, to remember who it'd been.

Or as a note to her daughter, like the name tag sown into clothes.

'It's complicated.' A finger to her temple. 'I keep my parents in here.'

Arlo looked at her head as if taking the measure – an oddly small head, Tess always thought, for the scale of losses it held.

'You're... to me you seem...' but he didn't know her well enough to settle on the word. He threw her an off-kilter glance. 'You seem balanced, I mean.'

'I'm not balanced. I just have large feet.' Actually, Tess had flippers and she straightened her legs to show him. 'I need them for swimming.' She'd learned to swim before she could walk. And she'd learned to walk on a deck of a houseboat that rolled with every gust of the wind. She was used to putting her feet against ground that fell away. She found out early that nothing was dependable, and if you took that into account, then you stayed upright.

Arlo kicked off his shoes and ripped off his socks despite the mosquitoes. Average feet, hairy toes, Tess noticed. They talked about feet, and compared sizes and the way their toes bent different ways. She showed him how to angle his feet for front crawl. They did breaststroke for a while in their deckchairs. Then they listened to dogs complaining about the heat, and to the sound of their own breathing. It was a still night, the hottest of the year so far, and no sea breeze. It was a gibbous moon and bright enough to soak shadows deep into the roof.

'I'm glad you've got your feet,' Arlo said. 'I wish I had a distinguishing feature. Something to put in my passport.'

Arlo had distinguished himself already. In forty years, he could be just like Stan: rare, ragged, built into her bones.

'What could *I* do with?' he said.

There were so many possible answers to that question, which was probably why he'd asked it. 'Some cool? Do you want to go inside?' Tess took Arlo's hand before she knew what she was doing – felt the heat and the damp and the fact he didn't flinch. Tess knew then that it was inevitable. It was just a question of how they got from here to there, and how long it took them.

They reached the ground floor and Tess went to the fridge. She stood by the open door and looked into that other world that was brightly lit and laden with possibility.

Arlo said, 'I like your freckles.' She had her back to him, which meant he'd already noticed them. 'They're like ellipses. I *like* ellipses. Nothing categorical...'

'You know, in Greek ellipsis means "falling short".'

'I like short things.'

Tess was short.

'Like your name. Is it short for something?'

It was way too early to divulge things like that.

'How tall are you?'

She was five foot two, which was two inches shorter than her grandfather, and why – with turn-ups – she could wear these trousers.

'If you're short, you have less far to fall,' he said.

'It still hurts though.'

13

'It depends what you're falling into...'

And, she thought, how fast. Arlo was turning out to be quick. Tess reached into the fridge and rummaged around for something solid. 'Are you hungry? Watermelon?'

They stood in the dark and ate, making odd animal noises.

And then, when they were finished and there was an awkward pause, Tess became aware of the darkness. She said, 'Would you like to *see* where I live? Shall I show you round?'

She found her torch and swung the beam briefly across the bare limestone walls and landed on her books: books about trees and flowers, birds and insects, *Managing Your Lawn*, Greek Dictionaries. Also coffee-table books on Kent and Dover Castle, part of her induction package when she took the job.

Arlo tipped his head to the side, reading the titles, making a show of taking them in, of being impressed by the lack of organisation. Then he turned round and narrowed his eyes against the shadows, trying to make out what else was in this room.

Which was not very much, and was why her torch was focused here. Also because books gave an impression of a person, didn't they? An overview?

'What are those?'

Those obscure shapes were bowls of figs. That afternoon they'd hung on trees, warm and wrinkled, and as she'd picked them, they'd sagged in her hand with the tenderness, she imagined, of an old man's testicles.

Arlo sniffed the air. Tess sniffed. It was earthy, ripe, rotten, rich. It smelt of the end of things and the start of things, which was exactly why she liked it.

Arlo said, 'You live in a garden shed. My father spends a lot of time in the shed. He goes there to soothe himself with his fossils.'

So, Tess thought, his father retreated millions of years and joined the dinosaurs, and Arlo was in exile on St Mira. 'And your mother?'

'Joy? She doesn't run away from anything.' Arlo scanned the titles for longer than scanning takes, which meant he was thinking things, weighing them up. Then he reached for a book. His hand was aiming, apparently, for *Managing Your Lawn*, and it almost got there. But it was caught in a contrary current, and landed instead on his belt. Arlo's fingers undid the buckle. And then he looked anxious, as if afraid his trousers would do something wrong, that they'd be crass and insensitive and fall to the floor.

Tess had thought something like this would happen, but not quite then. She didn't know where to look, so she looked at the top of Arlo's head. 'You're not wearing your hat.'

'I wear it to have something between me and the sky falling in.'

'And?'

'Vera said it wouldn't today.'

And maybe that thought gave Arlo courage because he pulled his shirt over his head and dropped it.

Tess's eyes moved downwards, past a face that was watchful and hopeful, to a caved-in English chest that never saw the sun. She stopped at his navel. It was small and round and dark. It could have been a full stop, only Tess didn't want to stop there. 'What happens after that?'

'Well, then there's the rest of me.' Arlo undid the top button, undid the zip and eased his trousers to his knees.

Tess's eyes followed them, saw thighs that belonged to someone else: a blokey bloke who was tough and outdoorsy.

'From all the cycling,' he said.

'Where do you cycle?'

'Away from the man I'm supposed to have been.'

The waistband of his underpants said ANDROS. They were grey and thin and local.

'What do yours say?'

'British Home Stores... On the inside... At the back.'

Arlo put his hands to Stan's button flies and undid them with caution, as if they might break. Kid-glove skin, Tess noticed. He eased her T-shirt over her head and cast it into the darkness.

Tess became aware of her breasts. They were small, and kept out of the way, and didn't need a bra, but were big enough to remind her she was female, if she ever checked in the mirror.

'You have big shoulders,' Arlo said.

Tess had shoulders like shelves. You could keep a library on them. Like a mantelpiece with her head as the central ornament.

'From all the swimming.'

'Where do you swim?'

Back to her mother, was what Stan used to say.

Arlo edged closer.

Tess said, 'You smell...' He smelt fleshy and she was about to say 'mammalian,' but changed her mind to 'like Stan.'

'You mean dead?'

'I mean familiar.' It was the Karelias cigarettes. In the torchlight, Tess caught the glint of sweat. 'Come down here. It's cooler.' She led Arlo to the mat on the flagstone floor.

They lay together in their underwear, touching where triangles meet.

Tess knew that in the morning, the glasses and deckchairs and bottle and shoes would be just as they'd left them up on the roof. But also, that the first light would be so dry and crisp and weightless, it would offer them up as dead things, as sloughed-off skin.

'I'm glad you brought me here,' Arlo said.

She listened to his breathing slow. She felt him relax into the hardness of the cold stone floor.

Wasn't that what they were here for? The cool?

*

Over the next twelve years, Tess and Arlo evolved into Tess-and-Arlo, into a hyphenated compound: hyphen, *enotikó*, under one. Tess swam in hidden mountain rivers. She saw

16

meteor showers and twice watched Mercury transit the sun. Arlo mapped St Mira, foraging for food that dripped from trees just asking to be taken. He climbed every peak of the island. And they grew closer, their bodies edging towards each other, so that these days when they came to Dover Castle on Midsummer's Day and drank wine and slept on stone, there were no awkward triangles. Their geometry had turned liquid, their level found.

They looked now over the castle wall, to where pitch black sea met the fairy lights of Mirapolis. Arlo reached out for Tess. He tucked her hair behind her ears – ears that on that first evening, he could have said were big, but didn't. Ears that, in Tess's lifetime, had been called 'curtain stays,' 'jugs,' 'no, no little espresso cups,' but which for Arlo, when he finally mentioned them, were parentheses. Because he liked words. They made her Tess-by-the-way. He said all the interesting qualifications came in brackets.

These days, Tess had shorter hair, but still Arlo tucked it behind her ears, not because it needed tucking, but as a reiteration of who they were.

And that, when Tess looked back, was the last gesture they ever made in their old life.

Because then came the flash, a line of light that curved and collected itself, and rounded into a gaudy bauble that hung on the horizon like an awful Christmas in June.

Then a thunder so deep it could have come from the start of the universe. Tess saw Arlo try to work it out, this thing that had happened that couldn't possibly have happened. She saw him want to run and not run. He went to the castle wall and stood between two suns, casting far-fetched shadows like something religious – like those paintings in the cathedral of Jesus riding rods of sunlight, delivering fantastical news to the world.

'It's Amyna,' he said.

Amyna was the military base.

'That was a bomb.' He took a deep breath and held it, his lungs panning the air. Then he turned to her with a face she'd seen only once before. It was the look Stan had the last time in St. George's and the nurse had broken the news. 'That's how worlds end,' Arlo said.

He was like that. He knew things. He could see into the future.

Then they watched the brief sun die. The sky browned. It turned the colour of old blood.

Midsummer slipped away from them.

And from then, their days grew shorter.

3.

List ALL the addresses you have lived at in the last fifteen (15) years, and give dates:

(1)   DOVEK CASTLE

KENTISH TOWN

MIRAPOLIS

ST. MIRA

JUNE 2009 - JUNE 2010

(2)   FLAT 4

1, EXODUS SQUARE

MIRAPOLIS

ST. MIRA

JULY 2010 — PRESENT

Other people, in other parts of the world, would have known what to do – a bomb would be ordinary, death everyday. But this one had fallen here, on St Mira. Tess and Arlo looked at each other now, as they had that first night, their eyes grasping, when there was nothing in this world except the self and the other and the pressing urge to live.

Tess took Arlo's hand and they went inside and down to the cellar. The light switch was broken, so they sat in the dark in the smell of a crypt, their bodies burning, their feet turning cold, the way people must cool when they die. They waited. They listened for another blast. Tess heard the drum of her heart. She felt the beat of Arlo's. They were thirty-eight years old and thirty-five. Added together, they wouldn't die young.

Tess stared into a darkness so complete it couldn't be measured. She'd only been down to the cellar once before, on the day she took the job at Dover Castle. She couldn't picture now how big it was, how far away the other wall. But she did remember thinking that every grave had already been occupied by the person who'd dug it. She said, 'Is this war?'

'It's always war somewhere.'

But here. Had it come here? Had war come for them?

If another bomb dropped, and landed closer, it would surely be the end. They'd die entombed in the debris of a make-believe castle. How long would they have? People lived for days under earthquake rubble, and in the back of locked lorries, beating on the sides for air. How much oxygen was in this cellar? How many breaths were left?

Tess took out her phone. The light from the screen turned her face ghostly blue. Two thumbs tapped out a message. To everyone in her address book: *Bomb on SM. Dont know what nxt. Loveyou xxx*

She pressed send.

Waiting for connection.

She tried again.

Still waiting.

Had the blast brought the network down?

So *was* this it? Would they sit in the dark to save the battery and wait for a connection and the world to end?

Then suddenly Arlo shuddered.

Tess leant against him. 'What are you thinking about?'

A shrug. 'Nothing.'

Arlo never thought about nothing, not even in his sleep. He said, 'What are you thinking about?'

They were sitting close enough to read each other's thoughts, except that down here, they'd become obscure. 'Everything,' she said.

When Tess looked back, what surprised her most was she didn't tell Arlo how much she loved him. Neither of them said it. Maybe saying last words would make them last words, then a second bomb would drop, and that would kill them.

So they sat in silence. Every so often, Tess picked up her phone, waited for a connection, checked how long it'd been. And every time, Arlo said, 'How long's it been?'

Except that one time he said, 'Shall we go?'

Though, if Tess allowed herself the truth, that's not what he said. Arlo didn't ask a question and there was no 'we'. He said: 'I'm going.'

Tess remembered that more clearly than anything. And it had shocked her: that when it came down to it, that's what desperation did – made everyone alone.

They cycled into Mirapolis through a frenzy of sirens, Arlo's pedals spinning orange, and slowing every so often so Tess could catch up. They reached the half-built houses on the edge of town, the concrete storeys added in the good times and abandoned in the bad. Usually they just looked ugly; now they looked like an aftermath. Police had cordoned off the main road to traffic, so Arlo veered onto the beach path and wound along the coast into the centre. Tess pushed her bike through the slip and shift of sand, listening to the unbroken beat of the waves and alarms set off by the blast, and Arlo bumped over rocks, his tail-light veering like a lost and distant star.

At Exodus Square, fire-engines pumped blue against the walls. The air smelt singed and pale ash had settled like the first sleet of winter. Tess glanced up at their block of flats. Most days, the balconies were flagged with clothing: Vera's black laundry, Rron's white lab coats, the Moros's latest made-to-measure. But they were empty now, cleared because of the fall-out. Even the workmen who'd been there forever, fixing the maple that had broken open the church, even they had gone – their tent abandoned beside the sandpit, the news left crackling on the radio.

Arlo took their stairs two at a time. At the first floor, the shuttered sound of the Moros's turned-up telly. Rron's door was open, TV voices flung into the stairwell. Vera was waiting for them, fretting on Rron's landing.

Tess said, 'Is it war?'

'They say an accident.' Vera looked wrecked, her deep lines deeper. She embraced them, the sleeves of her outfit hanging black like slackened wings. Then a nod towards the news. 'And poor Petris...' Vera drew them closer.

Petris, it turned out, was the baby killed by the bomb. He'd been alive a few weeks, and dead just over an hour, and apparently already a household name. Vera said, 'The only son of Maria, killed in the family home while being nursed through sickness.' She had one of those memories. Vera could hear something once and repeat it word for word. 'The distraught father, name withheld, is now in the care of relatives.'

Vera led them into Rron's flat. Usually she glided, her feet barely touching the floor, but tonight she was grounded, her tread dull. They found Rron on the sofa, moulded into his corner, his eyes fixed on the telly. Ringing his feet, whisky and bottles of beer. The mix had immobilised him. It had clung to his breath and filled the room and covered the traces of Cid-the-cat.

Now on the telly, a photo of Petris the day he was born, eyes clamped shut, fists clenched and thrown beside his head as if he knew life would be a fight. The details were repeated over and over, confirming Vera's account. They showed olive groves where fires were raging, farms alight and livestock blackened. The confirmed casualties were Maria and Petris. It looked as though everyone else had gone to the mountains, as was tradition. From the peak of Panorama, they'd watched their village burn and the midsummer sun go down.

Then the news cut to Parliament House. The Interior Minister had found a blazer and tie and he recited a scribbled statement that looked like a code you could almost decipher as he held the sheet up to the light. He told St Mirans not to be alarmed. This was a one-off, unintended detonation, and please stay at home and remain calm. It was an accident, a mishap, an error, misadventure, oversight... He dabbed at his forehead with a white hankie.

'So can St Mirans sleep safe tonight?'

'As safe as any night.'

'How can you be so sure?'

The Interior Minister skimmed his notes.

'Because if bombs can just go off, what other disasters can we expect? What else is not under your control...?'

'This was not a disaster. It was an unfortunate accident.'

'...Such as the election.'

The Interior Minister paused. He loosened his tie. He loosened his throat with a cough. The election was due in a couple of weeks and the result was on a knife-edge. 'What about the election?'

'There must be implications of a disaster like this.'

'What kind of implications?'

'That's what I'm asking you.'

'We have a national disaster just before the country goes to the polls...'

Because the party that had governed St Mira for decades was in deep trouble. After 2008 and the crash, they'd promised things would get better but failed to do anything to make them better: failed to tax the rich, failed to regulate the Frourio, failed to redistribute, failed to stop the lies, failed to prosecute. Just failed.

'We all know what happened in 2017...' The reporter meant the election that had almost wiped out the Labour Alliance majority.

'That was only because of what happened the year before.'

2016... That dark year when all around the world impossible things occurred. What happened on St Mira that year was the birth of the Firsters. The National Conservatives merged with the St Miran Patriots to form the St Miran First Party.

'So?' the reporter said.

'What?'

So, people had waited long enough. They wanted a change. 'So won't this disaster tip the balance in favour of the Firsters?'

What was this reporter trying to do? Tip the balance?

Then coverage cut to eye-witness accounts of the bomb. People squinted into the TV camera, offering up stories that got bigger and brasher as the broadcast ran out of facts: that light from the blast had lit up the Parthenon, that the boom was heard off the coast of Malta, that the ground shook in Libya. But no-one could explain why a bomb had gone off or whose it actually was.

Rron rocked back and forth, gaining momentum and finally defeating the drag of the cushions to flick ash into the ashtray. He smoked Blue Mountain, grown on the slopes to the south of Mirapolis and smelling of peat and wild sheep. He rolled his own identical cigarettes in thick, dextrous fingers, could work a fag across his hand like a drum majorette. He turned half a face to Arlo. 'Here we go again...'

'It's happened before?'

'Carnage!'

It hadn't happened before, but Rron didn't speak much English, and what he knew he'd picked up from the international press stand at the Mirapolis bus station. He spoke English in red-top headlines.

Arlo said, 'How many times?'

Rron reached for the plate of peanuts and scooped up a handful. 'Enough is enough.' He passed the peanuts to Arlo. It was his Guest Plate with the rinsed pink and brown flowers, crockery he'd inherited from his grandparents, handed down from Albania. Not that he had guests. Vera sometimes spent an hour here, and his nephew, Rrock, who'd taken over as caretaker when Tess had left Dover Castle. But since retiring from the Blood Board and becoming part of the sofa, Rron's life was basically: Rron, Cid, and Time and how to kill it.

He turned back to the telly where experts were taking turns to interpret the meaning of 'accident' and the Interior Minister's synonyms. Rron said, 'No news is bad news...'

'There *is* news,' Vera said. 'And it is that there is no news. Facts are shy. They take patience, and coaxing, and double-checking.' But then, Vera worked at the Records Office and knew how to do her job. She was happy with uncertainty if she knew that she knew all there was to be known.

Tess would know more in the morning. Though already she was sure that this story didn't add up. How, for instance, did they name the victims quite so fast? And get hold of the photo of Petris? And why a mother and baby, which just happened to be the symbol of St Mira? What the bomb scenario said to Tess was: there was an election coming up and this would alter the outcome.

But anyway. First thing tomorrow, the press release would be ready on her desk. Tess would translate it from Greek into English, and Duke – officially Dr Michail Kontos, Head of the St Miran Central Communications Office and her boss on the English Desk – would amend it, then Tess would polish it, and Duke would consider it and reinstate his gems. And then he'd send it out to the world's media, and a few more places than usual would report on events on the island.

Rron watched his clock. On its face, the St Miran red cross. Every schoolchild learned what it meant when they were taught the story of Mira and Georgios: the central circle as her birth canal; the four lines, the spill of original blood to the corners of the island. Rron's clock was a retirement present from the Board – though he still volunteered now and then, thanks to Vera. She'd told him he had to circulate, keep the oxygen of human company flowing in his veins. Also, Vera wanted more of his stories. Rron had always been full of improbable facts: that the iron in our blood comes from the death of supernovas; that it travels nineteen thousand kilometres every day; that cows have eight hundred blood types; that human blood contains 0.2 milligrams of gold.

Óchi!

Naí! And he'd thump his chest meaning *on my heart* – a sound that had thickened and dulled over the last couple of years. And now, Rron spent most of his days smoking on the sofa, his calves rugged with varicose veins and turning blue.

Arlo got up. He signalled to Tess that Rron was signalling – slipping off the furry boots that kept his cold feet warm. He flapped open a blanket and draped it over the sofa. He would go to bed where he sat. Cid had heard Rron too, and he slid into the lounge, taking them in with his citric eyes and cleaning out his claws while waiting for the final goodbyes. Then he went downstairs and out for the night, and Tess, Arlo and Vera went up. At her door, Vera tucked Tess's hair behind an ear. She'd picked that up from Arlo. Then she swallowed her into her black, silk wings. Vera had worn black since 2002 and Albie. And over the years, she'd found the colour practical because when are people not dying?

Tess stood in the scent of cedarwood, used to keep the moths away and 'immortalise my wardrobe,' Vera had once said. Vera used words like 'immortalise'. When Albie had died, she'd vowed to keep him alive by speaking his language. She was going to reach him through his tongue. Vera would read the entire English dictionary and learn the words for all the things she would have said if they'd have had more time. It was a *Complete Oxford*, stamped *REFERENCE* from the Mirapolis Central Library, lifted in 1982 to aid their courtship and never, somehow, returned. She'd only got partway through. But Vera still said things that were polysyllabic and dazzling and started with A to I.

Now she drew Arlo to her and whispered a while in his ear. When she handed him back to Tess, 'Sleep well my lovelies. And pray for Petris.'

Then the stairwell lights went out.

Arlo took her hand and they climbed up to their flat. He felt for the lock, did the Yale. 'At least the bomb was an accident.'

'Though accidents have consequences.'

'*Sometimes* have consequences.'

'Everything that happens shifts the world a bit.'

He did the mortice, then the shove to the right of the lock. 'Yes, the world shifts a bit. But not so that you'd notice.'

They went inside, turned on the lights and opened the windows. They re-lit the boiler, and set all the off-off-offs to on-on-on. It always took a while to come home.

Tess splashed her face at the bathroom sink, chose not to look in the mirror. 'What did Vera say to you?'

'Vera-isms.'

'Were they helpful?'

'I love the sound of her voice.'

Tess loved it too. She sounded like the sea. Her words ebbed in and out. They came and went with meaning, without meaning. But Tess knew what Vera-isms were: they were Vera telling Arlo to keep an eye out for Tess, to steady the boat and bring it safely to shore.

Tess went into the kitchen. She stood still and breathed. Finally, she could breathe. She looked around. This was where they lived. It was their flat with the passport-booth photos on the side of the fridge, taken in England their first Christmas back, kissing four ways and looking too young to be true; *HAPPY 12th!!!* written on the whiteboard in Arlo's teacher's hand; the mouldy potato they couldn't throw away because it was shaped like a heart. This was the flat they'd skipped out of with the bottle of Euphoria to go to Kentish Town and mark their anniversary in that already distant age before The Accident – and right now it looked exactly as they'd left it.

Tess sat at the kitchen table and stared at a radio that wasn't on. It told her the time, that it was very late – and very early – already tomorrow. She thought back to twelve years ago, and how, early the next morning, Arlo had made her a cup of tea, and had a cold shower – there were only cold showers in Dover Castle – then cycled back to this flat. For the next few days, Tess had relived events, distilling and improving them, becoming more adept at seduction every time. She'd looked Arlo up on the internet and found out what she already knew: that Mr A. Brown BA (Geog.) was a tutor at StUKCO teaching Certificate English in the afternoon and Business English in the evening. Also that he ran the Life in the UK course, which followed the bestselling *Life in the UK Test Handbook*.

Then, at the end of the week, Tess took out the mower and did lengths of Kentish Town, avoiding the strips on which they'd trod, and all the while in her head, the moment that Arlo had reached out a hand for the *Lawn* book. English lawns had decided it.

Tess could remember thinking that.

And then the blade had struck the cable, and at that moment, Tess was severed from her old life. Two hundred and thirty volts pierced her hands, ran up her arms and struck her with a blow so sudden and complete, it took her breath away.

And for a while, that was that.

When Tess woke up, she was in this flat. She was on the sofa in the sitting room, which from then on was going to be called the living room because 'you're going to *live* here, Tess, you're not going to die.' There was a bucket for vomit and a bucket for pee and a get-well sprig of clematis clipped from the side of the church. For days, Arlo emptied buckets and delivered bowls of mild food that didn't need chewing.

Then, one morning on his way to the Blood Board, Rron called by with a syringe. He took a sample and a long look at the woman who'd arrived upstairs. When he came back with the results, he looked satisfied. Tess was blood group A, as was eighty per cent of the island. '*That*,' Rron said, 'is the face of St Mira.'

Arlo had gazed at Tess, her profile drawn on the pillow. He said she *did* look like the woman on the banknotes – serene and highly valuable.

Tess was actually only a quarter St Miran. She was also a quarter English and half Greek. At some point that week, Arlo had told her she was lucky to have roots in so many places. He'd said he was sorry, but better to know now what she was getting into: 'My family doesn't really understand abroad.' His mother liked to travel, but only backwards in time, to the clarity and comforts of 1066. And his father, very occasionally, took the ferry to Calais, to look for fossils and pick chalk from *their* white cliffs, and think how strange it was that once we were all connected.

The Browns were extremely English, he said. The family tree hung in the hallway of their Dover home and it reached from the decorative frieze to the skirting. When visitors came, his mother – History teacher and genealogist – would pause to point out how many generations had occupied that part of Kent, how long the Browns hadn't moved.

'It's all right, Arlo,' Tess had said. 'It's OK to be English.'

Even his name. It sounded like Guthrie and Woody, but it was actually Old English. It meant 'protected town'. He'd been named after Hastings, the town where he was born. And Edwin, his brother, was Old English for 'rich friend.' Edwin had taken the meaning of his name to be the meaning of his life. He'd married into a fortune and bought a Grade 1 listed Manor House, where he lived with his two sons, Edgar and Edmund – both Old English. And now he did unaccountable things with money.

'Such as?'

'Making lots of it and keeping it for himself. I'm sorry, Tess, but I'm related to immense wealth.'

'That's all right, Arlo. It's OK to be immensely wealthy.'

'No it's not.'

No, it wasn't. But Arlo wasn't wealthy, so that was OK.

When Arlo was teaching in the afternoons and evenings, Vera looked after Tess. She put an ear to her chest and listened to her heart. Tess watched Vera's silvery head rise and fall like the wax and wane of the moon. Then one evening, when Tess was as good as well again, Vera propped her against the pillows to give her a view of the sea. They watched the scythe of the waves, which was lovely, but also sad, because Tess couldn't help thinking about her mother. Tess had been born with a caul. Sailors collected them as charms against drowning. But hers hadn't saved Isadora.

When Vera watched the sea, she thought of Albie. He was named for the Royal Albert Dock and came from a family that had worked on the Thames. 'Your caul saved *him* instead.' Luck could be fickle like that, she said, and generous. If it hadn't been for Tess's caul, Albie would have drowned and Vera would have lost her husband. 'Your caul saved my marriage.' As did the English dictionary. The separations at sea were fine. What she'd needed was a way to manage the times together. So they'd taken as a marriage vow: *We shall give each other a very wide berth.* Vera had lived her own life while Albie was away, and her own life plus his during shore leave. She'd been all over the world through his stories, had a whole wall of souvenirs. Though one time, Albie brought back Dengue. Vera had nursed him on their sofa, directly below where Tess was lying.

Albie had died.

Though Vera didn't believe he'd really gone. His atoms were still here, only more dispersed. Albie just took up more space than before. 'And now *you* live with us too.'

'For now.'

'For as long as you want.'

'I'm not sure how long Arlo will have me.'

'You know he has emptied Dover Castle? Your belongings are in the hallway. I think he is hoping you will stay for ever. It is why I tell you about keeping a marriage by passing like ships in the night.'

Tess still lived in the living room. Right now, though, she stared at the radio and listened to the low broadcast of Arlo's night-time routines brought to her from the rest of the flat: the snacks for beside the bed, the headtorch, the notepad and pen, the T-shirt for his eyes for when dawn came.

Whereas Tess just went to bed.

On the kitchen table, a pile of Arlo's marking. He'd asked the students in his Certificate English class to write a letter in the present simple telling a new friend about their daily routines – the things they always did, and always would. Tess thought: I set an alarm and get up at 6.30. I have a banana for breakfast. I drink a cup of tea. I do not go online. I avoid the news because I produce the news. I put on my Comms Office clothes. I wear linen because it is cool, and khaki because it is the colour of foot soldiers and I am one of a troupe of civil servants making the Office sound informative in the major languages of diplomacy. It is not a happy colour. It is a head-down, do-the-job colour. That is the way Duke runs Comms. I leave the flat at 7.30 and walk to work. I take only streets named for an event in St Miran history. I walk in chronological order. I ignore the Firster-man who holds out leaflets that most people take and some of them bin round the corner. At the Comms Office gate, I wave at Max and he waves back. Then work begins.

Always.

Tomorrow too.

Despite The Accident, Tess still had her routines.

Arlo came into the kitchen and sat beside her. He moved the marking out of the way and turned the radio so Tess couldn't see the time.

'That was the longest longest day,' she said.

'You know days are getting longer?' Arlo had read it in the newspaper. However many million years ago, days were half an hour shorter and there were three hundred and seventy-something of them in a year. They'd found it out from the growth rings on giant molluscs. Usually, Tess and Arlo would have said *Óchi! Naí!* But right now, it just added to the uncertainty. Tess wanted to say, 'You mean we can't even rely on the universe to deliver the days of the year?' But she didn't. Instead, 'What's your tomorrow?'

Arlo had *Life in the UK* tomorrow. He was on Chapter Four, 'A Long and Illustrious History': the six wives of Henry the Eighth in order. Queen Elizabeth. Mary. Famous Shakespeare quotes.

The Head of StUKCO, Mr Dee, had given Arlo a Scheme of Learning, which was to get through the book by the end of term. It meant five pages a lesson.

Arlo ran his eyes around the kitchen, the one room in the flat where their lives as a couple played out. '"All the world's a stage",' he said. Then his gaze landed on his students' homework. 'Once more unto the marking...' He rolled his eyes at Tess. 'To bed or not to bed...'

They went to Tess's door to do architraves, which was how they said goodnight. Actually, what they said was: 'See you when I see you.' Because sometimes Tess didn't go straight off, and then she'd tap on his door and hope he was still awake. If

Arlo heard her, he'd call her in and she'd say: 'Can I tell you something?'

'Tell me something.'

And she would.

And that was all it would take.

This time, though, Arlo said, 'Shall we sleep in my room? Or at least you start off in my room?'

Arlo's bed was under the window because it was cooler there with the breeze. Tess rolled against him and squeezed the soft tops of his arms. She smelt his neck, which was sweet and lived in. She smelt his sheets, which were salty and lived in.

Arlo's body stilled. Then said through the first breath of sleep, 'Between being and not being, isn't the answer to be?'

But hadn't we already been both? Mostly not here, and now briefly here we were, and then we wouldn't be again. Wasn't it just a question of how long between the two oblivions and how we chose to spend it? Tess rolled towards the window. Her eyes traced the dark body of the mountain, its contours drawn in moonlight: the shoulders, waist, the hip.

Arlo liked mountains because he was a geographer. He knew what they were made of and the slow cataclysms that had formed them. And because from the top, it was like a map, he said. They gave you a sense of place. You had context, became part of the world.

Also, Arlo liked mountains because at the top, you were on your way to heaven, nearer to those who were already there.

Actually, that was why *Tess* liked mountains.

She breathed deep, filling her lungs. On the balcony, the Angel's Trumpet signalled to the night pollinators – the moths and the bats – and the scent of desire sighed into the room.

Just out of sight, the highest peak of the Blue Mountains. It was where Mira, protector and progenitor, had lain with Georgios and peopled the whole island. And now, with a baby at her breast and an olive branch in her hand, she was the emblem of St Mira.

St Mira and St George.

Then Arlo draped an arm around her. She felt the beat of his heart. She felt it slow.

And then it began to rain. It was soft, and smothered the last of the sirens, and sounded like applause as it riffled the leaves on the balcony.

Tess said, 'Rain can move mountains. Water shifts maps. The shapes we know dissolve.'

'Yes, things dissolve.' Arlo sounded a long way off. 'But only in the end. It takes aeons, and you and I have time.'

4.

Have you ever been involved with, or accused of being involved
with, any political or religious organisations?

No.

Have you ever been convicted of any criminal offence (including
driving offences) in the UK or any other country, at any time?

No.

Tess lay tangled up with Arlo till the end of the rain, then slipped back to her room and slept to the alarm. She'd left him looking expectant, as he always did, because something worth noting would occur in the night. And last night must have been busy because now the Alpha flag hung on his door. In shipping terms, it meant: *I have a diver down; keep well clear at low speed.* What it said to Tess was: *Stuff going on in here. Please ignore.*

Tess ate a banana.

She washed and dressed.

She made tea, running the tap because of the lead, then filling the kettle to half. Three spoons of English Breakfast, which was posted over on a repeat bulk order. Tea was the last regular connection they had – apart from the once-a-month call to Arlo's parents – with the country they once came from. The rag-and-bone man crept round the block in his broken silver Mazda, his pitch unchanged for as long as she'd lived here. Up to that moment, life was pre-yesterday. It was ante-Accident.

Then, for the first time since she'd worked at the Comms Office, Tess turned on the radio to listen to the news. Maria and Petris were the only casualties; all other villagers had now been accounted for. Detonation had occurred five kilometres east of Amyna, not at the base as originally thought. The St Miran army was fighting the wildfires ignited by the blast, hindered by a summer that had broken all records. Smoke had turned the sky orange in Israel, Jordan, Lebanon. Anyone with a health condition please wear a mask. Then an interview with Hector Varela, leader of the Firsters, who repeated his long-running anti-mask rant: *St Mirans are a freedom-loving people. We will not be muzzled!*

And Tess turned the radio off.

She watched the timer time the tea, checked the sky, saw the colour of rain.

She wrote on the whiteboard: *Happy Anniversary + 1!* Because whatever the deep-down diver was doing, she wanted Arlo to surface to good cheer.

If rain heavy, please bring in the necessaries.

Arlo was good with plants. He claimed the first word he ever said was 'delphinium'. His mother loved to garden and she used to wheel the boys around Sissinghurst and point out the names of all the flowers, common and scientific. It was a firm grounding in Latin, she said, and you could build a whole empire with that.

Do they really want the six wives IN ORDER?

I love you (= present simple)

And Tess meant it in the present, at that very moment, standing in the hallway in her Comms Office khakis with Arlo doing his thing, whatever it was, on the other side of the door.

And loving him *was* simple.

Especially for such a complicated man.

Tess left the flat. Vera would already be on her way to the Records Office because she went by the seafront for the fresh air and horizon before a day walled in by archives. Rron was up too. Tess could hear him bonding with the telly. Mr and Mrs Moros had put up a sign: *Out of respect for Maria and Petris, we remain closed today. Open as usual at 10 tomorrow.* The Moros family sold cloth and advertised Made to Measure, and a suit was often on their balcony getting its first airing. Their real money, though, was in the big parades. Four or five times a year, you could hear their sewing machines whirring into the night, which was an order from the Church or the Scouts or the Masons.

Tess took her usual route: Catastrophe Alley, which was named after the earthquake and tsunami that laid waste to Mirapolis in 1600 BC. Then along the year of Mira's birth, via the martyrdom of George of Lydda – later St George – in 303. The rain had made mud of the ash from the fire, and cleaners were scraping it up on Willoughby Street. He was the man who'd arranged the exodus of the British in 1912 and in exchange had secured the Treaty of Friendship, guaranteeing in perpetuity the maintenance and safeguard of all British interests. At the time, that was Kentish Town, a string of red letterboxes and a liking for afternoon tea.

Tess crossed Junkers, formerly Fountain Square and re-named for the downing of a Ju 88 A-4. The captured pilot was the only German to set foot on the island in the whole of the War. The Firster-man had friends with him today, and they threw loud chit-chat against walls pock-marked by the weather. It was last night's bomb they were enacting, their cheeks exploding, arms throwing up shrapnel, their armpits damp even before the heat of the day.

At Plebiscite Circus – the decision not to become part of Greece – workers wound into the office for their eight o'clock start. One or two were wearing masks. Costas sat under the oleander and dragged 'As Lambs to the Slaughter' from the belly of an accordion. Tess paused at the newsstand. All the papers had front-page bomb-spreads. *The Enquirer* had somehow got hold of a picture of Petris being breast-fed. Left breast, swaddled child, the emblem of St Mira.

You couldn't make it up.

Though Tess worked at the Comms Office so she knew that quite often you could.

The flag on the cupola was at half-mast. She waved to Max, who opened his hatch and put his face out, ruddy and petulant, like the gatekeeper in *The Wizard of Oz*. 'Morning, Miss Tess.' He addressed every translator in the language of their Desk. Then he beckoned her over. 'I have to check identity.'

'You know who I am.'

Max levered his eyebrows in the direction of the security camera. For the first time ever, the red light was on. Mouthed through his moustache: 'They check the checkers.'

She handed over her security pass.

Max made a show of copying down the details, consulting his watch, noting the time in the ledger.

Was checking the checkers a good thing? Tess wasn't sure. And should someone check the checkers checking the checkers?

'But why?' she said. 'Not because of yesterday?'

'Because because.' It was Max's answer to everything. At his interview, the Head of Security had said: 'If someone asks you a sensitive question – even someone you know, even your superior – and especially a *why* question because, let's not forget, all *why* questions are sensitive: how would you respond?'

Because because.

Why?

Because because.

That had got him the job.

Tess ran up the front steps and took the brass handle in both hands, leaning back to let her weight swing the main door open. It reminded her of childhood and playgrounds, and she knew it was the last innocent thing she'd do all day. Usually, the atrium echoed to sensible heels ticking on marble, but this morning, it was mayhem. The corridors were strewn with cameras and mics – left to the TV Centre, right to Radio – and crews stumbled over their own cables in the rush to get hold of the news.

Tess crossed the chaos and went through the double doors into Translation. On the ground floor, French and German because of Europe; on the second, Arabic because of proximity and Spanish because of the conquistadors. On the third: Chinese since China's rise and Russian since recently. English had been the first to move in and had taken possession of the whole top floor. Translation was a small, familial place to work. Fourteen staff, two per language, enough to cover the rhythms of the island: the harvests, the rise and fall of the Frourio, routine press releases from Amyna.

Tess's desk was as she'd left it, which was empty, apart from today's first translation. Duke was always in the office before her, and was usually quiet and reading the papers, though today he'd settled in on the phone.

Tess read:

June 22, 07:00, Statement from the Prime Minister:

The events of last night are much to be regretted, not least the tragic loss of life. Several friendly nations have access to the facilities at Amyna. Enquiries are underway, and all parties are co-operating fully to determine the cause of the accident. A report will be released as soon as investigations are complete. The thoughts of the government, and of all St Mirans, go out to Georgios Papadopoulos, who has lost his wife, Maria, and their son, Petris.

Tess's task was to translate that from Greek into English, word for word, 'Nothing added, nothing taken away,' as Duke had told her on her first day, quoting an ad for St Mira's best-selling olive oil. The *new* news was the father's name. So, it was another G-and-M pair, the most popular coupling on the island. For years, until the internet and phones took over, peak viewing on Saturday night was *G&M*. It was a kind of *Blind Date*, where single men called Georgios in its various spellings asked women called Mira, or Myra, or Maria, or Mary, or anything reminiscent of the patron saint of the island, 'What would you do *if...*' The scenarios always involved good fortune because to imagine mishap was to invite mishap. And because St Mirans loved the sun and couldn't believe it might ever stop shining.

Duke gave Tess a few minutes for the translation, then opened his door a fraction. It was the sign that she should go in. She spun her globe, dotted with a felt-tip for St Mira. She watched the turn of the island slow and friction bring earth to a stop. It gave Duke time to get back to his seat and to keep the breadth of his desk between them. When she went in, she knew, his eyes would be resting on his Rudyard Kipling: 'Words are, of course, the most powerful drug used by mankind.' It was framed and placed in that corner of the desk where you'd otherwise have a photo of family, just a glance away.

She held out her translation and Duke set it aside without looking. They didn't say good morning. It was practice on the English Desk to pretend they never left the office. Sometimes, according to Max, Duke didn't.

'The Prime Minister's words are no longer relevant.' He still hadn't made eye contact. It meant Tess wasn't to speak. 'I have been on the telephone.' In fact, Duke had several colour-coded phones – red, blue, green and yellow – and they were lined up on his desk like something out of playschool.

'And I have new intelligence from key sources.' He moved his attention to the certificate of his Ninth Dan Black Belt in Taekwondo. Duke was a Grand Master. Today, he wore his red-and-white St Miran tie, which meant an official engagement later. He bought shirts a size too small which stressed the buttons and measured his time in the gym.

And still he didn't look at her.

'I am in possession of disturbing facts. Facts that are not attributable but are utterly reliable.'

Even for Duke, this was a long drum-roll. Tess shifted her weight. In any other office, she'd be asked to take a seat, but Duke didn't offer comfort to the people he worked with. Sometimes, Tess wished life was simpler and that she could just teach Certificate English to pensioners wanting holiday phrases, and recite royal successions and the wives of Henry the Eighth. She wondered what the correct order was. She wondered what kind of a man would have his wife beheaded. Duke didn't have a wife. At least none that he'd ever mentioned or that any colleague on any Desk had detected. Plus, he sent his shirts out to be pressed, and if he had a wife, she'd be the type who'd do that for him.

41

'The accident,' Duke said, 'was not an accident.' He was motionless after that. Duke was deliberate in all his movements, his muscles focused, including his tongue. He could ventriloquise anything. Duke could sound St Miran, or Greek, British or American. He could mimic the British speaking French. He could be a St Miran with a Smethwick accent. Duke could be anyone.

And now the silence must have lengthened long enough because his cold, globular eyes swung round till they stopped on Tess.

She knew not to contradict him. She wasn't going to say, 'But the Prime Minister's statement says it *was.*' So she came up with a wording that added nothing and took nothing away. 'It *wasn't* accidental.'

'The word is "deliberate".'

When Tess had first met Duke, he'd worn glasses and they'd warmed his face and softened the look. But then he'd made enquiries on the ground floor about German laser technology, and now he saw perfectly with eyes she knew from just below the surface of turbid garden ponds.

He placed a sheet in front of her. They were notes he'd made from his phone call. Anyone else would have scribbled them, but these were in the hand of a man who had total motor control:

- Warhead type: Mk82 Enhanced GP bomb
- Warhead: 500 pound
- Manufacture: Raytheon UK
- Accessible to foreign forces operating on base: UK, FR, DE
- Air burst 50m
- Secure comms intercepted 20.06, 21.06 confirm intent
- Casualties: x1M; x1F
- Area of collateral damage: 7 square kilometres
- Estimated loss in dollars: 12 million

'I want a press release in twenty.'

Duke was in a hurry. Tess said, 'Has anyone claimed responsibility?'

He tipped his chin to the sheet. '*Has* anyone?'

'But why would anyone want to attack St Mira?'

'Where does it say "attack"?'

So, we were looking at a non-offensive deliberate explosion. What was that? Sabotage? Theatre? And if so, who was doing the staging? Tess said, 'Why would anyone want to make trouble at the base?'

In her head: *Because because.* Duke, she knew, would say something more sophisticated than that. He had a PhD in Law. His answer would be referenced, precise and evasive. He said, 'How would *you* respond to that?'

If she hadn't been at the office, Tess would have said: you make trouble at the base if you get something out of it – such as unnerving an electorate and promising if elected to take back control. Or, if you want to oust the countries that use the base and get to use it yourself. A third of St Mira's income came from leasing Amyna. But maybe there'd been a better offer? Who would like a foothold in the Mediterranean? China? Not China. They were busy eying up islands in the Pacific. Russia? They had interests in Syria, but wouldn't they want a presence further west?

So, the Firsters, then. Or Russia. Or both.

That's what she'd have said if she wasn't at the office. But here she was in front of Duke, and he was getting bored. So she just repeated what he'd often made clear: 'My job is merely to put grammar around the facts.' The word 'merely' was one of Duke's favourites. He used it for all the important things. He enjoyed British understatement. Duke was merely Head of the Central Communications Office. He merely controlled all the information leaving St Mira in the world's leading languages. On difficult days at the office, Tess reminded herself that one day Duke would merely die.

He raised a hand towards the door, showing Tess out from his seat. 'Thank you.'

That was the nicest thing he'd said for a long time.

'Thank you too, Dr Kontos.' Duke was never without his title at the office.

Tess went back to her seat. She spun on it a few times. She had to get her bearings in this changed landscape. Till today, 500 pounds measured the export of olives, and the most violent thing that ever happened was a winter storm. But was St Mira now the stage for political theatre? Had the new world order just arrived?

Tess went online and found out that GP meant 'general purpose'. Also that 7 square kilometres was approximately the size of Gatwick airport. She took her time constructing sentences from Duke's bullets. She worked hardest on the 'comms intercepted' line because that was the claim that made the accident deliberate. How to word it to mean: someone says (though can't say who) that they heard someone saying (though can't say who there either) something or other (though can't say what)?

The rest of the morning, Duke spent on the phone, emailing her tasks through the wall. At just before twelve, Tess left what she'd done on her desk and went out for lunch. She knew that Duke would read her work in her absence and make a mental note of the things he didn't like. And then, when she handed it in, he'd peruse it as if for the first time, his amendments spooling from his silvery tongue, as if all spontaneous brilliance.

She headed to Dimitri's for a chat and the Daily Special, which would be the same as every day. They talked about the weather and the state of the world, and Dimitri would nod to the crucifix sticky with cooking fat. He'd wipe his hands on his dishcloth, which he wore round his neck as if running a café were a form of boxing. Sometimes, he'd heave his shoulders, which once had hauled in full nets of mackerel, as if the world were too confusing, he really didn't know.

Except today, Tess never got to Dimitri's. She was diverted by music being broadcast over the town. It was the folk song, 'Oh, Mira, Maiden Fair'. The song was reserved for National Day. Had today had been turned into a day for the nation?

Tess followed the music, which led her in the direction of Junkers Square. There were more people than usual in the lunchtime streets and everyone seemed to know each other. Or maybe just being here, heading this way, meant they recognised each other, they were here for the same thing. Volunteers were giving out St Miran flags and black armbands. There was something religious about it, a fervour in the air that Tess knew from Easter and All Souls' and parades made baroque by Mr and Mrs Moros.

She turned the corner into Junkers. The fountain switched off by the council to save on water had been turned into a stage – covered with decking and draped with wreaths. And there he stood in extravagant mourning with a black sash and fedora: Hector Varela. Didn't Tess recognise that suit? Wasn't that the one with the wide lapels that had hung on the Moros's balcony not so long ago?

Tess kept to the edge of the square, close to the pensioners who relaxed with their worry beads. She leant against the marble of the All Saints Bank. The walls were still gashed from 2008 when people took axes to get to the ATMs. Things turned bad that year, and although most people had recovered, some had recovered more than others. Some had recovered so much, they seemed better off than before 2008. Better off *because* of 2008. Hence the gated villas, the security guards and the private coast road to the Frourio. You could say: hence Hector Varela.

The man had always struck Tess as newly hatched: it was the overreaching mouth with the downturned corners, the punkish look of fifties hair loss; the eyes that hadn't quite opened. Except today he was wearing mirrored shades. He was facing south, and the sun lit up both lenses. Two suns, just like yesterday. Now he raised an arm for a wide sweep of Junkers. 'Ladies and gentlemen, I am deeply moved. Thank you all for coming. What a *momentous* show of support.' There were probably five hundred people here and they were all facing Varela. In their heads, the whole of Mirapolis could have been crowded behind them. 'We come in mourning, we come in sadness, we come in respect for two innocent St Mirans who perished last night. A mother. Twenty-five. A baby. Six weeks. And now mother and child are gone. And we knew them, didn't we. We knew them well.'

No we didn't, Tess thought. We hadn't heard of them till yesterday.

'I offer you two simple words: Maria.'

Pause.

'Petris.'

Varela bowed his head. Everyone took their cue – apart from his security detail, his men in black with their wrap-around shades and faces swivelling like mechanical toys.

After a while, Varela glanced at his watch.

Tess glanced at hers. Half a minute which would serve as one.

'Ladies and gentlemen, friends, we come here to mourn, yes, but we also come in anger – *righteous* anger – that this was allowed to happen.'

Murmurs from the crowd. The man beside Tess speeded up his worry beads.

'So how *did* it happen? In truth, we all know, don't we. Because of *foreigners*. Maria and Petris's family have farmed that land for generations. But who do they have as neighbours? Foreigners. Foreigners came and parked themselves at the base next door. In perpetuity, I might add.'

The British wanted Amyna because it had the only deep harbour on the island. They paid to use it, an arrangement guaranteed by the Treaty. But then they sublet to certain allies and that way got the money back. That was how Friendship worked.

'And where are *our* forces, the brave lads who at this moment are still fighting to put out last night's blaze? The heroes who risk their lives to defend the country of their birth? Packed off, round the corner, out the back, servant's entrance. And what do they have? A fine view of the mess of Africa, thank you very much.'

An eddy of swearing at that.

'Now, our foreign friends are supposed to stay on the base – that's the deal, as we all know. But do they? Not if they can get a pass, and how hard is that? And then squaddie wives come over, stay at the Holiday Inn, love it so much they don't want to leave.'

Not many foreigners settled on St Mira. The expat community was different from other places. There were no beaches for one, and no commercial airport, so you couldn't just get on a plane and be home in a couple of hours.

'Next thing you know, we've got whole families coming over – kids, grandparents, why-not-bring-the-in-laws – not a word of Greek, buying up our villas and putting a lock on the gate.'

A handful of streets in Mirapolis were known as 'Little Smethwick'. There was a pub that showed Premier League and ran a quiz on Friday nights. Also a fish-and-chip shop that had a deal with Mirapolis bus station – took their unsold papers and wrapped your chips in yesterday's UK news. The Germans had followed each other from a village in Hesse to one on the south coast, known locally as 'Dorf'. And the Greeks had come over in the millennial building boom when the government tried to turn St Mira into a tourist spot after all. They'd stayed on when it all collapsed and now they lived in the half-built resort of Parádeisos, its artificial beach claimed by the sea.

Varela said, 'When I'm in a bar enjoying a quiet drink and I hear *foreign*, I feel awkward. It spoils the mood. Parts of St Mira are unrecognisable, they're like a foreign land.'

Migrants to St Mira had stuck together, it was true, because the reality was it helped: with the language, with finding somewhere to live, getting into the tax system, the health system, getting a bank account, with finding work or even just finding a plumber. It wasn't easy being an immigrant – even a welcome one.

'*BUT!*' Varela put finger to the sky like a lightening rod for a higher power. 'In just under a fortnight, ladies and gentlemen, we have an appointment with history. We will tell this blood-sucking, soul-destroying, misery-inducing government exactly what we think of them. We. Will. Take. Our. Country. Back!'

Whoops of joy. Whistling. Someone had started to drum.

'Now, some of you, I know, have voted in the past for the Labour Alliance. That's understandable enough. They *seemed*, didn't they, the natural choice. They *presented* themselves as the ordinary, hardworking party of ordinary hardworking people.'

The Labour Alliance had been in office since the seventies. They'd introduced a universal basic income, free education, cheap public transport, and funded a health system that meant you could see a doctor or a dentist in a day. Until 2008 and things had turned bad and it'd all started to crumble.

'*BUT* is this government *ordinary* anymore? No. They are responsible for *extra*-ordinary failures. Like the base. Like Maria and Petris. Like the coming cover-up. Like the foreigners. And hardworking? No! Lax. Lazy. Incompetent. Time to be fired!' Varela slipped a hand into his jacket and waited till he'd pocketed all the applause.

'But that, ladies and gentlemen, is in the future. Two weeks. And a lot can happen in a fortnight. We are here today to respond to what is...' Varela's eyes swept the faces, his twin suns lighting up the crowd. '...nothing short of a national emergency.' He pointed into the audience. 'And I can see you're ready...'

Did he mean the guns? Several men were carrying rifles. Every family on St Mira had a firearm. They were brought out for births, marriages, funerals, feuds. All life events were marked with gunshot.

'Now, our friends in the media are already portraying last night's appalling attack as an accident. But they *have* not – and they *will* not – fool me. And they *will* not, I know, fool you. There is tangible anger.' He made a show of feeling it, rolling the air between two fingers as he must have felt the black serge as he put in his order with Mr and Mrs Moros. 'A lot of nonsense will be spouted in the coming days about "taking time," and "collating the evidence," and "verifying the facts," but I'll tell you this for a fact: we don't need time to know that the symbol of this nation has been desecrated.'

A gun went off, a pop into the sky.

Varela said, 'We will find the culprits and kick them arse over heel out of here. And until that glorious moment: Any. Single. One of them. Could. Have. Done it.' His gaze cruised the crowd. 'Shall we name them?'

'The frogs!'

'Of course.'

'The eighty-eights!'

'Thank you.'

'The yanks!'

'Could well be.'

Could it be? The U.S. had been in the Med for decades and they'd just expanded their presence in Greece. Did they really need St Mira?

'The fish-and-chips!'

'Ah, yes! Our dear and *longstanding* friends the fish-and-chips.'

Suddenly, the cool of the All Saints Bank was cold. Tess moved away from the wall. She turned her back to the rally, got out her phone, cupped a hand over her mouth, and dialled Vera's number.

Vera answered before it had rung: 'You know it wasn't an accident? They're saying it was an attack.'

'Who's saying?'

'They're saying it was the foreigners.'

St Mira had a population just under a quarter of a million. It was roughly the size of Wolverhampton. Almost everyone in the world was a foreigner. Tess was a foreigner. '*I'm* a foreigner.'

'No you're not.'

Tess had two passports. She spoke Greek and English. She had a St Miran grandfather and a half-St Miran mother.

'You come from here. You have relatives on the island.'

Vera had unearthed Stan's sister when Tess first arrived on St Mira.

'You keep up with family.'

Tess had gone to visit her. There was such a family likeness, she could have been Stan in a headscarf.

'You care about blood, Tess.'

Tess had described Stan's life in England, and his sister nodded as if she could imagine taking the tube to Tottenham Court Road, eating dolmades in the café in Coptic Street, and spending nights guarding Greek and Roman Life in Room 69 at the British Museum.

'This is your home,' Vera said. 'Your roots are here.'

Tess had drawn the family tree in the dust on the farmhouse floor: that was Stan, and that was his daughter, Isadora, who drowned. And here I am, Stan's granddaughter, your great-niece.

Not long after, Stan's sister had died.

Tess said, 'Last night, the bomb was an accident. This morning it's deliberate. No-one can establish facts that fast.'

'In my experience, it depends who does the establishing.'

Tess looked back at Junkers. Varela had put down the mic and was reaching for hands that wanted to touch him. People threw coins at the fountain the way they always used to, showering him with luck. Varela scooped them up and cast the coins back. '*Your* money, *your* good fortune. *Your* country, ladies and gentlemen.'

'You know they're blaming fish-and-chips.' Tess was a fish-and-chip.

'You are not a fish-and-chip.' Vera paused. 'And anyway, Tess, you *love* fish and chips. We *both* do. Fish and chips are our madeleines.'

Vera loved them because she and Albie had had them on their wedding night.

'Tess, you love fish and chips because of Stan. Because of the lido.'

Because after Isadora died, she'd gone to live with her grandfather, and he'd taken her to the pool to help her over the fear of drowning.

'Remember: fish and chips equals the man you love.'

She and her grandfather had sat in a corner eating cod and chips and watching swimmers get out of the water. 'That one still breathes,' Stan would say. 'And look, she gets out and laughs, even.'

Vera said, 'When you hear the word "fish-and-chip," think of Stan and what he told you.' Vera knew it off by heart: '"In general, Tess, things work out. On average in life, people stay alive."'

At the edge of the square, rifles tipped into the sky and let off a ripple of thunder. It was co-ordinated, orchestrated, a military salute.

A pause while Vera made sense of the sound. 'You're not *there*? You are not at *Junkers*?'

So, she knew about the rally too.

'What your grandfather said was true.' Vera's voice had stopped persuading. 'On average, in life, people *do* stay alive. But...'

What she said next was drowned out by gunfire.

In Tess's head: *...these are not average times.*

5.

Have you travelled to the UK in the last ten years? If 'yes' please provide details.

YES.

I SPEND CHRISTMAS EVERY YEAR WITH MY PARTNER AND HIS PARENTS AT THEIR HOME IN DOVER, KENT (APPROX ONE WEEK).

Do you have any relatives in the UK? Give name, nationality, relationship to you, permission to be in the UK.

YES.
1) JOY HARRIET BROWN
   BRITISH
   PARTNER'S MOTHER
   BORN IN KENT AND LIVED THERE ALL HER LIFE.

2) ELMER ALAN BROWN
   BRITISH
   PARTNER'S FATHER
   ALSO BORN IN KENT AND LIVED THERE ALL HIS LIFE.

3) EDWIN RODNEY RALPH BROWN
   BRITISH
   PARTNER'S BROTHER
   BORN IN THE UK, NOW LIVING IN SURREY WITH WIFE AND TWO SONS.

A week after the bomb, it was the monthly phone call with Arlo's parents, a ritual established twelve years before when he'd arrived on St Mira and rung to say he was here. Joy had entered it into her online diary: event: hear from Arlo; repeats: last Tuesday of the month; category: THE BOYS; colour: Brown; ends: never. Never, Joy had told them, because she knew from the lightness – and the gravity – of his last goodbye, that Arlo wasn't planning to come home.

The calls were scheduled for nine pm UK time, eleven on St Mira, which was when Arlo was back from class, and he'd eaten, and changed and shed the day from his skin. It was late for Tess with her six-thirty start, but the phone was on speaker, so she sank into the sofa and sipped at wine and let the sound of mother-and-son lull her into semi-sleep.

'Hello, Mum.'

'Hello Arlo my love hello Tess my lovely how are you both?' Said like that, one pent-up, unpunctuated stream of goodwill.

'Fine. Doing well.'

'You *sound* well.'

'We *are* well. And you?'

'Better for hearing your voice.'

The calls always started that way. Tess liked to listen to this kind of exchange: familiarity and tenderness offered across the breadth of a continent. She knew Arlo liked it too – she could tell from the way his voice dropped a tone. Also because he'd said so. The sound of Joy was something he'd known all his life, a voice he'd heard since his ears were forming, at eighteen weeks or thereabouts. His mother bounded him in time the way maps bounded him in space.

'And life?' she said, by which Joy meant *Life*. She loved the fact that Arlo was teaching History, following in her footsteps. And not just teaching History, but helping people pass The Life in the UK Test and become what everyone would if they could: a British citizen.

Arlo had already told her it wasn't like that, and repeated what it said on the StUKCO website: that there were many requirements for British naturalisation and passing the test alone was INSUFFICIENT. But just like his students who'd enrolled in hope anyway, Joy didn't believe it. She said it couldn't be that hard, could it? Britain was friendly, and the British were friendly people, and if someone had something to offer, why wouldn't they be welcome?

'It's not like that, Mum.'

'But surely with a hundred percent in the test? Surely with a perfect score, you know as much as anyone here?'

Quite a bit more, actually.

Now Arlo said into the phone, '*Life* is Henry the Eighth plus the six wives in order.'

'Divorced. Beheaded. Died. Divorced. Beheaded. Survived.' Joy loved facts, things that were fixed. It was why she loved Britain. It was an island, and you knew where the country began and ended, you couldn't move the goalposts like they did with Poland. She said, 'All Boys Should Come Home Please.'

At one time, Arlo would have taken that as double-edged, as an ill-concealed expression of need. But now, he just listened. He drank his wine. Arlo understood Joy. He understood his mother better than she understood him. It had been a complicated process and had taken time, though less than it might have because when Tess met Arlo, she'd understood it all in an instant.

Joy said, 'This latest business is a bit of a turn-up, though, St Mira being in the news. It's in all the papers.'

The bomb had been in the tabloids for several days, but now it had made it into *The Telegraph*. 'You're saying we did it deliberately.' That was how long Arlo had been away: he was now seen as St Miran by his mother. Joy said, 'Of *course* we didn't do it – deliberately or not.'

All week there'd been official denials from the countries on Duke's list. The French foreign minister had said: 'The whole of

France, the entire world, reaches out at this time of heartache. All French people feel your tragedy. We are all St Miran.'

Mais ce n'était pas nous.

The *Auswärtigesamt* in Berlin had issued a statement extending condolences and appending a spreadsheet detailing all military manoeuvres at Amyna with date, time and personnel involved, showing zero (Ø) activity for 21 June. It was signed and stamped by the Minister for Defence and submitted in original and in Greek, the translation by a state-certified translator.

For almost a week, the British had said nothing at all.

But when a TV reporter cornered a minister as he was heading into the Foreign Office, he'd snapped, 'Where? Oh *that*? It's not yet clear precisely what happened, but whatever it was, we categorically deny any involvement, and now if you'll excuse me...' And he strode off in the direction of Clive of India.

Joy said, 'It's categorical we didn't do it.'

Joy needed categories and order and the certainty of past events. 'What's done,' she liked to say, 'cannot be undone.' Lady Macbeth was a source of comfort.

Arlo put his glass down. He placed it exactly in the middle of the mat and Tess wondered if it was a sign. It was their long-standing policy to keep calls to the parents on an even keel. But his glass looked so much like a bullseye. Was Arlo about to strike?

'It *was* a British-made bomb, you know.' The investigation had named it as a Paveway IV, the RAF's go-to weapon and used in Afghanistan, Libya, Iraq, Syria.

'Just because we made it doesn't mean we dropped it.'

And that was what Tess thought too. The British were happy to sell their bombs for other people's wars. The arms industry made a fortune doing it – made billions from the Saudis alone. And that was the scenario Tess was settling on: a British bomb that found its way into probably Russian hands; Firster knowledge; a blast close enough to implicate the base while limiting local casualties. It was a perfectly choreographed show.

She'd said all this to Arlo, who'd nodded. 'Could be, could be,' though sounding less convinced than she'd hoped.

Now he said to Joy, 'The British *do* drop bombs, you know.'

Tess pulled herself up on the sofa. Was this because of the wine? They'd been splashing out recently, buying stuff that was more alcoholic and easier to down. Or because a bomb had fallen *here*: it was history happening to her son and he wanted to set the record straight?

'Granted, we dropped bombs on Hitler,' Joy said. 'But that was *Hitler*, that was a *good* thing.'

'The British military hasn't stopped intervening since the Second World War.' There'd been decades of peace that weren't peaceful at all in some parts of the world.

Tess could picture the Brown's sitting room, Joy on the edge of the sofa, Elmer's cushion suddenly uncomfortable, and the rumble of lorries on Maison Dieu Road deadened by double glazing.

'Such as?' Joy said.

'Starting with the Greek Civil War.'

'Never heard of it.'

'French Indo-China.'

'That was the French.'

'The Dutch East Indies.'

'You know who that was.'

And on Arlo went through the twentieth century with Joy protesting over him – through colonial wars, overt invasions and covert ops to help faltering regimes – till he got to the Falklands, at which point she said: 'We *won* that one.'

A cough from Dover. It was deep, which meant Elmer. Was he thinking it was time to intervene?

But Joy wasn't going to let him. 'Are they in *Life*, these conflicts of yours?'

'Is that all that matters? Would they be fictions if they weren't?'

Which was the thing with History: it depended on who you asked.

Tess tipped herself forward and raised her voice towards the phone. 'Elmer?'

'Yes, love?' He sounded pleased to hear her, though also some way off, calling back from the far side of the cricket pitch – the other deep fielder, there to catch stray balls hit too hard by Joy and Arlo, the batters in the family.

Elmer, meaning 'noble' in Old English, shortened to 'El' – in Spanish, a singular, masculine, definite article. And Arlo's dad was singular, and definitely the definite article: a once-shy, friable, hesitant man compressed by middle age into a solid family feature.

'Elmer, tell us what you've been up to.'

He didn't say a lot on these monthly calls. He was happy to chat in person if you caught him one-to-one, but had never taken to declaring to the ether. 'Well, I found a dinosaur footprint the other day.'

That's how singular El was.

'And they think it's a theropod.'

Gasps and congratulations from Arlo and Tess, which they kept up long enough to clear the air and take the edge off the call.

Joy said, 'T. Rex was a theropod.' She sounded glad to be back on safe ground too. 'You know, modern-day birds are descendants of theropods.' She could talk forever about Elmer's fossils. She loved them because they were certainties of the most ancient kind, facts turned to stone.

'And *you*, love?' Elmer said. 'I imagine work's been busy what with the...' but he didn't finish because the word that came next was 'bomb.'

Yes, Tess said, work was a little busy at the moment.

All week, the Central Communications Office had been in overdrive, translating a rising flood of government statements into seven languages. Words gushed out of the building. The

Prime Minister had taken to twice-daily briefings, each time sounding less sure of his footing, and more like the Firsters. He'd been talking about 'a swarm of people coming across the Mediterranean' and the 'justified sense of betrayal of ordinary St Mirans'. He promised that things would change.

Varela was on the campaign trail, criss-crossing St Mira, his press team tweeting and uploading coverage onto YouTube. He'd met Georgios Papadopoulos yet again, and laid another wreath at the site where Maria and Petris had perished. Varela handed over a cheque, the money 'donated by true patriots' for the restoration of the family olive grove and a permanent memorial to his loved ones. He even trekked with his team into the mountains – declining the offer of a helicopter from one of his party donors. Varela arrived exhausted, his jacket black with sweat, his 'appreciation renewed' of the toughness of the lives lived in the remotest reaches of our island. Also with a stash of forms to register to vote. He stood in front of a dry village well holding the reins of a ribby donkey, and said: 'When there isn't enough, who should get it? The people who've lived here all their life, giving of their blood, sweat, their tears and becoming part of this very soil...' He let a handful of dust trickle through his fingers. 'Or the people who've hopped on a boat and swanned in, who might have contributed, but probably not, and never as much as those of us actually born here.'

From the highest peak of the Blue Mountains, where Mira had supposedly lain with Georgios and given birth to the first inhabitants of the island, Varela laid out his vision for the country, and in it were only true St Mirans. 'Those of us who can trace our line back for generations, who have a St Miran name, and sound St Miran, and look St Miran. And that, you cannot fake. You cannot apply for it. You cannot pass a test for it. A St Miran passport cannot change where you're really from. True St Mirans are its indigenous people, its native people. You and me, for instance,' he told YouTube.

Tess and Arlo watched Varela's arm flourish along the horizon. The sky was stretched blue and taut and faultless. He was a performer, a preacher, a conjurer, a reader of minds and an alchemist of hearts. And it was only a week to the election.

Then a heatwave rose from Africa and swallowed the whole country. Temperatures hit forty-six degrees. It could have slowed the election campaign, but didn't. Varela appealed for vigilance against the heightened risk of fire. 'We all know how devastating a blaze can be,' and photos everywhere he went of Georgios and Maria's ashen olive grove ringed with wreaths and Bomb Weed already showing. The Prime Minister echoed the call for care, especially now that drought threatened water supplies, and he issued a ban on private sprinklers, sparking outrage in the press: it was an attack on the freedom of the private citizen, another blow from detached élites.

The whole week, it was too hot to be indoors. Rron volunteered at the Blood Board for the all-day air-con. And people came in droves, answering the Firster call for more local blood. They donated their half-litre of A and left with a thankyou picture of Maria and Petris. In the evenings, Rron went down to the square and took his favourite seat at Café Echo and watched the news on mute. Or else he sat with the workmen who were back at their sandpit, and bonded over ice-cold beer.

Everything that week was hot or cold, everything extreme. The government was fighting for its life, everyone knew that. Its majority had been dented in 2012 and almost wiped out in 2017, and right now everything was against them: the bomb, the wildfires, the sprinkler ban, the political winds that were blowing across the continent – look at Italy, Hungary, Poland, Austria, Finland, Sweden, the Netherlands, the UK. The Labour Alliance was in a corner. Government ministers appeared on panel shows and appealed to reason, reciting their track record and offering up the stats.

No-one took any notice.

A couple of days before the country went to the polls, they placed a bulk order of mugs that said *Controls on Immigration* and did their last TV interviews sipping tea.

Then, the night before the election, Arlo got home early from his Greek class. Tess heard him pounding up the stairs. He always hurried back because finally the week was over and his weekend had begun. But tonight his feet struck a different note. Tess held open the door and watched his head rise up the final flight, his face turned to meet hers, and it was thinner than it should have been. A kiss too brief to matter. 'I think we'll have to leave St Mira.'

'What's that?' In his hand, a St Miran flag.

'Mrs Moros gave it to me. They're celebrating already.'

The extended Moros family was at that moment arriving downstairs, vanloads of them from across the island, bearing sewing machines. They were turning the first two floors of the building into a workshop. It was the biggest Moros order Tess had ever known.

Arlo came into the flat but didn't take his shoes off. He put the flag in the bin. Then he took it out again because in his head, scenarios were already forming where a flag might be convenient, a useful prop. He sat at the kitchen table, reached for the notepad they used for shopping and wrote: *A Bomb Scenario Clearly Helps Patriots*. It was the wives of Henry the Eighth in order. Because that was the thing with History: there were so many ways of remembering it.

That evening, Arlo's Greek class had covered politics vocabulary such as *politiká*, *diplomatía* and *taktikí*. They'd watched the current affairs programme, *Dimokratía*. But the broadcast had been interrupted. There was *éktaktes eidíseis*, which was breaking news. The final opinion poll had been released and it was *katastrofikós* for the Labour Alliance, the biggest projected wipeout in St Miran history. Then the Prime Minister had appeared in the garden of his residence, panic in his eyes, urging people to 'see reason, see sense, look at the facts, vote with your head, not your heart.'

Varela would be Prime Minister in the morning.

It was the weekend. Tess wasn't at the office. But on Monday, the words of the by-then former Prime Minister would lie as an official transcript on her desk, and she'd translate it into English and Duke would scan it, and amend it here and there, and then give it back with a nod. He was nodding more often at the news these days.

Across the square, Aeolus, who was in the Mirapolis Reserves Military Band was squeezing the national anthem from his euphonium. For half a minute, he drowned out the industrial whirr of the Moros's sewing machines. Tess put the kettle on. She stood at the window and looked out across her flowerpots that were unwatered and dead forever and wondered what had happened. How could this lovely island have turned so sour? And so fast? Or maybe not so fast. Perhaps she'd been too busy perfecting statements at the Comms Office, being careful, considering every word, to notice the rage that year after year had been thumbed on a whim into phones.

Tess thought back to 2016 – that blighted year – when St Mira's centre-right merged with its far-right and the Firsters were born. Some took it as a license to be nasty. For a while, it was awkward speaking English in public. People turned to stare at them. Or else they moved out of earshot. She could remember Arlo being asked where he was from. 'Here,' was not the correct answer. They meant *really*, originally. And recently, Arlo's Greek had been met with a frown and an '*Eh?*' As a matter of principle, people weren't going to understand their language if spoken with a foreign accent. Tess had put it down to one-offs, to individuals. And she hadn't allowed herself the thought that a series of one-offs was, in fact, a trend.

The kettle boiled and Tess made tea. She sat at her laptop, checked her emails, deleted the messages from British Home Stores who were still trying to welcome her back as a loyal customer. Then she went to the BBC. The British government had made a statement about 'alarming developments' in the Mediterranean. Tess clicked on the video. The Foreign Secretary was dressed in black and spoke from notes like a hired-in funeral celebrant. 'We reject absolutely the unfounded slur in respect of the recent bomb-related event. Further, whatever the outcome of tomorrow's election, we expect the terms of the Treaty of Friendship to be respected and the continued protection of all British interests on the island.'

The camera moved in to frame her face, the lips razor-thin and jaw at a jut. 'The UK is a nation with the world's fifth biggest defence budget and is the second largest defence exporter. We've never shied away from acting, even if that has meant standing alone as we did in the darkest hours of the Second World War. We must be ready, where necessary, to use hard power to support our global interests.'

Tess held her head in her hands. What was it with the British? Did they never look at a map? Did they not see they were a small island off the coast of Europe with diminished influence and ruined credibility? And yet still they wanted the guns to defend an empire.

Arlo said, 'She's just trying to sound Churchillian. It's grandstanding.'

'But why pick St Mira to do that?'

'Why pick the Falklands to go to war?'

'But there's no election coming up.'

'A bid for the Party leadership?'

The Foreign Minister was rousing herself with her own oratory now: 'Wherever I go, I find that Britain stands tall. We have the world's finest Armed Forces, brave men and women that we are so truly proud of. Some still wish to cut Britain down to size and send her back to her shores. But to those I say that has never been our way. It is not in our nature. History has taught us that crisis comes when we least expect it.' A pause so dramatically long it must have been down in the notes.

Then said direct to camera: 'The aircraft carrier HMS *Prince of Wales* is currently visiting the Mediterranean.' A brief nod as she gathered her papers. 'She is just off the east coast of Malta.'

That was just off the west coast of St Mira.

Tess's heart sank. It was already going badly enough. Did the British really have to get the *Prince* involved?

When the polls had closed and the count was nearly complete, the residents of Exodus Square gathered for the declaration and the Victory Party. Neighbours who always seemed weighed down – with shopping, with infants, with worry – looked unburdened this evening. Under the maples, old men and dogs chewed their cheeks in their sleep. A screen had been set up with a sound system rigged to the church. The speakers that usually broadcast services to the overspill in the square were pumping out *kardiochtypi*, the local pop. The priest of All Saints sailed about, barely recognisable in slacks and a polo shirt, smelling of aftershave instead of Orthodox incense. Children kicked a ball around to decide who dropped the bomb. It was England versus France.

Rron's nephew, Rrock, was here. He'd cycled down from Kentish Town because Rron had told him tonight was historic and he'd regret it if he missed it, and Rrock worried about regretting things. Rrock was always surprising – just the bulk of him, a sudden, magnified man. Rrock had taken over as Gatekeeper of Dover Castle when Tess moved in with Arlo. He was perfect for the job because he liked to labour, but also to be alone. He used to grow fruit, his money mirroring the seasons. Now, he had an income that rose in line with UK inflation, and every year, an invitation to The National Trust Christmas Party, which he never dreamed of accepting.

Vera steered them to the back, and Rrock sat at the end of the row so he'd only have one human being to deal with, and that was his uncle. Tess was on Rron's other side because he'd given up speaking English these days and Arlo couldn't catch St

Miran slang issued on a puff of smoke. Arlo was next to Tess because that meant Vera was at the other end, and that was a sign: that the two residents of Exodus Square *not* born on the island, the only un-true St Mirans, were *with* them.

Tess looked across to Rrock. He was a careful man. He cared. Probably too much, especially about grass. He knew what the perfect lawn should look like because he'd studied the coffee-table books that came with the job. The lawn had been shipped over as slabs of turf, cut from the High Weald and kept alive through one hundred and fifty Mediterranean summers, and he worried about going down in history as the man who'd let it die. In the grass were the descendants of Kentish wildflowers.

Tess leant across Rron's lap and whispered, 'Rrock, how's the grass?'

In the heatwave, he'd become anxious about the English lawn. He didn't know if his sprinkler, supplied by The National Trust and the St Miran Heritage Society, was public or private and if watering was allowed. 'I tend it with all my heart.' When Rrock had first taken on the job, Tess had taught him about 'He loves me, he loves me not,' and four-leafed clovers. Rrock had taken it all so seriously. For the last decade, he'd waited for the man who loved him and a lucky clover to work their magic at the same time. He knew it could happen. It had happened to Tess. If he just waited long enough, and kept the grass alive, a man would arrive at the castle gate bearing a red rose.

Now in Exodus Square, the final exit poll appeared on the screen: a Firster landslide and odds on that the British had dropped the bomb. Tess turned to Rron, watched him draw on his cigarette and blow the smoke into the gap between their knees. Rron had picked the Cid-hairs from his shorts. He was wearing a shirt Tess hadn't seen before. A red one, blood-coloured. He looked hydrated from his week at the Board, and fuller in the face. Then she scanned the square. Lots of people were brightly dressed, ready to party. These were neighbours Tess had known for a decade, said hello to, waved to, liked. How many of them had voted to get rid of the foreigners? Rron followed Tess's gaze, and maybe he followed what she was thinking too because he put a hand on her knee and squeezed the way he did Cid's neck when Cid was fretting and he wanted to get him to purr.

At nine o'clock exactly, the Speaker of the Chamber appeared on screen in his black skirt and silver leggings to say: 'It is my solemn and humble duty to announce that with all votes counted and all seats declared, the St Miran First Party has won the election with sixty-seven percent of the popular vote and ninety-five percent of the seats.' Because the other thing the British had bequeathed, alongside post-boxes and afternoon tea, was First Past the Post.

Two-thirds of Exodus Square was on its feet, scoring the air with rattles and releasing red balloons donated to the party by The Plastic Shop. Arlo reached for Tess's hand and Vera reached for Arlo's. Rron ran hands through hair he didn't have and Rrock dropped his head to his chest.

Then Dr Apostol, psephologist, came on to interpret the results. She was famous for winning a gold medal at the International Maths Olympiad in 1986. For a while, she'd had her own TV show – was the local Carol Vorderman. She juggled numbers and showed how sixty-seven could so easily turn into ninety-five. Not that anyone was listening, or could hear her above the racket.

And then celebrations sank to a hush: Varela had appeared on screen. He was on a stage in the grounds of the Firster Headquarters, spot-lit and theatrical. St Miran army officers had put on their gongs and were glitzing up the wings. Varela had shaved his head – got rid of his fifties hair-loss – and now he looked sleek. He looked punchy. The spotlights caught Varela's eyes, made them moist and made them sparkle, in a way both beautiful and brutal. He surveyed the crowd as if seeing into every soul. Then a dip of the head in a gesture that could have passed for deference. 'My dear friends,' he said.

Varela looked different – not the Man With a Beer of the campaign trail. This was Varela with his hands on power: at ease, even-mannered, in control. He wore a steel-grey suit with narrow lapels. Were Mr and Mrs Moros sharpening their style?

The crowd was transfixed. They wanted to hear more. But 'my dear friends' was what Varela had to say. That *was* his message: all of you gathered here to mark this victory are my friends. The TV camera panned over rapt faces. Then applause broke out. Cheers. Arms were raised as people caught this moment on their phones.

Varela gestured for calm. 'I have an important announcement to make, and it is so important I will read it verbatim, word for word.' He reached inside his jacket, flashing red lining. He retrieved a piece of paper. 'And it pertains to the foreign presence on this island.'

Vera muttered to her feet, 'What does it mean "foreign"…? Does it not depend on where you are? On how you feel?'

Varela unfolded the sheet.

She said, 'I have lived in this town all my life, I have never been abroad, I wish I had been foreign more often.' Vera would have gone on, but a hush had taken hold. The night was still, and a cloud of red balloons was suspended over the square. The whole of Mirapolis, the whole island, held its breath. Even the birds got wind of it and fell silent.

'The St Mira First Party will waste no time in doing the job you have elected us to do. To that end, a taskforce has been set up to regularise the non-native presence on our island. We are calling this the "Minefield Policy". We wish to establish the principle that for foreigners, nowhere on St Mira is safe to tread until they have proven, beyond all reasonable doubt, their right to be here.'

Cheers exploded against the walls of Exodus Square and fireworks whooped somewhere off-camera. Tess bent over. She fiddled with her sandals, the buckle suddenly tight. Arlo was already down there, head in his hands.

Varela refolded the statement and put it away. 'The foreigners, of course, know who they are. But do *we*? The truth is: no, we don't. Things have been allowed to slide. And that's what we're going to remedy from our first day in office, from now, from as I speak. We are going to collect data on every single foreign person present on this island. Now, as you'll see...' Tess glanced up. Varela held a finger to the bottom of the screen '... the means to offer this information is already at your disposal.' A web address slid across his white shirt: www.my-local-foreigner.stma.

Tess didn't hear much after that except a banging in her head, which was probably her heart, and the scrape of chairs as people left the square. Arlo was still in brace position. Between their feet, ants ferried messages, and dead leaves, and dead ones of each other. He said, 'They're going to report us.'

'Not *you*.' Vera stroked his back. 'Varela doesn't mean *you*. No-one means *you*.'

'But if you're an exception, it's already too late.'

'It is not late. It is early. The evening light is lovely. We just sit here. We are in no hurry because we know no foreigners. We are all St Miran. We sit here and have no concerns at all.' Vera straightened her back and nodded benignly to the neighbours she'd known for decades who weren't quite seeing her, and swallowed night air as if it were champagne.

Rron said, 'I need a drink.' He stood, his red shirt rising like a late-released balloon.

'Sit down. We need all hands on deck.'

Rron's calves wobbled.

'Sit, Rron.'

Tess's eyes mapped the blue range of Rron's varicose veins, the valves weakened, the blood pooled backwards, struggling to make it up to the heart.

'Rron!'

Rron stood there, his small, flat feet pressed together.

'Sit!'

Tess watched his weight swing, his body waver. The point of contact with the earth was too small to keep him. Whichever way the wind blew, it would take Rron with it.

6.

What is your present work or job or occupation?

TRANSLATOR AND INTERPRETER (GREEK ⟺ ENGLISH)

What is the name of the company or organisation you work for?

CENTRAL COMMUNICATIONS OFFICE OF ST. MIRA (ENGLISH DESK)

When did you start this job?

2010

Have you ever worked in the media, government, public or civil administration, security or scientific research?

YES. SEE ABOVE.

The day after the election, Tess walked to the office, picking her way through streets littered with the fireworks that had punctured her sleep. The people who'd backed the Firsters had partied on for hours. Tess could tell which way her neighbours had voted from the lights that were on in Exodus Square. On every corner of Mirapolis, blackened cartridges and spent canisters had turned the city into a war zone. And yet Morning Glory still burst in purple along the ancient shoulders of the city as if nothing at all had changed.

Tess reached the Comms Office and waved at Max, who threw up his hands as people did at the market – the price too high, far too high. It was his way today of waving her through. Dear Max. He loved foreigners, and he didn't care right now that this was Day One of the Minefield Policy or that the checkers were checking the checkers. Tess went up to English and knew straight away that something was different. Then she saw the flag. It must have been put on her desk overnight. From today, every public servant was to work within sight of the red cross of St Mira. It was plastic, which meant it would last forever. Then Tess noticed the smell: the leftover traces of yesterday instead of chemical lemons. Had Duke given the cleaners a morning off so they could stay up and party? She could hear him in his office now. He was on the phone, his voice punchier than usual. Laughter too, which was entirely new. The translations were on her desk with a note that said: *URGENT. Within the hour.*

Tess spun on her chair, relieved by the momentary breeze. Then she spun her globe. All those foreigners, she thought, everywhere foreign, everyone a foreigner somewhere in the world. She'd spun it hard and the world wavered on its axis. The earth did that, and today it seemed she could feel it.

Tess re-read the word *URGENT*, checked the clock, took her time to water the cactus that didn't need watering. She lined up the pens in her stationery drawer, sharpened the pencils, arranged the felt-tips to make a rainbow. And then, through the door, the end of Duke's phone call. Tess turned to his paperwork. On top, a formal acknowledgement of defeat by the Labour Alliance and a statement of resignation by the ex-Prime Minister. Also Varela's address from the night before. She'd half-translated that in her head while waiting for the city to sleep. And then there was a new statement, issued by Mr Hector Varela, Prime Minister, at the Headquarters of the St Mira First Party at 04:00 hours. It was an addendum to the Minefield Policy:

The scale of the operation now facing us requires a triage of foreign persons on St Mira. The British were the first to establish their presence in this country, and as the government in London has been especially hostile in recent weeks, we have decided that British citizens will be our first priority. We are calling this the 'First In, First Out Policy.'

Tess didn't knock. She marched straight into Duke's office.

'Oh dear...' He swung round on his swivel chair.

'Oh dear, what?'

'Isn't that exactly what they say? That the British just march in without bothering to knock?'

'I'm not "the British".'

'True. You *are* British. And you are *also* St Miran. So there is no cause for alarm.' He leant back in his chair and studied her from the angle of his headrest. His eyelids hung soft and under-slept.

'This...' Tess held up the First Out policy. '...is pretty awful news.' Was she really expected to translate something that would directly harm people she knew? Names went through her head, faces she'd known for years.

Duke released a sigh, a long one, emptying his lungs. He had big lungs from Taekwondo. Tess sniffed the air when she guessed his breath had reached her. No hint of alcohol, but then Duke didn't like to lose control, which meant he rarely drank.

'"Pretty awful", he said, 'is a value judgement. I must remind you that in this job we do not evaluate. We merely translate.'

71

'This policy...' She waved it like a flag. '...is going to make *everyone* feel unsafe. *Everyone* feel unwanted.'

'Not everyone. Only the British. And that, clearly, is the government's intention.

'But doesn't it make *you* feel...' She wanted to say ashamed, worried, embarrassed, but Duke cut her off. 'I do not bring feelings to work.'

'Your *opinion*, then.'

'I do not have opinions – except on the technical quality of the output of the Office.' And then Duke told Tess to expect a demanding time. The next two months would be especially busy. The government was front-loading its legislative programme.

'While everyone's on holiday, so no-one will notice.'

'Not everyone. Not us, for example.' Duke said, 'The new government has impressive ambitions.'

'Isn't "impressive" a value judgement?'

'The *scope* of their ambitions impresses itself upon me, and what it might imply for our workload. I do not refer to the *nature* of their ambitions or what I might, or might not, feel or opine about them.' He took a sip of water.

That was Duke the lawyer.

He grasped his knuckles and made them crunch.

And that was Duke the Grand Master.

'Over the coming weeks,' he said, 'we will be dealing with *sensitive* matters that require *sensitive* handling. We must be aware that those receiving the information we release might be *sensitive* to some of it.'

'Sensitive' was not a word that often sprang from Duke's lips. Had it ever? It sounded strange coming from him. And he never repeated words in that way either. It was the politicians who did the repetition, nailing home the message. Duke was one for synonyms and touting his vocabulary. But now, the English Desk was to be... Tess thought: euphemistic, evasive, deceptive. Would we, after all, be adding here and there, or taking away if necessary, to appeal to the sensitivities of a world that was about to find out about the Firsters?

'How we present this initial stage will shape perception on the global stage. Tone is all.' He pursed his lips to soften them, the way singers do, and actors. 'The wrong tone, a false note, and the already – let us say – less than stable situation, could deteriorate. So, the utmost care, Tess, in *every* single detail.'

Duke made it sound as though a misplaced comma could start a war. But then, maybe it could. *Eats Shoots and Leaves.* Wasn't that British foreign policy all over?

Things moved quickly in the weeks after the election. Varela rescinded the Treaty of Friendship, to protests from Downing Street and a cameo appearance of the *Prince of Wales* off the St Miran coast. Officially, Britain wasn't going to be bullied. But on the grapevine, Tess had heard there was bewilderment at the Foreign Office: who were these Firsters? Where did they come from and so fast? What did they actually want? Shouldn't we just step back from this nonsense and wait for it to fade?

Everyone in Translation was contacted by their embassy and offered advice on navigating the Minefield. Everyone apart from Tess, who instead got an email from Brexpat – the network of British people living on St Mira. Brexpat organised the Christmas party she and Arlo never went to because they were always in Dover. Also pet-sitting and classes in watercolours. The secretary had written on behalf of the committee, paraphrasing UK government advice, and telling everyone not to worry, this was just a storm in a teacup, it would all blow over, and when were the British ever forced out of a country?

And then in August, came the 'General Prohibition on Foreign Languages in Public'. Everyone was expected to speak Greek. If you couldn't, you had to type your message into your phone and let Google speak for you. English disappeared overnight. Tess hadn't realised how widespread the language was until it was erased. Little Smethwick was hushed. Drinkers stayed inside the pub with the doors and windows shut and the aircon on. The family that ran the fish-and-chip shop gave up and left the island. Business had slumped anyway since Varela's speech in Junkers. In the supermarkets, the Exotic Food shelves were emptied, which meant gone was what Arlo called the Britshit: baked beans and Jaffa Cakes, lemon curd and sliced white bread that never, ever went off. Multilingual menus vanished and international papers disappeared from the bus station newsstand.

In the hallway of Tess and Arlo's block, a note appeared behind the locked glass of the noticeboard:

PLEASE USE ONLY THE GREEK LANGUAGE!

By order of Mirapolis Council

It was written in English and so, probably, in breach of the General Prohibition. And soon after, a note appeared beside it in a hand Tess knew from signs in the Moros's shop window:

As we finally have our great country back we feel there is one rule to that needs to be made clear to House residents.

We do not tolerate people speaking other languages than Greek in the flats.

We are now our own country again and the the Greek of St Miran's is the spoken tongue here.

If you do want to speak whatever is the mother tongue of the country you came from then we suggest you return to that place and return your flat to the council so they can let St Miran people live here and we can return to what was normality before you infected this once great island.

It's a simple choice obey the rule of the majority or leave.

You won't have long till our government will implement rules that will put St Mirans first. So, best evolve or leave.

God Save St Mira, her government and all true patriots.

Arlo wanted to take it down and report it to the police. Tess wanted to correct the typos then report it to the police. They only spoke Greek to each other outside now, and English at home, though quietly. On Sunday mornings, they had tea in bed, and caught up with everything that had happened, and wondered what might happen next, while in the background the World Service whispered to them about religion. Arlo would come up with the Firsters' next moves: they'll tag us. They'll lock us up in barracks. They'll put us on a plane to Rwanda. He'd say, 'Have *you* thought that too?'

And Tess would say, 'No, I haven't thought that.'

Of course she'd thought that.

Because wasn't it the nature of cruelty to take its cue from the cruel?

In early September, when the heat finally lifted and the frenzy of Firster initiatives seemed to slow, Tess began to believe that things might ease. She started to think about a holiday – somewhere not Greek-speaking. She wondered if it was too early to plan Christmas in England and book annual leave.

And then two envelopes arrived in their letterbox. They were official and identical and stamped with the new portrait of St Mira that the Firsters had commissioned – her breast obscured in this version of the way she suckled the nation.

Tess always picked up their post because she was first out in the morning. And she had permission to open Arlo's letters if they were Greek bureaucracy, or junk, or from Glasgow, which meant Student Loans. These were from the Registration Bureau. As part of the 'First In, First Out' policy and in response to the call for information on British citizens, the Bureau had updated its records, the letters said.

Please check the attached details are correct, then bring this letter and evidence of your competence in the Greek language (acceptable evidence is a certificate issued by a certified issuing body) to your Screening Interview:

On: Wednesday 7 September

At: 07:30

Gate: 6

Category: OTHER

Also bring valid photo ID together with the relevant Screening Fee (see table over).

NOTE: Appointments cannot be deferred as the Screening Process must be complete within the timetable set out in Paragraph Two of the Memorandum on the Regularisation of Foreign Citizens on St Mira.

It was a memorable sunrise the morning of their appointment, the sky copper in the east and purple in the west, like a bruise around the rim of the earth. Tess woke Arlo with tea. He was down the other end of the bed, which he did sometimes if he'd had a bad dream. Tess sat on the edge of the bed. Arlo took her hand – his cool from the night, hers hot from the tea, and they stayed like that till their skin had equalised. He must have known she needed his hand because of the blouse. It was a gift from Joy the year that sunshine yellow was in. It made her chin glow as if she were holding a buttercup. Tess had promised to wear it whenever she was feeling sunny. In fact, she wore it in times of gloom in the hope of a change of mood.

'I don't want to be regularised,' she said. It sounded like revised, like rectified. It made her sound like an error.

'It's just a bit of number-crunching, form-filling, hoop-jumping, some box-ticking...'

Tess thought: why does bureaucracy only work with compound nouns? She said, 'Why are we Category Other?' It meant they were an afterthought, last on the list and throwaway.

'Because we're uncategorisable.' It meant they'd defied labels and confused the bureaucrats. 'It means they don't know what to do with us.'

But that was exactly what worried Tess: what were the Firsters going to do?

Tess and Arlo walked to the Registration Bureau for their screening interview. The cicadas were quiet still, the morning too cool for them to sing. They arrived early, but already there were queues. Costas worked the lines with his accordion, playing *Rule St Mira* because this was public and people would feel obliged to give. Tess saw faces she knew. That was the landlord of the pub in Little Smethwick. His regulars were here too, looking bleary and dismayed – closing time faces after a match lost on penalties. And that brown huddle was the Condiment men. They always stood out because it was company policy to wear shades of the colour of the sauce they made. Except it wasn't a huddle; they were standing in pairs. Were they preparing for this interview with role-play?

Tess saw other Brexpat faces – Jeannie, for instance, who'd have taken the bus over the mountains from her village on the south coast. She clung to Emma – a white Yorkshire Terrier with a bow in her hair and named after her granddaughter. Jeannie's eyes searched the faces looking for someone familiar. And then they found Tess. Jeannie was usually a lightning-strike of a woman, electric in her dress and unmissable. But today, the spark had deserted her. Jeannie looked as if she was about to cry.

Tess and Arlo were called in at 7:30 exactly. It was a small, windowless Portakabin, put up in a hurry. Inside, one table, three chairs and a man swamped already by office boredom.

'Good morning. We're Tess Petrou and Arlo Brown.'

'I know,' said to the computer. He didn't have a nametag, didn't introduce himself.

They sat.

Tess studied him, the cylindrical head and waxy skin, like a votive candle. She said, 'I think I might have seen you at a StUKCO film night.' Tess had a memory for faces. She said, '*Four Weddings and a Funeral*?'

No answer. He was not in the mood for light banter.

She said, '*The Killing Fields*?'

He drew on his cigarette, let Blue Mountain smoke trickle from his nose.

The ban on smoking in public spaces had just been lifted. The freeborn people of St Mira, Varela had told the country, had an ancient and inalienable right to light up wherever they wanted.

'Screening fee.'

Tess counted the notes onto the desk, St Mira-side up. He re-counted them into a petty cash tin, and locked it. 'Forms.' He shoved aside his ashtray. Tess and Arlo were his first appointment and that heap of dog-ends was how he'd started his day.

Tess said. 'We have a correction. My partner's name is *Arlo*.' She spelled it out.

'I can't accept that information. The person concerned has to tell me.'

Arlo said, 'Harlow is a town in Essex.' Which was why they suspected Mrs Moros had reported them. It was how she said his name. Also because the Moros family had come into some cash. They were building an extension, expanding their business to meet new demand. And people who'd proved helpful in naming foreign residents were going to the banks for interest-free loans. The Firsters were appealing to self-interest with nought percent interest.

The man asked Arlo to spell his name. Then he put a finger to the keyboard and stabbed at *delete*. It was single digit data-entry and an enormous effort.

Usually in offices, desks were cluttered with photos of children that had since grown up and chunky mugs with jokes that were no longer funny. And on the walls, scarves of football teams you couldn't help supporting, and posters of bands that had were dead or disbanded. But this cabin still smelt of the glue that held it together. The walls were blank except for a clock and a sign that said: *No English*.

'Language certificates.'

Tess handed over her degree in Greek.

His fingers tried the thickness of the paper. He held it up to the neon and found it watermarked. 'Is it Ivy League?'

'That's the USA. It's from London University.'

'London doesn't count.' He flicked his eyes to Arlo, heavy-lidded, his gaze half-eclipsed.

Arlo gave him his certificate.

The man glanced over it. 'B2?' That was upper intermediate. 'You don't sound B2.'

Arlo had barely spoken.

He looked at the certificate again. 'It's from StUKCO.' And he handed the certificate back.

'So?'

'That's where you work.'

'So?'

'So very convenient.'

He aimed an index finger and dropped it from a height, making his keyboard bounce. 'You have to take it again anyway.'

'Sorry?' Arlo leant forward. He thought he'd misunderstood.

'Your certificate is three years out of date.'

'It's three years *old*. I took the test three years ago.'

'So it's out of date.'

'But the language hasn't changed since then.'

'But you might have forgotten it since then.'

Tess cut in. 'He's speaking Greek to you right now. You can hear he hasn't forgotten it.'

'And you, Miss...' He glanced at the form to catch her name again. 'Petrou? Is that true?'

'Through my grandfather.'

'But it's Greek.'

'He was St Miran.'

His eyes caught hers then and held them. He rearranged the flesh that had pooled in the seat of his chair. 'I'm sorry, but guidelines say you both have to re-take your certificates.'

'I can't retake my *degree*. And you can hear I speak the language fluently.'

'Guidelines say you might be reciting from a script.'

'I sound St Miran.'

'Guidelines say you might be acting. Christian Bale sounds American. Sean Connery sounds Scottish.'

Tess glanced to where the window would be if the cabin had had one. She was glad this was an early appointment. By mid-afternoon, the temperature in here would be unbearable. Tempers would fray. She said, 'I grew up with my St Miran grandfather. He sang me St Miran lullabies. He read me the Greek myths as bedtime stories. I brought his ashes home after he died. We spoke Greek *all* the time.'

Which was true, apart from when they spoke English. Mainly, it was medical English. Stan's vocabulary advanced as he got older. 'London has asthma,' he'd say. 'Streatham High Road suffers hypertension.'

Now the man had turned to where the window would be too. He looked wistful for daylight, or fresh air, or for whoever was talking to him in his head. And he seemed softer, his features melted.

Tess said, 'What's the minimum that would make you happy?'

'If only it were about happiness.'

'What if I do B2, like Arlo?'

He smiled at her then. 'Thank you. Very much. I am at a stage in my life where it means a lot to tick a box.'

On the day of their language test, Tess and Arlo made their way to StUKCO via the park where Arlo had his lunch before going in to teach. It had always been semi-wild and a lovely spot to start his working day: on the bench with his picnic while Painted Ladies dripped like condensed milk on the oleander and gold-foiled beetles careened around the tops of trees as if they were flying Quality Street. For years it'd been the Park of Peace and Friendship. Now it'd been renamed for Vigilance and Self-Defence and the lawn mown to 1.5 centimetres, which was the permitted length of boys' hair for the new school year.

Tess and Arlo joined the queue that wound through the gate, towards the glass-and-concrete modular block assembled in the sixties. They filed past the statue of Graham Greene, chosen by a former St Miran Minister of Culture because 'Greene understood that small islands harbour big stories.' When they reached Reception, Arlo gave his passport to the woman on duty, who was actually one of his students. She blushed, embarrassed to find out the date of birth and first name of her teacher. She gave him a number which would take him to his seat in the exam room. She wished him luck and said, 'If you can keep your head when all about you are losing theirs...' *If* was among the UK's favourite poems, according to *Life*.

Tess and Arlo went into the hall. It smelled as it always did, of plastic chairs and warm dust. Also, of Arlo. It was where Tess had first set eyes on him, exchanged her first hello – and he'd infused the room, and the room, him. And now, there he was a few rows away, among surnames that opened the alphabet, wearing his cap and waiting for the sky to fall in.

Jeannie was here, though without Emma this time. She'd been placed at the front because she'd be taking the simplest test, A1. The government had decided that if you were retired, it was enough to know a handful of useful phrases. Examples were: 'My name is...,' 'I come from...,' and 'Please call a doctor.' 'It is not enough,' a Firster spokesman had said, 'to say *kaliméra* and *kalispéra* over the fence to your neighbour and think you speak Greek. It is like sheep bleating at passers-by.'

And now, with everyone seated, Mr Dionysopoulos, Head of StUKCO and Arlo's boss, glided into the hall as if brought here by a force other than his legs. He'd come straight from the nineteenth century: a black suit and white wing collar, his face parchment-yellow, the features drawn with a leaking quill. 'My task is to ensure that this examination is conducted with no duplicity, laxity or impropriety...' He spoke with a command that was easy and practised, and in Greek because he had to, and slowly because he knew that almost everyone in this room would find it hard to follow. '...and that the results are reliable and fair.'

He scanned the hall for a reaction.

There was no reaction.

'I must also demonstrate the above, and so I draw your attention to the independent observers...' In each corner a suited man was making notes. 'And to the video cameras that are recording this event. I am also to remind you there must be no conferring and no leaving before the ninety minutes are up. If you wish to go to the toilet, you cannot. And now...' He cast his gaze a long way, as if towards the future though actually to the clock. He checked it against his watch. 'Please turn over. You may begin.'

The reading comprehension was an extract from the St Miran Constitution. The listening was a Varela speech. For the writing, you had to invite a friend to a traditional St Miran gathering, demonstrating knowledge of appropriate greetings, food and dress. The oral exam was one-to-one, administered by StUKCO staff and students.

Tess's examiner was Mr Dionysopoulos. He was in a room that caught the sun and where Arlo sometimes taught *Life*. He sat with his back to the window, his face obscure. On the table, a tape-recorder was running, the red light on. 'Good Morning,' he said. 'My name is Mr Dionysopoulos.'

For all the years Tess had known him, he'd been Mr Dee – as in D for Dickens.

'Good morning, Mr. Dionysopoulos.'

He'd become 'Dee' when he was sent to board at the oldest school in England. And the name had stuck. It had stayed with him all his adult life. Until now.

He motioned for Tess to sit. 'And your name is?'

She was the woman who'd been to his house for cream tea he'd made himself and Earl Grey from Fortnum's. She was the

82

woman who'd listened to his stories about what it was like to be sent abroad to school, how hard he'd tried to be English.

'My name is Tess Petrou.'

'May I have your mark sheet, please, Miss Petrou? Thank you.' And still he couldn't look at her. 'First I'd like to know something about you. What do you usually do at weekends?'

These days it was scour the news for better news. 'I enjoy keeping up with current affairs.' Tess told him the papers she read and the radio stations she listened to.

'Would you like to take up a new hobby?'

'I would like the news to improve.'

'Ah! It is the best of times, it is the worst of times.' Mr Dee had read all the Dickens novels. It was how he'd got through school – in a corner of the library, making friends with made-up people.

'Not the *best*, in my experience,' Tess said. 'But let's hope this is the worst of it.' For a while, she talked about London, and what Dickens must have witnessed, and how it all seemed to be coming true again.

Mr Dee's greying eyebrows hung on her every word. He nodded to the tape-recorder, as if wanting it to note his disappointment at how things had changed. It was why he'd left in the end, and returned to an island he knew only from childhood. London had lost its loveliness, he said. Where had the green and pleasant land gone?

Then Tess realised she'd just been speaking Greek as if she could – like a native speaker – and Mr Dee hadn't written anything on his mark sheet. She glanced at the clock. 'I think it's time to address the grammar.'

Mr Dee couldn't respond because there was nothing about such interjections in his exam script. So he said, 'In this part of the test, I'm going to give you two photographs.' He gave Tess two photographs. 'I'd like you to talk about the photographs for about one minute.'

Tess said, 'This picture is of Hector Varela, leader of the St Miran First Party and the Prime Minister of this country...' A pause to emphasise the connector. '...*whereas*...'

'Whereas.' A tick went down.

'...it is widely known...'

That was the impersonal passive. Tick.

'...that the other photo is of the former British Foreign Minister who has been elected...'

Passive. Tick.

'...by a tiny handful of people to lead the United Kingdom.' Tess said, 'Who knows where all this will end?' Rhetorical question. 'It should...' Modal auxiliary.

Nod, nod, tick tick.

'...not have been possible. If I were in England now...' which might have been the subjunctive, though Tess had never really understood that.

Mr Dee was watching his watch. 'Thank you, Miss Petrou. That is the end of the examination. You will not be told your grade until you receive your results.' He turned the tape-recorder off.

Tess took in his black jacket and wing-collar and thin black tie. In all these years, he hadn't escaped school uniform. She whispered across the desk as if a teacher might be listening. 'Can I ask you something?'

'I am not allowed to speak. The examination is over.'

'You're speaking now.'

'Only because you asked me a question.'

'Is StUKCO going to close?' Because Tess had heard rumours that all traces of the UK would soon be gone and the Office would promote St Miran culture only.

Silence.

Once, Mr Dee had told her that when he was at school, he would lie in bed for hours listening to the bells of Canterbury and try to hear his heart. He wasn't sure it was beating.

Tess said, 'Can you tell me *anything*?'

Even now, Mr Dee would go to bed and wonder at the silence. That was what happened in British public schools, he said: they filled your head and emptied your heart, and then you led the country.

'Please, Mr. Dionysopoulos. I'm worried. Arlo's worried. It'd help to know if he's going to lose his job.'

She watched the slug of his Adam's Apple, could tell he wanted to speak. But more than that, he wanted to be dutiful. And his duty at that moment was to conduct language exams as if everyone was equally strange to him. She said, 'Imagine it was *you* in this position.'

'I do not care to imagine.'

Which wasn't true. He imagined all the time. He'd spent his life taking refuge in other people's stories.

'Imagine it was Dickens, then. Or one of his characters, from whichever book it was.'

And that thought seemed to reach him. He turned to the window with those doleful eyes that could wet but never water. Outside, the sky was the rich blue Tess always wanted it to be. Two clouds, lipped at the edges, hung companionably. They could have been talking. Mr Dee was about to say something. But then a knock at the door, and the next candidate came in, and the moment was lost.

'Good morning,' Mr Dee said.

Tess stood.

He gestured to the seat. 'My name is Mr Dionysopoulos.' He spoke through Tess as if through air. 'And your name is?'

7.

What is your total monthly income from all sources after tax?.

APPROX EQUIVALENT OF £3,500

Do you receive income from any other sources including friends and family?

NO.

Do you have savings, property or other income (for example from stocks and shares)?

NO.

How much of your total monthly income is given to family members or dependents?

MY PARTNER AND I POOL OUR INCOME

NONE GIVEN TO OTHER FAMILY MEMBERS

WE HAVE NO DEPENDENTS.

How much do you spend each month on living costs?

NOT SURE WHAT COUNTS AS A LIVING COST

WOULD NEED ACCESS TO MY BANK ACCOUNT FOR DETAILS. CAN I HAVE MY PHONE BACK, PLEASE ?

A week later, the exam results arrived. Mr Dee had signed the letters himself. He'd used Indian ink and elaborate curlicues, all very nineteenth century. Tess had a PASS. Arlo had a PASS. The results were endorsed with the StUKCO stamp – the St and CO legible, but had someone tried to remove the 'U' and the 'K'? Tess pictured the results landing in the letterbox of everyone who'd taken the test that day.

And then the telephone rang.

Tess picked up.

'I've just mailed you something over.' It was Jeannie, and there was an edge to her voice.

'Are you all right?'

'I'm not sure.'

'Where are you?'

Jeannie was in town delivering Emma to the vet. She'd been off her food lately and hiding under furniture. Animals could sense when things were wrong, Jeannie said, and everything *was* wrong at the moment, wasn't it – what with the plague, and the war, and the Queen, and now all this.

And then her email came through. Tess read Jeannie's result while in the background, Jeannie recited how she'd put 'PASS' and 'SUCCESS' and 'CONGRATULATIONS' into Google Translate, but it hadn't been any of those. If she'd failed, they couldn't get rid of her, she had nowhere to go, she'd lived on this island for twenty years, this was her home. 'Last time I lived in England, Tony Blair was Prime Minister. *Pop Idol* was on telly. Gareth Gates was Number One.'

'They won't send you back, Jeannie.' Tess hoped they wouldn't. She thought Jeannie was safe for now, at least. The Firsters had taken on too much – they couldn't keep up with their own mayhem. She said, 'Why don't you come over? It'd be lovely to see you,' trying to make it sound like an innocent invitation, not the preamble to bad news. She checked Jeannie had their address and knew the way. Streets had been renamed right across town, road signs were only in Greek now, and Google maps hadn't caught up with the changes. 'We're ten minutes due south from Junkers.'

'I'm not good with a compass.'

'Follow the sun.'

'Won't that take all day?'

'The sun is in the south.'

'Is it?'

'For us it is,' Tess said.

Jeannie seemed cheered by that: the whole universe wasn't against her after all.

They waited for Jeannie to collect Emma and make her way to Exodus Square. Tess recorded A1 phrases into one of Duke's Dictaphones: he was keen on dictation and handed them out like candy. Half an hour later the bell rang, then the sound of heels and claws on the stairs, and Tess opened the door to an anxious Emma and vibrant, nervy Jeannie. Her golden hair fell in waves and broke on her shoulders, her lamé blouse splintering light. 'Oh, bless, Tess, you're a sweetheart, thank you so much, you don't know how much this means.' She spoke loudly and in English.

Tess motioned her in and shut the door.

Jeannie pulled off her shoes – some film-star kind of confection. Her breaths were shallow, her chest heaving. 'I could do with a break. I need a rest. But then, the whole world does.'

And that was the thing: there *was* no rest. And there would be no rest. It was turmoil for the foreseeable. That's what Tess had started to think – though she didn't say it to anyone, not even to Arlo.

They went into the kitchen and drank tea and ate biscuits, and chatted about nothing in particular. Jeannie wanted to know, but clearly didn't want to know, the contents of her letter. And then, when the preamble lagged and Emma whimpered into the quiet, Tess said, 'It's going to be OK, Jeannie. They're not going to send you back.'

Jeannie clapped her little hands together, making her painted nails flash.

Tess thought: they won't send you back because I won't let them, and she hoped that it was true.

Then she went through Jeannie's letter. 'This word here? It means...' She wasn't going to say 'fail'. 'It means you have to take the test again.' She gave Jeannie the Dictaphone and said to listen to it whenever she took Emma for a walk.

Jeannie reached for her necklace, a fine gold chain with an 'S' for Steve, her late husband. Also for 'stroke' which was how he'd died. They'd been married twenty years and he'd been gone twenty years, and since then, she'd been on her own apart from three Emmas, and the neighbours and Google Translate.

'You know I've got a memory like a sieve.'

'I know you can recite the bus timetables off by heart.'

Well, of course she could. She didn't drive, so she needed to know the buses.

'And you can remember what every customer said and pick up where you left off.'

Well, that was just part of the job.

'But those phrases I'm supposed to learn? For my name, I just...' She pointed to her chest '...and say "Jeannie". Everyone knows what "England" means. And for "Please call a doctor...", people know what a sick person looks like.'

Jeannie felt for the 'S' and worked Steve through her fingers. 'This language thing, it's not laziness. People just understand each other.' She'd left school at sixteen and been a hairdresser ever since. She'd spent her entire adult life interpreting signals, getting on, and making sense of garbled dramas acted out in the mirror. 'I might not speak the language, but I *do* communicate.' Jeannie still did the hair of her whole village. She was proof of ingenuity and what people could do when they were open and curious and wanted to understand.

Arlo refilled her teacup. Jeannie didn't seem to notice. She turned her face to the window. Outside, the sound of chainsaws.

They were taking down the maple in Exodus Square. 'I don't know what's happened to St Mira. It's all so different… It used to be lovely here. It was my paradise…' Then she ran a fingernail around her mug, tracing the pattern – a spiral that she followed anticlockwise, as if winding back time. 'I'm trying to place it… Was it around the time that you came?'

That was when the villas went up along the coast with their sprawling grounds and swimming pools and helipads. And then there was that hold-up. 'Do you remember the hold-up?'

Tess remembered the story, it was huge at the time: a farmer led his goats into the road, stopped a Mercedes and said to the driver: 'Your money or your life.' And the driver said, 'I don't have any money,' and took out his wallet to show him. The farmer said, 'So, where *is* it then?' and the driver shrugged and waved an arm to the ether. And so the farmer shot him.

They all upped security after that. And now they were fortresses guarded with dogs and cameras, with armed men and anonymity. James Bond hideouts that belonged to no-one. Or no-one traceable, according to Vera. They were owned by companies registered on islands that people had heard of but no-one could place on a map. Maybe Frourio men? More likely Frourio clients who had their fortunes made for them there. Some of them were probably foreign. And would they have received a letter telling them to be regularised? No. National law didn't apply to the slippery-rich and ultra-connected. The Firsters wouldn't be troubling them with an early morning appointment in a Portakabin.

Jeannie said, 'You know, they're empty most of the time. They're holiday getaways. Weekend pads. But you can't be in two places at once. Who needs two houses?'

The people who owned them thought they did.

Tess said, 'I wonder what happened to the farmer?' After the hold-up, he'd been a bit of a hero. It was just after the crash, and people were desperate. Things could have gone one way, but in fact they went the other. And now here they were, unwanted foreigners sitting at the kitchen table, their warmth soothing an anxious dog and eating shortbread Arlo had made because you couldn't get Walker's any more.

Jeannie shrugged. 'Still, people have earned the money, so they can do what they want with it, can't they.'

Except they hadn't earned it. Not really. They had money, and money made more money.

'They've worked hard.'

Not necessarily.

Arlo's brother had more money than he knew what to do with, and he hadn't worked any harder than Arlo. He'd just been a banker instead of a teacher.

Jeannie reached a hand under the table, feeling for Emma, telling her she was here. And then, 'And *you're* both managing OK, are you?'

Arlo said, 'We're not thinking ahead.' Which wasn't true. This morning, he'd been thinking about where he could work if he lost his job at StUKCO. 'We're trying to be practical.'

'Me too. But the bureaucracy never ends... It's letter after letter after letter...'

Tess knew what was coming next and it was something she hadn't mentioned to Arlo. So she cleared away the dirty mugs and made noise filling the sink.

'And that latest one from the Finance Office. Turns out I'm an immigrant.' It sounded strange to her. Jeannie had always thought of herself as an expat. '*You're* not immigrants, are you?'

Arlo said, 'Economic ones. Opportunists.' *He* was, anyway. He'd come for a decent salary and a permanent job.

'Well, as a...' Jeannie searched for the word that felt right to her. '...as a comer-to-this-country, I've got to prove I'll have paid enough social security from the beginning of time till the day I die not to be a burden on the state.' Something like that anyway. 'Have you had letters from the Finance People too?'

Tess said to the sink, 'Yes, we have.'

'Have we?'

91

'A couple of days ago.' Actually, a couple of weeks ago. And, actually, there was only one letter and it was for him. 'I've dealt with it,' she said.

Which was true and not true.

A letter had come from the Finance Office telling Arlo he was a British citizen whose salary fell below the required threshold and that therefore he was no longer entitled to reside on St Mira. It was part of the 'Nothing for Nothing' policy. Varela had said that 'only skilled foreign contributors' were welcome on the island. Tess had translated the official announcement, while in the back of her mind she'd guessed it meant trouble for Arlo. She'd wondered why she was doing it – translating for the Firsters. Sometimes, it felt like writing your own death sentence, like digging your own grave. *Because it's my job to translate, just doing my job.* That's what she told herself, and she needed her job more than ever.

Tess had taken the Finance letter to work, ignored Duke's *Urgent!* notes because since the election everything had been urgent, and wrote straight back:

I have lived with my partner, Tess Petrou, for twelve consecutive years. We form a single, stable household. Our joint income is DOUBLE the minimum threshold. I therefore DO meet the requirements for residence on St Mira. Please amend your records accordingly and confirm in writing.

Tess printed the letter, and re-read it, then removed the block caps because she'd calmed down by then. Should she take it home for Arlo to sign? She thought it'd just work him up. And Tess forged his signature all the time: birthday cards, Christmas cards, and this wasn't so different, just routine paperwork. Arlo's signature was easy to fake – A B and a line that trailed off, like a child learning the alphabet and then just giving up.

Tess signed. She folded the letter exactly and ran a nail along the folds. Envelope. Stamp. There. Done. And at lunch, she'd put it in the post-box beside the Comms Office gate, which was no longer Royal Mail red. They'd all been repainted, 'the colour of the dawn on the Blue Mountains,' a Firster spokesman had said. Pantone 307 C to the department charged with changing the livery of St Miran Post.

But then, a couple of days ago, the Finance Office had written again asking for Arlo's marriage certificate. He had to submit that for Tess's income to be allowed into his calculations. Tess had rung Arlo's caseworker, and a woman at the other end had said, 'Strangers cannot subsidise each other.' It was a bored, office voice.

'I know Arlo Brown extremely well. We're long-term partners.'

'In the eyes of the law, you're flatmates. All you do is share the rent.' And the government was keen on marriage. They'd held a Family First Festival in every neighbourhood of Mirapolis.

'Furthermore...'

Did people really use that word?

'...you are not blood and you are not married so I am not allowed to be having this conversation.' And the line went dead.

Tess told Jeannie not to forget the Dictaphone. She said to listen and repeat twice a day, every day, morning and night, which made learning Greek sound like dental hygiene. Tess and Arlo saw Jeannie out, waving her down the stairs with the farewell phrases that were on the recording, while in the background the Moros's sewing machines whirred.

They went onto the balcony. In Exodus Square, the maple had been dismembered. A dustbin van was scooping it up. For years, the vans had said: *Recycle. Reclaim. Reuse.* Now they trawled the city warning foreigners who weren't meant to be here: *GO HOME OR FACE ARREST.*

Jeannie emerged from their building, Emma in her arms. She cruised across the Square, flashing gold, and heading into uncharted waters. She glanced up and blew them a kiss. They waved till she'd disappeared round the corner of All Saints. Dear, brave Jeannie.

'What are her chances?' Arlo said.

She wore film-star heels but was as tough as old boots. It was why everyone in her village loved her. 'She just has to listen to the tape.'

They went back into the kitchen. Arlo finished off his shortbread. Tess topped up the sink for the washing up, and against the gush of water said, 'Actually, Arlo, I *haven't* dealt with it. We've got a problem with the Finance Office.'

And Tess explained.

Arlo listened, toying with the salt and pepper, with elastic bands and odd coins, moving them about like pieces in a game whose rules were unknown to him. And when Tess had finished, just silence. Then, without a word, Arlo got up and left the room. Tess heard the bathroom door shut, the sound of the lock which they never used, and then the shower run. Arlo was usually quick in the bathroom. But not today. He was taking it in, taking his time, being thorough.

Tess went back onto the balcony and looked down. For as long as anyone could remember, a maple had splashed shadows onto that Square. Now there was a crater, and into it a crane lowered a monument to the English exodus. Vera was watching from her balcony too. Rron would be inside, watching it live on TV. Mr and Mrs Moros were milling around down there, bearing cloth that soon, probably, would be used for an unveiling to fanatical fanfare.

When Arlo came out, he was dressed for the office. He'd shaved. It always made him look younger and earnest, as if he'd go knocking on doors and want to sell religion. Except he couldn't manage the righteous smile. Or any smile. 'So. What now?'

'Are you OK, Arlo?'

'I'm being practical. Not looking ahead. So, what now?'

Well, since getting the letter, Tess had checked the regulations. One option was for a family member to act as guarantor. But it was a large sum.

'Like bail. As if I'm a criminal for doing a legitimate job? For teaching *Life* and English?'

Tess said, 'I thought maybe we could ask Edwin?' She'd wondered about it a long time. She was an only child and so had no idea about sibling relations, but when it came to family, their options were limited.

Arlo spent a while looking at his feet, working the toes as if typing out his thoughts. 'What I don't understand is how parents can produce such different people. Same ovaries, same testes, two years apart, and they give birth to different species.' Then he said, abruptly for him: 'Oh, what the hell... All right, then, let's ask Edwin.'

'So, will you call him?'

'*I* can't call him. We haven't spoken in years.'

'Well, *I* can't call him. I've never met him.' Tess only knew Edwin from the family tree that hung in the hallway of the Browns' Dover home. Edwin Rodney Ralph. Born two years before Arlo. Married to Amaryllis, a descendant of James 'Paraffin' Young, the Scottish shale oil pioneer and source of Edwin's wealth. Tess also knew Edwin from the photos that Joy kept close. In fact, she kept both sons close; wasn't there a photo in every room? But Edwin was the son who'd been endowed: he had a body that played rugby and a face cast from geometry. His angles were protractor-exact, the kind that made things tessellate and rotate, that made the world go round. Whereas Arlo's face was not divisible by anything neat, a face of fractions and remainders. Elmer, the engineer, had mentioned it once to Joy, and she'd repeated it over family Sunday lunch, because it was so *true*. It was a *fact*, and it helped distil in her own mind the difference between the boys.

Arlo said to Tess, 'I don't know why Edwin isn't ashamed of his wealth. Why don't the rich just give their money away? They don't need it.'

'I think the rich don't feel rich. There's always someone richer. Plus there's the lifestyle that seems normal. Or earned. Or deserved.'

'Then maybe the rich need to meet the poor. Edwin, meet Arlo.' Then, 'On second thoughts, let's *not* call Edwin.' He'd answer the phone with something like 'Hey!' as if they were pals and chatted all the time. And Arlo would hear his smile down the line, would picture his bathroom-tile teeth – square and white and even. And Edwin would listen to his younger brother and make understanding noises, and then he'd say, 'How about this: do the maths, put it down in black and white – Excel spreadsheet for preference – and I'll see what I can do.' Arlo would have to make his case. It'd be like talking to a bank manager and applying for a loan. Arlo gave Tess a look that was meant to be care-free but came across as desolate.

She said, 'But you're happy, Arlo.'

'How do you know Edwin's not happy *and* rich?'

'Maybe he is. So, that's two happy men. Different men, happy with different things.' It sounded good. Tess almost believed it herself. She said, 'Or else we could ask Joy.'

'I knew you'd say that.'

'She has enough money for bail.'

'Please don't ask my mum. You know it'd come with strings.' Christmas would turn into Christmas-and-New Year. It'd be: come over for my birthday. 'Anyway, how do you know she has enough for bail?'

Because Tess had already rung her – just a provisional, test-the-waters, off-the-record call. She'd explained about the Law on Financial Self-Sufficiency, which meant foreigners had to earn the equivalent of £30,000 a year or they needed a guarantor.

Joy had said, 'Well, Arlo does, doesn't he?'

'This flat is free.'

A pause while she juggled figures at the other end of the line, guessing the rent and adding it to a salary she had no idea about. 'It's not that much to be earning, is it? Not at his age.'

Tess wanted to say: it's got nothing to do with age. Gone are the days of career structures and working your way up the salary scale. She thought: please don't say what you're about to say.

'You know, Edwin...'

Tess turned to Arlo now. 'I don't *know* she has enough. I'm just guessing.'

'Please never, ever ring my mum.'

'I won't ring her.' She'd email her instead and say: forget I ever called. Forget I said anything about you know what. And please NEVER MENTION IT. She'd leave the block capitals in. Possibly make them red. And she'd sign off: *Love T.B. xxx.* Joy didn't always do what Tess asked, but she never over-rode her in her capacity as a Brown.

Arlo put on the apron and finished the washing up, the radio on loud to cover the clamour in Exodus Square. Tess stood in the kitchen doorway and watched him. Arlo was at home in the kitchen. He became a different person here. He moved fast and focused and filled the room. Within arm's reach, his gadgets – the jam thermometer, stick blender, Japanese knife and knife grinder. Also the folder of recipes fine-tuned over time. Every day, he fed her. Arlo kept Tess going.

She turned her gaze to the elaborate ears of the bow that hung at his waist, 'If I were to say, "Will you marry me?" what would you say?'

'I'd say: that makes me the subject and you the object of the action. Did you mean it like that?'

Tess felt herself cave in. She leant against the doorframe. She thought: can't you just do what other people do? Say: *Yes! That'd be wonderful!* Or even: *No, thank you.* But grammar? This wasn't how she'd expected it. Tess had thought, many times over the years, about how she'd propose, and it was always early summer, a light breeze blowing and high cirrus clouds wisping the sky, which meant a warm front was coming.

She glanced at Arlo at the kitchen sink, his hands still dug into water. It wasn't meant to be like this. It was a once-in-a-lifetime question for a once-in-a-lifetime decision. And now that moment was gone, lost forever. Tess's eyes drifted across the walls, over cheap kitchen cabinets fitted years ago for StUKCO language teachers who probably wouldn't stay long. But Arlo had stayed, and Tess had stayed with him, and their fingerprints were everywhere. Usually, the kitchen seemed crazy and chaotic and inviting to her. Right now, it looked wrecked.

Tess pulled herself straight, then an intake of breath to rephrase the question. 'Arlo, shall we marry?'

'Why do you ask?'

Tess took a chair. She sat. She explained: they could pool their resources and get the Finance Office off their backs only if they were married.

'We *are* married.'

'Officially.'

'Officially, every year we go to Kentish Town and celebrate our anniversary. Plus,' he said, drying his hands on the apron, 'we vowed we wouldn't.'

'That was *then*.'

'Nothing's changed. Not between us.'

Twelve years had gone by. A lifetime had passed. 'We have reason to now.'

'It's a bad reason.' Then said to his reflection in the window as if to witness his own resolution: 'I am *not* getting married for the Firsters.'

'It'd be getting married for *us*.' Then Tess muttered – but audibly, because she meant it as a complaint but knew he'd take it as a compliment: 'Your bloody principles...'

'I'm glad one of us has them.'

'I have them too. And my principle in this case is: we have to find a way through.'

'By any means necessary?'

'Not *any* means. By *some* means. Such as those at our disposal.'

He turned to Tess. 'Can you imagine getting married? *I* can imagine it.' And he told her about the Register Office packed with Georgios-and-Mira pairs, the men in military uniform, the women like balls of white tumbleweed, already pregnant in the rush to answer the call to make native babies. 'I Pledge to Thee, St Mira' in orchestral version, and marriage vows you'd never agree to under any normal circumstances.

Tess said, 'Or else a small party with a few friends in Dover Castle?'

On the radio, the pips for the news. Arlo switched it off. For a moment, they listened to where a voice would be.

Should she suggest Gibraltar? John Lennon and Yoko Ono got married there. Or else they could elope to Gretna Green? Do it in secret in a blacksmith's shop, the marriage sealed on an ancient anvil.

Joy would love it if they got married. She'd already told Tess that. It would turn their relationship into a fact, recorded on paper, signed and dated. It would bring certainty. Joy would be touched and relieved that her son was officially tied to Tess, for as long as they both shall live.

It'd taken Joy five years to decide that Tess was more than a passing phase. It was twice as long as all his other girlfriends, and there'd been quite a few – far more than Tess had had boyfriends. Before Arlo, she'd dated her three foreign languages: Greek, French, and an Englishman learning Albanian. But now, in Joy's view, Tess had progressed from being Arlo's girlfriend to being his partner. In fact, his *lovely* partner. That's what she liked to say. And on Tess's fifth Christmas in Dover, Elmer had presented her with the Brown family tree. There she was, *Tess née Petrou* in flawless italics and linked to Arlo by a line of permanent ink. 'Congratulations, pet, you're one of us now.'

Tess knew Elmer would be happy if they got married. And especially happy for Arlo, because he'd made it work this time. He'd think: it's not easy getting on long-term with the same person. It takes years and diplomacy and thinking about. But Arlo had done it. Tess was a good person, which meant Tess-and-Arlo was a good thing. And if they wanted to get married, then good on them. At the wedding, he'd put an arm around his son's shoulder and regard the groom with a kind but distant curiosity, as if he were one of his fossils, an imprint of the boy he used to know.

Arlo said, 'Do you really want to be a *wife*?'

She'd rather be a wife than the partner of a deportee.

'I don't want to be a *husband*.' It sounded like husbandry, like raising livestock, like all the men he'd spent his life trying not to be.

That fifth Christmas, Joy had talked Tess through all the Brown men on the family tree – the husbands and fathers who'd passed the name on. She said 'Brown' originally meant 'to bear children.' 'And look at them all,' and she'd scrolled an arm down the generations. At the bottom, three inches of unwritten future. Not that she thought the family would stop at that point. She wasn't a catastrophiser, didn't think the world was about to end. Joy said you had to draw the line somewhere, and that for her was the skirting board.

Tess thought: *Husband. Wife.* Did it matter? 'Can we care less about words?'

'You *work* with words. You *can't* not care about them.'

'Or what other people think of us?'

Arlo didn't react.

'Or what *we* think of us?'

Silence.

The truth was: Tess would be happy to be married into the Browns. Through them, she'd have a family. Joy had spent years in the National Archive and had traced the line back to the Normans. The Browns were related to Capability, which Tess bore in mind when she fiddled with her plants, and which Joy honoured through hours on her knees in the garden.

And when Tess thought about her little branch of the Brown family tree, the thing that struck her most was that Joy had only a tenuous hold on all the men that mattered: she'd lost Arlo to St Mira; Edwin to the counties – only eighty miles west, but a side of England unknown to her. Her grandsons were photos on the mantelpiece. Even Elmer sometimes retreated to the shed where he ran his fingers over his fossils and felt alive and connected again. Maybe that was why Joy believed in God. Believe in him and he'd never desert her. He was the one constant man in her life, and she had the power to keep him. It made Tess sad. It made Tess want to make their Christmases work. They *did* work for Elmer because, although he didn't get that much from Arlo, he didn't need much either. They *didn't* really work for Joy because nothing was ever quite enough, and the more she wanted, the less Arlo could give. But the more Tess could give, the less she needed from Arlo. As a package, Joy got more than she'd ever had before. Tess-and-Arlo were a joint effort.

Tess knew all this because she was a Brown and Not-a-Brown. She was inside and outside.

Elmer was like that too. Plus he was an engineer and understood systems.

And the main thing was: Elmer liked Tess. Joy liked Tess. Tess liked them. And they all, in very different ways, loved Arlo.

'Arlo?' Tess said now.

His hands reached behind his back for the knot. He undid the tie and hung the apron up. 'Yes?'

'So we won't get married, then?'

'No.'

'Not even for the piece of paper?'

'A marriage certificate won't stop them. It'll be something else after that: they won't like my name, my face, my tax records, my health insurance, that I go to England for Christmas.'

'So what then?'

'We wait. We wait and see.' He glanced down. He spent a long time looking at his feet. When Tess had first met Arlo, she thought they were average feet, normal size, not much good for swimming. But over the years, she'd learnt to read them. Arlo had canary feet – instantly hot, instantly cold. If the weather was on the cusp of changing his feet knew.

He reached out an arm to Tess. 'Actually,' he said, 'let's *not* wait.' He picked up a bag and felt a trouser pocket for keys. 'Shall we start the day again?' He took her hand. 'It's Saturday. Let's go to the market. Let's buy lovely things and I'll cook us a lovely meal and we'll have a lovely time.'

They ran downstairs and burst into the daylight and ignored the crowd gathered at the monument because right then, those people had nothing to do with them.

My Arlo, Tess thought. Lovely Arlo, full of loveliness. Waiting was fine. One day they would get married. Some other time. Some other place. Maybe when they were old, and had nothing left to lose, or win, or do.

But before she died, Tess did, definitely, want to marry Arlo.

8.

Do you hold, or have you ever held any other nationality or nationalities?

NO.

What is your race/ethnicity/tribal group?

WHITE

Have your ever been fingerprinted in any country?

NO

Tell us any other information about your personal circumstances you think we should know.

SEE OVER →.

Arlo said they'd wait, and so they waited – they didn't know what for. Meanwhile, life went on. In outline, it was recognisable – work, home, work again – though everything was different. Arlo went into StUKCO, and each class, one or two fewer students came. Sometimes they emailed an apology: *I am sorry, but due to current difficulties with foreign nationals, I am unable to continue with the course.* Or else they mailed to say they were leaving the country and taking whatever English they had with them. No-one was going to the UK. In the past, some of Arlo's students had been taken on by the Smethwick Condiments Company and had relocated to the Midlands. But not anymore. It was almost impossible to get into Britain now. They were heading instead to small countries in the region with a language no-one expected them to know and where English was the lingua franca. English was a passport now to everywhere except England.

There was still the problem of the Law on Financial Self-Sufficiency. Arlo asked Mr Dee to change the way he was paid: could he increase his salary and Arlo would pay rent on the StUKCO flat instead? Mr Dee listened. He looked concerned, or maybe just dutiful. It was hard to read the tilde on his brow. He said he'd consult with Accounts, though they had responsibilities – to norms and expectations as well as the law – and so it would take time. He said, 'Do not be disheartened if I am unable to allow it, though do take heart that I try.' Mr Dee mentioned Arlo's heart twice in one sentence. Later, it felt like a warning: he'd sensed what was coming and Arlo should take care.

At the Central Communications Office, Tess got into work punctually and left whenever Duke released her, and tried not to notice the hours in between. There was an endless stream of government statements, which she read without reading. One thing she did notice, though, was more and more use of the passive: *All foreigners on the island have now been reported to the authorities. Illegal foreigners will be arrested and deported without warning.* It was as if no-one was responsible for the things the Firsters were doing. And, in response, Tess found herself entering a passive state of mind: these were just words moving from one language into another. She was distanced from their meaning, felt suspended above the act of doing her job.

At lunchtime, she had sandwiches at her desk these days. She'd stopped going to Dimitri's. Conversation had tailed off whenever she went in. And although Dimitri had told her: *It's not because of you and it's not about you*, what else could it have been? So now, instead of the Daily Special, Tess spent her lunch breaks with cling-filmed leftovers and the internet. She became interested in the weather – past trends, present anomalies, future doom. She found a site that let her track storms as they crossed the continent. She sat at her desk and watched lightning strike the heartlands of Europe. It was all very prophetic.

Mr and Mrs Moros conducted their business more visibly than ever. They greeted customers outside the shop, and took bolts of cloth into the Square to examine them by daylight. Their nieces, Fashion graduates in Milan, had come home to help with the family firm. Associations for the Defence of This and That were springing up across St Mira, and they all needed a uniform. Rron was talking more these days, spending time with the workmen and their radio. Foreign pop had been banned, and in its place, traditional dances in 9/8 time, *kardiochtypi* in 2/2 time and military marches in 2/4 time. The entire rhythm of the island had changed. Vera said almost nothing. She watched St Mira alter from her third-floor balcony – though mostly she came out at night when nothing seemed to have changed after all.

And then, finally, Tess and Arlo found out what they'd been waiting for. It was a letter from the Immigration Office:

Dear Mr Brown,

According to our records, your nationality is [BLANK].

You and ALL household members must attend an immigration interview. Each household member must bring their passport/s and proof of address. A household member is ANYONE living with you on a temporary or permanent basis, regardless of their relationship to you or their immigration status.

Tess rang the number given on the letter, but got a machine that wouldn't take messages. She asked at work and no-one had had anything like it. She rang Jeannie, who'd answered the phone in Greek. No, she said, she'd had nothing like that from Immigration, touch wood. But she did get a letter from StUKCO, and she'd passed the retake of her language test. She thanked Tess again. 'And if there's ever anything I can do, anything at all, just say.'

Right now, Tess needed help. 'I need help, Jeannie,' and she read the letter down the line. Jeannie made sounds as if sucking boiled sweets. And Jeannie-the-hairdresser, the woman who understood people, told Tess she understood how confusing it must be, and how distressing. 'I can hear it in your voice, love, I can picture you now,' and Tess saw herself cast left-to-right in one of Jeannie's mirrors with Jeannie in her raging colours standing behind her like a bush on fire. And then silence. Tess listened to her breath, an uneasy breeze blown from the south coast to the north, because this woman who could chat to anyone about anything couldn't think of anything else to say.

On the morning of their interview, Arlo woke Tess with tea. He'd been up all night, judging by the noises – the fridge door, kettle, the porridge pan – that had beaten a fitful rhythm through her sleep. He was in a brown suit, beige shirt, dull brown tie. He said he was trying to be overlookable. Actually, he looked like a package, like someone about to be processed, sorted, sent off – who knew where? They sat on the bed and drank Yorkshire Tea, their quintessentially English balm from Sri Lanka, India and Kenya.

It was raining heavily when they set out. Water scalloped down slopes in the road. They walked fast, jumping puddles, bending away from the spray of the traffic. They were going blind into this interview – no-one had been able to tell them what it was about. So Tess distracted herself with questions such as: do you get less wet if you hurry through rain, or do you hit as many raindrops, only quicker? Or should you just stand still and wait for the rain to stop?

They arrived at Immigration soaking.

They'd been to this office before, when Arlo got citizenship. But that was in the summer and the pebbledash façade made you think of the beach, and the brass veneer was sunstruck. Today, it was grey and still half-shuttered. The man at the door checked their appointment, told them they were early and they had to wait.

'Can't we come in? It's raining,' Arlo said.

'It's only water, do you not bathe?'

At nine-thirty exactly, he opened the door and pointed them through to Security. Arlo made the metal door beep. He always beeped at airports, though they never found anything metallic. He had a strong magnetic field, that's what Tess thought. He just had that kind of soul. The officer was suspicious of Tess's shoulders, took her aside and patted her down because something must account for the bulk. Then he said, 'Laptops? Phones?'

They took out their phones.

'Turn them off.'

They turned them off.

Communications with the outside world were not permitted in the building.

Tess and Arlo watched their bags disappear through the X-ray machine. Then Arlo's reappeared and was opened up and searched. An officer removed the contents item by item and Arlo had to explain them.

A hat. A scarf. 'That's a hat. That's a scarf.'

Tupperware. 'Food. In case we have to wait.'

A plastic bag of pills. They were for his for headaches. He could take them without water now, without even tipping his head.

'And that?'

It was a book. 'Something to read.' It was *The Lord of the Rings*, once voted the UK's best-loved novel, according to *Life*. Arlo didn't read fantasy, but maybe reality was getting on top of him.

'English isn't allowed in public spaces.'

'My bag isn't a public space.'

'But it's *in* a public space.'

So, what did that mean? That he could read the book, but only inside his bag?

Tess said, 'That's not very helpful.'

'I'm not here to be helpful. I'm here to make a challenging environment. And it's working because I'm pissing you off. Am I right?'

Yes, that was right.

Arlo picked up *The Lord of the Rings* and weighed it in his palm. It worried Tess that he'd chosen to read it, was three-quarters through already. Did he really need that much illusion to cope with this much life?

'A challenging environment. That's my aim at the end of the day.'

Arlo repacked his bag with the book at the bottom. It was unreachable there, unreadable.

'There you go, I've done my job.'

Just doing his job. Wasn't that what they all said?

And then Tess thought – and the thought troubled her – that she'd said as much herself.

They went upstairs to the Waiting Room and sat at the back on pine-veneer pews, as in a soulless, new-found church. On the far wall, where the pulpit would be, a TV screen listed threats to the nation. A voice that came from the bowels of the earth said

NO! to drugs, infectious diseases and illegal immigrants. In the corner, a yellowing yucca longed for water while rain thundered against the air-tight windows.

Arlo fingered his documents: his passports and proof of address in original and photocopied, and translated into Greek by Tess. She was preoccupied, trying to work out what this interview was for. She wandered to the front and turned for a glimpse of a face she might know. But there was only a handful of other people waiting. A couple of families were lost to their phones. A woman was reading a book in a script that seemed to drip from the line. Something Himalayan maybe? Tess wanted to go to where she was from. She wanted to ask: do they think your nationality's *[BLANK]* too?

Then a buzzer went and a voice said: 'Brown Room Four.'

There was no please. There was no 'Mister'. Arlo was no longer fully a person and this wasn't really a room. It was more the kind of low-lit cubby-hole Tess knew from border crossings. A smoked-glass screen stopped a couple of inches short to allow papers across the counter. No chairs, no hellos. Whatever this was, it'd be brief and impersonal.

They handed over their documents. The woman behind the screen reached out a lazy arm. Sewn onto her sleeve, the head of a Sea Eagle, the bird of prey that patrolled the coast of St Mira. From her wrist came the clammy smack of cheap scent – the type they sold at the market next to carpet cleaner and deodorant. She took a while with their papers. Tess studied her lowered head, the hair raked back, the parting tight enough to hurt. What was going on inside there? What story was she telling herself about these people from England? Then her face re-emerged as if coming up for air. 'Connection between the two of you?'

Arlo said, 'We're partners.'

'But single.'

'We've lived together for years.'

'How many children?'

'We haven't got any.'

'Zero children.' The number seemed to satisfy her. Was she glad the foreigners weren't breeding? 'Anyone else in your household, or is this it?'

Yes, Tess was it.

She slipped a sheet onto the counter and placed a paperweight hand on top. 'I am formally issuing you with this notice. Please confirm you have received it.'

'Yes, I've received it.'

She took her hand away and Arlo read:

DEPRIVATION OF ST MIRAN CITIZENSHIP

ORDER UNDER SECTION 40(2) OF THE ST MIRAN NATIONALITY ACT

It is hereby Ordered, in pursuance of the notice issued by the Secretary of State for the Home Department, that

Arlo BROWN

born in the United Kingdom

on 20 October 1986

be deprived of his St Miran citizenship on grounds that it was acquired through naturalisation and that deprivation is conducive to the public good.

Arlo swung his jaw as if he'd been punched. Tess took the sheet and scanned it. 'Ignore it,' she told him. She gave the piece of paper back. 'It's not true.'

A shrug of the officer's rounded shoulders. 'Sorry to break the news, but all naturalisations have been cancelled.'

'No they *haven't*.'

'It's the new law.'

'No it's *not*. I get to see all new laws and that one doesn't exist.'

'From tomorrow it does.'

110

'So it's *not* law then. And what you're doing right now is illegal.'

'"Efficient" is the word we use. The Immigration Office is on top of its workload.' She rocked against the spring of her chair. 'Anyway, by the time his paperwork's through, it *will* be law.'

Which meant that in the morning, this law would be on Tess's desk and she'd be translating it; *just doing her job.* She said, 'Why the hurry? Do you have some kind of target?'

'Only people like...' A nod towards Arlo, who'd bent down and was ransacking his bag for something. Maybe she was used to moments like this, the blind panic, the whatever-it-was that couldn't be found, because she reached for her cigarettes and lit up.

Arlo came back with paracetamol. He forced them out of the blister pack, put them on his tongue and swallowed.

The officer swallowed. Tail-end smoke coiled from her nose.

Tess took Arlo's hands. 'You have citizenship till tomorrow...' What could they do in a day that would fix this? 'Arlo, we *have* to get married.'

Tess got out her phone.

'No phones.'

She pressed the switch.

'Phones are not allowed.'

Why did phones take so long to start? Tess said, 'I'm calling my lawyer.' She didn't have a lawyer.

The officer put their documents back on the counter. 'Take care of your bits of paper. Things are hotting up on St Mira. You know what temperature paper burns at?' the orange tip of her cigarette hanging close enough to catch. Then she leant into a microphone. 'Brown audit complete.'

A voice crackled back from somewhere in the building.

'Roger. Sending them in.'

They went through a door that said *Do Not Disturb*. And they sat, undisturbed, in a room set up for families: a ring of chairs at the desk, a map of the world hung off centre, a box of scented tissues. Also a toddlers' playpen with a house in ruins in Lego.

They waited.

The door opened so quietly, Tess didn't notice. She didn't know how long they'd not been alone, how long they'd been observed from behind. She just sensed a draft, and turned to see a woman in military khakis with stars on her epaulettes and her long hair down. She didn't give her name. She didn't wear a name tag. She was slight and quick, and slipped to her desk as if her army boots were ballet shoes.

There were no introductions. She just took their documents and laid them out as if for a game of patience. Her eyes ran back and forth, figuring out how best to play them, these pieces of these puzzling people. She turned to Arlo. 'Why did you not renew your British passport?'

'Because I became St Miran.' He'd got a St Miran passport so he didn't need his British one. When it expired, Arlo had filed it as a memento in his Don't Throw Box, along with his degree certificate and his will. He'd left everything to Tess apart from his body, which he'd donated to St Miran medical science.

Also because why would he want to identify as British? Why would he, as he put it, want to be associated with a shrunken country adrift from the world that flattered itself with inflated stories as it sank into oblivion?

The immigration officer reached for his hand as if to console him. In fact it was to take prints. She pressed his fingers onto an ink pad and then onto his file. She did the same to Tess, a cool grip, instrumental fingers. Then she held out the box of tissues and they all wiped their hands. It was an odd moment of etiquette.

She picked up Arlo's St Miran passport. 'You are aware that from tomorrow, this...' She waved it at the clock as if making clear how little time between now and midnight '...is invalid?'

Tess said, 'Only from *tomorrow*.'

'But your appointment is scheduled for today, and so we proceed as if today is tomorrow.'

Then Tess saw the guillotine.

The officer stood. She slid the corner of the passport under the blade.

'Please don't do that.'

She gave the blade her weight.

It was harsh and final, like something you heard at the butcher's.

Tess felt sick. She reached for Arlo's hand, but found herself fingering air. Arlo's hands were in his lap. He was looking at his shoes. The toes were wet. His feet would be frozen.

The officer placed the passport on the table. 'I'm sorry,' she said, 'but you are now undocumented.'

She sat.

Tess held the clipped corner to the cover. Could they fix it? Would glue be enough? How did you cover up a join? Then Arlo took the passport and fingered it, stroked it, like something fond and newly dead. He stopped at the photo. It was from the booth in Mirapolis bus station. He hadn't thought about how he'd look for the next ten years – hadn't flattened his hair or straightened his collar. He'd just stared at the bulb waiting for the flash, and in his head, all the things he could do now that he was St Miran. He said, 'You know I got accelerated citizenship?' He'd made exceptional efforts to integrate, and 'a notable contribution to St Miran culture,' the award letter said. He'd written a song, 'No Island is an Island' – a kind of John Donne-meets-Abba. It was shortlisted for the 2020 St Miran entry for Eurovision.

Arlo said, 'I don't know what you mean: "undocumented".' He had plenty of documents: his StUKCO card. His credit card. A whole box-file of papers bearing his name, and he reeled them off – all the things that proved he existed and who he was.

The officer put her hands on the desk and clamped her fingers shut. She looked immovable, was going to sit it out, this list of meaningless credentials. This was a woman who wasn't going anywhere. And, actually, that was true: all uniformed servants of the state – police, army, immigration, border control – they'd all been asked to hand in their passports. No-one was to leave the country 'at a time of national upheaval'. The state needed all its resources.

She said, 'Undocumented means you have no document that legally recognises your presence in this country, or your right to leave it.'

Tess said, 'So, he can't stay and he can't go?'

A nod to that.

'But I'm *British!*' It sounded so odd coming from Arlo, the man who'd do anything to leave Britain behind. He turned to Tess: 'I *am* still British, aren't I?'

She said, 'Does Arlo have any legal status?'

'He's not stateless.'

'That still sounds like a non-thing.' Tess looked at him, his jacket hanging open, his tie loose, a package ransacked, a man undone.

'The good news,' the officer said, 'is that if you're British, you can apply for a passport online from anywhere in the world...' A glance at the floor. '...but, unfortunately, not from St Mira.' The Firsters had blocked access to the UK government site. Arlo could always try for an Emergency Travel Document from the nearest British Embassy. That was Albania. One obstacle was time. Everything was an emergency now and Tirana was overwhelmed. They were double-checking applications from St Mira because they'd been asked to. He might be able to speed things up in person. But how to get to Tirana with no travel documents?

Tess glanced up at the window. Was that north? Was Albania that way? It was overcast and there were no clues in the sky. But at least it had stopped raining. For a while, she knew, the world would shine. The grey slate of the pavement would be turned to silver and everything would look magnificent.

'And you, Miss...'

Tess turned to the officer. There were three stars on her epaulettes. What did that make her? Inspector, Superintendent?

'You have *two* passports, which isn't *so* unusual. And *two* names... which really *is*.' She threw her gaze over Tess as if to net her. Tess stared back, picking this woman apart. She had freckles. You didn't often see them on St Mira.

'Here...' She held up Tess's St Miran passport. 'You are Tess *Petrou*.'

That handful of dots could have been Gemini.

'And here...' That was her British one. 'You are Tess Isadora *Matthews*.'

Which meant that freckle would be Castor and that one was Pollux.

'Can you explain?'

'I changed my name.'

'Legally or whimsically?'

'By deed poll.'

'Why?'

'I'd just turned eighteen. I could.'

She held the passports open at the photos and moved her eyes between them, matching feature to feature, tying these two women up.

Tess said, 'Plus, in England, I had to spell "Petrou" all the time.'

'And "Matthews" is English.'

'As English as it gets.' Though ancient Hebrew, originally, and the name came to England with the Normans.

'And "Isadora" comes from Greece.'

Also from her mother.

Because the truth was: Tess had changed her name because she wanted to revive her. She hadn't been able to save Isadora from drowning, but she could save her from oblivion. Now she brought her back to life every time she said her name.

'Isadora Matthews is my mother's name.'

Her mother: the woman in the photograph, in the bathing suit with the swimmer's legs. It was the only photo Tess had of her. She was leaning against a rock and she wore big, round shades and was smiling into the sun. *St Mira* it said on the back. Handwriting. Her mother's, probably. *1983*. Was Isadora about to meet Nikos? Or had she already? Was Tess already growing in that flat stomach?

'You don't mind being a double?'

If you wanted to be the image of someone, it would be the woman in that photo. If any woman in the world could become your mother, you'd want it to be her. She looked eternally happy. Always the sun shone on her. And she'd stayed that way all of Tess's life. Even now, when Isadora would have been sixty-two, she was still in a bathing suit in her twenties.

'My mother's dead.'

'I'm sorry.'

Tess nodded. Usually, she waved a 'sorry' aside and said, 'Oh, it was a long time ago...' But not this time.

'You must have been close.'

'Mothers and daughters usually are,' though Tess couldn't remember it. It was so long gone. And that photo was the only trace Tess had of her. Stan had cleared out all her mother's things. He couldn't bear to live with his dead daughter.

'Is she buried in the UK?'

Isadora was in the Thames. Stan said she was happiest in water. He'd cremated her and cast the ashes into the river from Chelsea Bridge, in sight of Battersea Power Station, close to where she'd died.

The officer held out a hand. In her flattened palm, Tess's British passport, as if it had just landed there. Or was about to be released. 'So, to confirm: your British passport is in your legally recognised name – the name on the deed poll: Tess Isadora Matthews, born in London on the twenty-third of April nineteen eighty-four.'

It was Easter Monday that year.

It was St George's Day every year.

'And your St Miran passport...'

'I got it here. They asked for my birth certificate. I gave it to them. They issued the passport to Tess Petrou.'

Across the desk, an intake of air, then a slow release of breath. That was recognition. What had happened with Tess had happened to other people, she could tell. It was the way discrepancies arose, immigration records blurred, one person became two.

'And your direct St Miran relative is...'

'My grandfather, Konstantinos.'

'And where is he?'

'Scattered on St Mira. It's why I came.'

'And *his* birth certificate?'

It was in the Records Office. Vera had unearthed it when Tess had first arrived. But when Konstantinos left Mirapolis just after the war, he was paperless. He'd got in a boat going anywhere, and landed in Folkestone unable to prove who he was, or wasn't.

'Did your grandfather have siblings?'

Stan had one sister, now dead. And she had two daughters, now in a convent and bound by a vow of celibacy. Tess's line of the family line stopped there – in a draughty, white-walled monument to privation in a cleft between two mountains.

The officer looked hard at Tess, then put a finger across her lips, as if this was a secret, it's between you and me. 'People with more than one passport are either criminal, rich or interesting. Lucky you. In times like this you can't have enough passports.' She felt the British one and fingered the cover, the gold lettering worn away, EUROPEAN UNION as good as gone. She flicked through. 'It's one long weather forecast.'

Arlo said, 'There are only four cloudless days in the whole passport.' He knew such things because of *Life*.

She turned the pages, reading it like a picture book. She reached VILLAGE GREEN. 'Are there really places that look like this?' She sounded wistful. For a moment she was off duty.

Arlo said, 'In Kent there are.' The Browns used to tour local villages on Sunday afternoons. Joy wanted to take the boys to all the Norman churches so they could marvel at the history, at how long England had been Christian, how rooted the family faith. Then they went to the pub and ate ready-salted crisps and flicked wasps off their orange squash. Or else they watched a game of cricket played on the village green.

Then all of a sudden, Arlo sat up, his face bright. 'Games can last up to five days but still result in a draw!' He'd put on his *Life* voice.

The officer heard the change of tone and watched him closer.

He said, 'The idiosyncratic nature of the game and its complex laws are said to reflect the best of the British character and sense of fair play.'

'*Please*, Arlo.'

'You may come across expressions such as "rain stopped play," "batting on a sticky wicket," "playing a straight bat".'

Tess hung her head.

'"Bowled a googly" or "it's just not cricket".'

Silence after that. Tess's eyes rested on the cheap, white finish of the desk. Under the desk, Arlo was fingering a hand as if it hurt.

Then Tess turned to the officer. 'I'm sorry, but everything that's happened has been so unexpected, and is so confusing and difficult, and if I need to get back to you, who should I ask for?'

'We don't have names.' A shrug of her stars. 'Though, of course, we all have the same name. Aren't we all cousins on St Mira?' The officer stood. She went to a machine under the window. She placed a card on the flatbed and pressed a button. Something hummed. Over her shoulder she said to Tess, 'I saw in your passport: in an emergency your contact person is Arlo Brown.'

'And vice versa.'

'And if something happens to *both* of you?'

Tess picked up her passport. She turned to the inside cover. It was comforting – that row of Hardy cottages, the oak leaves, the wording: that in the Name of Her Majesty, all those whom it may concern were required to afford the bearer – which was her, Tess Isadora Matthews – such assistance and protection as may be necessary. 'Nothing will happen to *either* of us.' She reached for Arlo's knee. His trousers were damp, the hems dark.

The officer returned to the desk. 'Mr Arlo Brown. You have your invalid St Miran passport. You also have your expired British passport. And now you are to have this.' She handed him a card. There he was: his wide-eyed St Miran self, a number that ended in his date of birth, and stamped at an angle in ink that had bled: *UNDOCUMENTED.*

Then she produced a checklist and flicked a pen across the boxes. 'This is to confirm I've explained what has to be explained, withdrawn what has to be withdrawn, issued what has to be issued, and that you understand and agree. Do you understand and agree?'

Silence.

She dug her signature into the form and dated it. Her name was illegible, the kind of scrawl you use to get a pen to work. She stood. Tess thought it was to shake hands. In fact, it was to tidy up her desk.

Tess said, 'What do we do now?'

'You leave.'

So that was it? The interview was over? All done, everything settled, except nothing was settled. 'Leave? And go where?'

Outside this room was where Arlo was allowed and wasn't allowed, where logic no longer applied. Couldn't they just sit here protected by a sign that said *Do Not Disturb*? Tess wanted no more disturbance. She glanced at Arlo. He was close enough to touch but felt miles away. Her eyes turned to the tissues that someone before them had taken, to the wrecked house, to the tilted map on the wall. There was a whole world beyond St Mira and now it was out of reach.

9.

Do you have any friends in the UK?

YES

If 'Yes' please provide their full name, nationality, address and telephone number.

NOAM GERALD LANGBERG

BRITISH

ADDRESS: SHORT-STAY ACCOMMODATION, MIKAPOLIS, ST MIKA.

PHONE NUMBER: STORED IN MY PHONE UNDER 'CONTACTS' AS : NOMIE

NOAM LANGBERG IS AN OLD FRIEND. HE IS FORMERLY OF THE UK FOREIGN OFFICE AND NOW AN INDEPENDENT CONSULTANT AT NOAM LANGBERG INTERNATIONAL.

<u>PLEASE</u> CONTACT NOAM LANGBERG ABOUT MY CASE

The Immigration Office had been right: acquired citizenship was annulled overnight. When Tess got into work, the 'Regulation on National Clarity' was on her desk, along with a commentary from Varela. 'At long last,' he said, 'the blood of true St Mirans is legally protected. The fact has finally been acknowledged that this island is riddled with fake St Mirans.' On the wall opposite Tess's desk, a map had appeared. It was the new Firster Projection. St Mira was now at the centre of the world, the coast teethed with cliffs. 'I'd don khaki,' Varela said, 'pick up a rifle and head to the front lines to root them out.'

Tess sat.

She didn't have the energy to spin the globe and wish herself somewhere else.

She closed her eyes and listened to her own breathing. It was what she'd done last night when Arlo hadn't slept – not at all, as far as she could tell. And maybe he'd wanted Tess to be disturbed because he'd made his porridge with the kitchen door open and knocked the spoon against the side of the pan, banging out a protest. In the morning, the Oscar flag was hanging from his door. It meant: *Man overboard.*

Piled on the kitchen table, every document Arlo had been able to unearth to prove he existed. She didn't know he'd got a Duke of Edinburgh Silver Award, or represented Kent at the World Scout Jamboree in 1999. His Last Will and Testament was on the top, his body no longer donated to St Miran medical science. He'd scribbled that out and put: *Cremate me, Tess. Scatter me wherever.*

Wherever. He'd stopped caring. Now the decision was hers. And where would *wherever* be? Not the UK. Not St Mira. To the winds, then? To the world?

But, no. She wouldn't be scattering Arlo. It'd never be the right place, or the right weather, never the right moment, always too soon.

Tess hadn't felt like breakfast after thinking all of that. She'd left home without eating. Hunger was getting to her now though. She opened her packed lunch and skimmed the Regulation:

Our intention over the coming weeks and months... We shall... In due course... This will allow enough time for those affected to make alternative arrangements for their legal status.

Tess thought: shall, will? In due course? Those were statements about the future, but it was already happening. She put her sandwich down and knocked on Duke's door.

'Morning, Tess. How are you?'

'You never ask me that.'

He indulged her with a joyless smile. Then, 'Are you wearing flowers?'

Tess had decided to give up on khaki. She didn't want to look like one of his foot soldiers, like a Firster recruit in Moros kit.

'They suit you,' he said.

'They're foxgloves.' Foxgloves were poisonous, which was how she was feeling when she put it on this morning. Tess placed the Regulation on Duke's desk. 'Can we fact-check this? It's talking about the future, but it's happening now.'

'The future, clearly, is the tense in which the government wishes to express itself.'

'But you can't just make facts up.'

'Of course you can. The whole world has been doing it for years.'

'But the fact – the *truth*, as we used to say – is they are already implementing the policy.'

'Oh? Can we fact-check that?'

'Yesterday, Arlo was told he was no longer St Miran. I was there when they took away his citizenship.'

'Oh? I am sorry to hear that.' There was no regret in his voice. No surprise either. Did Duke somehow know already. He said, 'But you still have *yours*.'

'We're not talking about *me*. We're talking about my partner. *Him. His* citizenship. "I" is not the subject of every sentence.'

'I understand that.' He turned to his computer where his self was cast dark on the screen. 'Your partner, of course, is still British...' He put his hands on his knees and glanced between his legs. Duke had taken to wearing deck shoes, as if the Central Communications Office were a cruise ship and here he was being carried somewhere glorious with a view from his window of the open sea. '...for what that might be worth.'

'Being British would be worth a lot, if Arlo still had a valid passport.'

Duke looked shocked, but only theatrically. And momentarily. Only in the way lawyers allowed anything onto their face – via a reckoning of what's expected and what they're going to say next. He said, 'That was a little thoughtless of him, to let it expire.'

'Arlo assumed the world was sane. That it was predictable. That rules still applied.'

'That was unobservant of him.' Duke observed her. He seemed more curious than sympathetic. Maybe he was asking himself how she was going to react to this turn of events.

Tess thought: what would *you* do in this situation, Duke? He lived in a world where you looked after Number One. It was dog eat dog. She said, 'Do dogs eat dogs, Dr Kontos?'

'Sometimes. To reduce litter size.'

He didn't have a partner. He didn't have a wife. He did have a bulldog, though – a small black French one called Marine. She'd seen them in town together. Tess said, 'What would you do if they started rounding up dogs, Dr Kontos?'

'All bonds are transient.' He turned back to his screen. 'All ties contingent.' He started typing. And that was that.

Tess spent the next hour not translating the 'Regulation on National Clarity' and listening to Duke emptying filing cabinets and feeding papers into a shredder. Finally, the whirring stopped and he came out with two large bags for disposal. He said, 'Tess,

I have been thinking about what you said, and I want to impress upon you: it is a mistake to be overly attached to truth. What matters is what we *believe* to be true.' He spun her globe idly and watched it slow. Then he put a finger to the USA and the world stopped turning. 'I love America. Do you know why?' He clapped a hand to his chest as if about to recite the 'Pledge of Allegiance'. 'The freedom to believe. Millions think the sun revolves around the earth and there's no such thing as evolution. They believe they are the greatest nation on earth, and forty percent have never left the country to find out otherwise.' He leant forward, his tie tonguing her desk. 'Have you ever done jury service, Tess?' It was one of the delights of life in court, he said, to watch the sway of the jury. The lawyer for the prosecution makes his case and twelve faces nod because for sure the defendant is guilty. Then the lawyer for the defence makes his case and the faces nod because for sure the defendant is innocent. And you watch them file off to the jury room to consider their verdict with a look of bewilderment – like children shown a magic trick – because something impossible has just happened: they are convinced both of the defendant's guilt *and* innocence. And now they have the task of giving up one of those beliefs – through reason, ideally, though that was rarely so. 'It depends on the crime, but generally men convict and women give the benefit of the doubt.'

He looked at Tess. 'You look doubtful. Do you have a question?'

'Do you want me to take the rubbish down?'

He glanced at the bags he'd put at her desk. Prompt disposal was a new Firster initiative. Every day, someone from the Clean Country Force collected the rubbish. They wore an olive green uniform designed by the Moros's nieces with a Milanese flourish to the flare.

'Would you mind?' Duke said.

'Is it our past you've shredded?'

'As already noted, the future is the tense of the times.'

For the next couple of days, Tess was busy translating legislation that shifted the kaleidoscope of life on St Mira. They were enforcing silence in public on Sundays – which was pressure from the church. They were removing the limit on guns per household, which was the hunting lobby backed by the church. And they were taxing dogs by weight, which was the Finance Office raising quick cash, and which angered Duke, but only mildly because Marine fell below the taxable threshold.

Duke was busy over those two days too – networking, preparing, shopping – though Tess didn't know that yet. All she knew was that on Friday morning, she went into the office and found his door open. She thought the cleaners had forgotten it, and that Duke – for the first time ever – would get into work after her. But, no, here he was, reclining in his armchair, arms on the rests, his eyes shut. 'So, we're wearing poppies today.'

Was this a game? Seeing through closed lids?

Duke was in a new outfit. It was the same as usual – light shirt, dark trousers – only something was different. Tess couldn't quite put her finger on it, except that money was involved. Duke had acquired a Look. Had he been looking in a Look Book?

She said, 'What are you doing?'

'Nothing. Which is, of course, *something*.' And still his eyes were closed.

She went to shut the door.

'Please leave the door.'

She left the door. Tess went to her desk and shifted her chair to be out of his line of sight when he finally opened his eyes. And then Duke leapt to his feet, burst in, and did a circuit of her room. He came to rest against the far wall, which put him into perspective – wide Taekwondo shoulders, small deck shoes, a V-shaped man, which in this mood, he would probably say was V for virile and she would say was V for very self-congratulatory.

He said, 'Thought association, Tess. Are you ready?'

And still the games.

'How about we begin with...' His gaze lingered on her. '... with your poppies... with *red*.'

Tess didn't like his focus on her chest. She crossed her arms.

'Come on,' he said. 'Thought association: red...?'

'Cross.'

'St George.'

'England.'

Duke clapped, as if she'd got it right. Then he wanted to do it again, only with Tess starting with red.

Tess didn't want to play, but Duke was insistent. 'So, *red*, then...'

'Bull.'

'Dog.'

'England.' Duke looked pleased. 'You see...?' And he was off again. 'Red.'

'Nose.'

'Farce.'

Tess thought: England?

'You see where all roads lead?'

Tess thought about England. She glanced at the map. Britain had been cast to the edge of the earth in the new Firster Projection. How was Arlo ever going to get there? She said, 'What are they going to do with undocumented people?' What was the plan: deport them? Detain them?

Duke pushed his weight away from the wall. 'I am not at liberty to say.'

'But you *know*.'

'I am not at liberty to say that either.'

One thing Tess knew was that undocumented people lost the right to work. Because Arlo no longer had a job at StUKCO.

Earlier that week, he'd come home with a docket. It was pale green, and watermarked with the head of St Mira, and reminded Tess of the postal orders she used to get for her birthday –

quaint and of limited promise. It was actually Arlo's 'Notice of Termination'.

Arlo had told Tess how Mr Dee had called him into his office and sacked him with immediate effect. 'I am required to rationalise the workforce. You are not needed here... No, that is untrue, you *are* needed here.' He'd glanced up, his eyes missing Arlo by a fraction. 'But I have been informed, and I am not allowed to let you stay. You are an Undocumented.'

Arlo said, '*Person. The word is still an adjective.*'

Mr Dee seemed embarrassed. It was hard to tell if it was what he was doing to his member of staff, or what he'd just done to the language. Mr Dee focused on his mug. It used to be a Platinum Jubilee mug, but that had vanished and his new one was plain olive green. 'On the matter of personal effects...' as if Arlo were dead. 'Please remove them all. This is your last day.' He said Barbara would see him off the premises.

She was the StUKCO Bureau Chief. That was the title she'd given herself when she'd got the job as Secretary, and it had stuck. When she typed, the office rang with machinegun fire. She marched down corridors, her heels sparking. And in the yard, she chain-smoked and cast lipstick-red butts at the feet of Graham Greene.

Barbara had no choice but to let Arlo go. That was what she told him when she said goodbye. And it was hard for her because secretly she was in love with him. Or so Tess thought. And so Arlo thought. But she was a battle-axe who chose her battles, and she wasn't going to fight Immigration.

Mr Dee said he'd see Arlo's classes through to the end of term. 'The next lesson in English is...?'

'Future Perfect Simple.' Which was ironic because Arlo's future was looking neither perfect nor simple. And in *Life*, he was about to teach 'Leisure'. It had sections on Gardening, Shopping, Pubs and Night Clubs, Betting and Gambling, and Pets.

Mr Dee said, "'There are famous gardens to visit throughout the UK'". Like Arlo, he was primed to recite. 'Kew, Sissinghurst, Hidcote, Crathes Castle, Inveraray Castle, Bodnant, Mount Stewart...' Mr Dee sighed – at the sheer joy of lists, at the sadness of their parting. 'Leisure is what you have a lot of now, Arlo.'

He nodded. 'I'll have gone in an hour.'

That was the Future Perfect Simple.

Barbara helped Arlo clear his desk and pack his belongings into a cardboard box. She went out to the yard with him. They stood for a while and she wreathed them in smoke and Arlo smoked passively.

'Cold?' she said.

'No, not really.'

'Happy?'

'No, not really.'

Barbara loved *Brief Encounter*. It was why she loved Arlo. She'd been to every showing of it over the years.

'It wasn't brief, though, was it?' Arlo said. He'd worked for StUKCO for 3324 days. His Postal Order gave the exact length of employment. Arlo turned his face towards the gate. "'And I got out at Ketchworth and gave up my ticket and walked home as usual. Quite soberly and without wings. Without any wings at all."'

Barbara looked away, her eyes watering. She pulled at a lid as if a tear could hurt as much as a piece of grit.

Duke came over to Tess's desk. 'For reasons I cannot reveal, I have not been able to be forthcoming on topics on which you have touched. But...' He held a sheet to his chest. 'This is not officially released until tomorrow.' He turned it over so that Tess could see.

Was he leaking something to her?

It was a list of names – Brexpat-looking names, as far as she could tell across the desk.

'The British government is sending a vessel to evacuate key personnel.'

There were forty of them, numbered and arranged alphabetically.

'It will dock at Mirapolis Port this evening. The evacuees will gather at the Cargo Gate, from where they will be collected and taken home.' He put the sheet on her desk.

Tess checked the Bs for Arlo, then scanned down in case they'd misspelled him. She checked for Matthews. She checked for Petrou.

And while she was still checking, 'You are not on the list.'

You. Funny word. Was that you, Tess; or you, Tess-and-Arlo? English was vague like that. Not like Greek, or Albanian, or French, or German, which addressed specifically: you singular or plural; you formal or informal.

Tess read the list again. She knew quite a few of these people: staff from the Smethwick Condiments Company. Holiday Inn. That man was in insurance. And was that the whole contingent from the Frourio? No military – even though that was how all this had started: with who had the right to use the base. The army was making its own arrangements to keep its top brass safe.

Tess said, 'Am I not key?'

'You are needed on this Desk.'

Passive. No-one doing the needing – though there was only one other person here.

And was Arlo not key?

Duke said, 'You have a role here, Tess. You are embedded.'

She didn't like the syllable 'bed'. It made her think of fellows; and making it and lying in it. It was a piece of furniture she preferred not to imagine in relation to Duke. But what he probably meant was: he liked their arrangement. He wouldn't want anything to happen to Tess, or for her to leave, because then he'd have to recruit a replacement, show them the ropes, break them in. Tess pulled on her leash from time to time, like

Marine. But he enjoyed the resistance. It kept him on his toes. Using your opponent's resistance against them was how you won in martial arts.

Duke said, 'Things will happen that you cannot change. I want you to know this. It might become turbulent for your boyfriend, but it need not be turbulent for you.'

'He's not my boyfriend. We're as good as married.'

'But not *actually* married. In fact. In *truth* – as you would say.'

'That doesn't lessen the obligation.'

'But it *does* lessen the liability.'

Duke had never met Arlo. He'd shown no interest and never made enquiries about Tess's family or personal life. But then, no-one he worked with had a personal life. They were at the office, or not-at-the-office. Everything about them was defined by the CCO.

Duke said, 'You and he are on different trajectories now. He is most definitely *not* St Miran and you most certainly *are.*'

'You mean I have a passport.'

'You have the *blood.*'

She stared at his odd, blank face. Duke seemed to have come from no-one. Whoever his parents were, they weren't trophy-parents you talked about, or ones whose names opened doors. He had the kind of background the ambitious left behind. Duke's closest ties were to the International Taekwondo Federation and the Harvard Alumni Association. Occasionally, he flew to the States for a reunion, and he always returned looking well fed, but also deprived. He'd pace his office as if the walls were too close and St Mira too small for him.

Poor Duke.

Merely Duke.

Maybe once upon a time he'd thrown those American men over his shoulder and now they sat on committees deciding the fate of the Western world.

Duke went into his office and shut the door. She thought the games were over. But a few minutes later he was back, this time rolling a suitcase.

'Are you going away?'

'A quick trip abroad.'

There were no quick trips from St Mira, unless you had private transport. She scanned his luggage – compact, unlabelled, no clue as to where he was going.

Duke said, 'You do not mind staying till lights out?'

Was this trip the reason for his new Look?

'And answering my calls?'

He'd never asked her to do that before – left her in charge of the entire English Desk.

He went to the door with his small black suitcase. It sat at his ankles not unlike Marine.

What did he want? Duke never gave anything without expecting something in return. She said, 'When will you be back?'

'You will serve most ably until I am.'

Would she?

'Won't you.'

And then he left. She listened to the sound of his suitcase recede along the corridor.

Tess didn't like his compliments. She didn't trust Duke's trust.

That evening, Tess and Arlo took the bus to the port. They sat at the back and watched night-time Mirapolis shrink and thin and tumble into darkness. At the edge of town, a string of car dealerships: new cars, then used cars, and then just the tyres. Ahead, the lights of the dock glowed orange and spun drizzle. They reached the Cargo Gate – a concrete yard with silos and rusting girders, chained-up ponies tonguing sticky puddles, and St Miran flags slapping at the wind. The evacuees and their families had packed the only café. They looked pale and laden, barricaded in with luggage. People cast glassy stares at the plastic windows. They sipped from paper cups. On the giant telly, out-takes of sporting accidents: skiing overshoots, cycling pile-ups, sailing disasters. No-one was speaking.

Tess and Arlo took shelter in the bus stop. They weren't going to join the evacuees. They didn't want to explain to people they knew, or half-knew, that yes, they were British, but no, they didn't count as key to whoever had drawn up the list. And no, they weren't trying to cadge a place. They were just interested in who'd been chosen and how this evacuation was taking place, because if Arlo could get out of St Mira, it would surely be like this.

Arlo looked out to sea. 'I was born British, and the one advantage of that is your first language is English. You've got a ready-made job almost anywhere in the world exporting the language. Until you haven't. Until it just ends.'

Tess listened. He sounded thoughtful. His face was placid in the shadows. She looked up to the sky. There was Saturn, and there was Jupiter, both beautiful.

He said, 'So, here we are at the end. Or *an* end, anyway. Life is turning out to be just like *Life*.' The Handbook had a timeline that began with the Stone Age 6,000 years ago and ended on 31 January 2020 when the UK left the European Union. 'Sometimes, time just stops.'

'And sometimes it goes on forever.' Which was why Tess loved the stars. They did change; they all expanded, cooled and became red giants – but only eventually. She said, 'Look, that's Perseus, slayer of monsters.'

'Anyway, what is *Life*, really? Just a sad little pamphlet.' Arlo didn't teach it anymore so he didn't have to pretend. It was, he said, 'a statement of the arrogance of a shabby little island that can't see it no longer rules the world.'

Tess said, 'Look, that's the Little Bear.' Then she said, 'Look, what's that?'

Arlo followed her finger, and rising over the horizon like a new constellation, a sprinkling of lights. They grew larger, and took on shape, and turned yellow. Then a hull emerged from the darkness and a chimney whipping smoke. Someone must have seen it in the café too because everyone stood and looked out to sea. There was the grinding of gears and the choke of an engine stalling, and the dented bow of the *Pride of the Strait* glided towards the dock.

Then a quiet commotion as people gathered their luggage and children and pets and went out to meet it. They formed a queue up to the water's edge.

Tess scanned the line. 'They've arranged themselves alphabetically.'

Arlo said, 'They've sent a cross-channel ferry.'

Then a gangway unfolded and a uniformed officer skittered down. He shook the hand of the figure at the front of the queue. It was Mr Aldridge – Head of the St Miran Division of the Smethwick Condiments Company. It looked as though Mr Aldridge had had the pick of who'd leave with him: there was Harris and that was Tom Johnson. He was evacuating his pub quiz team. No Mr Kilic, though. Perhaps he'd been asked to hold the fort – a foreigner used to foreign things, who knew how to keep his head down while tracking events on the ground. It was coming up to the company's busiest time of the year. The olive harvest was about to start and would go on past Christmas. But could they still buy from local growers? And how would they ever get the olives out of the country? Brown sauce had a long shelf-life. They'd have supplies in the warehouse to last a couple of years. But if this chaos went on... These were the questions stamped over Mr Aldridge's brick-like face – red brick, very West Midlands.

Under the dim lights of the ferry, the officer checked Mr Aldridge's ID: his face against his passport photo; his name against a list. Then a tick, and a wave up the ramp. At the top, the same procedure. They'd set a checker to check the checker. London was taking no risks with who got onto the *Pride*. Tess watched the alphabet shuffle forward. She watched the rain pit the sea and the wind churn water. When the queue had gone, the officer radioed a message to someone inside the ferry. Then he ran up the gangway, turned to the dock and saluted into the darkness.

Arlo said, 'My parents took the *Pride of Something* ferry for their honeymoon to France.' It had been choppy that day. Elmer wasn't deterred by the weather, though. He'd spent the crossing leaning over the railings and imagining the animals that had once walked where the Channel now was – woolly mammoths and rhinos, elk and lions – leaving their bones in the mud. Joy had recited Churchill. It was the 'We shall fight on the beaches,' speech. And that was how his parents had begun their marriage: dreaming of dead things, and battling for England.

Eventually, the *Pride of the Strait* hauled herself round and headed out to sea. Tonight, the evacuees had been a quiet, exclusive queue. By tomorrow, they'd be the headlines.

The next morning, the evacuation was all over the British papers. It was a 'discreet withdrawal,' according to *The Times*. *The Sun* had front-page pictures of our 'heroes snatched from the jaws of hell.' There were photos of the ferry, which had reached Catania overnight and from where the Famous Forty would be flown home. It was sunny on Sicily and the quayside welcome was bright with reflector blankets and a brass band playing. Seagulls hovered over the *Pride* like helium balloons. There was talk about what would happen next and how the British and St Miran governments might resolve their differences. Then Tess read:

> *Noam Langberg, Director of Noam Langberg International, said he was 'delighted to be working alongside the British government to secure a solution to the St Miran question.'*

Noam Langberg?
She knew Noam Langberg.
The last she'd heard, he'd been fast-streamed into the Foreign Office and stationed in Albania with special responsibility for

what he'd called 'small lumps of rock in the Med.' But now, apparently, he'd done that and moved on.

Tess Googled Noam Langberg International, and there he was, Founder and Director of a company based in The Strand: 'We are policy experts. We are delivery practitioners. Working shoulder to shoulder with political leaders and governments, we provide support, develop radical-yet-practical policy solutions and drive real and lasting change.' And this weekend, NLI was hosting roundtable talks with stakeholders in the conflict.

Was that where Duke had gone? Was he in London?

Because the English Desk did play a role: statements made by the Firsters were translated by Tess and signed off by Duke. The exact words offered to the British were decided in their office. Maybe Nomie would want meanings that could be troubling to London to be made untroubling. Unpalatable messages could be sweetened. Was Noam Langberg right now sweetening Dr Kontos?

Tess clicked on 'About Us' and found his photo. 'Oh, *Nomie...*' she said. 'You're so *old.*'

Nomie had lost all his hair. His face had slumped and coalesced. In that central, softened morass she could just make out the man she used to know. The same smile, though, held a little too long before the shutter went and looking just short of meant. She would never forget his fading smile. It was the one thing of Nomie that Tess had carried with her because it'd faded so abruptly over her.

Because before the Foreign Office, Tess and Nomie had been a couple. They'd met at university as language partners, exchanging Albanian for Greek. They'd met a few times that way, then their partnership had extended its reach, after which they just spoke English.

Tess spent a few minutes roaming around her ex's past: the projects he'd been involved with, the professional memberships he'd accrued. Then she saw 'Send us a Message'. Should she send a message? It was an open invitation. Strictly speaking, it was an imperative. Tess wrote:

Hello Nomie,

It's been a while and I do hope you're well. I see you've been asked to help out with the St Miran situation. We (my partner, Arlo, and I) could do with some technical assistance. Would it be OK to give you a ring? It'd be good to catch up.

Best wishes to you and

Tess couldn't remember his wife's name. Kirsty? Katie? Chrissie? Something plosive and unpleasant. He'd probably have children now too, so she just put:

yours.

What Tess had liked about Nomie was his round, open face with its far-flung features that invited exploration. Also that he had two living parents and had grown up with both of them, which was a form of human relations that was new to her. And that he was learning Albanian, which had three genders, six cases and many moods, including the admirative. Once upon a time, he'd seduced her in that mood.

What Nomie had liked about Tess was: she spoke perfect Greek and sang St Miran songs that bit into your heart and filled it with longing. Also, that she was even shorter than he was. Other things too, which he'd told her at the start, but which she'd forgotten now, because the start had been overshadowed by the end.

A week later, Tess got a message back from NLI:

We are unable to deal with individual enquiries. For advice on your specific situation, contact the British

Embassy in Albania. Please note that due to a recent surge in enquiries, replies may take longer than usual.

It was ten at night when that message came through. Arlo was in his room, and the Oscar flag was up. Tess put an ear to his door, but whatever he was doing, he was doing it quietly. She went onto the balcony to breathe the scent of night-time air and trace the fine scythe of the moon. From downstairs, the catch of a chair and a cough, which was Vera saying hello.

And that was enough.

They sat a while together, one above the other and the moon above them both, gazing at the sky and trying to read the future. Today was the alignment of Venus and the sun. Vera had told her that. She said Venus was the planet of money and the planet of love.

It was the same sky over Nomie, if he cared to look.

Was Venus also the planet of ex-love?

Tess went back inside, turned on her computer, and from his website, wrote another note:

Nomie? Are you there? It's me, Tess. Remember?

Her outstretched finger hovered over 'Send' – over her past with Noam Langberg and whatever might be left of its purchase.

10.

Have you engaged in any activities that might indicate that you may
not be considered a person of good character?

HAVEN'T WE ALL DONE SOMETHING WE REGRET ?

Tess and Arlo didn't listen to the radio in bed anymore on Sunday mornings. The BBC had been blocked. And in every other language, even ones they didn't speak, they always seemed to catch the news and got the gist just from the tone: it was bad everywhere. The entire world was in freefall. So, instead this morning, Tess listened to her heart, which was faster than it used to be, easily alarmed. She listened to Arlo's breaths, which were intermittent sighs these days, the air grabbed at and then relinquished. Dear Arlo: thinner, older, quieter, with the five-day beard and the hair that was out of control because no-one would cut it. And Tess listened to her thoughts. There might have been a Law on Sunday Silence, but it could do nothing to still the clamour in her head.

And then the doorbell rang. It was so brief it could have been an accident.

Tess glanced at Arlo. 'Religion?' Because only zeal got people up at this hour. They were going to ignore it, but then the brief bell again. Did God's messengers sometimes ring twice?

They grabbed the clothes that had been cast onto the floor – they'd given up folding things; who cared anymore. They put them on: his, hers, it didn't matter which. Then Tess and Arlo went to the door like twins washed up on the broken shores of their morning. Tess leant an ear to the door. She wanted to say: we don't believe. We'll never believe. God is a fiction. Go away. Instead she said, 'Hello?'

'It's me.'

Vera. And speaking Greek because English would carry down the stairs.

Tess undid the chain, the lock, the other lock, and opened the door. And as soon as she saw her, she knew something was wrong. Vera looked shrunken, as if she hadn't slept.

'Rron and Rrock are in hospital.' Her voice was dry, her eyes misty. She was in her black cape, the big hood up, like something from a fairy-tale that didn't end well. 'You didn't hear the commotion in the night?'

Arlo had taken a pill.

Tess had heard something, but wasn't there always mayhem on a Saturday night? Fist-fights, pot-shots, gangs combing the streets.

Vera said, 'They set fire to Dover Castle. Rrock was inside.'

'But he got out?'

'He jumped.'

'But he's alive?'

'Rron gave blood. Litres of it.' Vera's eyes were rimmed in red. Was that fatigue or had she been crying?

'But he'll pull through?'

'I pray.'

Vera didn't believe, but she did pray – not to God but to whatever goodness was Out There, to clemency in the stars. She said, 'They're claiming a scalp they haven't got. These are all over town.'

At first glance, it looked like a standard 'In Memoriam': black-edged, a grainy photo, a line of text saying who the person had been, and details of the funeral. They were printed by the family and stuck to lampposts, one death layered on top of the next in directories of local loss.

But this wasn't done *by* Rrock's family; it was *for* the family. It was meant for Rron. And it was meant for the whole of Mirapolis too because everyone in town would see it. Vera said, 'I wanted to tell you as soon as possible, before you went out and saw it for yourselves.'

In Memoriam

Rrock Murad

† 5th November

Keeper of Dover Castle
British collaborator

ST MIRA FIRST!

140

The paper was damp. It'd rained in the night and the ink hadn't run. It was a professional job, put out quickly. Whoever had done it had money.

'And Rron?'

No answer.

'But he's OK?'

'He needs his cigarettes.' Vera patted a pocket – she was on her way now.

It was chilly on the stairwell. Arlo's feet were bare. Tess knew that they'd be frozen. She put an arm around his waist and pulled him to her, exchanging heat for cold. Then she thought: British collaborator? 'Isn't that what I'm doing, collaborating with a British man?'

'You're co*habiting*. It's not the same.' Arlo sounded so close. Then he said, 'Dear Tess,' which sounded like the start of a letter, as if they were apart and reaching for each other from a long way off. 'Tess isn't in danger, is she.'

'Of course not.'

'And Rron doesn't blame her, does he.' Because Rrock only took the job at Dover Castle because Tess had given it up.

'No.'

'Or blame us.'

'No.' A pause. 'Well, yes, he does blame you. But not for long. And not *you*, exactly. Not you *personally*.'

'But what about impersonally?' – as nameless foreigners?

'Rron just wishes the British had never been here because without the British, there'd be no Dover Castle and this wouldn't have happened.'

Which to Tess didn't seem reasonable, but at this time on a Sunday morning and shocked by the news, did make sense.

Then Rron's cat appeared. He stopped just short of the top step, placing himself between his neighbours, his eyes brimming with judgement. Vera bent down mouthing things to him. She was looking after Cid till Rron came out of hospital. The appearance of the cat had softened her tone. She sounded for a moment like herself again.

Tess said, 'Vera, can we come wi...? But she knew straightaway that they couldn't. They wouldn't be welcome at the hospital. So she said, 'When you see them, Rron and Rrock...' Tess spoke to Vera's chest, a direct appeal to her heart. 'Please..' She wasn't sure what came after that. Which verb would make things better?

'I will.'

Then Vera took their hands. They stood in a ring as they all had, once upon a time, when they were young and the world was easy, making wishes, chanting chants. They agreed to be careful. They agreed not to worry. They agreed it would be all right in the end.

Then Vera followed Cid downstairs. Tess listened to her feet, past her own flat, past Rron's flat which was empty, past Mr and Mrs Moros who'd be getting ready for church. She waited for her to call back up, to say something reassuring or funny, to undo the news.

But Vera didn't.

Instead, the sound of the door as she went into Exodus Square, which was plastered with Rrock and silenced by law.

Later that day, there was a Zoom with Dover. Joy started the call with none of her usual exuberance, no 'Hello Arlo my love hello Tess my lovely how are you both'. Instead, 'We're worried about you. We've heard the news.'

Usually, Joy avoided Zoom because it was like putting your family in a glass cage, she said. It was like visiting them in a zoo. The phone was Joy's thing – the physicality of the voice, the other person vibrating in her ear. It was intense and intimate, almost pillow talk. But this time she'd wanted to see them, to be certain they were all right. Joy's face looked chalky and craggy, and smeared too – like the Dover cliffs after rain. Had she been crying?

'We're here! We're fine!' Arlo waved in wide arcs as if cleaning windows.

'There you are, thank God!' And she really was thanking him. She would have been praying for Tess and Arlo. And this Zoom was proof that God had delivered again. If you didn't stop believing, he always did his bit. God understood the value of reliability. He'd had a plan right from the start and had carried it out, no messing: all the major tasks of creation completed within a week. Joy loved God for that.

She said, 'We heard about the fire. You know someone died?'

'Injured,' Arlo said.

'But still...'

Yes, but still. Rrock had third degree burns, damage to his spine, and questions over whether he'd ever walk again. Rron had given five litres of blood.

Joy said, 'But are you two safe?'

Well, no, not really. Hating foreigners was government policy now. And every Monday, Arlo had to report to the Immigration Office to be reminded of how hated he was. Tess wasn't allowed to go with him, but she knew what happened: the man on the door being difficult; Security searching his bag; the Immigration Officer rolling his finger on the inkpad – always the same finger, the ink starting to stain. And when he came home, he didn't want to talk, just went into his room and put the Mike flag up: *My vessel is stopped and making no way through the water.*

Arlo said to his mother, 'We *feel* safe, don't we.' He'd shaved for this Zoom, and Tess was in her sunshine-yellow blouse. He reached for her hand and a gentle squeeze because that was the line they'd agreed on.

Joy said, 'You know it was Bonfire Night that they did it? Do you think that was deliberate?'

Tess couldn't imagine anyone on St Mira knowing the significance of the fifth of November unless they'd done Arlo's *Life* course. She thought he might recite the *Handbook*, how people remember, remembered. But Elmer got in first. 'They've

143

evacuated some people. The top forty, wasn't it?' Which sounded like the Official Singles Chart.

Arlo said, 'They got the key people out.' Someone in Whitehall had been asked to draw up the list. They'd have thought: finance, trade, power, influence, class. People like us. People I went to school with. They didn't want their kind of person to be locked up, deported, put at risk or even mildly inconvenienced. It would be like abandoning family. When you had to choose, people weren't equal. Values came shining through, lighting up the hidden corners of the heart.

Joy said, '*You're* key to us.' She leant forward, filling the screen with the undyed roots of her hair. 'We want you to come Home.' She said it as a proper noun, as if you'd find it in the index of an atlas between Hollywood and Honolulu.

Coming Home.

In Arlo's lap, two pieces of paper – notes for this conversation:

- *Don't Talk About*: No job. No passport. No way out. Forget Christmas.
- *Do Talk About*: <u>Them!</u>

'Tell us about *you*,' Arlo said. 'How are things?' Joy and Elmer were wearing poppies for Remembrance Sunday. They were in their seats on the sofa, always the same ones. Tess felt fond of that piece of furniture because at Christmas, she sat next to Elmer while they watched whatever was ringed in the *Radio Times*. Sometimes, she watched telly with her eyes closed and let Elmer turn into Stan. They were similar like that. It was the warmth she loved, and the immobility, like sitting next to a rock that every so often breathed.

'Fine. Fine. Same as ever,' Elmer said.

'We'd be happier if you came Home. Not permanently, it doesn't have to be forever, just till things calm down.'

Arlo went still. 'It might not be that straightforward.'

'Can't you just take annual leave?'

Joy was practical. And solutions came so much easier when you didn't know the facts.

Tess said, 'There's no way my boss would let me have time off. There's too much going on.' Then her eyes found the ghost of her face in the screen. It was exactly how she felt at work: thin and see-through, always at the office and less and less there.

'And you wouldn't consider coming separately?'

No, they definitely wouldn't. They'd agreed on that too. Whatever they did, it'd be together.

Which was bad news for the Browns, but also good. They weren't about to see their son, but Arlo and Tess had each other, the two of them were inseparable, no matter what.

Joy rocked on the edge of the sofa. Finally, she said, 'If you can't come officially, you could always come anyway.'

What did she mean?

'Get in a boat and come over. That's what people do.'

And thousands of them died.

'Head for Sicily. Then get on a plane.'

And how to get to Sicily?

'Sicily's not that far.'

It might seem close on a map, but look in that direction from here and all you could see was water.

Joy said, 'You'd be escaping war... violence... social unrest... threat to life and limb...' It sounded rehearsed, their many claims for sanctuary. 'They couldn't send you back.'

Yes they could. St Mira would hardly count as dangerous when people were sent back to Afghanistan, Iraq, Somalia – countries the Foreign Office warned you not to go to.

Suddenly, Tess wanted this Zoom to end. There were only so many half-truths she could handle. She turned her face to the window. Outside, swallows filled Exodus Square with flight. They were heading for the Sahara. Some of them would have spent the summer on the rafters of English barns. But now the weather had turned. It was nine degrees in Dover.

Arlo pressed on with questions about Them! And Joy talked about the grandchildren, and Edwin who'd been up Everest to raise money for some fatal disease, and people whose names rang a bell, but not loudly. Arlo listened, and Tess and Elmer slipped into the shadows of the conversation. Elmer had stopped blinking, which meant that in his head, he was somewhere else – maybe in the shed, turning over fossils.

After a while, Tess heard Joy's voice slow, her stories drying up. Then an exchange of farewells, all four of them echoing *Take care! Bye! Love you! Miss you!* till those were exhausted too.

Arlo said, 'It's the button at the bottom, Mum. The red one.'

'Will you do it, please?'

Because for Joy, pressing 'End' was too painful. It would be like terminating her own son.

A few days later, Tess was at the Holiday Inn. Noam Langberg International, on behalf of the Foreign Office, had invited British citizens to an Outreach Evening 'to offer reassurance in the light of events on the 5th of November.' Brexpat had emailed a warning not to go: 'All things foreign are clearly a target, so gathering in one place to discuss safety rather defeats the object.' But the event was being fronted by Noam Langberg himself. It was a chance for Tess to speak to him directly and there was no way she would miss it.

Tess lingered in the Holiday Inn lobby before going into the meeting. She loved lobbies, all the languages, the splash of Everywhere. The 'Ode to Joy' on pan pipes brushed against the ceiling. Guests lounged in a string of easy chairs, forming an archipelago. In this enclosed, dim-lit space, the rest of the world had been forgotten. How nice, Tess thought. She wanted to be one of those islands. She wanted to draw up a chair, and lean her head on the headrest, and fall into a different geography.

Instead, she followed a sign that said: *NLI Event, Blue Room.* At the entrance, a man spent a while checking her passport. He rummaged in the gape of her open rucksack and asked if she was carrying anything sharp, combustible or toxic. Nomie was taking no chances.

The Brexpat email had had an effect: the room was mostly empty. End-of-row chairs had been taken, and a small group had clustered close to the door. These were people, she thought, who'd book plane journeys early to get seats by the emergency exit. They were the ones who'd read the safety card and glance over their shoulder when the voiceover said, 'Remember, your nearest exit may be behind you.'

As a backdrop to the stage, a screen set the tone for the evening: *Be safe. Be unseen.* And people had taken the message to heart, sinking low in their seats, shoulders rounded, making themselves small. Except for Jeannie. She was there, light-bulb blonde at the front. She mouthed, 'No Arlo?'

No, no Arlo.

Tess lipped back: 'Busy.' Actually, she'd asked him not to come. She hadn't seen Nomie for years – not since his wedding – and she didn't want to overload the moment. It was already enough to say, 'Hello, how was the last decade?' She didn't want, on top of that, to introduce her partner and his problems.

Tess sat.

She was in the back row, a table with give-away water and NLI freebies behind her: pens, fridge magnets, calendars. When Nomie had got the job with the Foreign Office, he'd been so happy with the posting. There were more than two hundred islands in the Mediterranean he'd told her: Gozo, Ponza, Uzunada... Tess had never heard of them. 'Think of all that fishing. All the sailing.' And now, apparently, he was still in the Med, only an independent actor – a specialist in the region and a fixer for hire on the ground. He could do what he liked – get his hands dirty, speak to the unspeakable, cover his tracks – and leave his client innocent of all but best practice and compliance with relevant law.

Then night fell suddenly, the way it did on St Mira, the blue of the sky matching the twilight blue of the walls. A side-door opened, and Noam Langberg took the floor to a clatter of uncertain applause. He received it with both hands, as if the endorsement were deafening. Then he grasped the lectern and leant down into the mic. Nomie was taller than he used to be. Was he standing on something up there? 'Ladies and gentlemen, thank you all very much for coming. You will be fully aware of developments on St Mira since the election in June, and most particularly of recent events in Kentish Town. Indeed, it's why you're here.'

Nomie sounded posher than Tess remembered. The Foreign Office had altered his vowels. But his eyes still did that weird thing – followed the trajectory of his voice, as if speaking were flyfishing. Nomie had been an angler. He liked to watch and wait. He was a hunter at heart. Predatory. Fishing was supposed to be a sport, but it was actually deceit with intent to kill – and Nomie was a natural.

He said, 'You will have been disturbed by the attack on Dover Castle and will of course be seeking details.' Because since the first reports, there'd been no updates at all. Social media was full of it, and there were photos of Rron beside Rrock's hospital bed and Rrock in bandages, rigged up to a drip, his lashless eyes stuck to the camera. But, officially, it was as if the attack had never happened. Someone high up had decided with someone else high up that it was best if Dover Castle went quiet.

Nomie said, 'But my primary task this evening is to build trust and nurture confidence so that you can continue to live your lives on St Mira – as many of you have for years.' That comment had landed just above Tess's head and he'd chosen not to acknowledge her. She was in Nomie's line of sight and he was going to be blind.

Soon, he was in full swing, telling the room that negotiations were underway, and that there was broad consensus on a constructive way forward... His voice had the lull of a school assembly – familiar and vacuous – and Tess's attention wandered away from Nomie's words and onto him.

Nomie was dressed in blue: dark trousers, dusky shirt, subtle shades of tie. Had he dressed to match the walls? Was he demonstrating his message to be safe and be unseen? Then she remembered he'd worn blue at his wedding too – trousers that were drain-pipe tight because skinny legs looked longer, he'd always claimed, and his bride – what was her name? – must have believed him. A thin tie and small lapels, which made him look like a man on the make as he walked down the aisle.

His bride was in something that could have been a wedding gown, or might just have been a trail of laundry. It was hard for Tess to distinguish between high-end fashion and accidents. They'd made their way towards the altar of St Mary le Strand, Nomie with a swagger as if he'd snatched something valuable, and she tripping over the chance to marry into the Foreign Office.

Nomie had invited Tess to the wedding – not as a guest, but as part of the ceremony. He'd asked her to sing one of her lovely St Miran songs, something that would 'raise the heart of everyone there, and pierce it.' He'd asked her because 'I *like* you Tess, I really do, and no hard feelings.'

'O.K.'

What was she thinking of? Tess wasn't thinking. She was still in the fug of rejection. The end had been fast and brutal.

They'd just left university and Nomie had said it would be in her own best interests if she calmed down and dropped the ditsy act. He was being Fast Streamed and his screening interview was coming up. They'd ask him about partners, and he wanted Tess to be as... He'd hesitated over the word. '*Appropriate* as possible. Acceptable to the Service. You know, less...' Nomie had never finished that sentence. Tess had, though, to herself. What he couldn't bring himself to say was: please be less like who you actually are, less of an orphan raised in two languages by an immigrant on a council estate.

In the end, Nomie had brought in reinforcements to end their relationship. He'd got his parents involved. Stephen and

Veronica lived in Exeter. He was an academic and she was monied – related in some way to Greek shipping and a distant cousin of Jackie Onassis. They came up to London when Stephen gave a lecture. He was a world-renowned expert on the colon. When Nomie had first told Tess this, she'd found it fascinating: visceral and life-saving. In fact, he was a linguist and his subject was the punctuation mark. It paid, though, his forensic, polysyllabic probing of two dots. They had a house on the south coast, a yacht and membership of the sailing club, and a pied-à-terre in Bloomsbury, which Nomie used as his student digs.

At Nomie's suggestion, his parents had invited Tess to dinner. 'What should I wear? What should I say? How should I be?' she'd asked him.

'Just be yourself.'

It was what he'd wanted: for Tess to prove, with witnesses present, that she wasn't a suitable wife.

After dinner, walking home, slipping on autumn leaves and in the rich scent of decay, Nomie had pointed out the booby traps his parents had set: that syllabub wasn't 'dessert', it was 'pudding'. It wasn't 'bubbly' that had made her talkative, it was 'champagne'. She shouldn't have been 'bursting to go to the toilet'; you excuse yourself and ask staff the way to the loo. He'd explained his mother's thoughtful looks, and what those pauses had meant. Tess was really upset. Nomie should have warned her that this was *her* screening interview. She could have mugged up on British class etiquette.

'There, there.' Nomie stroked her hand with the back of a finger like you do with a bird got by a cat that you know is going to die.

And the next day, Nomie said, 'I'm sorry, Tess, but I'm letting you go.'

Had he said 'sorry'? It was hard to remember now.

What she did remember was the 'letting go,' as if Tess had been his employee and her services were no longer needed. Or as if she'd been captive all that time, his hostage.

'Why?'

No answer. He cast his eyes left, which happened to be westwards, towards Exeter.

'I know why. It's your fucking mother, isn't it.'

He said, 'You didn't come across as a terribly diplomatic wife.'

Veronica. Tess would never forget the name. It was Greek for 'she who brings victory.' Veronica was going to make sure that her son triumphed in life, and that meant her family money was going nowhere near a woman from Wandsworth Council. Her grandchildren would be heroic and have long legs and that meant not breeding with Tess.

She wondered if at that point Nomie had already met Catriona – yes, that was her name – because very soon after, she was invited to sing at their wedding. And Tess had said yes because... because she wanted to know what she looked like, this wife he'd chosen instead. And because she was still in love with Nomie, or maybe just furious with him – the feelings were strangely alike. And because she wanted to sing him something fitting, to send him into marriage with the contents of her heart. It was listed in the service as a St Miran lullaby. Actually, Tess sang a wife's lament for her drowned sailor husband. No-one knew except Tess. Though maybe Nomie, and possibly his mother, caught one or two words which were the same in the dialect and modern standard Greek: 'drown,' 'die,' 'pain' and 'eternity.'

Occasionally, over the years, when Nomie had sprung from nowhere into her mind, Tess had wondered why she'd sung that lament. It troubled her. What did it show about her character? That if pushed, she wasn't the person she'd like to be, that deep down, her moral world was messy?

And now Tess's attention came back to the room and the end of Nomie's talk. He was reminding people of the key safety rules: be unseen, head down, fit in. No English in public places. 'And please: remember you are abroad. You are guests in this country.'

No they weren't. Some of them had citizenship. All of them had the right to be there. Or *had* had the right.

Nomie thanked people for coming, for braving the dark and the weather. Any questions, please go to the NLI website and submit them there. 'Good night,' he said. 'And good luck.'

In Tess's head: *Would the last one out please turn off the lights.*

Stunted and stunned applause, and before anyone could approach him, Nomie had made his exit. He must have known Tess would follow because he'd already reached the lobby before she caught up. Over his shoulder: 'Not now.'

'When then?'

He went to the door. 'I'm busy. Contact Tirana.'

But Tess had already done that and the automated response said the matter was important to them, and they would deal with it as soon as possible, but not before Calendar Week 03. That was January next year. So then Tess had gone back to Nomie's website. She'd written messages explaining the situation with Arlo – saying less, then saying more, trying to sound light and breezy, then cool and business-like. The replies began: *While there is much to appreciate in the case you make...* And ended: *We know you will find this response frustrating and disappointing, but...*

Tess said, 'You've seen my messages.'

'My staff deal with those.'

Tess had spent longer than was good for her staring at the online stable of long-haired women who worked for Nomie, willing them to lose their cemented smile and tell him to do something. She said, 'You understand the problem.'

And it was getting worse. Arlo's mood had shifted in the last few days. Lying to his parents about what was going on seemed to have brought the truth of it home to him. He was quieter. Thoughtful. And he often had the Juliet sign up: *I am on fire and have dangerous cargo on board. Keep well clear.*

Nomie cast a quick eye around the lobby as if thinking: is anybody watching this? Mr Noam Langberg of NLI, formerly of the Foreign Office, being collared by a woman in a second-hand Parka who doesn't seem to own a hairbrush. He pushed through the door.

'Where are you going?'

'To where I'm staying.'

Which obviously wasn't the Holiday Inn. 'Where's that?'

'You know, Tess, this is the first time in years that we've spoken, and I am instantly reminded of why I didn't marry you.'

Tess followed Nomie out. He turned towards the Old Town. A wind was blowing. The boats in the harbour swung their hips as if this was Hawaii, not St Mira heading into winter.

'Arlo and I have to get out.'

'There are no plans for further evacuation.'

'Unless you're key. How do you become key?'

Nomie tried not to smile. 'Key' was apparently not something you could *become*; it was a state you were born into. It was like being 'appropriate' and 'acceptable to the service'. He said, 'Your current position is not unenviable. I hear you work for Dr Kontos.'

So *had* Duke gone to that meeting in London and met Nomie there?

'I hear you're his secretary.'

Was that what Duke had called her? Or was that Nomie's slight?

'He struck me as practical. Clear sighted. Far sighted.'

What had Duke been saying?

Tess turned to the night sky. Yesterday was a full moon. Some people called it the Beaver Moon, though its other names fitted better right now: the Mourning Moon and the Frost Moon. 'I need your help.'

Said to no-one, 'The situation as it stands does not require a crisis response.'

'*I'm* in a crisis.'

'The FCO would consider a crisis response *if* – and I quote from publicly accessible data, so do look it up...' Nomie looked at her. He used to have big eyes that were open and interested. Now the lids hung half-closed, ready to guillotine the conversation. '...*if* there were an incident in which large numbers of British nationals were killed or injured. Or, *if* there were events such as airport shutdowns and volcanic ash.'

Yesterday, it was a total lunar eclipse in some parts of the world, the moon dim and dusty red.

'Or if there were civil or political unrest which caused the FCO to advise you to leave the country, which it hasn't.' Nomie tried to move off, but Tess stood in his way. She was eclipsing him, blocking out his light, cutting off his path.

'Tess!' It was the first time he'd said her name, and the tone brought it all back. She was being inappropriate, dismissed, split up with. Nomie had picked up a decade later exactly where he'd left off. 'Come on, realistically, what are we looking at? A political circus that is international norm and one *non*-British, *non*-fatal injury.'

Though what Tess was looking at was Arlo: undocumented, unable to stay and unable to go, unemployed, and very unhappy.

And now she looked at Nomie. He was older than his online photo, his face dented and shadowed like the seas on the moon. She said, 'How are you?'

'Busy.'

'How's Catriona?'

He started at the sound of her name. Maybe he was surprised that Tess remembered it.

'She's here with me.'

'And the children?' Nomie must have them.

'At school.'

'They must be… what… how old now…?' as if she had any idea.

'Twelve, ten, eight and seven.'

So, four of them. She said, 'And how's Veronica?'

'She died.'

Oh good.

'A few years ago. Dad's alone. He sends greetings, by the way. He asks after you from time to time.'

'He remembers me?'

'Some of the things you do, Tess, are quite unforgettable.' Then Nomie raised an arm to an empty taxi. He opened the door and spoke to the driver. Tess couldn't hear what he was saying, but everywhere in town was within walking distance. Nomie was brushing her off, letting her go again.

'So I'll see you, then,' she said to a slamming door.

Nomie put a hand to the window, which was half a wave and half to screen his face – a royal kind of sleight.

The taxi took off, didn't bother with the lights, ducked and dived as if it were a car chase, not deserted Mirapolis on a Sunday night.

Tess turned to look out to sea, at the lights of the boats far out in the water, in weather that was turning unkind. She flicked up her hood and dropped her hands in her pockets. She listened to the seagulls fighting with the wind, rattled, hoarse, raw.

11.

Have you ever received medical treatment in the UK?

NO

Did you have to pay for the treatment?

N/A

Tell us about any medical conditions, disabilities, infectious diseases or medications you should be taking.

NONE

Tell us about those things for your ~~spouse~~ PARTNER

ARLO BROWN WAS REGISTERED WITH AN NHS GP WHEN HE LIVED IN THE UK.

UNTIL THIS YEAR HE WAS IN GOOD HEALTH. HE NOW NEEDS URGENT MEDICAL HELP.

Tess reported to Arlo what was said at the meeting with Nomie, and he listened, rocking on his heels. In his head, she thought, Arlo was at the meeting with them, altering the outcome. 'But it wouldn't have made any difference if you'd been there.'

'It would have made me real. He'd have seen me.'

Except, he wouldn't. Nomie couldn't focus on individuals. They were too small, too particular. He only understood people as statistics.

'I could have explained why we need his help.'

But Nomie wouldn't have heard.

'I've just been caught up in circumstances.'

'He doesn't think like that.' All Nomie would have seen was someone who'd made bad decisions, who'd brought it on themselves. Successful people were like that. They thought they were hardworking, talented, deserving, and you weren't. Whereas what they really were was connected, ruthless and lucky. They always overlooked the luck.

Arlo had gone quiet after that. He spent a lot of time on his own chain-smoking, the smell of Karelias filling his room and leaching under the door. Sometimes, Tess heard music, sometimes a tinny American YouTube voice, sometimes Arlo talking to himself. When he appeared, his eyes were black, the pupils dilated, the look of a man on a mission who'd spent too much time in the dark. And always, the India sign was up: *I am altering my course to port.*

Tess wasn't sure what that meant until she came home from work and found the kitchen furniture stacked in the hall. She thought Arlo was cleaning the floor. He'd done a lot of housework since losing his job at StUKCO, and now the flat seemed bigger, lighter, somewhere you wouldn't want to leave. She took off her shoes, ready to tiptoe across damp lino. Instead, the floor was covered with paper and Arlo was on his hands and knees.

'I'm mapping us,' he said. 'Finding out where we are.'

The maps were large-scale, detailed, printed from his computer and sticky-taped together. And they were blue. He'd covered the floor with the Mediterranean. 'I need to know exactly what's out there.'

Water was out there.

And up against the kitchen units, the edge of nearest landfall. Arlo had drawn pencil lines from Mirapolis to the coast of Malta, Sicily and Crete. The shortest, he said, was from St Mira to Capo Passero. 343 kilometres. It was the distance from the middle of the floor to where they kept the saucepans.

'I don't think it's quite like that.' At sea, you didn't measure distances with a plastic ruler. The Mediterranean wasn't flat and pastel blue. It had waves and tides and currents. It was cold and the water was salty.

Arlo said, 'People are crossing it all the time.'

Was he planning the unofficial return his mother had suggested? 'You can't make an escape with Google Maps.'

'St Mira's an island. The place is packed with boats. The harbour's full of them. The marina's jammed.'

Was Arlo thinking they could hitch a ride? Ask someone to take them along? Tess suddenly felt the weight of her office bag and tipped it from her shoulder to the floor.

'Fishermen are out every day.'

'It would be people-smuggling.'

'It would be taking us on an educational fishing trip.'

'This is St Mira *now*, not St Mira back then.' That kind of thing happened when they'd first got here. But that was an economic crash ago. An election ago. The Firsters had made it clear they wanted to know exactly which foreigners were on St Mira, where they lived, how they supported themselves, and to oversee departures. Anything else was irregular. Punishable. A bad idea.

'We could ask Vera.'

Vera would know someone who'd smuggle them out because Vera knew everyone. But that would mean whoever it was collaborating with the British, and that put them in danger.

'So, we pay them,' Arlo said.

'A lot.' And Tess wasn't going to turn to Joy again. She was already Arlo's guarantor for the Law on Financial Self-Sufficiency. Joy had asked Edwin, who'd paid his mother, who'd transferred the money over.

'Not *that* much,' Arlo said. 'People are broke. They'd settle for anything.'

But Tess wasn't going to bargain down with someone's life. She went to the sink and turned on the tap. She watched the water rise up a glass till it was half empty then not quite so empty. She took a sip. 'So, suppose, then... Someone takes us out in their fishing boat – and then what?'

'We land... wherever... we find some kind of official... and we explain. We tell them I'm British but don't have a passport and you're British and St Miran and have two, and we've escaped St Mira together because we're a couple and we're cold and hungry, and is there a telephone because we need to call home.'

Tess could picture the officer's face – the doubt, the boredom – when they heard all that. How many times had people turned up, confused and exhausted and trying to tell a story in a foreign language they didn't know or were too tired to speak?

She leant against the sink and looked down at Arlo's maps. The nearest landfall was Sicily. That meant Italian. And what did Italy do with migrants? Hadn't someone just said they were going to repatriate and sink the rescue boats?

Arlo rocked on his haunches as if trying to stand. 'I have to get away from St Mira. And I want you to come with me because you have to get away from Duke.'

Tess turned her back and rinsed a water glass that didn't need rinsing. She knew what was coming next because what followed from the word 'Duke' these days was a certain line of thought.

'You know he's in love with you.'

'Duke doesn't do loving, except possibly of himself.' Tess wasn't even sure he loved Marine. He admired her obedience and docility, the qualities he expected in those around him.

'He's interested in you.'

'No he's not.' But Duke did know things about her past he could only know if he'd talked to Nomie – and only if Nomie had told him.

'He's trying to come between us.'

Duke had asked Tess to take Marine for early evening walks, and that meant giving her his housekeys and Tess getting home late. She knew what it signalled – all three of them did – this unsupervised access to his home, the encouragement to bond with his dog.

'He wants something from you.'

'No he doesn't.'

'Yes he does.'

Yes, he did. Something.

Arlo said, 'He doesn't have a wife...'

Duke had a housekeeper. She prepared his evening meals, and in the morning cooked breakfast to order. Duke was fond of his housekeeper, but he couldn't get together with her because she was already married to somebody else for whom she did the same.

'And he doesn't have a girlfriend...'

Tess had poked around his villa, cracking doors open. She'd found a gym, a sauna, a TV lounge, a room for his sporting trophies. Marine slept on his king-sized bed, on a pillow trimmed with French lace and embroidered with an 'M'. It was 'M' for 'Marine'. Also for 'Michail'.

Arlo said, 'He's not gay.'

'I know he's not gay.'

'How do you know?'

'He's not capable of being gay.' He didn't have the heart for it. He had Taekwondo. He got physically frustrated and took it out on martial arts. But it was family first on St Mira now. Not married by Duke's age, and it counted as odd. And it wasn't safe to be unusual anymore. And when you were in danger, what did you do? Run or hide. Was Duke trying to hide behind Tess?

For a while, they listened to the sounds of the house – water in the pipes, Vera's washing machine, and in the distance, the ebb and flow of the Moros family. Then Arlo said, 'I've been thinking about *Ancora*.' That was the boat that Albie had used to sail from Sicily to St Mira. Vera kept it as a shrine to her dead husband and dusted it, polished it, talked to it in *Complete Oxford* words.

Was Arlo really thinking of doing a runner? Did he want to escape on *Ancora*? 'We don't know how to sail.'

'I've been teaching myself.'

Was that the YouTube American he'd been spending time with?

Arlo said, 'Sailing's not hard. It's just a clock face. Between ten and two is the No Go Zone. Then there's beam reach at three, and down wind at six.'

Tess took off her watch. She wanted to change out of work clothes. It was getting late. She wanted to stop.

He said people have been sailing for all of human history. 'It's just wind and water on a sail and keel.'

No it wasn't. It was dangerous. It was a few planks of wood between you and death. Tess said, 'We have no idea how to navigate.'

'You're good with the stars.'

Yes, she knew the constellations, but how to read them to tell which way to go?

'And if we get into trouble, I can swim. You can swim amazingly.'

She said, 'Twenty-five thousand people have gone missing in the Mediterranean and they all got into a boat telling themselves they could swim. It's a graveyard.' The seabed was littered with unclaimed bones.

'If we got into trouble, we'd be rescued.'

'No we wouldn't. This is Europe, remember.' Frontex didn't do search and rescue; they did surveillance and return. 'People die of thirst waiting to be rescued from the Mediterranean.' St Mira wasn't close to where most boats went: Morocco to Gibraltar, or Libya to Italy, or Turkey to Greece. But now and then an orange life jacket washed up in the marina and one of the staff hooked it out and threw it in the bin.

Tess glanced towards the window. Out there, a half-moon and Jupiter – an inch from each other and 600 million kilometres apart. Arlo sat in his mosaic of sea, clinging to a knee as if it were flotsam. '*You* can leave anytime.'

'I know.'

'We're only going through all of this because of me.'

She knew that too.

Tess came and sat beside him. She didn't mind. She could manage it. She held his hand. It was cold and weighed nothing, as if a gust of wind would take it. Then she thought that Arlo might mind, though – that they were in this fix because of him. And that worried her. She said, 'Don't do anything alone. Don't get in a boat without me. Don't disappear on me, Arlo.'

'Don't worry.'

She squeezed his fingers. 'We've got to stick together.' And as she said it, the thought occurred to her for the first time in this mess that if they stuck together, they were stuck.

Arlo did ask Vera if they could borrow *Ancora* and take the boat back to Sicily.

'No.'

'No because it wouldn't be borrowing; you'd never see *Ancora* again?'

'No because I don't want you to drown.' She said, 'Do you know what it takes to sail a boat? Albie was a born sailor and the sea nearly took him many times.' But she was prepared to lend *Ancora* for a day. To Nomie. It was Tess's idea: offer a jolly that played to his weaknesses – for sailing and fishing – and get to speak again to the only man with any power to help.

It was three weeks since the Outreach Evening, a Sunday morning, early for Tess, but late for a father of four. And now, here Nomie was, in a Barbour and flat cap, with rod and tackle over his shoulder, as if he were after trout in the Tamar, not trying his luck in the sea.

'Morning!' she called to him.

He put a hand to his cap.

'Clear skies. No rain. The perfect day for it.' She had no idea if that was good sailing weather.

A cautious nod from Nomie. He stood some way back from her – maybe twenty paces, duelling distance? Tess stood in the smell of sea salt and dead fish while he eyed her, maybe having second thoughts about the wisdom of this trip.

'I'm glad you accepted.'

'My wife persuaded me. I made the mistake of mentioning your offer.'

Tess turned towards the water. Tied-up fishing boats shouldered each other. In the distance, the blue and white sway of the marina. The whole coastline was hazy with rigging. There were, she thought, so many strings attached to boats.

At school in Devon, Nomie had been captain of the Angling Club. It was a posh grammar school with its own stretch of river. Noam Langberg was often seen with a rod and fly, which made him the butt of gnome jokes. It was difficult being short at St Brendan's, he'd told her once. To survive, you either had to be funny, pugnacious, or an angler – make people laugh, beat them up, or avoid them – and Nomie had taken the fishing route.

She said, 'A quick coffee before you head out? And then I'll leave you to it.' She'd promised Nomie she wouldn't detain him, she wasn't going to take him hostage for the day. She'd offered a local guide who'd show him the best fishing, but no, he'd said, he wanted to think. He wanted to be alone. With four sons and a wife, he didn't get to think that often.

They went to The Snack Bar and Tess ordered. 'You're looking well,' she said.

Nomie didn't rise to the compliment.

She took in his flat, round face – like a compass. Today, Nomie's eyes had a force to them, a look of intent, as if no matter what distractions – such as Tess – turned up, he was implacably drawn to wherever he was heading.

'How did Catriona persuade you?'

'She said I work too hard and a bit of the old hobby would do me good. She said I know you. Or *have known* you. She said you were harmless.' A sideways glance at that. 'She said "Imagine it was me in that situation" – not that my wife would ever get into such a situation. It's a very Tess-esque kind of fix. She said you must be having a tough time of it, and five minutes won't hurt. She says hello by the way.' He checked his watch – a complicated, jet-setting kind of face that told the time in several places.

Then the coffee came. Tess added sugar and Nomie didn't, just as it used to be.

Tess said, 'The *Pride* is back.' The ferry had arrived in Mirapolis a few days ago, but it hadn't been reported in the news. No-one had got on the boat and no-one had got off. But lights were always on and people moved about as if they lived there. You could see them through binoculars – Tess had done it – relaxing in the lounge with what looked like pints of beer. And eating in the canteen – chips with their fingers. There were rumours of hearing English-type laughter from the deck.

Tess said, 'Are more people being evacuated?'

'As made clear at the Outreach Evening, this is not a crisis.'

'So why's the *Pride* here, then?'

Nomie picked up his coffee and put it to his lips. 'It is an offshore office. A floating bureau. The *Pride* now deals with immigration.'

'I thought that was Tirana.'

'Tirana was overwhelmed. And Albania is too far away. We needed a dedicated local solution.'

The people Tess had seen, he said, were Home Office staff. They were from UK Visa and Immigration and the Passport Office.

'So Arlo's passport is...' Was it within swimming distance?

Nomie drained his cup. He returned it to the saucer. 'Your partner...'

Could Nomie not bring himself to say Arlo's name? Would that make it too personal and her partner too real?

'...must apply for a new passport through established channels.' A finger traced a crack in the melamine tabletop. 'There *are* established channels. *I* established them. I have consolidated all immigration issues into one place and anchored it just along the coast.' He laid his palms on the table and thrummed his fingers. 'We just have to wait our turn in the queue.'

'But it's urgent, Nomie. Arlo's not well.' In fact, he was really ill. The last time he reported to Immigration, he'd been detained and strip-searched. Since then, he'd stopped eating, stopped sleeping, and refused to talk – except for outbursts of fury when he talked about ending it. He wouldn't go to the doctor, so Tess went for him. Arlo had been taken off their lists.

She said to Nomie, 'If he can just get a passport, he'll be official. He'll exist again. He can get medical help and get some rest. We can *both* get some rest.' She glanced over Nomie's shoulder. The clock on The Snack Bar wall said five minutes were up already.

Nomie sat in silence. He'd pushed back his chair, crossed his legs and turned to face the sea. He tapped a foot. He seemed to be counting. 'There have been, to date, three thousand two hundred and one St Mirans making a claim to a British passport. There are thirty-seven staff on the *Pride* who will be dealing with those claims. Do the maths.'

Tess couldn't divide by thirty-seven. Nothing divided by that. And anyway, Arlo was British *already*. He was *still* British. All he needed was the paperwork.

'Granted, your partner's case is relatively straightforward. *His* misfortune is everyone else who got in the queue before him.'

Tess watched the seagulls cruising up and down the water's edge, crying to each other over the hope of fish. 'How many of the three thousand will get a passport?'

Nomie pursed his lips – thin lips, nothing to them, she remembered that now. 'My best guess? Not one of them.'

'So, the *Pride* came the first time to get people out of St Mira, and the second time to make people stay.'

'*Enable.* Our procedures enable people to clarify their legal right of abode, namely on St Mira and nowhere else.'

Tess picked up her coffee but found she'd already finished it. 'Look, Tess...'

She tilted the cup, watched the grounds take a while to register gravity.

'It's a complicated business. I've got immigration staff who'll be conducting interviews – forensically detailed – some of them over several days.'

'You'll be *keeping* people on there?'

'They'll be *berthed* for the duration of their interview. It's a processing centre, not a detention centre – though even if it were, it wouldn't be a first.' Then he straightened his back, making himself tall for a short man. 'I've arranged interpreters who can speak every Greek dialect. I've taken on lawyers who know immigration law here, there and everywhere. I've got doctors – specialist paediatricians – who can tell how old a child is just by X-raying their teeth. I've got the Whole. Damn. Shebang.'

Tess had never heard anything like it. 'I don't believe you.'

'Unfamiliarity should not be mistaken for improbability.' He looked at her a while as if weighing something up. 'All right, then, I will share with you, Tess. I will enumerate what I've been contracted to do.' He splayed five fingers as if having his nails done. 'One: get key people out. Done. Two: process the wannabees. That's what the *Pride* is for, and the task is about to begin. Three: allow the Firsters enough slack for their domestic purposes – such as blaming foreigners for the country's problems. That's ongoing. Four: manage reaction in the UK media. Also ongoing. Five: keep the military base open to British forces and annul other bids for its use. Difficult in the extreme. And that, Tess, is what all this hullaballoo is about. The British want unfettered use of the base. The Firsters want to keep their new friends happy. My job is to make the incompatible compatible and manage reactions on both sides.'

Nomie retracted his nails. He paused to catch his breath. Maybe he also heard his stomach because he said, 'I didn't have breakfast this morning. I'm going to order a bite.' He signalled the owner over and asked for the house special in Greek with an Albanian accent.

'Not that I mind being in demand. You know my client list. You've been on my website often enough.'

Did Nomie have tracking stats?

'You know the reach of my work: I shape the debate and offer expert practical advice, fully cognisant of the modern world and the bold steps needed to achieve radical and realistic change.'

Tess could recite that too. It was Nomie's Mission Statement.

'And then I bill them.'

'How much?'

'Enough to sustain my lifestyle.'

A plate of charred sardines appeared in front of him.

'And the truth is: I *love* it when shit hits the fan. Shit is my bread and butter.'

Tess looked at the sardines. They were branded with an identical barcode, their eyes milky-yellow. 'You mean, the worse the problem is, the better it is for you?'

'The more stakeholders there are, the greater the conflict of interests, the more intractable the problem, the more I can invoice.' Nomie said, 'You know, when you join the Foreign Office, you're taught that your job is to promote British interests and British values – values of fairness and justice and democracy.' A trace of a smile, as if it struck him as quaint. 'It's partly why I left. On the outside, you don't have to be old-school. You just do what's really respected: you go where the money is. That's the only value now – maybe the only value there really ever was.' His fork hovered over the fish, picking where to start.

Tess turned away. She looked east into the sun, which had cast everything in black and white. Boats heading out to sea left checker-board patterns in the water.

Nomie said, 'I'm an enabler, a fixer. Like all fixers, interme-diaries, agents of any kind, I facilitate a transaction and make money from it.'

'*And* make money from it? Don't you mean: *only if* you make money from it.'

'I don't help because I want to *help*. I help because it gives me an income.'

'So it's *not* help, then, not in the usual sense. It's the sale of assistance.'

'Help is a commodity, and I trade in it. And, by the way, that *is* the usual sense. Long gone are the days of doing good just to do good. Tess, come on...' He sounded impatient. 'Wake up to how the world works.'

Tess closed her eyes. Once, she'd bought a book called *How to Get On In Life*. But it wasn't about self-advancement; it was about getting on with people. Liking them. It taught you how to generate feelings of goodwill. She did it now, letting her insides go quiet and waiting to feel warm towards Nomie. In the background, the slap of the sea and The Snack Bar radio set to *kardiochtypi*. Tess said to herself: I wish Nomie well. Go well, Nomie. You are a living being, like all of us. A being in human form – though only just. She tried not to want him to drown.

Nomie broke the silence. 'Oh... *Tess*... How old are you?'

She opened her eyes and stared at him. 'Same age as you, plus six months.'

'And still fond and dreamy as ever.'

Close up, Nomie wasn't so fresh-faced. Under his eyes, a tidy stack of lines, a neat sheaf of the years. His eyes watched her, flitting back and forth like beads on an abacus. You could almost hear them click.

She said, 'Do you ever do anything for free?'

'I don't *have* to do anything for free. And do you know why? One: I've avoided ever asking for favours. I have no personal debts that can be called in. Two: I always balance my books and I do nothing that HMRC doesn't know about. Three: my personal life has been impeccable. Squeaky clean, thanks to Catriona. I am, therefore, *obliged* to do nothing for free.' He forked up another sardine. Tess watched him. He ate slowly, thoroughly. Even the way he chewed seemed calculated.

She said, 'Do you ever *choose* to help for free?'

'You mean volunteer?' He swiped at the corners of his mouth with a paper napkin. 'Catriona sponsors goats in Malawi. I've made a charitable bequest in my will.' Nomie seemed to be thinking about it, though, the strange idea of helping for nothing. 'When I was setting up the business, I *did* take on some loss-leaders. Even one or two projects simply because I believed in them. But now? I have so many contenders for my attention that I only ever take on the biggest payers – which are essential, of course, with current financial responsibilities.'

'You mean four sons.'

'And their schooling, and our health, and our pensions, and our homes.'

Plural homes?

Nomie finished off the plate. 'It's simple: I work. I earn money. I keep my family going.'

Tess thought: is that what your world has been reduced to – your family? Are they the limits of your care? How small you

169

have become, Nomie. How self-absorbed. She said, 'So, family comes first.'

'Always.'

'And who, or what, comes second?'

'I have nothing left for anything after.'

Nothing for people like her and Arlo, then.

'Look...' He picked up his fork but found nothing left to eat, so he prodded the air instead. 'The UK doesn't want problem people either.'

'Arlo isn't a problem person. He's a person with a problem.'

'I do politics, not social work. And at this point in my career, yes, I am very much post issues like Arlo.'

At last: he'd said his name.

Tess thought: this was a man who'd slept with her, who many years ago had dreamt his dreams on her pillow. And he couldn't find the wherewithal to care. It was too much effort, and it didn't pay. She said, 'Empathy is such hard work.'

'Ton of bricks. And I'm not a natural labourer.'

And if it were paid labour, the kindest people in the world would also be the richest – and then, probably, they'd give their money away.

Then the owner of The Snack Bar brought the bill – a till receipt held down with boiled sweets.

Tess said, 'There you go, that's a kindness. *They're* given away for nothing.'

'You know very well they're not. They're factored into the price of the coffee.' Nomie dropped his sweet into Tess's hand. '*That's* free, though.'

She left it in her palm, an awkward thing weighing on her, sitting there like a full-stop because with that he'd won the argument. She didn't want to thank him, but what else could she do?

They went to the water's edge and stood by *Ancora*. Tess looked down. In the water, their shadows merged. A breeze blew and their outline rippled. They lost their shape – even Nomie. In the right element, even Nomie was a moveable man.

He set down his bag with all his kit. 'One of the things I most like about fishing, aside from the quiet, is the connection.' Nomie was talking to his shoes – boating shoes with thick rubber soles. 'People have been fishing since people and fish began. With sharpened sticks and barbed poles, mind you.' It was a real skill, he said, because in water, things are never quite where they seem. Light passes from one medium to another and tricks you. So you have to train yourself to think differently. You have to know something to be other than where your brain places it. 'I learnt the principle first through fishing. And I learned it the second time at the Foreign Office.' A shoe kicked at a stone and it landed in the water with the sound of something final. Then Nomie picked up his bag and stepped onto *Ancora*. He looked for balance and couldn't help himself: he reached out to Tess to steady him.

She took his hand. Hello again, she thought, after all these years. It'd slipped in easily. Familiarly. Bodies remembered each other; you never really broke the bond.

Then a smile so fleeting she might have imagined it. 'You still have Orion's Belt.' He meant her freckles. To Arlo, they were ellipses. To Nomie, they were Orion – in Greek mythology a hunter.

Then Nomie found his footing. Tess untied the rope and threw it to him. She watched him move about the deck, making himself at home. Nomie raised the sail. He'd have a good day on the water. He always knew which way the wind was blowing. And, on cue, a breeze came, moving him away from the quay. Then Nomie stood and looked back at Tess.

He didn't wave, so she didn't wave.

She watched Nomie grow smaller, take on shadow, turn the colour of the sea. She thought: the light from Orion's Belt takes 1,500 years to reach the earth. When you looked at the night sky, it was ancient history you were seeing. It was already over, and yet right there. And Tess-and-Nomie were also history, and not quite out of reach.

12.

Please give details of specific events in which you were personally
involved that relate to you deciding to leave.

SEE OVER.

After Vera said 'no' to Arlo's plans for *Ancora*, he'd folded up the Mediterranean and thrown it away. The kitchen had turned cold after that. It became a place where they unwrapped ready meals and ate them without noticing. Tess often found him in there, his eyes fixed on the pans, which is where Sicily would be, his toes clamped to the edge of the chair as if he might jump. And tonight they sat at the table with a frozen pizza, thinking their own thoughts and failing to find anything to say.

Then the ping of a text on Tess's phone:

Appt Imm Off. Tmrw noon. Access 03-12. Do not divulge 3 party. Do not respond.

She turned her back to Arlo and read it again. Then a glance at the calendar on the kitchen wall. A white goat stood in December snow – being safe, being unseen. It'd lifted its head from grazing, alarmed by an intrusion.

Was this good or bad?

Tess turned round, saw the brown stains under Arlo's eyes, under his armpits, on his fingers. What was she to do?

She watched him play with the jigsaw remains of his meal. Was he a third party? There was nothing party-esque about him. 'I've just had a confidential text,' she said.

'So why are you telling me?'

'Because most likely it's about you. It's from Immigration.'

'Why can't it be about *you*?'

'Because I'm legal.'

Arlo shut his eyes.

Tess said, 'I've got an appointment tomorrow.'

'It's Saturday tomorrow. Public offices aren't open.' A languid arm reached for his cigarettes. He pulled out a paper and a thread of tobacco. 'Roll up, roll up,' which he said every time, as he must have when he was fifteen, giving smoking the air of a travelling circus. Arlo had given up Karelias. He couldn't afford them, he said. But Tess thought it was more than that. It had to do with Stan, with no longer feeling entitled to remind her of a man she adored.

She reached for the kitchen window and pushed up the sash. Outside, the sound of gunfire. On Friday evenings, the football stadium was used as a shooting range. Almost every man on St Mira owned a gun, and if you signed up for target practice and gave a litre of blood, you could join the Citizens' Army. They were backup for the military, guarding infrastructure, being present on the streets, leaving bullet holes here and there, making their mark on history.

Arlo dragged hard on his cigarette, then watched the tip flare and dwindle. He liked playing with fire. 'More bad news would be very bad news, you know that Tess.'

Somewhere outside, rubber was burning. Tess watched Arlo smoke. Sometimes she wished she did too, that she could temporarily reduce the flow of oxygen and loosen her bond with Arlo's difficult world. 'Or else it could be *good* news.'

'Could be. But probably not. When did we last hear any good news?'

Well, Nomie had got in touch after the sailing trip. He'd sent a photo of a swordfish laid out against a tape-measure, which at 152 centimetres was the same length as Tess. Catriona had cooked it for dinner. Tess had felt a pang of remorse that such a beautiful shock of silver had passed through the stomachs of the Langbergs so that she could have a brief chat with Nomie. She said, 'Noam Langberg's been in touch.'

'But he isn't going to help.'

Nomie had *voluntarily* communicated. That was surely good news? Tess said, 'The food parcels are good news.'

Joy had set up a 'Taste of Home' WhatsApp group and they sent packages out to St Mira. They came via Athens to get round the embargo, and now Tess and Arlo's hallway was stacked high with Britshit. Tess said, 'You love Britshit.'

'No, *you* love Britshit.'

Which was true. It was soft and sweet and didn't need teeth, and reminded her of grandad Stan, who used Warburtons to take stains off their Wandsworth Council walls. She glanced at Arlo's plate. He'd barely eaten. She tried to make sense of his leftover pieces of pizza. Was that a compass he'd made with them? Or a sun? Or just something exploding? She said, 'What are you thinking about?'

He gazed towards the window and spoke over gunfire. 'That while you're at Immigration, someone will come round here and I'll be disappeared. Vanish. Never heard of again. The appointment is just a ruse to separate us.'

Tess reached for his lighter, felt the teeth of the spark-wheel under her thumb. This was what happened when you couldn't keep off the internet. Some people couldn't get enough of plane crashes or murdered wives or missing children. Arlo was drawn to every form of state-sanctioned abuse.

'I'll be pushed off Forget-Me-Not Head. I'll be just another suicide.'

The cliff was to the east of Mirapolis, the drop sheer and the top blue with flowers in the early months of the year. It was the forget-me-nots that drew people, and the fact that the sea barely entered the cove, even at high tide. It was the perfect place for people who wanted to die but also wanted to be claimed.

Arlo said, 'They'll hang me from a lamppost. Or from a tree. A note in my pocket.'

Tess had tried to persuade him to unsubscribe from all the groups that somehow had got hold of his email address and filled his inbox with arbitrary arrest, false imprisonment, torture and execution. But he'd refused. 'You mean, you want me to unsubscribe from life?'

'You don't *have* to know about it.'

'Yes I *do*. It's happening.'

'But not *all* of it, every day, before breakfast.' It choked him, the enormity of it. The impossibility of doing anything about it. He started every day unable to breathe.

Now Arlo took one last, long drag on his cigarette, flicked the butt outside and pulled the window shut. The shooting stopped. In the quiet, Tess listened to the tick of their kitchen clock. Usually she tried not to hear it. She didn't like being reminded of time all the time. But right now, it was reassuring. Clocks ticked on through every disaster and were still ticking when you came out the other side.

She watched Arlo pick at his fingers – nails bitten, the skin raw. 'Please don't,' she said.

He put a nail to his teeth and tore so hard that he drew blood. Tess reached across the table and scooped Arlo's hands into hers. In another version of their story, in a parallel life, it was the gesture she made when she asked Arlo to marry her. But here and now, she just held them, his fingers stained with the two things that kept him going: blood and tobacco.

He dropped his head.

'You know what to do, Arlo. You've always known. You improvise, you find a way out.'

'My last way out didn't get very far.' His eyes grazed the kitchen cupboards, which was where the Mediterranean had broken against reality. A careless shrug. 'If I've improvised my life, I can improvise my death.'

'You're not going to die.'

'No, *you're* not going to die. Don't universalise your good luck.'

'No, I *am* going to die. Sometime. We're *all* going to die. Sometime. But not yet.'

Arlo shook his head. 'I'm sorry, Tess.' He sounded exhausted. 'I'm not a natural liver of life. It's such a difficult thing to do, such a slog – for most of us, really, except we're too afraid to say it. Some people just seem to know how to live, but for the rest of us... we spend our whole life learning. And I just don't have the patience.'

'You know, your death...'

'...is what happens to other people. Yes, you've told me before. Which is why, if you're thinking of ending it, best to have a small social circle.'

Tess wished it wasn't so hard for Arlo to be Arlo. She didn't think Joy and Elmer had been bad parents. Sometimes, parents were just the wrong match for their child. Not a mix-up in the hospital so much as a mix-up in the general order of things. Arlo wasn't meant to come out of Joy, and when he did, she and Elmer didn't know what to make of him, couldn't make of him what they wanted. Arlo was always fretting to go.

He looked her in the eye then. 'If it wasn't for you, Tess, I'd be out of here like a shot.'

Tess glanced at the clock. It was 8.32. She wanted to remember this moment: Friday night in Mirapolis, the kitchen smelling of warm oven and home-grown basil, the fridge door an archive of notes and tokens, the table ringed with wine and splashed with candlewax, their hands soft and known to each other. It felt like a life you'd want to hold onto.

And then, suddenly, Arlo pushed away his chair and stood. He went to the sink and ran his finger under the tap.

'Do you need a plaster?'

'No. Who cares if I bleed? It's the wrong kind of blood anyway.'

He meant O, not A.

Then he poured himself some water. He was drinking everything these days from his *Life is a Gift* mug. It'd arrived in a food parcel along with the Britshit. Usually, he wouldn't touch mass-produced sentiment, but now it summed everything up: *Gift* meant 'poison' in German.

That night, Arlo drank whisky, took paracetamol, and slept. And maybe he took a sleeper too because in the morning, Tess did her routines loudly and Arlo didn't stir. She wrote on the whiteboard: *If you go out, leave me a message.* Then she clattered with her shoes and was about to leave the flat when

Arlo's door flew open. He was in boxer shorts from weeks ago and a T-shirt from Amnesty. 'What are you doing? You said not to do anything alone...' His cheek was creased from the sheet, like an old wound, a slash in the face.

'I'm going to the Immigration Office, and I'm going alone because the appointment's for me.'

'And what if you don't come back?'

'I'll only be gone an hour or two.'

'I'll be dead by then.' Was he carrying on an argument he'd been having in his sleep?

Tess said, 'I'll be home in time for lunch.'

'What if I'm not here when you get back?'

'Nothing's going to happen, Arlo. And there's always Vera downstairs.'

'So is the Moros gang. So is Rron.' He didn't trust them. And Rrock was downstairs too, staying with his uncle and serving as a constant reminder of the attack on Dover Castle. He used the stairwell for physiotherapy, hauling himself from landing to landing with some kind of harness Mr and Mrs Moros had run up.

Tess checked her watch and opened the latch. She caught the smell of cat. Cid was marking his territory up to the fourth floor now.

Then Arlo got between Tess and the door.

'I'm not *not* going,' she said. 'Something will come of this appointment. Something after it will be different.' That was all Tess wanted: for something to change.

Arlo leant forward, his face close. She caught the fug of alcohol and unbrushed teeth. 'If I'm not here when you get back...'

'I wish I'd never told you about this appointment.'

'If I'm *dead* when you get back...'

'Don't do this to me, Arlo.'

'What?'

'Mess with me. Make life harder than it already is. I hate it.'

'See?' A flick of his chin at her. 'Even *you* hate me.'

'I hate *it*, not you. I hate what you do.'

'I *am* what I do.'

'I hate what you *sometimes* do. Like this. Right now.'

'Well...' He put his hands on his hips, his fingers close to touching, he'd grown that thin. 'I hate what *you* do quite often.'

She didn't say: *Such as?* but that must have been what he heard in his head because 'Such as...' he said, '...be so bloody optimistic it's depressing. Such as: please people all the time. Such as: be so nice and kind and understanding. I don't want you to be kind. I want you to get a gun. That's what we need. You can't defend yourself with kindness.'

She'd always thought you could, that if you lost that, you'd lost everything. But maybe what they needed right now was kindness and a gun.

Tess moved forward. 'I'm going or I'm going to be late.'

Arlo shrugged. He stepped back from the door. 'Okay,' said lightly. He'd given up, given way, just like that.

Except she knew him too well to believe it.

'Well fuck off then.'

'Arlo, *please*...'

He put a hand to his mouth and gnawed at his fingers, trying to draw blood. Tess brushed past him, catching his elbow on her way out. *So bleed then*, she thought. She stepped over Cid, who'd been drawn to the ruckus, and she took the stairs so fast she nearly fell. Arlo's voice came after her, filling the stairwell with the first English that had sounded there for months: 'Cremation, not burial. And I don't want any fucking mourners.'

'Don't worry,' she called back, 'there won't be.'

Tess threw open the front door, and ran into daylight. On Saturdays, the St Miran Maidens League used the Square as a parade ground. Teenage girls in gym skirts were weaving figures of eight and blowing tunes through pink kazoos.

When Tess got to the far side, she glanced back at the house. She hoped to see Arlo with a look she recognised – a kind kind of expression. But he wasn't there. Instead, Vera had come onto her balcony. She wanted Vera to reach out her arms and wrap them round thin air, a huge hug, big enough for two. Instead, they stood and watched each other. Neither of them knew how to sign this moment. They didn't wave. Why would they? This wasn't a goodbye, it wasn't a hello, and there was no happiness.

When Tess got to the Immigration Office, the metal shutter was down. It was sprayed with *GO HOME!* and hung with a message in English and Greek to come back only with an appointment. She took the alley down the side of the building and found the only other door. It was the staff entrance and had a keypad. Tess entered 03-12 and heard a click – thin, metallic, final. It could have been the sound of a trigger. Then she leant against the door and shouldered her way into darkness.

'You're late.'

Tess knew that voice. She let her eyes adjust, then Arlo's Immigration Officer emerged from the shadows. Beside her, a Christmas tree stood shackled in silver tinsel. 'I was about to decide you weren't coming. That would have been most unfortunate.' Then she walked at a clip down the corridor, pausing at junctions and looking left and right as if expecting traffic. But the building was deserted. The smell of floor polish made Tess uneasy. It was the smell of an institution when you weren't meant to be in it.

They went down to the basement, past doors that said *HAZARDOUS* and *HIGH VOLTAGE* and *NO ENTRY* and stopped at a door that said nothing. Inside, abandoned filing cabinets, bent chairs, broken fans and cardboard boxes, the walls bubbled with water and the air laced with acid.

Tess stood and waited. The officer's eyes fell on her, but didn't seem to see her. Tess knew the look. It was the focus on something rehearsed being played through one last time. It was the look of a diver at the end of the board, then a deep breath, in and out, and 'My name is Agnesa.'

'What does that mean?'

'It means I remember our previous conversation.'

Tess remembered it now too. She'd asked at the last appointment what she was called and hadn't got an answer. But why a store cupboard to be told her name? 'Why exactly am I here?'

'Ah, *that* question… Don't we all ask it?' She glanced up to the white-tiled ceiling, to where, beyond this building lay a blank December sky. 'God can answer it, if you believe in God?'

Tess had never believed in God, though at that moment she wished she did. She needed some benevolence – she didn't care where from.

'How's Arlo?'

Tess thought of him gnawing at his fingers like an animal chewing on its chain. 'He's unhappy. I'm unhappy. It's what happens when you live with someone.' Though, actually, she said it with a question mark. She was asking: *Do you know what I mean? Do you live with someone too?*

But she was giving nothing more away.

Tess watched her. For an instant, it was like glancing in a mirror: the same alert reserve, the same look of intense neutrality – the kind of face you present to a border guard when trying to resemble your passport. Tess said, 'We had a row this morning. We never row.'

'About what?'

'Me coming here. He didn't want me to come.'

'But you did.'

'I please people, apparently. All the time. I'm *endlessly* nice.'

'But you didn't please Arlo.'

No. He was beyond pleasing. Tess was starting to think he was beyond rescue. 'Arlo has to leave the country, but he can't.' Because of you, she thought. Because you took away his St Miran passport.

'Because of me,' she said.

Because she worked in Immigration, and those were the rules, and she chose to follow them.

Agnesa put a hand in a pocket and stirred keys. 'What would you give for Arlo to get out of St Mira?'

'You mean he *can*?'

'*Could*.'

Tess scanned her face looking for clues. What was the *if*? What did this woman want? 'I don't have any money.'

'Not money.'

What else was there? She didn't have special access. She didn't have classified information. 'I don't have anything else.'

'You have more than most people.'

'Such as?'

No answer.

What did Tess have that she didn't? For a while, they exchanged looks. Over their head, the neon hummed. It cast shadows on the officer's face that beat her up and left her bruised. Tess felt suddenly exhausted, battered by the morning. She abandoned the guessing game. 'So, have it, then, whatever it is. I'll give anything for Arlo to get out.' Then she changed her mind. 'No, I'd give *everything*.'

Agnesa nodded. Everything seemed to cover it. She took down two chairs and tested them with her weight. She sat, arranging herself, looking for comfort in warped plastic. Then she focused on her fingers, the way newscasters do before raising their face to camera. 'I have to inform you there is a clear and present threat to Arlo's life.' Her voice was unhurried, her expression untouched.

'How immediate?'

'I called you in on a day we're closed to tell you.'

'Have you told the police?'

'Arlo has to be removed from the sphere of danger. That includes the police. He has to disappear.'

Wasn't that what Arlo had said – that he'd be disappeared? 'You mean he has to go into hiding?'

'More thorough than that. We have to remove him from their calculations.'

'Whose calculations?'

'The people who are after him.'

Tess knew about the militias. She read the papers. They were above the law and below the law. They were full of lone egos chalking up hits via encrypted message: anyone who crossed them; snowflakes, fags, foreigners; people in the wrong place at the wrong time; people who didn't know to keep their mouth shut if they didn't like what was going on.

For a while, there'd been resistance. But not for long – they didn't have the guns or the killer instinct. Now they'd stopped fighting and were on the run instead. But if they were caught it was summary justice. The morgue was full to overflowing.

'Arlo's name appears on certain lists.'

'You've seen them?'

'Let's just say I have prior knowledge. Thirty-eight years of it.' She'd lived her entire life next door to the men in those militias. 'They're planning a sequel to Rrock. Something symbolic. Kentish Town. And I suggest that we…' She reached for a cardboard box. '…do the job for them.' She removed the lid. 'If Arlo wants to leave St Mira alive, first he has to die.'

Inside, his death notice:

Arlo Brown

Fake St Miran
Polluter of our culture

Executed † 3 December
Hanged from the Majesty Oak

The Mob

Tess looked at his photo and wanted to cry. It was the one in his St Miran passport. She looked into his eyes – full of excitement, brimming with hope. How long since she'd seen those?

'I decided The Mob should get him.'

The Mob was a militia that drew loners who liked to hunt – who killed deer, bear and lynx in the mountains, cut off the head and hung it on the wall, ate the meat and fed their dogs the bones.

Tess read the notice again. 'Fake St Miran.' Otherwise known as 'naturalised citizen.' 'Polluter of our culture' aka 'teacher of English and *Life in the UK*.' 'Hanged from the Majesty Oak.' Tess could picture the tree – the fissured bark, the tinder fungus lodged like seashells, the ground rusted with leaves and rough with scattered acorns. And Arlo hanging, his feet inches above English lawn, in sight of Dover Castle. She said, 'What happens when you hang?'

Agnesa rocked in the give of her chair. 'If the drop is short, you're strangled. It's slow and painful and ugly. If the drop is long, your neck breaks. It's quick and painful and ugly. With a very long drop, your head comes off. Urine and faeces. Struggling. Swollen tongue. Erections sometimes. Brain death in a few minutes, the heart stops in ten to fifteen.' The British were experts at it, she said. The *Official Table of Drops* had turned hanging into a science. 'It's still used in some of your old colonies. There are one or two copies lying around St Mira.' She laid her arms along the arms of her chair, squaring everything up. 'And after the death, there's the question of the body.'

The body? Was that what Arlo was about to become? Tess lived with *the* body. She loved *the* body. She was going to save *the* body. What was it doing now, she wondered? She hoped it'd had breakfast and washed and was calmer and...

'It will be in the morgue tomorrow. It will have to be identified, though not by you. Someone independent. With official standing.'

Nomie? Had she earned a favour with that fishing trip? Would 152 centimetres of Sword Fish buy her a lie?

'A native St Miran.'

So not Nomie, then.

'And not a friend.'

So not Vera – though she'd have done it. She'd have gone to the morgue in her permanent mourning and shed real tears for everyone in there.

'No neighbours.'

There were no other neighbours.

'Neutral.'

Tess thought: Mr Dee? The man who'd fired Arlo? Wasn't that proof he had no vested interest?

'Someone you can trust.'

'To tell a lie?'

'Not exactly. To imagine themselves, briefly, in another version of events and believe them long enough to sign a piece of paper.' She paused. 'And free tomorrow lunchtime.'

'That's rather specific.'

'Because it's specifically a good time to identify bodies. There are helpful staff on Sundays who clear up the excesses of the night before.'

Tess knew what Mr Dee would be doing on a Sunday lunchtime. He'd be writing up vocab from his tapes of the BBC. He liked to imagine he worked for Auntie, writing reports for *From Our Own Correspondent*. Sometimes, he spent Sunday afternoons actually writing them. He had a drawer full of unsent dispatches from Mirapolis to Bush House.

'When you get back from the morgue, the death notices will already be up. There will be a reaction, of course, from neighbours and friends. They'll talk among themselves, but probably not to you. On the whole, people avoid the bereaved. If anyone offers condolences, you lower your head and accept them. Say nothing. It's what's expected.' She rearranged herself in her chair. 'There's the problem of the news, of course. A British death would be most unfortunate – if it's reported, which it won't be. I'm taking care of that. *Your* job is to take care of his family. Let them know in a roundabout way they are not to be alarmed.'

Tess nodded. She could do that. She worked for Duke. She knew all about not saying what you meant and not meaning what you said. She did it for a living. 'When does Arlo find out he's dead?'

'When I tell him.'

'But you *are* taking him to safety?'

'Yes.'

'Where?'

'You don't need to know that.'

'So how do I know he's safe?'

'I thought you'd decided to trust me.'

An involuntary glance to the door, the paint chipped where awkward weights had been shifted in and out. Tess said, 'How long before I can see him?'

'I can't say.'

'But he *will* get out of St Mira?'

A wordless sound it was hard to interpret, fractionally more yes than no.

'With a valid British passport? A real one, not fake, in his name, with a photo that looks like him.'

She nodded to all those things.

How would she manage that? How would she procure with such apparent ease what had eluded Tess so long? 'Do you know Noam Langberg?'

'Everyone does. He's in all the papers.'

'Professionally, I mean.'

'It's my job to know everyone involved with St Miran Immigration.'

So Agnesa was getting a passport from Nomie – in exchange for what? 'What does Mr Langberg want?'

'What do we *all* want? Outstanding immigration issues resolved as soon as possible. Procedures speeded up. Everyone being exactly who they are. No-one claiming to be someone they're not. And the *Pride* sailing away from our shores and home in time for Christmas.'

Tess wasn't sure what to think. She'd tried so hard to persuade Nomie and got nowhere, and now, suddenly, the knot was untying, this woman was sorting everything out. 'Why are you doing this?'

'It's my job.'

'But for nothing?'

'I'm a salaried employee.'

Tess said, 'You don't have to get Arlo a passport.'

'Yes I do. St Mira doesn't want a problem Brit.'

'You didn't have to warn me he's in danger.'

'We don't want a dead Brit either.'

Tess cast about, hoping for clues in the abandoned office equipment, the unmarked cardboard boxes, trying to work out what this was all about. 'But if it's all as straightforward as that, why down here in the basement on a day the office is closed?'

'Because we're about to do something illegal. We're about to stage a death. And we're doing it under pressure of time and in extremely hostile circumstances.' She checked her watch. She decided time was up. 'I hope it goes well tomorrow. Regards to Mr Dionysopoulos. He's doing us a favour.'

Tess shook her head. 'That's not possible. I didn't mention his name and you can't read minds.'

'But I can set parameters that lead only to him.'

It was all so efficient, so worked out. What had Nomie told Tess once, years ago, when he was signing up for the Foreign Office? *Diplomacy is the art of letting somebody else have your way.* Was Agnesa the consummate diplomat?

Agnesa closed Arlo's box, and put the box back on the pile.

'How much of this do I tell Arlo?'

'Give him the good news. Say that he's getting a passport. But spare him the details. He's in no state to hear them.' Then she went to the door, flicked off the light, showed Tess out and turned the key in the lock. They retraced their steps up to the ground floor and an unlit Christmas. At the staff entrance, she leant on the safety bar and opened the door to the chill of December air.

Tess stepped into a world that felt brash and relentless. She listened to the grind of Saturday traffic, the lorries that ploughed through the centre of town because the Great National Bypass still wasn't finished. She caught the smells of the countryside carted to Saturday market: manure, sweat, blood. She knew the whole of Mirapolis would be there, bargaining and bartering, no-one getting anything for free. And hard against the harbour wall, roped-up goats would mourn their final day and chickens would pick at dust till the moment their throats were cut.

Tess gestured back inside, to the darkened corridor, to what had passed between them. 'Agnesa?' It was the first time she'd said her name. It meant lamb. Like lambs to the slaughter.

'Tess Petrou?'

'You're not getting *anything* from this?'

She took a while to answer. She was raised on the doorstep as if on a pedestal. In this pearly light, there was something angelic about her. 'When we give, don't we always get? Isn't that one of the laws of the universe? It might be chaos down here. But up there...' She turned shiny eyes to the white of the sky. 'Up there, they still have laws.' She looked like one of those glazed figurines you could buy in the market, gaze rolled heavenward, heavy and hollow and invested with all the hope you had.

13.

When did you last have contact with your ~~spouse~~? PARTNER

AT THE UK BORDER. WHEN WAS THAT? I'VE LOST TRACK OF HOW
MANY DAYS I'VE BEEN HERE.

Where are they now?

YOU KNOW THAT.

Tess thumbed her address book for Mr Dee – found his work and home numbers and the number for his mother. He'd given that out over the months that she'd been sickening because more often than not he was there. Tess picked up the receiver. Mr Dee didn't own a mobile. He didn't want to be tagged, he said. He was available at the three most significant sites of his life – home, work, and at his mother's – but not everywhere, such as the garden, where a tin of his mother's ashes had been buried this summer. He liked to spend time under the bitter-orange tree thinking about bittersweet things, such as marmalade, and mothers, and England and if he'd ever go back.

Tess started to dial and then paused. She still hadn't worked out how to put it to Mr Dee, this invitation to the morgue. She went to the window. In Exodus Square, mourners were gathering for the funeral of Mr Pantazis, who'd died aged ninety-one. The death notices were all over town. The whole of Mirapolis knew him because he'd worked fifty years in the Main Post Office, and on retirement, for St Miran Heritage. He'd been posthumously named a National Treasure, and next year, he'd appear on a postage stamp. Rumours were that today Varela would deliver the eulogy.

Tess called Mr Dee at home and listened to the other end ring. She watched the priest join the men in Café Echo. They put away their scratch cards and gave him their attention as he regaled them with the volume and persistence of a drunken man.

And still Mr Dee's phone rang.

Then Rron appeared in the Square. And Rrock. He was standing unaided these days, though listing, his skin sallow, his cheeks cracked, the ends of his trousers gathering at his ankles. He played with worry beads like a boy with marbles: flick, flick, flick.

And then Mrs Moros slid out of her shop followed by all her nieces. They wore shiny black outfits and slinked across the Square like something poisonous. Trailing behind them, Mr Moros, crumpled and thin, like a skin the women had sloughed off.

Tess gave up and rang StUKCO instead. Maybe Mr Dee had gone into the office? But a recorded message said they were closed at the weekend and for Frequently Asked Questions such as our New National Curriculum, please visit our website. She tried his mother's number in case he was there, still sorting things, or on a pilgrimage – who knew what rituals people had with their dead mother? But the number wasn't recognised.

She could have rung Mr Dee yesterday, but she didn't want to give him time to say yes to the morgue, then imagine the consequences and change his mind. She tried him at home again, held the receiver under her jaw, went back to the window. Down in the Square, the priest was leaving the café. He walked towards the church, his sheet of silver beard catching the sun, his back straight as a rod – the perfect conduit for the word of God. The church doors opened and mourners streamed in. Tess saw candles and candelabras, the nave sparkling with drops of light such as heaven might look when Mr Pantazis got there. A man sang, his voice broadcast into the Square, sounding sad and delicious. In the background, a deep bell swayed.

She was just about to give up when Mr Dee answered. He'd been in the garden and had only just become aware of a sound that wasn't religion. He lived in a sleepy valley of chapels and orange and lemon trees that on Sundays sank under the slug of the church. 'I've been thinking about you, Tess,' he said. 'I've been wondering how you are.'

She was worried about Arlo. She hadn't seen him since their row, since the *No fucking mourners*, which still bothered her. And the *Don't worry, there won't be*, which bothered her just as much.

Arlo's response to the row had been to hide. When she'd got back from Immigration, he'd put a ships sign up. It was T for Tango: *Keep clear of me* – and he didn't come out of his room.

But she knew he was alive anyway, because in the early hours he'd blasted the flat with *Scary Monsters*. He got Bowie to break the Law of Sunday Silence. Tess had put in earplugs. That was the first time ever they hadn't said goodnight. She didn't sleep well, had got up and made porridge in Arlo's pan and wished she had one of his pills. He hadn't emerged this morning either. His room was quiet, but Tess knew he was still alive because of that Arlo forcefield, the psychic turbulence that permeated the flat.

She wanted to tell Mr Dee she was fine. In reality, Tess was in trouble – though reality was harder to pin down these days. She was trusting Arlo's life, and possibly both their lives, to a woman not given to explanation and known only as Agnesa. She was following Agnesa's instructions because her instincts said to trust her – though Tess wasn't sure she could trust her own instincts. That was how she was: the woman who could stand on rolling boats had lost her footing.

Tess said, 'Would you like to meet for lunch, Mr Dee? Have a chat? Have a picnic?' She knew he loved them. When he'd lived in London, he used to go to Brunswick Square with a Fortnum's wicker basket and dropped accidental crusts for the pigeons because Camden said you shouldn't feed the birds.

'In the park?' She had in mind Great Martyr's Park. It used to be the Beautiful Game Park till the Firsters changed its name. It had a strip of football pitches, and amateur matches were held every Sunday till the Law of Sunday Silence. The Park also happened to be next to the stadium, which was next to Mirapolis morgue.

Mr Dee said he'd be delighted. He hadn't seen Tess for such a long time and there was so much to catch up on. He'd bring the hardware. Tess would bring the Britshit. They could sit side-by-side and eat and remember. Or else they could eat and forget.

Tess arrived early and chose the bench near the stadium that also had the best view of the morgue. The bench used to be in honour of Mario, the St Miran striker who'd now left the country to play for Galatasaray. He was a hero till this year, when he'd been downgraded to a national disgrace and his plaque had been vandalised then officially removed.

Tess watched the black figure of Mr Dee trudge up the path. His shoulders were curved under a weight of care, or maybe caution, or maybe just the rucksack. He'd come without his picnic basket, had chosen not to be seen with the 'F' and 'M' of Fortnum and Mason, was not going to risk in public the letters of a foreign language.

Mr Dee was never a man to hurry. Each step bore a thought – a tentative one, formed slowly. But today it took an age for him to reach her. Tess hadn't seen him since *Chariots of Fire* and something serious had happened to Mr Dee since then.

They shook hands, a long, heavy shake as if this was goodbye, not the first hello in months. 'How are you Mr Dee?'

A sigh that brought a hint of Fisherman's Friends. It was a taste he'd acquired in London. 'Ah, Tess… I told you once about my heart?'

She remembered that – that he lay awake at night wondering if it was there.

'Well, it's true. I *do* have one.'

Of course he did.

'And it hurts.' A hand pressed to his chest.

Did he mean literally or metaphorically?

'It sits heavy. It is ill at ease in my chest.' Then he pulled at an earlobe. 'Do you see this?'

Was he showing her a wrinkle?

'It is a sign. It is called Frank's sign. My doctor told me. It turns out my heart is in trouble. I have a troubled heart.' A glance in the direction of the morgue. Then Mr Dee embraced her. He held onto her. He'd never done that before. He put his nose to the top of her head and inhaled as if Tess were oxygen. Pressed this close, she could feel his heart racing – sick or anxious, she wasn't sure which.

It took a while for Mr Dee to release her. Then he busied himself, emptying his rucksack and arranging a tablecloth, and napkins, and silverware on the bench. They ate Tess's Nutella sandwiches, which counted as British even though it was Italian. They drank Coca-Cola from champagne flutes. And all the while, Mr Dee reminisced about picnics in WC1 – how he loved to sit under the low boughs of the Brunswick Plane, and read Dickens, and look across to the Foundling Museum, because he often felt lost in London, but in that spot, he felt found again. He told Tess that the Brunswick Plane was planted in 1796, twenty years after losing America, five years before taking Ireland, in the reign of George the Third, then George the Fourth, William the Fourth, Victoria...

Teaching *Life* engraved habits like that. Arlo could do it too.

Dickens himself would have known that tree, he said. Maybe he even sat under it and watched people pass. Maybe some of them got into his books.

Then Mr Dee fell quiet. They watched the church on the corner of the park empty after the service. Families were dressed in their Sunday best, the adults starched and one step closer to salvation, the children starched and bored. They filed past the bench, doffing a head to Mr Dee because an older man in black must mean religion. It would be a day for mistaken identity.

'So, Tess, how are you?'

She said, 'Arlo's not so good.'

'No?'

'He needs help.'

'Oh.' Mr Dee dabbed his lips with a napkin. 'Well, perhaps I can offer it. I've been wanting to make amends. I'm sorry for what I did.'

So, something serious really *had* happened to Mr Dee.

'I made a mistake rationalising the workforce.' Mr Dee gazed across the park to where a child in the strip of Mirapolis United sat on the side-line, playing in his head the game the priests had banned. 'A strange phrase that, *rationalise the workforce.*

Cowardly, it strikes me now. Short-sighted, too.' Though it wasn't so hard for Mr Dee to rationalise what he'd done. He'd thought – and hoped – that Arlo would be the end of it, they'd know where to draw the line. But no. Next they came for the St Mirans who were *enabling* foreign influence. 'I'm suspended while they check my background. I'm being retired at the end of the year. No pension for my time at StUKCO.'

They sat without speaking, gazing in the direction of the stadium. In all the time she'd lived on St Mira, Tess had never been to a match there. Even though she liked football, even though she still supported Stoke City because of Stan and his namesake, Stanley Matthews.

Then a van approached and drove down the lane that led to the morgue. It did a three-point turn and backed up to the entrance.

Mr Dee had seen it too. He swung a foot, kicking up gravel. '"What passing-bells for these who die as cattle?"' He projected his voice, but only quietly, only as far as the Law allowed. 'Wilfred Owen, 1893 to 1918, *Anthem for Doomed Youth*, *Life in the UK*, chapter five, a Modern and Thriving Society.'

'Arlo among them.' Tess said. 'He's officially – but only officially – no longer with us.'

Mr Dee turned a quarter face to Tess, an eye meeting one of hers. 'Well, then, my deepest official condolences.' He looked at his feet: black patent leather, the polish dimmed, a fragment of gravel stuck in the stitching. This was a man who no longer cared about shoes. 'Since when?'

'Yesterday. And if you want to help Arlo, you could...'

'Yes. Yes, I can.'

Did he know?

'I've done it a few times already.' A group of former students had performed Monty Python, 'The Spanish Inquisition,' in English, in front of Firster offices.

Python was part of *Life*.

'The young don't believe they're ever going to die. But after that, they had to be...'

Tess said, '..."removed from their calculations". She leant back, finding the place where Mario had been. 'Are you telling me what I think you're telling me?'

'I don't know what you're thinking.' He looked away and up to the clouds. 'It's a great thing, the privacy of the mind.' Then Mr Dee checked his watch. 'I must get going, or...'

But he didn't finish. He folded his tablecloth and the napkins and wiped the silverware clean. It felt like the end of an operation, all surgically efficient. 'I'll head straight home from there. I must appear affected by events, be appropriately distressed.'

'You really don't mind, Mr Dee?'

'How could I mind?' Then a hand to his heart, as if that's where his mind was. 'Facts are important. Truth is important. But I live in a country where both mean nothing.' He lifted the rucksack onto his back and edged it around, making it comfortable.

When Tess got back to the flat, the hall-light was on and a ships sign up. Arlo's shoes lay where he'd last kicked them. His jacket hung on his hook. The air was rank with coffee left too long on the hob. But Tess knew that Arlo had gone. The pressure that had built up day after day had been punctured. The flat no longer felt about to burst. Cid had known too. His emerald gaze had followed Tess as she'd passed Rron's door. Had that been delight in his eyes? *Ha, ha, look what's happened, he's left without you.*

And because Tess was so certain, she could knock on his door despite the ships, and call his name, and know she'd get no answer, and go inside. Arlo's unmade bed was made, the creased sheets pulled flat, the duvet plump. A damp towel hung on the back of a chair. A window was ajar, fresh air creeping through the fug of weeks. Tess flicked through his clothes rack making the hangers clack: his winter coat was missing, his hiking boots gone. Tess lifted his pillow, hoping for a note. Instead, she found boxer shorts and his Amnesty T-shirt. He'd folded them. At the last minute, he'd become Arlo the Scout, Arlo the Duke of Edinburgh Silver Award holder. He'd arranged his bedclothes for someone else to find. It meant Arlo wasn't coming back.

Tess jumped when her phone rang. She glanced at the number – one she didn't recognise. It didn't even look St Miran. 'Arlo?'

Down the line, the sound of heavy rain. She knew it wasn't raining, but still her eyes flicked to the window.

A voice said, 'I will talk and you will listen.' It was a man's voice, but sounding manufactured, somehow untrue. 'Go immediately to Eastern Square. Bring one small bag. Pack all valuables: laptop, phone, money, passports.'

Passports plural? Who was this? Someone who knew she had two. 'Agnesa?'

'Speak to no-one.'

'Is that you?'

A pause. Wherever they were, rain was still falling. 'And switch off all the lights as you leave.'

Was someone watching her? Could someone see into the flat? Tess stood by the window and scanned Exodus Square for a face she knew. But it was deserted now the funeral was over, just a scatter of candles flickering by the church. 'Who's calling?'

Then a long drum of thunder, bold and brilliant. A click, and the line went dead.

Tess walked to the central station for the bus to Eastern Square. In Departures, the smell of bleach from the toilets and warming meat that was served for all-day lunch. She knew Rron came here sometimes – when Blood Broth was on the menu – and he caught up with colleagues from work. Old men sat under the click of the board, listening as if to the draw of the lottery.

They glanced at the tumble of placenames, at journeys they were never going to make.

It was a long ride to the last reach of town, into the blanket of low-rise flats, colour-coded so you knew where you lived, the paint chewed off by the weather. The flats had long been forgotten by the council, but remembered now by the Firsters. St Miran flags necklaced the balconies. Posters of Varela had been plastered over windows. It must have been dark inside, but what did it matter? Varela was all the light they needed.

Eastern Square was the end of the line. It was the kind of place you could be yourself in public and no-one would notice: you could be lonely, wanting to be alone, or the friend of dogs and strays. You could be out of work, looking for work, in need of a drink, in need of love, in need of small change. Or just waiting for the bus.

It took a while for Tess to spot Agnesa: a woman in a hoodie, the black hood up, and jeans ripped at the knee. She was sitting in the bus shelter leafing through a magazine. Tess took the seat beside her. Agnesa didn't register her presence except to cast an eye over Tess's bag, and cross her legs the other way.

'Was that you on the phone?'

Agnesa flicked the pages of the magazine, making the glossy paper tick. She was reading *The Week*. It was impossible to buy that on St Mira now, except at the Holiday Inn – flown in via Amyna for the few still entitled to read foreign news.

Tess said, 'Why the male voice?'

Agnesa stopped on a spread of 'charming thatched cottages'. They could have sat around the VILLAGE GREEN in the fairy-tale of Englishness in Tess's British passport.

'And why the downpour?'

Silence.

She took a sideways glance at Agnesa. So, this Immigration Officer with the crisp, fitting uniform and the glory stars on her epaulettes was trying to blend in in Eastern Square. How long had she been sitting here? Tess turned to Agnesa's knees, the skin pressed hard to the bars of white cotton. It was intimate and hypnotic and read like a message: that in truth Agnesa was not Agnesa; this was somebody else.

Then a bus pulled up and Agnesa stood. The doors wheezed open and they got on. She offered two tickets, which the driver tore, and Tess followed her to seats at the back. They sat sideways to the motion of the bus, and swung through empty streets out of town. Tess watched Agnesa in the window, her face dipped into the magazine.

'Why are you reading *The Week*?'

'I'm not reading.'

It was true. She'd stopped turning the pages. Her eyes were fixed on an ad for Omega watches. The cogs were cast into space like original stars that had measured time since time began. Omega. The last letter of the Greek alphabet. The End.

Finally, Agnesa said, 'Did he leave a note?'

'No. Should he have?'

'No.'

Tess focused beyond the glass. The road this far out was unlit. Every so often, a neon sign flicked past for a petrol station, tyres, emergency repairs. She thought: Arlo *had* left a ships sign though, and – now she thought about it – one she didn't recognise. Tess took out her phone, checked online, and there it was: H for Hotel. It meant *I have a pilot on board*. Pilot? She turned to Agnesa 'Where are we going?'

'As far as we can.'

Tess hadn't taken this bus before. She kept her eyes on the digital board, the scroll of the route in squared-off lettering: *Olive Co-op, St Benedict Church, First School, Village of Amyna all passengers dismount.*

The civilian airfield next to the base was fenced off, razor-wired and lit with building-site floodlights. They were constructing a spectacular new terminal here, a grandiose Firster project with a control tower shaped like an olive tree. This was where Varela flew out on his charm missions and welcomed the world's most unsavoury leaders, sweet-talking them and signing friendship agreements, offering access to the Med. But for now, it still had St Mira's old innocence. It could have been a school playing field – touchlines painted into the grass, a runway that looked like a 100-meter track, and the blue glare of an all-glass building that could have been the swimming pool but was actually Departures.

At the gate, CCTV cameras fingered every direction. Signs said *Restricted Zone. No photographs.* It was windy up here, windsocks snapping. The rumble of trucks was blown over from the base. In a Portakabin, two men in uniform were tipped back in their chairs, deep in cards. It was a quiet night, not many travellers. It'd be a long, focused game.

Then a chair fell forwards and a hand of cards fanned face-down on the table. An officer came to the window. 'Passports.'

Agnesa didn't have a passport. She'd had to surrender hers as a servant of the state. Instead, her Immigration Office ID slid under the glass.

The officer looked at her, then at her photo, then her again. A deep gaze into her eyes as if trying to hypnotise. But it went on too long, an absent stare, his mind still on the game. 'Passenger's name?' in a voice amped and tinny.

Agnesa said, 'Tess Matthews.'

Tess handed the passport over.

He glanced down, a finger skimming a list. Not a long list, and Arlo's name would be on it. Then the hum of a machine picked up by a mic. A nod, an arm reached for a button, and the gate clicked out of its latch.

They walked to the terminal, Agnesa half a step ahead. Hunkered down in front of the building, a squat, grey plane. The cockpit was lit, the pilot seated. So that was how they were getting back to England. It looked made of lead, too heavy to fly. Then an abrupt drop in her stomach like a sudden loss of height. 'The flight *is* to England?'

Was that a nod inside her hoodie?

'What time does it leave?'

At that moment, the cabin lights went on, a strip of yellow circles puncturing the dusk.

Arlo would be here already, in his winter coat and hiking boots, dressed for English cold. He'd be drinking something strong if the building had a bar. Arlo hated flying. He didn't believe it was possible for gases to hold up solids. Every successful flight was an exception to the rule. 'Look,' he'd say, taking something from his pocket and dropping it on the floor.

The door to the terminal building opened at their approach and slid shut behind them. It was warm inside, fan heaters blowing air so that men in suits didn't need coats and could arrive for business looking freshly pressed. At a kiosk, tall rakes of magazines hung like flags of the world. The scent of fresh coffee mingled with cologne. Around the edges of the room, greying men she half-knew from the papers wore cufflinked shirts and concerned themselves with broadsheet news.

But no Arlo.

'Where is he?'

Agnesa motioned for Tess to follow her. She knew her way around this building, and made straight for a door marked *Personnel Only*. She flashed her ID at a woman in uniform, who nodded acknowledgement without breaking her stare.

Beyond the door, the corridor was cool. It was windowless. The walls were blank. They were beige. This was something to do with Border Control. Agnesa rapped at a door that said *Female*, and when she got no response, went inside.

It was the kind of room Tess knew from cervical smears: a curtained cubicle, a sink with taps you didn't have to touch, soap dispenser, green paper towels. A table with trays for your clothes and belongings. 'Bag in this one,' Agnesa said. She wasn't making eye contact. Her gaze was patrolling the room at waist height. She hooked Tess's backpack onto a finger, gauging its weight and put it into a tray. 'Remove your clothes, please, to your underwear.'

'Is Arlo doing this?'

'No watch. No jewellery.'

Tess went into the cubicle and undressed. She took her phone from her jeans and found texts she hadn't heard come in. One was from Duke: *Keep Monday night free*, which she deleted. And one from Vera: *Is that you?*, which she kept. She could have dumped her clothes in a pile, but didn't. She folded them and lined up the edges as Arlo had under his pillow: scarf, anorak, jumper, T-shirt, socks, trousers. She was marking the end of a life too: Tess Matthews was getting on a plane to England and never coming back.

She pushed the tray under the curtain. Tess listened to Agnesa sorting things, double-checking. Then, 'Wait one moment, please.' The door opened. A sigh of air, and a sharp slam as it shut.

And so Tess waited. Her eyes traced the pattern in the curtain: a red-and-white splash of blousy flowers, probably poppies, maybe peonies, the kind of thing Joy would wear.

Joy.

Would they see her tomorrow? London tonight, Dover in the morning?

Tess caught the sound of a toilet flushing. She tuned in to the hum of the light, made harmonies with it – thirds and fifths – she and the neon sounding monastic.

Then the click, she thought, of a latch. 'Hello?' she said.

No answer.

Tess pulled her feet from the chill of the floor and clung onto her knees. Funny knees. Big joints because of the breaststroke, the right one scarred from a diving board fall. She reached for her feet, the nails sharp, the toes cold. She revved them up like a motorbike. She remembered how she and Arlo had flirted with their feet on the roof of Dover Castle. Flipper-feet... a distinguishing feature... something to put in your passport.

All that time ago.

How long ago *was* it?

Tess turned to her wrist, found a strip of pale skin. How long had Agnesa been gone? 'Hello? Are you there?'

Silence.

Tess swiped the cubicle open, the clatter of curtain rings sounding like the snap of applause. On the table, a tray of clothes: Agnesa's ripped jeans, a black hoodie, stuffed there in a hurry. Tess threw them aside, found her St Miran passport and a UK passport, the dark cover stiff, the ink so new it smelt sweet. It was in Arlo's name, issued in Tirana, dated yesterday.

Tess yanked at the door knowing it'd be locked and found it open. She put her face into the corridor. Left. Right. Left again, as if checking for oncoming traffic when the truck had already hit. The lights were off now, the beige walls murky. Tess could have been stuck in the bowels of anywhere.

'Agnesa!' Her voice sounded full in this empty space. It was the third time Tess had said her name aloud. The first was only yesterday: *You're not getting* anything *from this?* she'd said. And now she had the answer. She called 'Tess Matthews!' but only for the echo.

She got dressed, pulled on jeans and a hoodie that was sour at the armpits. Agnesa must have been scared at the end. She felt around in the pockets, found the screwed up ticket from the bus ride here, enough change to get her home. And in the jeans, a note:

There were two of you and now I am one of them.

Here is the best I could do for Arlo.

This way we all have a chance.

Yours,

Tess Matthews

Yours. Yes, mine, Tess thought.

Agnesa had written in English, had already changed languages, become Tess's other self. She'd penned the note with an italic nib, black ink, cartridge paper, the hand confident, a bravado to it. It'd been written in advance, it must have been, this whole thing planned.

Tess opened Arlo's new passport. With that same kind of flourish, a statement on behalf of the Queen, as if she'd never die: *Her Britannic Majesty's Secretary of State Requests and requires in the Name of Her Majesty all those whom it may concern...*

Was that what Tess had just done? Fulfilled the request and afforded Agnesa 'such assistance and protection as may be necessary'?

Had the Firsters been onto Agnesa?

Had she just disappeared?

14.

Passport number, place of issue, issuing authority, date of issue, expiry

MY PASSPORT WAS CONFISCATED AT THE UK BORDER.

YOU HAVE ALL THESE DETAILS ALREADY.

Please give details of any previous passports, covering the last ten years, including where these passports are now

N/A.

The village of Amyna had given up on its Sunday. The bungalows that dotted the road were shuttered up and silent, the 24-hour mini-market dark. The shop window was dressed with faded food in cans and plastic, in brine and in a vacuum, and with ads for discount phone calls to places far away. Beside the shop, the village payphone. Tess stood in a slurry of fag ends and watched drizzle spit against the glass. She dialled Nomie's number, let a fingernail trace a flash of initials graved with steady patience.

Finally, he picked up. 'Where is he?' she said.

The briefest of pauses then, 'Hello, Tess, I'll just get him.' It was Catriona, her voice unruffled, unhurried, still shaped by marriage to the Foreign Office. Nomie took his time coming to the phone. Tess watched her credit being chewed up, her bus fare home disappearing. Then a scuff at the other end of the line. 'I hope this is important.'

'Where is he?'

'Which *he*? You're referring to 50.4 per cent of the world's population, minus me, given you know where I am.'

Thank God she didn't marry this man. Tess said, 'The only *he* I care about. The only *he* I've ever discussed with you.' She turned her face away, to sky wiped out by the weather. 'Well, thanks, anyway, Nomie.'

'My pleasure.' He sounded genuinely pleased. 'What for?'

'For shafting me big time.' She could feel him wince. It wasn't his kind of phrase. Too graphic. Too clearly a breakdown of civilised means.

'I thought the problem was I *didn't* do things for you, and now, apparently, I *have* done something.'

'A passport for Arlo. I have it in my hands right now. Thank you – at long last.'

'Don't thank *me*.'

'And for disappearing him.'

'Where's he gone?'

'You tell me.'

Silence.

Then a figure emerged from the darkness. For a moment, it was Arlo. And then it was just a stranger coming down the road, hood up, hands in his pockets.

Nomie said something over his shoulder. Catriona must have been hovering. Tess said, 'You're probably going to claim you don't know Agnesa's on that flight and is right now on her way to England.' More coins into the phone. 'So where is he?'

'I honestly don't know, Tess.'

She took his honesty with a pinch of salt. Nomie probably avoided outright lying as a matter of professional practice. Lies came back as liabilities. But he'd misrepresent the truth without a second thought. 'You *do* know, Nomie. You know everything and everyone on this tiny island. And if you don't actually know, you certainly know someone who does.'

'Thank you, darling.' Away from the mouthpiece, the sound of a sip. Pursed lips and sherry, probably, always a favourite tipple. A pause while Nomie let it go down, while he decided how to play it, what to say next. 'I'm so sorry, Tess.'

She never believed so-sorrys. At work, she used the phrase herself: *So sorry not to have responded sooner.* It was the standard phrase of the unapologetic who knew good form. 'So sorry for what?' she said.

'Isn't an apology itself enough?'

'No. Please specify your remorse. Please enumerate your failings and regrets.'

The stranger, it turned out, was braving the rain for cigarettes from the machine. He pushed coins into the slot, thumped the side, and a packet tumbled down.

Tess said, 'What if I pay you for the information? What's your hourly rate again? How much would make it worth your while to tell me where Arlo is? To *share...*' as types like Nomie were fond of saying.

'I'd help if I could.'

'You can do better than that.'

A pause while he thought. 'I'll help if I can?'

Grammar. What was the difference? Arlo would know. It was the sort of thing his students learnt for tests.

Then the stranger came over and offered her a cigarette. Maybe he wondered who she was, this woman speaking English on her own in the dark in Amyna. Or maybe he was just glad to see her, this other human being.

Tess knew the packet: Karelias. She took a cigarette.

He clicked his lighter. A long flicker of orange, his hands close to her face.

She nodded, mouthed a thankyou, then a long draw, holding the smoke, and she watched him walk away. She felt instantly lighter. Weaker. Sadder. She stood for a moment in a veil of her grandfather's smoke. She leant against the payphone, the cold metal probing her shoulder. 'Do you remember that time you came to Streatham, Nomie? Stan was very ill, it wasn't long before he died, and I was in hospital...' What was it? The thing with the diving board?

'One of your scrapes. Yes, I remember. And I came down to help. Stan. Stoke City supporter. He wore the scarf in bed.' Nomie's voice had lost its edge. 'Yes, I liked Stan.'

'And there was nothing in it for you. You stayed with him even though there was no money. No career advancement. Nothing.'

Nomie had stayed a whole week in Streatham. He'd sat beside Stan's bed and fed him pitted olives and talked in his studied Greek about the ancient myths. And Stan had listened, and nodded against his pillow, and hadn't corrected him – not on his grammar, not on his misremembered stories. And then Stan had told Nomie the names of all the birds that came to visit him. And the names of all the flowers on the balcony. And that Tess was short for Tenderness. He called her Tenderness because her birth had been so easy. She'd swum out of her mother's body on broken waters, her face glistening, diving into life. Then the midwife had wrapped her in a towel and handed her to Isadora. He called her Tenderness because she'd slept all night and smiled all day. She'd looked with interest at strangers' faces and reached for their proffered fingers. Such creatures were created from time to time. 'She is Tenderness because she is so tender, and because the world needs more of it.'

Tess pulled again on the cigarette, watching the tip shine. 'You were a good soul once, Nomie.'

He exhaled down the line. It was a wordless response, but not an empty one. In the end he said, 'What would you like me to do?'

She watched the cigarette dim. In truth, she didn't know. She dropped the butt and smothered it. 'Maybe put yourself in my shoes.' A pause. 'No, not that.' Because Noam Langberg in her shoes would still be Noam Langberg. 'Be me, briefly. Be Tenderness.'

For a short while they said nothing. The credit counted down. The line buzzed. The drizzle fell. In the distance, the village church chimed the half-hour, sounding for no-one. And Tess's coins ran out.

Tess went to the bus stop and waited, hoodie up. She tried to shrink inside Agnesa's clothes, detaching her skin from the rain. In her head, she replayed the conversation with Nomie. His surprise had sounded genuine – insofar as anything about Nomie was genuine. In which case, he'd had nothing to do with tonight and Agnesa had acted alone. She'd stolen Tess's passport because she had to get out of the country. But why bother with a passport for Arlo?

Tess angled her face to the sky, to where she thought the plane might be. 'Why did you do it, Agnesa?' Because you *got* a passport so you *gave* a passport? It was a fair deal?

And then the bus came – same driver, same pop playing. She tipped a handful of coins into the tray, the coppers the payphone hadn't accepted. He scooped them up in a fist, and nodded her onto the bus. Occasionally they did that at the end of the day, when they'd been driving the same route over and over, because who was counting now?

Tess sat at the back, sideways on, same as last time. She put a hand on the seat beside her and felt the absence. *Where are you?* Tess glanced at her reflection lit in the window, and there she was, Agnesa's ghost. Tess Matthews was up in the clouds, and Agnesa had vanished, was dead, would not be coming back.

And the word 'dead' made her think of Stan, and of how Nomie had looked after him. She remembered the day he'd died – that the hospital had rung and said in a voice that was slow and even that she should come quickly. So she'd got in a cab – Tess never took a cab – but they were quick, weren't they? Then she'd sat in traffic jams while the driver made small talk in the rear-view mirror, and she'd watched the minutes tick by. How quick was quick when it came to dying? Did the dying really wait for you to come?

Stan's eyes were closed when she got to him. He was sipping at air as if measured out as medicine. His skin was ruckled – like lain-on sheets, like the bedding he rarely washed because laundry made him feel out of place, he knew he wasn't home. And because unwashed sheets were human, saturated with life, the nearest thing his nakedness had to another body.

Stan's mouth was open, his tongue slung back. Tess said into his ear, 'I'm here.' Then she tried again in Greek. She took his hand, like something from the autumn, the kind of thing he swept up from the balcony.

She said: 'Stan.'

She said: 'Konstantinos.'

She said: 'Tenderness.'

And waited.

A trolley clanked down the corridor. Dimmed voices the other side of the curtain.

Then a snatch of air, as if a shock of recognition. Was that how long it took for a dying mind to hear?

211

Tess watched his chest, waited for the out-breath. Seconds passed. And more. Divers could hold their breath for as long as it took to harvest pearls. How far down was Stan?

For a long time, he'd seemed almost-alive. Tess thought: all I have to do is rewind these last few minutes. She closed her eyes and in her mind travelled faster than the speed of light, overtaking events, and turning round and undoing them.

And each time when she opened her eyes, Stan was still there, slightly deader.

Stan was dead.

In the end, a nurse came in and said it: 'He's dead now, love. He's gone.'

It was the first time Tess had witnessed the beginning of something as long and endless as forever.

She'd rung Nomie from the hospital and told him the news. And with Stan gone, Tess had no-one. Her grandfather was dead; her mother was dead; her father was missing; no siblings; no children.

'You have *me*,' Nomie said. 'I'm here. Flesh, blood, warm, alive. Me. Here. Here. Me.'

He'd meant it when he said it. And he really had been there at that moment. But not for long, not even till the end of the call. At the end, he'd said, 'You have my sincerest condolences.'

It was shortly before the Foreign Office.

It wasn't long before Catriona.

When Tess got back to Exodus Square, the lights were on and everyone was home. She climbed the stairs, through the fug of the Moros family's gamey dinner, through Rron's smoke and Vera's silence, and put the key in the door.

And nothing happened.

She took it out and tried again. Then she checked the bunch: were these Agnesa's keys? But no, it was the *Dover, England* fob and keys she recognised: front door, front door, office door, bike, can't remember. Then she spotted the business card stuck at the top of the jamb: *SECURED. DO NOT ATTEMPT TO ENTER.*

Looking back, all Tess could remember after that was sitting on the stairs in the dark and tears dripping onto her knees, hot and wet through Agnesa's ripped jeans. And Mrs Moros yelling up to stop her English noise, and Cid passing by to see what the fuss was and pissing against the doorframe.

And Vera.

Vera put an arm around her and said, 'Come, Tess. You get chilblains and grief if you sit here any longer.' She didn't care if the neighbours heard her English. It was the language in which to mother Tess, the language she'd used with Albie in his sickness. She said, 'It will be all right in the end.'

Would it? And how far off was the end? 'But what comes between now and then?'

'What comes first is you find safe haven with me,' and she stretched out an arm and led Tess down a flight as if tugging a stricken vessel into port.

Vera's hallway was lit and warm and dry. Tess felt instantly exhausted. All she wanted to do was close her eyes and sleep. Vera led her into the bedroom. 'Your clothes are wet, you must change,' she said. 'Also, I cannot help noticing that your clothes are not your clothes.'

And Tess told Vera what had happened.

'But why go to England when she speaks Greek?'

'Because Tess Matthews is British. Because in Greece she'd be allowed to stay ninety days, and then what?' These days, the only place you could make a life with a British passport was Britain.

Vera unlocked the wardrobe. It was black enamel inlaid with mother-of-pearl, a wedding present from Albie, picked up in a flea market, but old and valuable. He'd seen such things in Hong Kong. Inside, a rail of black garments, worn and formless, that hung like a roost of bats. Vera spent a moment choosing things for Tess, releasing the scent of cedar, and laid them out on the bed.

It was Vera and Albie's double bed. On Vera's side, a Hornblower novel, *The Happy Return*, and on Albie's, a miniature of rum. Vera believed in the possibility of impossible things. Or, at least, she believed we knew only a fraction of what there was to know, that science didn't cover it. If time could dilate and length contract, why couldn't Albie return? One day, the sailor would come home from the sea.

Tess changed. She slipped Arlo's passport into the voluminous folds of whatever it was she was wearing, and drifted in a cloud of black to the kitchen. Vera had already put the kettle on and Britshit bread was in the toaster. Tess willed it to tick faster. She hadn't eaten since Mr Dee and the picnic.

When everything was ready, they took the comforts of England through to the other room and Tess lay on the sofa – the sofa where Albie had died – and Vera sat on the arm. They were like two widows in mourning. And maybe Vera had the same thought because, 'In your case,' she said, 'he is only officially dead, not really dead. I saw Arlo leave.'

'Which direction?'

A finger zig-zagged the air. She meant the maze of alleys at the back of the house, used by teenage lovers till dusk, then lone men with guns, and Cid. 'Big coat. Small bag. Big hurry.'

What did that mean? That Arlo had gone urgently to somewhere cold with plenty of amenities?

'The point is: he is gone. He is *as good as* dead. We all...' A finger ringed St Mira. '...know what is going on.' She took a bite of toast. 'Or half-know and do not ask the rest.'

And weren't humans good at that? Especially now. Times like these were perfect for sleights of the mind.

Then Vera jabbed a finger downwards. 'Neighbourhood Watch *certainly* knows.' Vera was in Neighbourhood Watch. She'd joined to keep an eye on them. Mr and Mrs Moros were in it. Also Rron. Plus the owner of Café Echo, and the man who ran the Plastic Shop and his doll-like wife, who blinked with effort under inch-long lashes and smelt freshly unwrapped from cellophane. The priest was the Chair. He sat at the head of the table and raised his hands as if he were the resurrection and started each meeting with Matters Arising. He compared the work of Neighbourhood Watch to the all-seeing eye of God. He recited from the Bible: *You shall not take vengeance or bear a grudge against the sons of your own people.* He said it again to emphasise his point: 'Your *own* people,' his beard propped on the table like a silver mirror to the room.

Vera said, 'Neighbourhood Watch changed the locks on your flat soon after you left. I texted you.'

Tess remembered now. When was that? Was it this afternoon and a lifetime ago when she was in the cubicle at Amyna? And she hadn't answered because she was distracted – half undressed and thinking she was about to meet Arlo. Tess ran a fingertip round the lip of the plate, circling the pattern of roses. 'He has to be on the island somewhere. He can't have gone. I have his passport.' She fumbled in her clothing and gave it to Vera. 'Agnesa left it for him.'

'But why would she do that?' Vera tested the stiffness of the cover. She held it open under her desk-lamp. 'Watermarks O.K. Optically variable ink.' She slid it sideways under the light. 'Holographic devices in order. No second laminate. Random fibres on...' She flicked through. '...every page.' Vera licked a finger and failed to smudge ink. 'No damage around the photo.' They both lingered on the image of Arlo. It was him, but not him. It was Arlo in twenty years' time – his hair cropped and white, shadows under his eyes. Ageing wasn't going to be kind to Arlo.

Tess said, 'Do you think it's real?'

Vera would spot a forgery. She'd had an entire career at the Records Office, spent every working hour handling documents. She'd forged things for Albie. He'd arrived on St Mira without a birth certificate and they needed it before they could marry.

But that meant applying to England. So Vera had speeded up the process. Faking her fiancé was how she'd learned her craft.

She rested Arlo's passport in her palm and viewed it like a rare species, a genuine find. 'But why would Agnesa do it? She's one of them.'

But maybe also *not* one of them.

Was Agnesa a servant of the state who wouldn't serve anymore? A saboteur in uniform? They were the best possible kind – insiders with access who could alter events.

Vera gave the passport back. Tess was about to kiss it. Instead, she caught a whiff of it. It was damp from all the rain. It was the smell of the platform at Gatwick, black with drizzle and slippy with discarded *Metro*s. It was the smell of the train to Dover, full of damp people with damp umbrellas talking into phones. England was wet and cold and dark. It was the ideal environment for the spread of viruses and the depletion of vitamin D. And yet no-one seemed to mind.

Vera said, 'What will she do, this Tess Matthews, when she lands?'

What Tess did every December, she imagined: smile briefly at the border guard, remember where she'd just flown from, and try to resemble her passport photo.

'Does Agnesa look like you?'

'Enough like me.' Probably. Tess hoped so. 'She's short. Freckles. Definitely got the ears.' Tess glanced at the clock. Agnesa would have landed. She might well be showing her ears right now. Look: curtain stays, espresso cups. She wouldn't speak, not even a thank you. An accent might raise questions. So she'd arrange *The Week* to stick out of her bag, and beam positive thoughts at the border guard. And then what? Once she was through, she'd change her money, maybe pick up a sandwich from M&S, and step into a foreign country and try to make a life.

Try to make a life.

Yes, please keep Tess Matthews alive. She hoped she was warm enough in an anorak and scarf. Tess hoped she'd make her way to the Browns. She wanted to say: take Thameslink to Redhill, then Southern to Tonbridge, then Southeastern to Dover Priory. Walk from the station to Maison Dieu Road. Pick up flowers for Joy on the way – something extravagant and distracting – and explain it all to Elmer. Focus on Elmer. Elmer will understand.

Or maybe none of that would happen. Maybe Agnesa would go up to Passport Control and say she was seeking asylum.

And they'd offer a blank, unhelpful stare, ask how she got this British passport and want to know where she was really from. Then they'd check the Safe Country of Origin list, and St Mira would be on it. It wouldn't have been updated since The Firsters and The Bomb – that bomb, which was never mentioned now, had been completely forgotten, its job done.

And then what would happen?

Tess had no idea.

Did anyone?

Vera went to the window and gazed into the darkness. Tess got up and stood beside her. In the distance, harbour lights swung with the wind. One or two fishing boats were risking the sea. Between the clouds, the moon was big. 'Newly into Taurus.' Vera's voice had turned prophetic. 'A sense of safety depends on stability, which at this moment is not easy to secure.'

Vera's horoscopes were always true.

'One must accept change as part of life.'

Tess knew that. Everyone knew that. But Vera made it sound like a message from the stars.

Then she turned to Tess, her face suddenly tired. 'I am sorry to say I too have news. I have had a letter from the council.' She went into the kitchen, her feet heavy, the tread audible. She returned with two tumblers and a bottle of wine. It was half-drunk, corked with kitchen towel, so dark it was almost black. Vera was awkward with the pouring, just flicked aside the spill. 'They intend to disinter Albie. They want no foreign corpses on St Miran soil.'

'They can't do that.'

Vera drank. 'He is be sent back to where he came from. Albie is to be repatriated on the *Pride*.'

Tess was about to say: Noam Langberg. He won't let that happen. He could stop it. He could help.

But of course he couldn't.

Of course he wouldn't.

And, anyway, it turned out Vera had already asked him. Nomie had been to the Records Office to talk about the Accelerated Programme to Resolve the Immigration Logjam. That was the three thousand two hundred and one St Mirans claiming Britishness by descent and the right to be on the *Pride*. Nomie had promised the UK and St Miran governments that APRIL would be wrapped up by December.

He'd briefed Vera's team on the legal routes to citizenship – two days of PowerPoint flow-charts: born in the UK yes/no; born before 1 January 1983 yes/no; to a British mother, British father, married yes/no; had a grandparent in crown service; born in a British colony at the time when the country was *still* a colony yes/no...

Nomie had summarised with a take-away message: *EAR*. It meant Efficiency. Acceleration. And if in doubt Reject.

At the end, Vera had approached Nomie and told him about the order to send Albie back on the *Pride*.

He'd tidied up his papers as she spoke. 'Well, if those are the wishes of the St Miran government, it is my job to fulfil them.'

'And what about the wishes of the British government?'

'Do you not keep up with the news, Mrs Vertete? As far as London is concerned, dead immigrants are fine. It's the live ones that are the problem.'

Now Vera rested her head on Tess's shoulder. Had she ever done that before? Tess said, 'When will you...' How to phrase it? Be reunited with Albie? But that came across as religious. Take delivery of him? That sounded like a package from St Miran Post.

But Vera knew the question. 'A week to ten days. They do the other British graves first.'

'Do what with them?'

They were burning the Victorian soldiers' teeth and grave wax. And St Miran Heritage was donating the headstones to the National Museum. They were opening a permanent exhibition on 'The True Story of the British.' They'd have the original Treaty of Friendship and a portrait of Sir Henry Willoughby on a rearing horse. Also, a red letterbox and a tea-set used by the civil service with plaster-cast scones and jam. There would be photographs of the donkeys exported from the island, whose descendants for years gave rides on Margate beach.

Vera knew all this because St Miran Heritage had sent a man to the Records Office to see what they held from the period. They wanted facts: how much oil the British stole, how much it was worth, how many St Mirans died extracting it. 'And it's true,' Vera said. 'The British came here and were a law unto themselves.' The British weren't seafarers because they liked sailing. They didn't send ships to the four corners of the earth to make friends. They went to rob. She topped up her glass. 'And the museum can quote me if they want to. But I'm deeply sad, to the bottom of my heart, to be forced apart from Albie.' Vera took another slug. 'I will take care of his bones for as long as I'm allowed.' And she'd see him off the way he'd arrived on St Mira, sailing him in *Ancora* to the *Pride*. 'I loved his bones. I married his bones. These bones...' she raised an arm and her sleeve fell back to the elbow. Vera was thin – thinner than Tess had ever seen her. '...These bones have made love with those bones.'

Tess felt the ribs of her glass, felt their coolness dig into her hand. She took a sip of wine that was raw and dank and meaty.

'Will Albie be fit to travel?' She had no idea how much of a body was left after twenty years in the ground, but surely his remains wouldn't survive however long it took on the *Pride*?

'He is to be put on ice.' He'd been booked a place in the walk-in freezer and would stay fresh next to the food. Vera coughed. Something had caught. She knocked on her chest, the sound dull and tangled. 'When you and Arlo get back to England – because for sure you will find Arlo and for sure you will go back...' She turned watery eyes to Tess. 'Every so often, will you lay flowers for Albie?'

Dear Vera. Tess reached out a hand. Vera took it. A firm grip. Always a firm grip.

Laying flowers for Albie was how Tess and Arlo had met.

And then a veil fell across the sea. It'd started to rain. Soon it was heavy, blocking out the harbour lights. On the Blue Mountains, this would fall as snow. Their peaks were already white. In the morning, the road would be impassable, the south coast cut off from the capital, the island sliced in two.

Then the rain hit land, sweeping down roads and swelling in the gutters. In Exodus Square, the candles for Mr Pantazis stuttered in their lanterns and went out. It was his first night in the earth, the soil fresh, not yet compacted. This rain would fill the graveyard. His flowers would be upturned, his coffin unsettled.

Against the drumming of the weather, church bells rang, a long peal across the town in a staggered stab at the time. Tess thought Vera would raise a toast – to these two widows, to unearthing their dead men – that their glasses would collide, sounding thick and resilient.

But she didn't. Vera's eyes were flooded. Vera was out of words.

15.

Do you fear returning to the place you were previously living?

YES.

Who do you fear for?

MYSELF.

ACTUALLY, I FEAR FOR ALMOST EVERYONE THERE.

What do you believe will happen to you if you return to the place
you were previously living?

IT'S ALL IN THE NEWS.

The next morning, Tess walked from Vera's to the office, taking her usual route along the history of St Mira. She kept her head down, paying attention to the pavement to dodge the puddles from last night's storm and not be distracted by the posters of Arlo. His death was all over town. At Plebiscite Square, Costas had drawn a crowd with his accordion and people were in the mood to give: tomorrow was the Feast of St Nicholas of Myra – the man otherwise known as Santa Claus. Tess reached the Central Communications Office and Max buzzed her in. He didn't make eye contact, though. He would have seen Arlo's posters too, and he knew that the news was either true or untrue, and either way, best not to get involved.

The building was hushed. There were no heels ticking down corridors, or distant ringing of phones, or confidential undertones creeping along the walls. The Feast of St Nicholas was a public holiday, and everyone was making a long weekend of it.

Except Duke, of course.

And therefore Tess.

Duke would be in already, and busy. There was no end of things to tell the English-speaking world. One in six of humankind, 1.3 billion people were hanging – Duke liked to think – on the Desk's every word.

But when she got to the office, instead of a stack of translations, a card was propped against her computer screen. The envelope was black and the handwriting textbook – Duke's exemplary control. *Tess Petrou* it said in white ink. Had he bought a special pen just for that? From his room, the shriek of coffee beans shattered in a grinder, then the release of steam, and the dull thuds of a barista. Soon the English Desk would smell of Oasis, which is where Duke bought his beans. It was his favourite café for the outdoor seating with all-day sun, invisible staff and customers there to be seen. Also for the view of the marina and the yachts, mostly belonging to money-men, though one of them his.

Tess opened the envelope. The card was a lily – *Lilium Candidum* it said on the back. Duke had picked a botanical drawing, the parts dissected and labelled in Latin. A lily was appropriate: the flower of death. Popular at funerals. Lethal to cats – just licking the pollen could kill them off. For a moment, the idea of lilies lingered in her mind next to the idea of Cid. She opened the card:

Dear Tess,

My sympathies for your loss es.

Yours,

Duke

There was a small gap between the 'loss' and the 'es'. He'd pluralised them after some thought. And her losses *were* more than one: her partner, her other self, her flat, her security, her sense of where to turn next. But how much did Duke know of all that?

She re-read the inscription. It was the first time ever he'd signed off 'Duke'. Till now it'd been Dr Kontos or just a tight flick of the pen that was uniquely his. And now, suddenly, he'd skipped first-name terms and was going by his nickname. The lurch unsettled her.

And *yours*? Duke wasn't *hers*. And if he was offering himself up, then she would refuse. Because yours was a possessive. And possession was so often meant as reciprocal: I am yours and you are mine. No thank you, Dr Michail Kontos.

Then Duke glided into her office with two cups of espresso. His hands were motionless as his legs moved – the way raptors shift their bodies with their eyes pinned on the prey. He put the cups down. 'My sympathies for your losses.'

He'd said that already.

He passed her a coffee. 'Yours,' he said.

That word again.

'I am aware of Arlo's...' Duke paused. He put the edge of the cup to his lip – a robust lip but gymnastic enough to meet the demands of his languages. Was he waiting for Tess to complete his sentence, to utter the delicate word herself?

'His what?'

'His... change of state. I know that he is, in one form or another, no longer among us.' Duke was dressed in a sombre suit. It was dark blue when caught by the neons and black away from the light.

Tess cupped her cup and sipped. It was just the kind of coffee a Taekwondo Master would make: it sat on your tongue being mindful for ages, and then without warning, kicked you in the teeth. 'Where *is* Arlo, Dr Kontos?'

'As already indicated, at one remove.'

'But removed *where*?'

An airy turn of the wrist and a flash of gold as his Phi Alpha Delta cufflink came into view. Ever well connected, down to the cuffs of his sleeves. 'He is, as souls often are, between worlds, awaiting the evolution of their narrative arc. He is in limbo.'

'Which is where?'

'The Fields of Asphodel.'

But Tess didn't want mythology. She wanted GPS coordinates. 'You *do* know, don't you.' Duke knew everything. Somehow.

'Tess, so many questions.' He seemed impatient. 'What did curiosity do?'

'Lead to the world's greatest inventions.'

'But you are not a cat-person, are you? You prefer dogs. You bond with Marine on your evening walks while Cid soils your doorstep.'

How did he know about that? Via Rron, the Moros family, Neighbourhood Watch?

'My sympathies also for the loss of your flat.'

So, Neighbourhood Watch, then.

And not just the flat, but everything in it – their books, clothes, personal possessions. Tess would have to persuade whoever had secured the door to let her in and claim them. She'd tell them: I *am* St Miran. I *am* one of your own people. To Duke she said, 'Have *you* ever lost, Dr Kontos?'

An eyebrow lifted briefly which, for a man with total motor control, counted as surprise. Tess had never asked such a personal question and it took a while for him to answer. 'In truth, not often. The World Taekwondo Championships. Seoul 1989. Silver by two points.'

'I mean family.'

'There's Marine, of course. This Marine is my fifth.'

'And parents?' He was old enough to have lost those.

A blank look, as if it was such an odd idea: he'd never had parents so how could he possibly have lost them?

What was it with the people Duke had come from? Were they dead or just embarrassing?

Duke finished his coffee. He cleared his throat. 'Now, Tess, I have a proposal.'

She didn't want a proposal.

'You got my text.'

She remembered it now. What did it say?

'About tonight.'

Yes, that was it. Could she make up a prior engagement? Something unavoidable she had to do with Vera?

'*Je propose dîner chez moi.*'

Tess rarely heard Duke speaking French, but that was so convincing, it could have been his first language. She knew he had a talent for Anglo-Saxon, was a master of words that were guttural, brief and brutal. But he was just as at home in the language of romance and diplomacy. It made her uneasy – the way he could be anyone, from anywhere, wanting anything. She glanced at him. His eyes were coated with something sticky, like the glue-strips used to catch flies. 'Dr Kontos. Thank you very much for the invitation, but I'm rather tired after recent events.' Last night, she'd lain awake for hours. The moon had pressed through the blinds printing messages in barcode she'd tried but failed to decipher. And from the other side of the bedroom door, the sound of Vera snuffling like an animal – busy and troubled in her sleep.

'I understand your fatigue. It is perfectly natural. So just come and relax...'

Had Duke ever said that word before?

'It would be good for you.'

'Good in what way?' The only thing that would do her good was finding Arlo.

'As in the opposite of bad.'

Tess turned to her computer screen, saw her black figure reflected in the glass. What did Duke want, in fact? Who was he inviting: a human – any human; or a woman – any woman; or *this* woman sitting at the desk – her, Tess Petrou?

'It will be informal, merely the two of us.'

So, not a dinner party and no display involved. But also no defence against whatever he might try.

'Just you and me and Marine, of course.'

It was true: she *had* bonded with Marine. She was innocent, willing, hopeful. Marine didn't scheme like Duke. She wasn't entitled like Duke. She ran after balls, begged for treats, loved you for no reason – none of which was like Duke.

Duke picked up the coffee cups and took them back to his office. He leant for a moment against the door frame, awkward in his attempt to be casual. 'So I shall see you at eight.'

Shall he?

Tess rocked against the spring of her chair. Eight was late. She'd be hungry by then. She'd have to eat before she left.

Duke's office door closed. A tap ran over the coffee cups. And soon he was on the phone.

Dinner with Duke and Marine the Fifth? Tess thought: *Once more unto the breach, dear friends, once more; or close the wall up with our English dead.* She didn't know she knew that. Was that Henry the Fifth? She must have picked it up from *Life*.

And that brought back Arlo.

She tried to tune into him, sense his magnetic field. She was sure brains could talk to each other – if you wanted it, if you focused – that thoughts met in the middle. She remembered his ship's sign: *I have a pilot on board*. If not an aeroplane pilot, then maybe the pilot of a boat. Was Arlo stowed away offshore? Maybe already on the *Pride* and waiting for her to join him? She reached an arm to her globe. He was somewhere here – she was looking at him right now. Tess spun the earth and watched the continents blur. Spin the world fast enough and there were no countries, no borders, nothing to try and cross. Surely, through space, the earth *was* spinning fast enough. Viewed from there, all this belonging and not belonging, this right to be here and denial of right – it all just melted away.

Tess arrived at Duke's villa a little after eight, in that margin of lateness that didn't need excusing, but meant – if Duke chose to examine it – that she was in no hurry to be there. She rang the doorbell. In her head, what Vera had told her: 'This is not dinner. This is reconnaissance. You are going undercover to find out things about the man you work for.' The door opened and there they were: Marine keen as ever and Duke looking nothing like her boss. He was barefoot on his hardwood floor, in creased chinos and a polo shirt open at the neck. A momentary pause as he took Tess in. She'd come in a black polyester jumpsuit. Vera called it her body-bag: a long zip down the side and epaulettes that could have been handles. It was intended for social events to deter unwanted advances – the perfect foil for *dîner* with Duke: morbid and synthetic.

'Well well,' Duke said.

And Tess stepped inside.

He took the anorak Vera had lent her and hung it on a hanger. He took her shoes, put them on the shoe rack and offered her slippers that were still in their cellophane. He bent down to stroke Marine, tugging at the roll of skin at her neck. 'We are both *very* happy to see you.'

Happiness looked peculiar on Duke. From here, Tess had a bird's-eye view, a relief map of this newly glad man. His skull was domed, the contour lines mathematical, the hair cropped close and no signs of thinning. Duke did nothing by chance, and he'd chosen to do this – to show part of himself. Would he be giving her a tour of the most appealing aspects of his villa? How odd would this evening be?

He said, 'I have rustled up something to eat. The meal awaits us in the Crow's Nest.' Tess followed Duke right to the top of the building, being startled by mirrors in unexpected places, thinking for an instant that other people lived here, that Duke had family.

The stairs opened into an all-glass turret that tilted with the flicker of candles. She'd seen it from the street. It was like a lighthouse – except usually dark, not helping anyone home. Duke led Tess to the window. Outside, the lights of fishing boats dabbed at the water. The houses along the street glowed rich and warm. His neighbours in miniature flitted to and fro. Duke lingered a while – and longer than it took to propose a view. What was he showing her, actually? Or was she being shown?

'Please.' Duke gestured to a floor that was spread with cushions in a careful arrangement meant to seem chance. 'Make yourself at home.'

No, she wouldn't be doing that. Duke was her boss and he wanted something. Tess wasn't sure what, but she didn't want to give it. She perched on the edge of a cushion and watched Duke wrestle with his. Cushions seemed new to him, something of a challenge. Was that a Taekwondo lock? Then he reached for Marine and placed her in front of them, holding her still as if for a family portrait. He cast shiny eyes at Tess, as a proud new father might, saying *Look what we have made*. 'So, here we all are.'

Yes, here they both were, plus dog.

He offered Tess rum punch.

Tess declined. Vera had warned her off alcohol.

Duke poured two drinks anyway – in goblets made from olive wood, the pitcher embossed with Mira and George. He had all the paraphernalia.

Then Duke served his stew. It was the traditional meal eaten before mid-winter, the whole family gathered around one big tureen. It was made from the oldest goat of the flock and olives too small to market. Tess picked around the cubes of meat that had settled at the bottom of her bowl, brown and sad, and which she pieced together in her mind to a once-happy creature that leapt over rocks and could bear snow and wind and baking summers and, from the highest peaks, could see all the way to Africa.

Duke ate his meal. He fed goat-fat to Marine. Then he looked around, his neck mobile, the vertebrae compliant. 'Such a commanding view.' The turret was octagonal, one window-pane for every compass point. A deep breath, his polo shirt filling. 'I *love* it here.'

Within a few hours, Duke had offered the words 'Duke,' '*dîner*,' 'relax,' 'welcome' and now *that*. He was revealing a whole new vocabulary. But why?

'The Nest would be the perfect spot from which to watch the boat race.'

Tomorrow, on St Nicholas's Day, it was the yearly free-for-all of St Mira's fishermen and sailors, racing to circumnavigate the island. Varela would fire the starting pistol, he'd award the prize money at the end, and in between, there'd be drinking, pairing-off and feuding. By tomorrow night, some new St Mirans would have been conceived and others would have died.

Tess said, '*Would* be the perfect spot?'

'Because we will not be watching. We will be working.'

Of course. It was a public holiday, and they would be in the office.

'Varela is going to open festivities with a speech. A big one. The transcript is already on your desk.'

'Saying?'

Duke shrugged.

Duke never shrugged.

'Very much the same as usual.' His tongue reached for something lodged between his teeth. That was unlike him, to show discomfort, have a body-part other than perfect. 'But more... blatant.'

Blatant? Wasn't that word pejorative? Hadn't he just made a value judgement on a text they were merely translating? Why was Duke openly breaking his own rules?

Tess said, 'More blatant in what way?' She knew how he'd answer: *As in the opposite of subtle.*

Except he didn't. 'Varela will tell us to breed for the nation. He wants *only* St Mirans and *more* St Mirans.'

The word 'breed' startled Tess, who startled Marine, who looked up from her sleep. Tess took a sip of punch. Breeding made her think of sheep, and goats, and dead goats in stews. She tried to put the word out of her mind – it didn't fit here, in such close proximity to the man she worked for. But Duke had gone quiet and it kept on echoing: *Breed. Breed. Breed.*

It wasn't something Tess could imagine him doing. But then she *could* imagine him doing it: rhythmic and relentless, stopping only out of boredom, winding down like a mechanical toy. Or else he'd be combative, doing it Taekwondo-style, climbing off when he was twelve points ahead.

Maybe, somehow, he'd sensed her thoughts because he climbed off his cushion and patted himself down. He stacked up the bowls: his, Tess's, Marine's. 'It is the Our Own speech.'

'Our own *what*, exactly?'

'Exactly. *Own.* Such a tricky little word. Perfectly clear when used as a verb, clear when used as an adjective, but as a pronoun? Our own *what*?' He glanced towards the window. The moon was yellow and chipped at the edge. Soon it'd be full. 'Our Own,' Duke said, 'is a rallying call to native St Mirans.' They were going to use Neighbourhood Watch to finger the incomers and fly-by-nights, the parasites, oddballs and queers. That was what

Varela wanted, briefing off the record. 'They will look into the background of every single person on the island. The Records Office will have a new Genealogy Bureau.' Duke stretched out his legs and reached for his feet, folding himself in two. What was he doing? Showing Tess how flexible he was, this man who at the office never bent the rules? 'It will take them a while, but that will not worry them. The Firsters have forever. They will get round to us all in the end.'

The idea of forever seemed to tire him. Duke surrounded himself with cushions and surrendered to foam. Marine settled herself, hot and heavy, against Tess's thigh. Tess watched Duke. He let his eyes close. His face went blank. The collar of his polo shirt was splayed open. A hairless chest, from here. Nipples you noticed. Pockets empty – no cash, no keys. The bunch of cloth at the crotch. What an odd man, she thought. She'd worked for him for over a decade and had no idea who he was: Dr Michail Kontos, Head of the CCO, Taekwondo Grand Master, son of no-one, married to no-one, sleeping with no-one as far as she knew, and devoted to Marines. And now, suddenly, he was unguarded. Was this a moment of unsolicited candour?

Duke's eyes opened a fraction. 'So, tell me about *your* own.'

No. It was transactional, meant in exchange.

'What about my own?'

He eased himself onto an elbow. 'Tell me about you Petrous. There are thousands of you.'

Twelve thousand on the island, according to Vera. It was the tenth most common surname. Tess would be related to all of them, probably, somehow, to some degree, way back. Plus all the women who'd married and lost their name – the ghost Petrous of St Mira.

'Tell me your family stories,' Duke said. 'Tell me the tales that are repeated time and time again until they're true.'

Tess took a mouthful of punch, which gave her time to think. What was she prepared to tell Duke?

'Tell me father stories.'

'I never met my father.'

'Grandfather stories, then.' Duke picked up his drink to raise a toast. 'To...'

Tess didn't supply the name. She was letting him nowhere near Stan. Instead she said that her grandfather's sister had owned a farm in the Blue Mountains, close to the peak where Mira and George had given the island the first St Mirans. She glanced over her shoulder to mountains that were rounded and soft after yesterday's snow and shedding yellow moonlight.

There. The Petrous. End of story.

'Come, Tess, there must be more. Every family has more. There is always more. And tell me in your St Miran Greek. Stories sound so much better in the language in which they happened.'

Duke drank.

Tess emptied her goblet. She let her gaze wind round the grain of the olive wood, getting lost on the knots that marked it like fingerprints. She said, 'My grandfather's sister had twin daughters.' They were Agathoklia and Agathoniki, and they'd wanted to learn to read and write, so they'd run away to the convent. They'd become nuns and taken a vow of celibacy. Also a vow of silence and refused to speak to Tess when she went to find her family. Instead, they'd written her notes in an ancient script that only nuns could decipher – prayers for her wellbeing, the Holy Mother had said, and now would she please return to the worldly world and leave well alone.

Duke listened. He inhaled, carrying the story into his lungs, into his blood. It would settle soon in his bones. Marine was wheezing in her sleep. Her mouth had lapsed, the tongue fallen out. It hung against the floor in a pool that glazed the tiles with something sweet and meaty.

Pools made Tess think of swimming. She said, 'The Petrous are good swimmers. We've got flipper-feet. I used to swim for Streatham. My mother swam the Thames every morning.' At the back of her mind, the thought that her mother wasn't, in

232

fact, a Petrou; she was a Matthews. Also, that she'd died from drowning. Tess's gaze dropped to the floor. Her huge feet hung from the body-bag. Her eyes moved across to Duke. He had big feet too. Perfect for balance, for Taekwondo, for winning world medals and Grand Masterdom.

And then Tess slipped into silence because talking about feet was what she and Arlo did. And here she was with Duke, having an OK time, considering, and she really should be going. Tess tried to stand.

Duke reached out to steady her. The last time he'd touched her was also the first time he'd touched her: at the end of the interview a decade ago when he'd told her straight off he was giving her the job. It was the same cool hand and confident grip. What job was he giving her now?

Duke said, 'The facilities are all yours.'

Yours. That word again.

Tess said, 'I'm going home.'

'You *have* no home.'

But she meant to Vera's.

He stood at the top of the stairs, not blocking her way, not helping her go. 'You spoil it, Tess.'

Had there been an 'it' to spoil?

'It is too late to leave, the middle of the night. Look at the time.'

She glanced at Vera's watch. Where had the evening gone?

'There are patrols out there, fully armed, just waiting for something to shoot at.'

Tess went down. She reached the hallway and found her shoes. She found her anorak. Then, as if to make Duke's point, the sound of an army truck grinding down the street.

She swung her anorak on a finger. What were her options? Ten minutes across town dodging patrols – or...? She glanced at Duke.

He reached for a doorhandle and pushed it open. 'This is the Guest Room.'

Why did Duke have one of those? Did anyone ever stay? As far as she could tell, this was a man who found company in mirrors.

He said, 'It does not help if you leave.'

Did Duke need help?

'Please?'

Was there pleading in Duke's 'please'?

'The Guest Room is also Marine's room if she prefers to be alone.' Maybe Marine heard her name and took it as an instruction, because she went inside and jumped onto a stool that let her clamber onto the bed. It was queen-sized with a pearly-white coverlet and a blanket embroidered with a bone.

Then gunfire – close and automatic and loud enough to set off car alarms. Tess took out her phone, texted Vera and got a text straight back: *OK, but lock door.*

Tess said, 'Do you have a key?'

'I do.'

'Do you have a spare toothbrush?'

'I do.'

And that sounded like marriage.

Tess tested the key in the lock. She looked in the cupboards. She checked under the bed for she didn't know what.

Duke said, 'There are clean towels in the bathroom. There is water in the fridge. There is fruit in the bowl. We have in-house communications. If you need anything, dial 0.'

Just like a hotel. *H-for-Hotel*, Tess thought. She glanced at the bedside clock. Six hours in Hôtel de Duke and it'd be time to get up for work.

Then Duke wished her goodnight, wished Marine goodnight, and let the door close.

Tess listened to footsteps moving about, tracking him over her head. What did Duke want? Maybe a woman under his roof for a night. To have someone staying who wasn't a girlfriend, but almost could be – who, if he repeated the story often enough, in the end would be.

She listened to Duke's night-time routines: the flush of a toilet, the hum of something electrical, a long time running a tap. He edited his body like he edited their texts – with meticulous attention to detail. And was that the sound of press-ups?

Tess stood at the window wrapped in Vera's body-bag. The town looked different this far after dark. It'd lost all its colour. And Tess felt lost – couldn't place which way to Exodus Square. Posters of Arlo wrecked by the weather hung from telegraph poles, and walls were shot with dots and dashes like a drive-by message in code.

She checked her phone and read tomorrow's headlines: Varela would announce the Our Own policy. The Foreign Minister was on a whirlwind tour of Russia, Poland, Hungary, Italy, making arrangements for their new embassies. It was the best olive harvest in living memory. A family of ten had been rescued in the mountains. In England, snow and ice were about to hit. There were rail strikes. Postal strikes. Nurses strikes… Tess watched time go by. It was late, well into tomorrow, already Saint Nicholas's Day. Today, children would leave shoes outside doors and adults would fill them with gifts. Nicholas was the patron saint of children, and sailors, and unmarried people.

Over her head, the press-ups finally stopped. Duke would be climbing into his king-sized bed alone. She pictured him lying spreadeagled, trying to fill it up. Tess reached for the phone and dialled 0. The sound of ringing came through the ceiling. Duke wasn't quick to answer. When he did, she said, 'I need to know what you need, Dr Kontos.'

Was that a sigh? 'Need is best avoided. It makes one vulnerable.'

The passive voice and an indefinite pronoun. Duke could come up with things like that at this time of night. He said, 'Anything else?'

Tess turned to Marine the Fifth. Already she felt like some kind of Sixth. What was Arlo's mnemonic for the wives of Henry the Eighth? *A Bomb Scenario Clearly Helps Patriots.* So, here they were, H and P, Catherine Howard and Catherine Parr.

'Only, sleep well,' she said. But Duke hadn't bothered waiting; the line was already dead.

Tess reached for the scruff of Marine's neck and rubbed it as Duke had done when she'd first arrived. Marine curled round her, reading it as affection. Actually, it was to feel the flesh, how thick it was, what it would take to sever.

16.

Have you ever said or written anything that justifies acts of
violence; or tries to make others commit violent or serious
criminal acts; or encourages hatred between communities?

NO .

Tess was woken by the bedside telephone. A voice told her this was her alarm call and that breakfast was served in the Breakfast Room. It sounded flat and mechanical but was actually Duke. She took a while to find her bearings, to register she'd spent the night with Marine and just a few feet under her boss. How had she let it happen?

She threw off the covers, then straightened the bed, making it unslept in again. She let the shower run right through her and dried herself on the corner of a towel so as not to wet it. Tess got dressed in yesterday's clothes and paused in front of the mirror. She wished that face belonged to somebody else – that a stranger had made this mistake.

Tess flitted into the Breakfast Room and found Duke at the counter in a slate-grey shirt, his face grave for a festive day. He'd already finished breakfast and was now consuming the day's papers. He was reading all the news, in all its angles, in all the languages he knew. 'Sleep well?' he said.

That wasn't a full sentence, which meant Duke wasn't concentrating; he wasn't really asking. But no, it'd been a long short night wracked with dreams of scouring St Mira looking for Arlo – and getting warmer, and warmer, and then the jolt and joy of finding him, and waking with her face buried in Marine.

Tess took a chair at the other end of the breakfast bar and scanned the buffet prepared by the housekeeper. In the background, what sounded like the BBC. Had Duke found a way to unjam the signal? She listened to a voice she thought she knew, and it brought on a wave of loneliness and homeliness and a yearning for a Full English even though she didn't eat meat.

Tess drank tea. She drank coffee. She fed sausages and bacon to Marine.

Then, finally, when Duke had finished reading, 'Did you sleep well?' he said.

Tess's eyes swept the spread of papers: five languages, roughly four titles each, which meant twenty newspapers. Had

Duke slept at all? She knew she was supposed to say 'Yes, I slept wonderfully, thankyou,' and compliment the bed. Instead she said, 'What *is* the news?'

'Varela is the news. Our Own is the news. His speech is much anticipated. The whole world, apparently, wants to hear what he has to say.' Duke delivered that as a newsreader would, trying to sound neutral while reporting on disaster. He spooned the last juice from his breakfast bowl. Had he chosen the Medley of Native Fruits?

Duke went onto the terrace and stood beside the ornamental pond. He stared into its depths as if they also held news. He stayed there long enough for Tess to think that for Duke it had already been a difficult day. Goldfish glanced back and forth. Every now and then, they lipped at the surface as if they knew that other life was out there and they came up to gasp at it. Did goldfish really have a memory of three seconds? Tess hoped so, that their dark, round world was ever made anew.

And then Duke checked his watch and suddenly it was time for work. Now he was in the hallway saying goodbye to Marine by way of the scruff of her neck. Soon his housekeeper would be calling back to clear away breakfast and take her on a morning walk.

Duke put on his shoes.

Tess put on hers.

'Thank you,' he said.

Tess listened to the intonation. That wasn't a thankyou.

'You were helpful yesterday.'

And that didn't sound like a compliment. Which meant he was making a bid for something, that was an opening move.

He did up his laces – a complicated knot, one that would never work loose.

Tess found her coat.

And here it was, what Duke wanted: Tess was to wear this thing he held.

'I have an anorak.'

'This is a Burberry.'

It was camel-coloured, double-breasted, belted, ghastly.

And still his arm was out there. 'Come, Tess, you spoil it.'

Was last night's 'it' still there to spoil? What *was* this thing that had to go so well for him? What did Duke need so badly?

And wanting to know the answer changed her mind. Tess took the coat and put it on. For a moment, they stood in front of the mirror like awkward twins in identical macs. 'They are trench coats,' he said.

Were they going into the trenches?

Duke opened the front door and they stepped out to a tall white sky and a blustery day. It meant the weather would be changing. Duke kept close to her shoulder, their pace matched – they could have been a couple and married for years. Soon they arrived at the sea. This stretch of water was clogged with yachts, the air matted with masts and rigging. Along the waterfront, red and white bulbs hung between lampposts. At dusk, they'd wash the pavement with the low-watt glow of the flag. In Great Martyrs' Park, a funfair was already in full swing. The big wheel turned against the sky. From the top, you'd see Amyna, maybe all the way to the ends of the island. From the big dipper, the gasps of people who wanted to die and come back again, to be Jesus for the length of the ride.

Junkers was cordoned off and the crowds diverted to enter the square from the back. But the man from the Public Order Office seemed to know Duke, or be expecting him, and he raised the tape so they could duck under. Duke reached for Tess's hand, but she'd sensed the move coming and angled out of the way. Instead, he hooked her arm and steered her towards Oasis Café, and didn't let go till he needed his hand to greet the couple who were waiting for them.

Tess recognised the face: it was Mr Pappas.

'My good friend, Mr Pappas.'

He worked in the Firster Press Office.

'And wife.'

Hello wife.

She was heavily pregnant.

They'd kept four seats at the best table in the café, with a view of the stage where Varela would speak, and the big screen that would broadcast events of the day. Duke and Mr Pappas sat close and addressed the air in front of them, which was actually talking to each other. It seemed easy, as if they chatted all the time, could pick up without thinking where they'd just left off.

Mrs Pappas sat next to Tess and away from the table because of her bump. She patted her tiny hands together, and leant over in a move Tess knew to be complicity. 'Duke told us he *had* someone.'

So, this was Duke's 'it': he was showing her off. They were performing the-morning-after-the-night-before.

Mrs Pappas said, 'How long have you known Duke?'

'I've worked for Dr Kontos for a decade.'

She leaned over, her lips so close they grazed an ear. 'I'm just so glad he's normal.'

Yes, not gay, not asexual, not alone, not dangerous to know.

Mrs Pappas rested fingers on Tess's forearm. It was meant as intimate but felt intrusive. 'We've all been wondering about you.'

All? How far had this deceit reached?

Tess wrestled off her Burberry to reveal herself. Look: Duke's beard – dead underwear and Vera's body-bag. Polyester. Cheap. Second-hand.

Mrs Pappas understood display. 'Delightful! Is it upcycled?'

No. Resurrected.

Mrs Pappas was in a stiff white confection and looking like Italian meringue. It had to be one of the Moros's.

'So tell us *everything* about you.'

Tess saw Duke's head tilt and an ear turn in her direction. What was she to say? She'd done jobs for Duke she didn't like before – elided, omitted, contrived with him. But this lie was about herself.

Mrs Pappas saw the hesitation and maybe read it as embarrassment because she stepped in to fill the gap. 'I'm a wife and homemaker!' She said it with an exclamation mark, as if it surprised her, this role she'd played for years. 'He...' She pointed to an upturned navel. '...is our sixth.'

Tess tried to imagine it: yet another life tied to your placenta, your body permanently occupied, your nipples savaged, and six children plus a husband eating up all your time. She couldn't think of a single positive thing about having six children, except it wasn't seven.

'And with him comes the Silver Star.'

That was the Firster Family Drive and they'd set the bar high; you needed ten for Gold.

They were still deciding what to call him, Mrs Pappas said. They'd named all their sons after the Gods: Adonis, Ajax, Apollo and Atlas – a pantheon of alpha males. But these were exceptional times, so perhaps they'd make an exception. 'We have "Hector" in mind.'

After Varela. Was this birth to deify him?

Then a boy appeared at Mrs Pappas's shoulder – pale skinned, dressed in black, and spectral. She didn't offer his name. He just stood behind her like the sigh of a son.

Tess leaned round. 'Did you get something nice from St Nicholas?'

The boy's eyelids sank shut.

'We can't fill an orthopaedic boot,' his mother said. Tess was about to glance down but instead watched water seep through his lashes. 'It would only make the infirmity worse. Be kind, and people take advantage.'

Or maybe they just took comfort.

'Off you go,' she said.

He backed away from his mother.

'But stay within sight! Over there!' Mrs Pappas pointed to the kerb where seagulls fought and stray dogs picked at litter. Tess half-listened as she talked more about her children. She watched

Duke and Mr Pappas, their legs spread, their coats unbuttoned and spilling over the chair. But she kept being drawn to the boy who'd found a puddle and was balancing in it, standing on one leg. Mrs Pappas realised she'd lost her audience. Her gaze followed Tess's to her son. Then her husband must have heard the silence of his wife, and soon everyone was looking at the boy and the puddle.

'I'm being an island! My foot is St Mira!'

Mr Pappas fingered him over, and he waded out of the Ionian Sea watched by anxious dogs. He stood in front of his father, his knees buckled as if he'd already been kicked.

'This country is not an orthopaedic boot. Say you're sorry.'

'Sorry.'

'Apologise to all the people you've offended, and that's everyone present.'

'Sorry everyone.'

Tess said, 'I'm not offended,' but the comment seemed to be lost. Mr Pappas was pushing his son in the direction of his mother, who grabbed him by the wrists and said, 'What is St Mira, Atlas?'

So, that was his name.

'One of the most beautiful countries on the planet, mother.'

'What are our landscapes?'

'Our landscapes are unique.'

'Ranging from...' She was tugging at his arms, beating out a rhythm like a playground game.

'...from wild coastlines and lofty peaks to rolling hills and expansive lakes.' His cheeks were streaked where the tears had run.

Tess said, 'Mrs Pappas, that description fits much of Europe. And the Americas. And Asia. And...'

But she just ploughed on. 'What's our favourite native plant?'

'The olive tree.'

'Bring English lawns here and what happens?'

'They wither and die.'

'Where do they thrive?'

'Where they come from.'

'Where should they be sent?'

'Back to where they belong.'

Tess looked away. All around her, camel-coloured St Mirans, the women with pearl earrings and shades resting in long hair, purses with gold chains nudged onto the table. And here was Tess, the ragged English lawn.

'This country, Atlas, this St Mira...'

'...is an ancient land, full of myth and tradition.'

Were they reciting from *My First Book on Nativism*? Tess said, 'Mrs Pappas? Aren't all countries full of myth and tradition? And if you look at the science, there was once a supercontinent that broke apart, which means that all land is the same age, that all lands are equally ancient' – roughly speaking, give or take a few plate tectonics.

But Atlas didn't want his mother corrected; he just wanted it over. 'Our wildlife is glorious! Just look at our native birds, flowers, trees, animals!' His mother released a hand. Atlas thought it was to let him sweep an arm across the nation's flora and fauna. Actually, she needed a finger to flick away an ant.

'Her architecture, some of which still stands after more than a thousand years, forms the fabric of the land. Quaint villages, thatched roofs, our towering cathedral: every brick, every stone tells a story. And it is the story of our ancestors! May I stop now, mother?'

Mrs Pappas sank back in her chair. 'Thank you, Atlas.' He'd redeemed himself. She was glowing and exhilarated.

Then the ant crawled back. Her finger hovered over it, the nail mother-of-pearl. And down it went and waited, the way Tess had pressed a finger when she'd had to give a print.

Mrs Pappas rested her hand on her belly knowing a kick would come. 'What a great country!'

And there it was, the kick.

Tess said, 'Is any country great, though, Mrs Pappas? Aren't all countries… complicated?'

But it was Duke who answered. 'Tess! You complicate things!' He excused himself from Mr Pappas. 'You know the importance of simplicity, of clarity. It's how we do our job. We're bold. We present the truth with confidence: great. Proud. Land. Blood. Our. Own.'

Was the truth monosyllabic?

Duke rested a hand on Mrs Pappas's shoulder, weighted enough to assure. 'Tess is one of us. She didn't just…' Duke didn't finish. But what he meant was the kind of thing Varela would say: she didn't just wash up here on holiday and overstay her welcome. She didn't pass a little test to wangle herself a passport and call herself St Miran.

'Tess's Petrous still live in the ancestral village. It's on the peak where Mira gave birth to the first islanders. Tess is a great-great-great…' His wrist spiralled back through time. '… of St Mira herself. Her many-times grandfather was St George.'

Duke leant in further.

So did Atlas. Tess felt his breath on her neck. He whispered, 'Is that true, Miss Tess?'

She looked at him – big eyes, enlarged pupils, he'd see anything in the dark. She whispered back, 'It could be true. And it will become true if it's said often enough. And it's what people want to hear, which is often more useful than true.'

Now Duke was expanding into last night's stories. 'You know, our Tess used to swim for England. Her mother swam the entire British coast. The Petrous of St Mira could swim all day, catching fish with their bare hands. Sometimes they swam all the way to Africa.'

Mrs Pappas turned to Tess and smiled, her face like cracked porcelain. 'You must be proud…'

No, she was embarrassed. She didn't know what to do: go along with Duke's fabrications? Set the record straight? Instead, she shifted her chair and sat out of the ring. She took Atlas's hand, his skin milky for St Mira, not often in the sun. 'How are you?' He was tall for his age, and reduced himself by hunching over like an ancient widower, a gnomic priest.

'Lonely.'

'Where are your brothers?'

'Marching.'

'Where is your sister?'

'Cheering them on.'

'Didn't you want to join them?'

'It's not allowed.' He scraped at the pavement with the side of his boot, a raking sound that alerted Mr Pappas. Atlas read the line of his father's jaw. He stopped raking, crossed his legs, and stood on his own foot. Then he glanced at Duke. 'I like stories.'

'What's your favourite?'

His eyes swung across to his father – a blank stare, as if he didn't know him. 'Once upon a time, a boy was born with a bad foot. He was ignored and abandoned by his family. And then, years later, he met his father by chance, but didn't recognise him. And do you know what?'

Yes, she did. The story went on after that, but Atlas stopped there. Patricide was what interested him.

Now Duke got up. 'Time to go, Tess.'

Mr Pappas was startled. 'You're not *off*?'

He buttoned up his mac. 'Duty calls.'

Tess stood. She made goodbye noises. Mrs Pappas waved her tiny hands, like little baby-fists. Atlas looked stricken.

'You're not giving up the best seats in the house? You'll be metres away from the man himself.' Above them, a drone ploughed back and forth, relaying footage of Junkers. Crowds had spilled into surrounding streets, a red-and-white hand fingering Mirapolis.

'We have Our Own to translate, don't we, Tess, and to deliver to the world without delay.'

Mr Pappas was still protesting. 'You do not have to be so diligent! You do not have to be so good! Stay and be a bad boy. Be outrageous. Entertain us!'

You do not have to be good.

That was a line from a poem, wasn't it? Tess couldn't remember the rest of it now, but she'd liked it once. Everyone had. She'd had it in the kitchen so she could read it while waiting for the kettle to boil. And reading it was soothing, like drinking tea before you'd had your tea.

You do not have to be good.

You *do*, though, don't you? Good was still good, wasn't it? Or at least good was still better than bad.

'At least *hear* the speech first, man! Witness history. *I was there. I heard it in the flesh.* It's the kind of thing people will tell their children.'

Would Duke be having children?

Mr Pappas said, 'It's a public holiday, for Heaven's sake!'

'And we are *not* the public. We *serve* the public, don't we Tess.'

She put on the Burberry, tightened the belt.

She wasn't sure who she served anymore.

Tess and Duke took the back route to work. They walked without talking, Tess listening to the sound of the crowds ebb away. When all she could hear was the clip of his shoes, 'Do you think they bought it?' she said.

Duke walked on. He was in brogues, narrow at the toes, his wide feet finding a way to fit in. 'Mr and Mrs Pappas have a house full of exquisiteness. They buy nothing unless it is perfect.' There was something of the workhorse in the way he moved – blinkered, diligent, tired and tireless. Did that mean Duke would have to try again?

When they reached the Office, Max was in his shed, on duty today only because they were. He was looking glazed and happy – a New Year's Day kind of face of too much alcohol, not enough sleep, and far more optimism than was ever warranted. 'Good morning Dr Kontos-Tess!' as if it were a double-barrelled surname. He had a six-pack of beer and was watching events on his phone. 'What a proud day!'

Max certainly seemed proud. Or delirious. And delusional. And drunk already.

Tess followed Duke up the steps and through the main door. 'Do *you* feel proud, Dr Kontos?'

'What I feel is irrelevant.'

But even so...

'One must merely *appear* to feel.'

'Aren't emotions hard to fake?'

'How long have you known me?'

'I've worked for you for a decade.'

'I studied Law, Tess. I am professionally trained to express little beyond mild surprise and passing contempt.'

They took the stairs up to the English Desk, turning on the lights as they went. The building was deserted but still she dropped to a whisper. 'I find the claims of St Miran greatness a little overblown.' She watched Duke feel in a pocket for the key. 'Don't you?'

He unlocked the door. 'You mean this unique, beautiful, quirky country with its proud, brave people *et cetera et cetera*?' He went inside. 'All that matters is that it is *believed* one believes.'

And there it was again, the passive voice and indefinite pronoun. 'One? You mean *you*?'

'And anyone else who wishes to live undisturbed, to sleep well at night.' Duke went to his room and shut the door. Soon the sounds of coffee, and from his computer, the cheering crowds on Junkers. Other than that, the entire building was silent. It was just the two of them in today. No-one else – no cleaners, interns, no ambitious new appointments – was working on this public holiday. No-one else had to try this hard.

On her desk, Varela's speech. It was two sides of A4, slim for all the billing. Tess lifted the cover sheet: 'Friends, St Mirans, fellow patriots, defenders of this land.' Usually, he opened with 'Ladies and gentlemen,' but not today. Everyone who'd hear Our Own was taken to be one of our own.

Tess turned on her computer. The screen told her it was 8:58 on the 6th of December and that she was Tess Petrou. Usually, she didn't notice any of that, she was straight into Word and work. But on a day so full of guile, she was glad of these small certainties. She liked the reminders that there were dates and times, and that this machine she'd worked on for years knew who she was.

Tess turned to the livestream from Junkers. Sparks fountained from the edge of the stage, fake thunder clapped, and Hector Varela appeared like something miraculous. He was in a silver-grey suit that shimmered as he circled – glitzy and oracular, a man bearing light. The crowds loved it. Tess heard the roar in triplicate – from her own computer, through Duke's door, and against the window, a dampened wave washing up from the Square.

'Friends... please... Please, my friends...' and Varela beat his arms up and down, which could have been to still the applause, but was also what you did to fan a fire. When finally there was a hush, 'St Mirans, fellow patriots, *staunch* defenders of this *proud* land... You have come here today with your *dear* family and *good* friends and *old* neighbours – people you know and love and trust.'

Tess glanced at the script. All those adjectives were embellishments, compliments showered on the crowd.

'But if you look around you... Go on,' he said, 'look around you now...' The camera zoomed in on craned necks, expectant faces. '...you'll see mostly strangers. Maybe a face or two you know, but mostly strangers. And yet these people are *not* strange to you, are they.' He turned his face upwards. And suddenly, the white sky broke and the sun shone down. It was if God himself were a familiar stranger, and it made the moment brilliant.

'Every single person here looks like us, speaks like us, thinks like us, they *are* one of us, and that is why, my friends, I can tell you exactly what you're feeling. You might be in a crowd of many, many, many thousands, but you feel *safe*. Safe Among Your Own.'

Tess expected guns to go off. But no. The crowd was stilled by mention of safety and no-one was firing anything. Varela let the quiet sit there, and while he did, Tess checked the transcript. He'd delivered that last phrase capitalised and it was written capitalised. Firster orthodoxy was now in title case.

'St Mira isn't the biggest country on the planet, I'll grant you that.' Varela stretched arms as far as he could. 'You can travel end to end in, what – fast car – an hour? But this gem, this jewel of an island is *ample* for her *own* people. And that is who it belongs to. You.' He pointed to someone in the audience. 'Yes, I mean you.' The camera followed, framing a man who looked astonished that Varela had singled him out. 'St Mira's yours.' His finger picked through the crowd. 'And you, it's yours. And you. And you.' He skated over Oasis Café. It didn't need to land where Mr and Mrs Pappas were sheltered under parasols, where Firsters met bankers, met the papers, met the army. Everyone there had known for years they already owned St Mira.

'And so, my friends, we've just demonstrated – for the cameras, for the record – that we can *instinctively* identify Our Own. We just *know*, don't we, and that's part of human nature. But what about the great philosophers, the historians? What do they have to tell us? Here's a definition from the Father of History himself. One: you must be of the same ancestry, share the same blood.'

Tess leaned closer to her screen. That wasn't Rron, was it? Had he painted his face with the St Miran flag? It must be Rron because that was Rrock, sad and monumental and made-up too.

'Two: you must engage in the same religious practices.' The camera cut to the priest from Exodus Square, his face ruddy, jowly, flooded with pride. 'Three: you must share the same customs. Four: you must share the same language, the so-called *native* tongue. End of story. Simple. Unarguable. Brilliant, thank you Herodotus. Now, was that hard? Can we all count to four? And yet there are people out there who'll tell you what I've just said is racist. Is it? No. Because to be racist you've got to be *anti* other races. We're not *anti* anything. We're *pro* St Mira. We're *pro* Our Own.'

Varela paused. He dropped his head. A cloud had passed over and without the sun his suit didn't shine. It'd turned iron-grey, so he waited with his message like a nail to be hammered home. 'Fact is: we are loyal and dedicated to our own family, pack, tribe – call it what you will. But we will not be guilt-tripped into caring about abstractions such as "humanity". We are tired of having our heartstrings pulled by vague notions such as "the world".'

And maybe the world was vague to Varela, up there on the stage, suspended between the clouds and the truth. His audience could feel the earth under their feet, but that was the solidity of St Mira, its certainty reaching only as far as the coast. And maybe they were too transfixed by Varela to notice the horizon – that line in the distance where blue met another blue, where one medium met another, where difference shaped the world.

Varela said, 'Fact is: for morality to function, the limits of the pack must be clearly defined. There must be an "us" and a "them". Fact is: the cries of a friend – one of *us* – causes pain. The cries of an enemy – one of *them* – evokes, at best, indifference. Fact is: primitive or not, when we hear of a plane crash, our first question is, "Were there any St Mirans involved?" And then "Were there any children?" Reprehensible? Some might call it that. But it is also *natural*. Fact is: our pack is rightly the limit of our concern. And that's as far as it ever need go. All we do is cripple ourselves if we experience pain on behalf of...' His downturned mouth failed to find the word, there were so many things not to care about. '...every single ant in the grass.'

Ants.

Varela's world would teem with them. They'd invade his property, dirty his food, spoil his fun, stink when he trod on them. Best use a bait, let them carry the poison back to the nest where they could die among their own. Tess reached for the button and switched Varela off. She'd heard enough of him, declaiming his own Genesis, making a world that was insular, incurious, fearful, hateful. She stared at her screen, a cool cobalt blue, a colour to dive into and swim away.

If only she could swim away.

Tess went to the window and looked at the sea. The water was dark and racing boats clamoured at the starting line. By the end of the day, all of them would have sailed round St Mira and mapped the limits of the only world that mattered. Down in the fairground, the big dipper dipped, the big wheel turned, and tiny figures milled about – thousands of them, too many to count. Call them dots, or ants.

Or people.

Tess picked up her globe and cupped it in her hands. It seemed to float – far too light for what it was. There were eight billion people living on this globe. And all you had to do, according to Varela, was care about your pack. He'd relieved his audience of the effort of the rest. But eight billion minus a pack was an awful lot of carelessness.

Tess listened for sounds from Duke's room, heard Varela's voice muted by the office door. Then came the sound of a pistol shot, which meant the boat race was off.

Tess found a pen. She picked up Varela's speech and wrote on the cover sheet:

Fact is: I refuse to translate this. Gone to lunch.

Then she picked up her globe and put it in her bag. She didn't really know why, except it was a present from Arlo, and she couldn't abandon it, the world being so often abandoned.

17.

Have you been granted a UK visa in the last ten years?
YES.

Have you ever been refused a visa for any country, including the UK?
NO.

Have you ever been detained, either in the UK or any other country,
for any reason?
I'M BEING DETAINED NOW.

Have you ever been deported, removed or otherwise required to leave
any country, including the UK, in the last ten years?

NOT YET.

Tess didn't go to lunch. She walked out of the building into wind that brought the roar of Junkers, and to Max waving in delirium, and rang Vera. 'I've just walked out of the office. Can we meet?'

'What has Duke done?'

Not Duke. It was Varela. And Our Own. And the ants. Especially the ants.

Vera had decided not to listen to the speech, but she had, she said, just walked *into* her office. 'Mr Langberg rang. An urgent meeting, couldn't wait, apparently.' He was in a hurry to wrap up APRIL. He wanted to finalise the passenger list for the *Pride*.

So, Nomie was working on a public holiday too. It was what people did when they had a point to prove – in his case, that he was a very busy man, met deadlines, and that other people's free time was his to dispose of.

The meeting was at eleven, Mr Langberg was punctual, they'd be done well before twelve, Vera said. Then a pause. Tess could hear her thinking. 'This meeting with Mr Langberg is private and confidential. But perhaps not for you. Among other things, it concerns you.' She said she'd leave her office door ajar and gave Tess the code to get in. 'A ringside seat on the methods of Mr Langberg. Slip in while I make him feel at home.'

Tess lingered on the corner by the Records Office and watched Nomie approach. He was smiling to himself, possibly talking to himself, his briefcase swinging, looking demob happy. He wore a homburg today, which gave him the air of a throwback. He'd come in fancy dress, as a Foreign Office by-gone. He rang the Records Office bell, and when the door opened, he took his hat by the crown and dipped his head as if bowing out of the project.

Tess gave them a minute to reach Vera's office then let herself inside. It was dark and quiet, and anonymous without the receptionist who remembered the name of every visitor, who was her own private Records Office. Tess took corridors that cooled as she went deeper into the building. They'd been redecorated since she was last here and dazzled now with local landmarks, like the hyper-real images that greet you at airports, sponsored by global banks. In the background, the pound and grind of a building site. The Genealogy Bureau was going up next door.

Close to Vera's office, Tess caught the sound of her voice enunciating over a warming kettle. Tess moved closer, saw the door wedged open and two figures shattered by frosted glass. She listened to Vera make tea. Then the crackle of plastic as she rummaged through a box. 'A chocolate bar? A packet of crisps? Or Mr Kipling?' But Nomie had just eaten, thank you all the same. They made conversation about the perfect brew – warming the pot, the pros and cons of cosies, how long to let it draw. 'Milk? Sugar?'

'A splash and no thank you.'

Nomie had sweetened his tea until he applied for the Foreign Office. Then someone had told him that two heaped spoons were an uncommonly common amount of sugar and not something Fast-Trackers did. Along with Tess, he'd given up sugar in his tea in the cause of career advancement.

Then Nomie got straight down to business. 'So. The passenger list for the *Pride*. I know we agree on the first item.' The clink of a teacup returning to its saucer. 'I've been involved in many repatriations in my time, but none of persons in your husband's particular state where speed, naturally, is of the essence.' He'd had Albert's remains re-identified via dental records, he said. Then there was the English translation of his death certificate, Permission to Transport, the Cargo Waybill Number, Customs Clearance, Handling Charges, Airport Transfer, and the same again for the airlines. It would have been much quicker, he said, to have repatriated solely by air, 'but, as you know, that option is now closed.' All flights from St Mira had been halted until further notice. There'd been a security breach at Amyna – no details given except that heads had rolled. So, the *Pride* would sail to Lampedusa, where it would unload its cargo, Nomie said, then make its way to England.

So, Albie was just 'cargo' to Nomie. And Lampedusa. No hero's welcome in Messina as there'd been for the Famous Forty.

'I checked in person that the *Pride* can ensure the integrity of your husband for the duration of the voyage.' The cross-channel ferry had a walk-in freezer. Once the body was on a plane, it was all routine.

Tess saw an arm pass something across the desk, then the sound of riffled papers. Vera said, 'Is this the bill?'

'Fully itemised.'

A pause as she read. 'You put in an awful lot of hours, Mr Langberg.'

'Your husband's return was an awfully difficult thing to achieve.'

'And that is an awful lot of pounds per hour...'

'Expenses that are covered, I suggest, within the budget for the *Pride*.' A sip of tea to allow that point to sink in. 'It means that *you* do not pay, Mrs Vertete; the British taxpayer does.'

So, Nomie was doing Vera a favour. That was kind of him. And unlike him. Wasn't that too good to be true?

Vera topped up their tea and tried again with the snacks. A pause while he assessed the offerings. 'I think I'll take the Bounty, if you insist.' For a while they drank and ate. Nomie made some kind of mumbled joke. A brief spark of laughter. The mood was convivial, but also false. They both must have known that more was coming. The moment felt ready to implode.

Nomie said, 'I take it you have someone in the UK to meet your husband on arrival?'

'Tess and Arlo will take care of that.'

'*Will* they?'

'Will they *not*? Given there are no flights out of the country, they have to leave on the *Pride*. I assume Tess and Arlo are on your passenger list. I assume – given your many, many connections – you actually know where Arlo is.'

For a while, Nomie didn't answer. Then, 'Well...' He could make one syllable brim with good intention. 'I can certainly make enquiries.'

'You mean you have not done that yet?'

'Please, Mrs Vertete, do remember how busy I am. I am dealing with an inter-governmental crisis. I can't be distracted by every single...' He didn't finish.

Ant in the grass, Tess thought.

Nomie said, 'My role is to look at the big picture.'

'And what *is* your big picture, Mr Langberg, except the sum total of little pictures? Of individuals needing help?'

'I am sorry, but I honestly, honestly, honestly have no idea where Arlo is.'

Was that too many honestlys to be honest? Or was it so many it had to be true? Nomie took a bite of Bounty. Silence. They all listened to him chew. When he'd finally swallowed, 'All I know is that Arlo has become... *elusive*... in the way a number of people have become elusive in recent weeks. And that Tess somehow got it into her head that she and Arlo would be on a plane out of Amyna. She seemed to think she'd been double-crossed, that she'd been used somehow.' Tess watched Nomie's shoulders shrug – a slow, exaggerated abandonment of responsibility. 'What can I say? What can I do? Such are the times we live in. Tess has a dreadful tendency to believe in human goodness. Charming, but very old-fashioned.'

She looked at her shoes: they were old, twelve years at least. She'd bought them to come to St Mira. Her eyes tracked the column of light from her feet up to the window. Outside, the Genealogy Bureau rose in a prism of glass. Soon, the building would be open to the public, and you could sit at a computer, under a Mediterranean sun refracted into clarity, chart where you'd come from, and leave with a certificate of Ancestral Proof.

Nomie said, 'I am aware you've been inundated with requests to prove Britishness, but time is no longer on our side. The *Pride* sails in under a week.'

'We have completed all the paperwork.'

'So that's that, then.' Nomie moved as if about to stand.

'And of the last twelve cases, five did not meet the relevant criteria...' The sound of Vera's fingers finding their way through paperwork. '...but the remaining seven *are* genuine...'

'Or so you believe.'

'...and have a legitimate claim to naturalisation by descent, and therefore the right to be on the *Pride*.'

Nomie picked up his Bounty and bit. He took his time finishing a mouthful. In the distance, the noise of the building site and the alarm of a truck reversing. 'In my experience, Mrs Vertete, would-be immigrants are ingenious. Surprisingly so. Determined. Fearless. Resourceful. They won't give up. Do you have a wastepaper basket?'

'They are would-be *citizens*.'

Then the sound of metal and the crackle of a sweet wrapper screwed up and landing in the bin.

'And why, Mr Langberg, would Britain not want brave, imaginative, determined people? Surely those are traits your country would welcome?'

'Those are the qualities that made us. That is what the British *are*. But not all bravery is equal. Nor equally desirable.' Nomie sat back in his chair and considered the pile of papers. 'Your cases would have to be closely scrutinised. Interpol. Europol. Due diligence and all that.'

'My team has been scrutinising for weeks. We have all worked many, many hours of overtime to complete this task.'

'And I shall do my utmost to expedite matters on the British side. As you've seen in relation to your husband, I do deliver on what is within my power.'

Nomie's words sounded reasonable enough. The problem was the intonation. It lacked finality. A 'but' was coming.

'But I cannot guarantee the cases in question will be on board the *Pride*.'

'They are not in question.'

'I will be as efficient at you have been, but...'

'The world does not need efficient people, Mr Langberg. It needs kind ones.'

'...one thing I *can* guarantee is that this process will take as long as it takes.'

'And the *Pride* leaves in days.'

'And citizenship is a lifelong responsibility. It's a privilege, an asset the value of which we will defend. The British people want to know that newcomers are appropriate. It's not something you can just...' An arm roved the desk. '...pick up from Waitrose. Citizenship isn't for sale.'

'These days, *everything* is for sale. The passport trade is worth billions a year, and you know it.'

'Do I?'

She said, 'Malta. Cyprus. Grenada. St Kitts and Nevis. Dominica. St Lucia...'

'And what are they? A handful of hot tatty islands. Britain is *not* one of those.'

No, Tess thought. *It's a tatty cold one.*

Nomie said, 'We do not sell Britishness.'

'Of course you do.' Silence after that. When Vera spoke again, she sounded tired. 'What has your country become, Mr Langberg?'

'Only more of what it has long been, I suspect.'

Tess leant her back against the wall. Soon the cold breached the body-bag. She stared across the corridor to a photoshopped St George. He'd just slain the dragon. Soon he'd be beheaded, named a martyr and made a saint. In years to come, his cross would bring tears to the eyes of people with an inflated attachment to England.

Vera said, 'Mr Langberg, these seven people are of British descent. They have relatives in your country. You should know their names at least.'

'No thank you. Names won't mean anything. Names are details and I don't deal in those. If you could forward the cases through official channels.'

'They have the right to a British passport. Under the agreement between our governments, they have a right to leave on the *Pride*. My team has completed the paperwork and it is there at your elbow.'

Nomie moved his arms away and pinned them behind his chair. 'Mrs Vertete and Team. Your work ethic in relation to APRIL was admirable. Your efforts were thorough.' Which meant they were a problem for Nomie. And he'd switched to the past tense. For him, APRIL was over. 'But those seven people would have turned into a horde of foreign criminals by the time they got to the UK. I have relations to manage. I have news to contain. Can you imagine the headlines? "Borders Open 7/7." "The Seven Deadly Sinners." "The Dance of the Seven Veils," because according to the *Mail* they'd all arrive in a burqa.'

'The headlines depend on which paper you read.' Vera folded her arms. After a while, 'Please do not look at me like that.' Nomie looked away – he did that at least. 'And, no, I am *not* mad. I simply have a sense of justice, which in this world is often taken for madness.'

'Mrs Vertete...' It was a conciliatory opening.

But Vera wasn't going to be cajoled. 'These people have a legal right to settle in the UK.'

'Then they should use legal channels to assert it.'

'You mean go to court?'

'Now you exaggerate. Now you catastrophise. I mean seek legal advice.'

'But that costs, Mr Langberg.'

'And the British, in truth, only want among their number, those who can afford a decent lawyer.' Nomie stood. The back of his head rose above the frosted glass like a yellowed moon lifting over the horizon.

'One last thing,' Vera said, 'before you go.'

Nomie didn't sit.

'Tess.'

'I knew you'd say that.' For some reason – maybe because in this whole process Tess was his only discomfort and he needed four closed walls – he went to shut the door.

'I leave my door open. I am open – to things, to people. Leave it open, thank you.'

Nomie held the back of his chair and rocked it. 'So, what about Tess?'

'She has to leave.'

'She's free to, isn't she? No-one's stopping her. Daily sailings to Italy, Malta, Albania, Greece. She can take her pick.' An arm pointed over Vera's head, which was also the direction of the port.

'With Arlo. They both have to be on the *Pride* when it leaves.'

'Oh? Why?'

'You *know* why. Because it is *not* safe here and it *is* safe there. Because the UK is the only country where Arlo has the right to settle, and therefore the only country Tess can settle. And her UK passport is currently unaccounted for...'

'She didn't tell me it was lost.'

'It was stolen.'

'And reported, I hope.'

'Yes, she reported it.' Which Tess did – to Vera. 'And the only passport in her possession is a St Miran one. And to get into the UK...'

'Not my problem.'

'Tess needs a visa.'

Silence.

'Mr Langberg?'

And still the chair rocked back and forth, back and forth.

Vera said, 'The Treaty of Friendship provides for the safeguard of *all* British interests.'

'Ms Petrou and Mr Brown are of *no* interest to the British.' Then the rocking stopped and the legs of the chair landed on the floor. 'You know the simple answer, don't you.'

'Yes. It's the answer to everything: money. But Tess does not have a spare two million to buy her way into your country.'

'No. So if she can't get in as an investor, is she a Skilled Worker?' And Nomie detailed the unlikelihood: that under the points-based system, Tess would need an offer of a job from a Home Office licensed sponsor. A job at level RQF 3 or above. A minimum salary of...'

Vera cut him short. 'I know the rules, thank you. I have been immersed in UK immigration for weeks. I do not need you to recite the rules. I need you to do the right thing.'

'The right thing, as you so quaintly put it, and the law are probably incompatible.'

'They often are. There is only a passing resemblance between justice and legality. There is much criminal behaviour in the world that has yet to be criminalised, most of it regarded as quite normal.'

'Listen, Mrs Vertete. If Tess wants to live in the UK, she needs points. Seventy of them. That's the long and the short of it. Of which she currently scores, what, ten? For being able to speak English.'

'And what about everything else about her? That she is so able and willing and funny and generous and...' Vera choked to a stop. Dear Vera. She didn't have to say that. 'How much do those things score? What is the point of a points-based system if it does not let the kind people in? If a good human being does not make a good citizen, then what does?'

'You're getting angry and you're directing it at the wrong person.'

'No, I am directing it at exactly the *right* person.'

'I don't decide the rules.'

'But you *do* enforce them.'

'I'm just doing my job.'

'And what about your conscience? What about enforcing that?'

'Lots of people make a living from things they don't consider one hundred per cent ideal.'

'Does that make it right? That the world turns on people selling their soul?'

'So what *should* they do?'

'Something else. Something better. Decide against.'

The goodbyes were brief. No handshakes. Tess ducked out of the way and watched Nomie head towards reception – his stride long, his briefcase light, unburdened by needless paperwork. She waited till the sound of his footsteps had vanished then went to Vera's office and slid half a face inside. Vera's eyes were closed, her palms pressed together and against her lips. On the desk, two unfinished cups of tea.

Tess tapped on the door.

Vera glanced up and then away. Her eyes were moist. They sparkled. She looked heroic, like a black-and-white film star, a Joan of Arc, going to her death on a pyre of paperwork.

'Vera?'

'You heard, yes?'

'Is everything all right?'

'No, everything is not all right. The world is not all right.' She suddenly stood, the legs of her chair catching on the floor. She went to the sink and picked up the soap. Vera slid it through her fingers, was thorough in washing her hands of Nomie. Said to the mirror: 'We need the people who *can* say yes to say yes. We need the people who *can* make a difference to make a difference. People make a difference. We make or break each other.' Vera had such a kind and familiar face, although – distracted and upset like this and inverted in the mirror – also a face Tess really didn't know.

Vera dried her hands and went back to her desk.

Tess said, 'Can I make you tea?'

But English tea was no consolation. Vera had just performed The Rite of Tea, and where did that get her?

Two stacks of manilla folders sat on her desk. She said, 'These are dead in the water.' Tess took the folders and read the names: Angelos, Diamandis, Kouris, Thanos, Williams. They were stamped DECLINED, and clipped to the front, a note of the reason. She sifted through birth and marriage certificates, divorce decrees, tax returns, bank statements, exam results, driver's licences – the dry, bloodless collage of five complicated lives.

Vera cleared her throat. 'They have to go, as some might say, "back to where they came from". Then she looked at Tess as if confused. She checked her watch. 'You are not at work.' Vera had lost track of time. 'You still wear the body-bag. How did it go with Duke? You are not fired?'

'No. I'm just... not at the office. Not...' Not until she had to go back. Not until... Tess really didn't know.

Vera fingered her neck and pulled out her necklace, the red coral gemstone, a present from Albie. Against that suit, she looked like a Black Widow, though Vera had no venom for anyone – only outrage, only fight. She turned to the cases that Nomie had ignored. 'What do you think he will do about these?'

They both knew that Nomie would do nothing. He'd just let time run out.

Vera scooped the folders up. She clamped her arms around them and held them to her chest. Rescuers did that when pulling people from the sea. Always you kept their mouth above water. You did it even when you knew they were dead because maybe they weren't, maybe they weren't. She said, 'Noam Langberg must have had a heart once, because once upon a time you loved him.'

Which was true.

But it was long, long ago in a land far away.

Nomie's heart was the stuff of make-believe.

Tess and Vera spent the afternoon filing away the paperwork, and it was dusk before Tess got back to the CCO. Max's shed was shuttered up, the lights in the building off. But Tess knew that Duke would still be working. Today of all days he'd be there, proving himself, protecting himself, translating Our Own as if one of our own.

Tess let herself in and paused in the cool of the atrium. She glanced up to the highest windows, the glass rippling moonlight. She held her breath. Tess knew this feeling: it was the moment at the bottom of the swimming pool, peaceful and other-worldly, before the press of suffocation, the urgency, the strike of relief.

She held the handrail to climb the stairs, feeling the weight c what she was about to do. She paused at *2: Arabic and Spanis* and listened to the sound of her own slow breathing. She listen(for Duke, caught a rush of typing. Then Tess reached *Engli.* The doors were open and Duke was leaning over his compu forehead shining, sleeves rolled up, his fingers beating the k(

'Dr Kontos.'

The clatter of the keyboard stopped. He turned, alarme the sound of a voice. Then his expression settled when h(who it was. Duke swivelled in his chair, taking Tess in expected a list of all the ways she'd failed him today, and the Desk, and failed herself – a dissection that was qui measured and brutal, of the kind only lawyers deliver.

Instead he said nothing.

Tess wasn't used to a wordless Duke. She said, 'It wa lunch.' Six hours, in fact.

Still Duke didn't respond. He spread his hands on h working the cramp out of his fingers.

'I was at the Records Office.'

'How is Vera?'

'Busy.'

He sighed. Duke wasn't a sighing kind of perso was lazy. Duke always made the effort to verbalise h

up the cuffs. Then he got up, walking stiffly. He must have been at the desk for hours. He moved into the other room, went to the window, stared into the night. And looking at darkness seemed to shift his mood. 'I know you did not like Varela's speech. If it is any consolation, *I* did not like it either. But did you hear what he said afterwards?'

No, she'd been at the Records Office listening to Nomie defend the indefensible.

'You have it there on your desk. It's tomorrow's headline. Varela said, "The Firsters control the streets. We control the courts. We control the media and we control the narrative."'

For once Varela had told the truth.

'And I helped them do it.' Tess had translated the Firster narrative into the world's most spoken language. But now she had stopped. 'It's why I no longer work here.'

Duke turned round. 'A conscientious objector?' That made him smile. Then a sharp clap as if to wake her up. 'Come, Tess. This is peacetime.'

'No it isn't.'

Duke's face skirted the room as if looking for somewhere to land. 'So, where are you off to? The moral high ground?'

'If you want to call it that.'

'Boggy up there.'

'I've got big feet.'

Tess wasn't giving way, and that seemed to annoy him. He worked his fingers, making the knuckles crack. 'Well, if this *is* war, you know what will happen, don't you. In war, things turn brutal. Tender things suffer. *Tenderness...*' He leant towards her. '...gets hurt.'

So, he was naming names now. Who had told him about Tenderness? That indiscretion had to have come from Nomie. Well, *she* could give him names too. 'Does the name Ioannidis mean anything to you?'

A thoughtful pause. Duke shook his head. 'No. Not a thing.'

It was Duke's mother's maiden name.

'Or Vasilis Michail Kontos?'

Because that afternoon, when she and Vera had done the filing, and Tess was in the 'K's looking for Kouris, she'd spotted a name she knew. Her fingers had backtracked and stopped on Kontos. She'd found a birth certificate for Vasilis Michail Kontos. Born in Athens.

Drop the Vasilis and you got Duke.

Duke's body had stilled. 'Vasilis Michail Kontos is my father's name.'

'Anyone else's?'

'And *his* father's name.'

'Yes, it's your family tradition. It runs uninterrupted along the male line.' Tess shifted her weight, lent on the desk the way lawyers did. 'Let me put this scenario to you: Vasilis Michail Kontos *senior* and Irene Ioannidis have a son, also Vasilis Michail, born in Athens in 1965.'

'I don't think so.'

'In 1967, the Colonels come to power in a coup in Greece and the Kontos family flees. They arrive on St Mira as refugees, a country they choose because they speak the language.'

Duke turned away. He sat on the edge of her desk, his face tilted up at the clock.

'The father is a journalist by profession – it's why he fell foul of the Colonels – but on St Mira he does odd jobs on building sites: Mirapolis is expanding at the time. Irene raises her son. Vasilis Michail soon learns Greek as spoken on the island. He fits in. He does well at school – exceptionally well – his parents have raised a fighter and a survivor. He goes to university, then wins a scholarship to Harvard for his PhD. That's when he drops the Vasilis. It sounds too Russian for those circles with the Cold War still going. He returns to St Mira as Dr Michail Kontos and applies for citizenship via naturalisation. He's excused the language exam, given Greek is his first language. He scores one hundred per cent in the Knowledge of St Mira Test and is granted a passport in 1990.'

Duke said, 'That is one full minute of defamation. I could take you to court on that.'

'I haven't finished.'

'You have no evidence whatsoever.'

The evidence was at her feet. 'I've spent the afternoon in the Records Office.' Tess had lifted Duke's paperwork, slipped it into her bag without telling Vera. 'I've pieced it all together, the entire arc of your life.' Dr Michail Kontos: refugee, immigrant, naturalised citizen. He was no more St Miran than Arlo.

Tess went to the window. Down there, the pin-prick lights of Mirapolis. The big wheel was lit and turning slow circles. The Genealogy Bureau burned with floodlights. Across the water, the finishing line for the boat race was marked by the rock of buoys. Soon the winner would be home.

She said, 'Finding out was chance, in a way. Pure alphabetical coincidence. I was looking for Kouris and stumbled on Kontos. Though it was also *not* chance. Because last night you said, "They will get round to us all in the end." *Us* all. Not *them* all.' It was a careless admission for a consummate linguist.

Duke didn't react. He was still watching the clock.

Tess thought of the condolence card he'd given her: *My sympathies for your losses* he'd said. And now Tess could enumerate all his losses: four Marines, the 1982 Taekwondo Gold Medal, his home, his security, his past – buried for years in the Records Office, erased from public view.

And now he'd lost his cover.

'My sympathies, Dr Kontos, but I know who you are.' She looked at the clock. The movement of the hands made time visible. The seconds passed. Together they watched time run out.

18.

Do you have any other evidence to confirm your identity?

YES, BUT IN ST. MIRA.

Do you have any documents or other evidence relevant to your decision to come to the UK, your family life, or other personal circumstances that you wish to submit?

YES, BUT ALSO IN ST. MIRA.

If so, how long will it take to obtain them and what language will they be in?

I CAN'T SAY HOW LONG IT WILL TAKE. HOW MUCH LONGER WILL

I BE IN HERE?

THE DOCUMENTS ARE IN ENGLISH AND/OR GREEK.

Over the next couple of days, Tess formalised her departure from the Central Communications Office. She put her resignation in writing and was invited into Human Resources, where she surrendered her office keys and her ID and handed over her internet passwords and signed a declaration that no CCO property, physical or digital, remained in her possession. Then she was told that Duke had pre-empted her: she was already suspended pending dismissal for gross misconduct. Max escorted her off the premises without saying a word. Tess didn't want it to end this way. In the version of events in her head, Max said, 'But *why*, Miss Tess?' And she said, 'Because because.' Because that would have made it all right.

Tess spent the rest of the time with Vera in the Records Office, helping out with admin. But it was also to avoid the noise in Exodus Square. The flat where Tess and Arlo used to live was being stripped and refurbished, and a native St Miran family would soon be moving in. There were plans to reconstruct Tess and Arlo's kitchen in the National Museum. 'The events of today are already historic,' a museum spokesman said. They wanted to show how the foreigners on the island had once lived – the foreign food with the foreign smells that filled an entire building. The foreign radio. The foreign language filling the stairwell. The teaching materials on the kitchen table that spread the language like a foreign plague.

And then, one morning, as they were getting ready for the office, Tess got a text from an unknown number:

You are cordially invited to a meeting. Holiday Inn. 8am sharp. Horizons.

It'd only been a couple of days, but it seemed she'd waited for ever for this: Duke's next move. Vera must have sensed the change of mood. 'Trouble?' she said.

For sure there was trouble ahead. Tess showed her the message.

'Nomie,' said as if a certainty. But then, Vera didn't know that she didn't know all there was to be known. Tess was sure this was Duke, and a meeting with him was unlikely to be cordial. She didn't want to spend time with a Taekwondo Grand Master who was on the defensive – and on the attack.

'There is no such thing as a free breakfast, just like no free lunch,' Vera said. 'But you *must* go. Nomie has something for you.' Did Vera think their meeting in the Records Office was about to pay off, that Nomie had had second thoughts?

'And what do I have to give in return?'

Vera hesitated. Tess was sure she had no idea what she had on Duke. But Vera *did* know that Tess must have something, or else why the invitation?

And Tess knew exactly what she had: Duke's papers were in her bag. The copies she'd made – because because, because who knew what was coming – were in the back of Vera's wardrobe.

At the Holiday Inn reception, Tess checked the hotel directory. Downstairs was the Treasure Trove Bar. On the terrace, The Captain's Favourite Café. And on the top floor, where she expected to find Horizons, the restaurant was called The Lighthouse. So Tess went to ask the man at the desk. A smile lit at her approach. 'Ms Petrou?'

How did he know?

'You're looking for Horizons?'

And that.

Tess glanced over her shoulder for who else might be here. Santa waited in his grotto for pre-school children. ABBA was on low and sounding oracular. Fairy-lights flashed in code.

'Ms Petrou.' Not a question this time. 'Thank you for keeping the appointment.' A glance at his watch. 'It is very nearly eight, so if you don't mind, I'll get straight to the matter in hand.' He placed his palms flat on the map of Mirapolis and leant his weight against them. He was wearing white gloves, thin cotton ones, the kind worn for fragile manuscripts – or stolen goods.

'It is believed you have in your possession...' Did his eyes just slide over her bag? She reached an arm across it. '...something of interest to someone you know.'

'Who do I know?' How did he know Duke? Who was this man? She read his name-badge. *Jan*, it said. Was that Jan as in January, as in two-faced Janus? She scanned his face – too bland to fix with an age, too bloodless for clues. All that struck her was how forgettable he was. Would she recognise him if she ever saw him again? The pin on his lapel said he spoke English, Greek, Italian and: 'Do you really speak Albanian?'

'Why might I not?'

'Not many people do.'

'Albanians do. And there are 2.9 million of them.'

And Nomie. Was Jan a Foreign Office pal? He had the kind of accent that would once have been Home Counties but had drifted to no-place over the years.

Jan bent down and reached an arm under the counter. Behind him, the hotel noticeboard said it was 07:57, 24 degrees and there were *SORRY NO VACANCIES*. He brought out a brochure and placed it on the counter. *Our Rooms*, it said.

'I don't want to check in.'

Jan opened the cover. 'Here, Ms Petrou, we have our best – and final – offer.' His eyes were on the page. Tess glanced down:

Noam Langberg International – offer of employment

Name: Ms Tess Petrou

Post: Senior Analyst (St Miran Affairs)

Start date: immediate

Salary: £25,600 per annum

'And if you'd care to turn over?' Even with gloves he didn't want to touch the page. 'To enable an enjoyable and longer stay...'

It was a UK visa. Tess was being allowed in under the Skilled Worker Programme. It was valid from... She searched for the date. It had been issued yesterday.

Jan closed *Our Rooms* and put the brochure away. 'So.'

So. Such a short word, and usually an invitation, yet the way he'd said it had put an end to bargaining.

He clasped his hands and placed them on the desk. His fingers were still, the skin, she imagined, would be smooth, the nails trim. Not a worrier. He was a man used to exchanges like this. She said, 'Who are you working for?'

'My employer.'

'Is that Noam Langberg, or Michail Kontos, or both?'

'Or neither. And one of those permutations is certainly true.' He tugged at his sleeves as if his jacket didn't fit. Had he been loaned it just for this job?

Jan said, 'It is suggested that there is an exchange.' Tess listened to the passive. Foreign Office, he had to be. Or ex. A lone wolf, like Nomie. A fixer without the ties. She said, 'Why should I believe your rooms are genuine?'

'Why believe they're not?'

'Because no-one has done anything honest for as long as I can remember. Because everyone is out for themselves. That's how the world now works.'

'Except for you, Tess. *You're* genuine.'

Was that a compliment? Coming from him, it felt like a trap.

'And the documents in your bag are genuine.'

Had someone been watching her? Had she been followed? Or was that just a shot in the dark?

They stared at each other with empty poker faces. Now she looked more closely, Tess saw his eyes were acid-green. They reminded her of Cid, of a cat that soiled doormats and played with drowned rats. She took a step back from the desk. She wanted to work it out, think through the moves, the *what ifs* of this situation. But she wasn't good at games like that: there were so many unknowns, too many variables. Instead, Tess found herself listening to the music. ABBA sang 'The Winner Takes it All.' She knew all the words, first verse to the last. Right now, it felt as though the gods were throwing dice. She waited for Jan's face to give something away. How did all this end? Was it win-win if she played it right?

Jan reached under the counter and put *Our Rooms* back on the desk.

Tess opened the brochure and fingered the documents. She had no idea what she was looking for except for something that didn't look right. She thought: what would Vera do? Tess pictured her checking the thickness of the paper, feeling the letterhead, pressing a damp finger against the signature and seeing if it brought off ink. Tess knew that signature: two brash capitals, N and L, the rapid trailing off after. It was quintessential Nomie – all seismic show. Tess said, 'Mr Langberg fixed this up very quickly.'

'It was promptly arranged.'

Which confirmed the speed if not the actor.

So, if she'd got this right: Duke wanted to swap his past for Tess's future. He wanted his records back as soon as possible and Tess out of the country and out of the picture. And he'd contacted Nomie to make it happen. It would have cost Duke a fortune: Nomie issuing an employment contract to Home Office standards. A fast-track visa. Recruiting Jan as intermediary. Swift compliance with a scheme he'd know only in outline.

Jan cleared his throat. 'So, if you're ready, I shall take receipt of the documents in your possession, and you accept *Our Rooms*, plus a key to your suite.'

'There aren't any vacancies.' A nod to the noticeboard.

'There are *no more* vacancies. Yours was the last booking.'

'Well, I'm not checking in.' Tess glanced towards the exit, to the revolving door and guests shuffling as if shackled in and out of the Holiday Inn.

Jan said, 'The suite comes with the job.'

Tess listened for a voice telling her what to do, but all she heard was ABBA. The winner was taking it all and the loser was about to fall. Agnetha had such perfect enunciation, she made everything clear.

Tess undid her bag and took out a folder. Here it was then: the truth about Duke. A manilla cover, unmarked and unremarkable. She placed it square in front of Jan. He gave this moment a moment's pause, as if the front desk were weighing scales and he was waiting for the needle to settle. Then he picked the folder up, didn't check the contents, slid it into a drawer and locked it.

Another glance at his watch. 'So...' This time the word was an invitation. 'You'll be staying on the top floor. An unobstructed view of the sea. On a clear day, you can see all the way to Europe.' He gave Tess a key. The fob said *Honeymoon Suite*. 'I'm not married.'

'If you'll follow me.'

'Where are you going?'

'I'm proceeding with the procedure.'

Honeymoon Suite? Did that mean a wedding?

'Which means the lift.'

In the lift, Jan pressed the top button. Then he clasped his hands behind his back, pulling wide his jacket. He was taller than she'd realised. Tess's eyes were level with his heart – if he had a heart; if any of them did. Her eyes drifted from Jan's chest to his lapel. So, he was a fixer in four languages. She knew one sentence in Albanian: 'I love you' – thanks to Nomie. In the early days, he'd often said it. Tess thought it was to be romantic, to give himself mystery. By the time they'd split up, she knew that saying 'love' in a foreign language put distance between you and the meaning of the word, took away its weight.

The lift was slow. It crept through the hotel. Tess imagined floor after floor of mirror-image rooms, and in the bathrooms at this time of the morning, guests leaning into their reflection and wondering how they came to look like that. Tess let her gaze blur, caught her out-of-focus self in the mirror. Behind her shoulder, the ad for the hotel beauty salon:

Relax, rejuvenate, find another you!
Make-overs our speciality!

And a photo of... that wasn't Jeannie? Tess looked closer. 'That's Jeannie. I know her.' Had she moved to Mirapolis? Was she a hairdresser here now? And why hadn't she told her?

Jan shrugged as if to say: *Doesn't everyone know everyone on this tiny island?* He didn't look at Jeannie. Instead, he watched the floors go by, the numbers lighting and going out, till there were no more numbers and the lift came to a stop. They waited for the doors to open – long enough for Tess to think that being stuck in a lift might all be part of the plan. Then the clunk as the lock disengaged, and Jan gestured her out. He nodded to a bell-boy, who nodded back.

'What's he doing here?' Did he work the lift or work for Nomie?

'People who wait for a living spend their whole lives wondering that.' Jan headed down the corridor. It was carpeted in pastel pink and scented with honeysuckle. He stopped in front of a door. 'And here our ways part.' So this was where his contract ended, with delivering Tess to the Honeymoon Suite. And into whose hands? The door had no spyglass, so she pressed an ear to it instead. She heard the hum of a faraway hoover, the sound of Jan's footsteps deadened by the carpet, of a lift going down.

Tess slid the keycard into the lock and shouldered the door open. She put her head inside. She expected to see Nomie in an easy chair, arms crossed, face stony, ready to make it clear just how much she'd put him out, and exactly what was expected now that she was on his payroll.

A chair was in her line of sight, but it was empty. Tess moved inside the room. There was no-one on the bed. Nor under it. Nor in the bathroom. Nor in the wardrobe. Nor behind the curtains. Where else did they look in the movies?

Tess stayed beside the window. Outside, the sun shattered on a choppy sea. Shipping containers were making their way to China. The ferry to Italy had just left the port, shrouded in a cloud of gulls. She sat at the desk and laid out her paperwork, put it in order, lined it up. She was slowly piecing things together. These four documents would give her a new life: her St Miran passport, a UK visa, Nomie's employment contract, and from Agnesa, the British passport for Arlo. The only thing that was missing now was him.

Tess checked the minibar and came back with chocolate, then lay on the bed and ate it. She kicked off her shoes, but didn't undress; sooner or later there'd be a knock at the door. She picked up the remote, put on the telly, found the news but didn't want to know it. So she scrolled through the channels – spent a while on betting, jewellery, football, cartoons – then settled on static and listened to electric crackle. One percent of that was big bang radiation. Tess knew things like that. Also, that the sky at night was dark because light from billions of stars never ever reached the earth. Also...

And there it was: the knock. Who was it – Duke or Nomie? There was no time to wonder or to hide, except under the covers, because already there was the sound of the key in the lock and the drag of the door on the carpet.

Then the clunk of a trolley as wheels bumped over the trim.

Tess curled under the bedspread and listened to the sounds of Room Service. She caught the smell of cigarettes. The cleaner had just had a fag. She listened to the flush of the toilet and the lid of the pedal-bin ring against the wall. Then the hiss of an aerosol, and the scent of make-believe sea misted out of the bathroom.

Through a gap in the covers, she eyed the fresh roses and the bucket with the dewy champagne. She fingered the gap wider and watched the cleaner clean: a man in olive overalls, a medical mask and a cap stitched *HI*. She watched him hoover. It was exactly the way she hoovered – bumping into the furniture as if it were an inconvenience and couldn't it just get out of the way? He emptied the bins that had nothing in them. Then he picked up her shoes, put them together and tucked them under the desk.

He paused.

He took a shoe out again and searched inside for the size.

Then he turned to the bed, her shoe in his hands. There was something of Cinderella about it. 'Tess?' Arlo said. 'Is that you?'

Later, when Tess thought back to what happened next, she remembered Arlo's silver-blond hair, and running her hand through it, and thinking this is what it'd be like when they were really, really old. Fifty years from now, when it hurt too much to move and their past was another country glimpsed in dreams, they'd lie fully dressed, feeling the perfect seal of their cheeks, foot locked onto foot, the angles complementary, the pieces matching, the puzzle of the other solved.

Tess said, 'How many years since we last saw each other?'

According to the bedside clock, today was Friday 9 December. They'd been apart six days. Tess put her nose to Arlo's neck. She thought: *I want to marry you.* The Holiday Inn was in his pores. She said, 'You smell of cleaning fluids.'

And Arlo told her what had happened: how the day after their row, after blasting Bowie, and in the morning, Tess went out, Arlo had got a phone call. It was a man's voice, but odd somehow, and hard to understand with a thunderstorm in the background.

A man in a deluge? That sounded familiar. Had Agnesa made a call to Arlo too?

He was told to go to the Holiday Inn. "'Leave no notes,'" the caller said. "'And leave now.'" But Arlo didn't want Tess to come home and find him gone. He didn't want her to worry, so he'd put up a ships sign. It was: *I have a pilot on board.* It was: *H-for-Hotel.*

It was a message so obvious, Tess hadn't seen it.

She replayed that morning in her head: when she was meeting Mr Dee in the park and briefing him on the morgue, Arlo was leaving for the Holiday Inn. For the last six days, he'd worked as a hotel cleaner – in the kitchens, in the laundry, servicing empty rooms. Everyone on his cleaning team had been in the morgue, was back from the dead, and now on their way out. Every night, somebody had gone. None of the guests cast an eye in their direction. It was the perfect cover, hidden in plain sight. 'Service staff,' he said. 'No-one wants to see them.'

Jeannie lived at the hotel too, in a suite with Emma-the-dog. She was part of this whatever-it-was, this network, this string of vanishing acts. And Jeannie, who loved to chat, never said a word. In fact, Jeannie no longer spoke English – apart from 'I show you the photo, I do you the photo, you are happy with the photo,' in an accent that was hard to place. When Arlo was in the salon, they'd apparently never met. Then she'd turned up the music and avoided Arlo's eyes as she'd shaved and bleached him to the beat of *kardiochtypi.*

Tess ran her fingers through the crisp tinsel of his hair. She thought: *I want to marry you.*

Arlo watched her, his eyes moving from her hands to her arms to her chest. 'Why are you dressed as Vera?'

And Tess explained. Or tried to: why she had no clothes of her own. Why they had no flat anymore. Why she had no job anymore. 'And I'm not Tess Matthews anymore, either.'

That story took a while. As he listened, Arlo ran a palm across the bedspread, smoothed the ruckles, traced the satin flowers that had been strewn across the start of a hundred marriages. 'So, she's making a new life, as a new person, with a new name, in a new country. Is that really possible?'

Stan had done it, from St Mira to the UK, all those years ago. But he'd never got over it, the losses stayed with him. Tess pictured Agnesa leaving the plane and stepping into England – and then what? 'I hope she's safe. Or safer. And less afraid.' She got out of St Mira, at least.

And now, so could Arlo. So could they both.

Arlo's passport was the new kind, the blue kind, with the photo that Jeannie had made him resemble. Arlo ran a finger across the back – felt the rose, the thistle, the daffodil and shamrock. He flicked through, the pages stripped of design, the cover so dark it was almost black. It was the sort of thing you gave out to remember the dead. Then he recited *Life*: "'As Protestant ideas spread, a number of poets wrote poems inspired by their religious views. One of these was John Milton, who wrote *Paradise Lost*.'"

Were they going back to Paradise Lost? Or was Paradise Lost St Mira?

They were leaving on the *Pride*, Tess told him, sailing to Lampedusa and flying back from there. 'All you have to do is get on the ferry without anyone asking questions. And all I have to do is come with you. You're a Brit going home. And I'm a St Miran, immigrating to the UK and starting a job approved by the Home Office. It'll be easy.'

It wasn't going to be easy. Not with Nomie at the heart of it all. 'I just have to keep Mr Langberg sweet.'

'What does that mean?'

Tess didn't know yet. But whatever he wanted, she'd have to give it to him. Her right to be in the UK depended on Nomie.

'You mean, you're his servant? His slave?'

No, she'd be paid. But still... They propped themselves against the headboard and pondered the possibilities that the visa opened up for Nomie – having Tess on a leash and her right to be there cancellable on a whim.

Then Arlo rolled the edge of the duvet and gripped it as if it were a safety bar. He stared straight ahead, like on the big dipper at that pause at the height of the ride. They both knew what was coming because it'd always been coming, and now here it came, here it was: 'Or else we could get married?' he said.

Tess felt the slow tip forwards, the gathering rush of the fall, her insides losing their grip, the world turned upside down.

And then stillness, and sickness, and then here they were, still breathing.

Tess said, 'I thought you were never getting married.'

'Never was back then.' Because gone were the days when you could reliably say that something wouldn't happen.

Tess thought: The Big Dipper. Also called the Plough, and Polaris, and the Pole Star. Enslaved people who'd managed to escape used the Big Dipper to show them the way north.

'If marriage would get you out of Nomie's grip,' Arlo said.

But would it make any difference? Would the British let her stay just because she was his wife?

'They'd have to, wouldn't they?' A pause. 'Wouldn't *we*?'

Then they opened the champagne and for a while they drank, drifting in and out of whatever they were thinking. Tess turned her head in Arlo's direction. She saw him sideways on, the angles of his face such a known horizon. Tess remembered when he was just Hello Man, the man in the fisherman's cap who'd turned up at Dover Castle and she'd wanted to ignore him. She had no idea, when she'd taken the key from the hook, she was opening the gate to the man she was going to marry.

Then Arlo turned to her. He raised their hands, their fingers locked, as if they'd won something.

Soon those hands would be wearing rings.

Tess was sure she wanted a ring. She wanted to be Mrs Brown. She wanted any protection going for an immigrant in England.

They jumped at the sound of the telephone, then stared at it, alarmed by the reminder of the outside world. For a while, they let it ring. Then Tess reached out an arm and held the receiver to her ear.

'P for Papa.' It was a man's voice – deep and accented. 'Blue Peter.'

Tess put her hand over the mouthpiece. She repeated the message to Arlo. He said, 'All persons should appear on board. Voyage about to begin.'

Tess said to the caller, 'Is this *it*? Are we...' Was their future about to begin? Which meant Duke was already in possession of his past. Duke: who had to have known about this hotel, who'd have known all along where Arlo was, he'd set everything up so fast. And now he'd let Tess have him. 'How much time do we have?'

'None.'

Then Tess thought of Vera. She had to call and tell her to go to the dock. They couldn't leave St Mira without saying goodbye. 'How do I get an outside line?'

'There are no outside lines.'

'There have to be. That's what phones are for – they let you speak to people in other places.'

'Not in your case.'

'A message then. And urgent. Are you ready?' She didn't wait for an answer. 'Vera. Vertete.' Tess delivered the words singly down the line. 'Records. Office. Dock. *Pride*. Now.'

A grunt from the other end.

Did that mean he'd got it? 'Did you write it down?'

'Such things are not written down.'

And then the line went dead.

19.

Please give us information on how you travelled to the UK from your
home country.

PLEASE SEE OVER.

Please give details of anything that happened to you en route to
the UK.

SEE OVER.

A minicab was waiting for them outside the Holiday Inn, the rear doors open. Tess bent to get in, for a split second hung there, startled by a shadow.

'Vera?'

She was in the front seat, her face like a painting Tess knew from the cathedral: bewildered, ecstatic, lit from inside. 'I have no explanation...' Vera said. A release of her shoulders as you would at a miracle. 'The cab was just ready to take me too. He was outside the flat...' They'd set off without a word, and then she'd realised they were going to the Holiday Inn. And that had worried her. 'Perhaps something happened at your breakfast meeting and I was being called as next of kin.' But no. Nothing was wrong. In fact, everything was exactly right. She turned to Arlo, reached around the headrest, her arms out as if in rapture. 'You look wonderful!'

He didn't look wonderful. He looked like his passport photo: someone punched by events and drained and dreadful. But her eyes were fluid, and maybe through the blur she meant it was wonderful to see him.

'But how...?' Vera's eyes flicked between them. 'When...?'

Tess didn't answer. A glance in the direction of the driver. He was in reflective shades, his chin tilted upwards. He was watching the exchange in the rear-view mirror. How much could he see behind all that shine?

Then the cab moved off, which started the radio, which told them the news. The rumoured sightings of Maria and Petris in Athens were 'fake news' a government spokesman said, 'and a slight against the dead and a dishonour to this nation, which continues to grieve them.' The photos of Maria and Petris circulating on social media were 'pure fabrication, the work of AI.' He said it rote, untroubled – so what if it was the truth; who cared anymore? Tess glanced out the window, caught sight of the sea. Had Maria and Petris been spirited away just before the bomb? Maybe taken to Greece and paid to keep quiet? Were they part of Firster theatre too?

She turned to the road. They were heading east, in the direction of the dock, keeping close to the water. It wasn't the quickest route, but there was almost no traffic – a desolate stretch of concrete pitted and cracked by cargo trucks. She watched the driver drive: mindful of speed, aware of what was behind them, as if he'd only just passed his test. She said, 'I take it you know where we're going?'

Was that a nod?

Tess studied the driver. He was wrapped in a scarf, cap and jacket – more layers than needed for a job in a vehicle with heating at his fingertips. She sat behind his brown shoulders, their hump and breadth somehow familiar, like the South Downs on an autumn day. There was something English about him.

Then they stopped at a junction and he leaned forward checking for oncoming traffic. His neck was long, an ear appearing out of his scarf. Didn't she know that ear? Hadn't she seen it before? Wasn't that line a sign of something? She tapped on the glass. 'You're not...'

'I am licence number 4570.'

Arlo sat up. 'Mr Dee? What are you doing?'

The way was clear, and the cab moved off. 'What I should have done sooner.' Mr Dee had been uniquely qualified to teach *Life in the UK* – what with his memory and Anglophilia. But things had changed and so he had changed, he said. He did this now. It was his new duty: not *Life*, but something for the dead and resurrected.

They neared the dock, and there it was: the *Pride of the Strait*, a long, white tin-can of a vessel, the hull hollowed where something had hit it, the chimneys leaking black. Mr Dee pulled up and cut the engine.

They all listened to silence. No-one knew what to say.

Then Arlo wound down his window, letting in the clamour of a gang of gulls. '"That the lowest boughs and the brushwood sheaf, Round the elm-tree bole are in tiny leaf..."'

Mr Dee's chin lifted a fraction. "'While the chaffinch sings on the orchard bough, in England – Now!'" He took off his shades, the skin around his eyes soft and folded and fingered like a favourite map. 'It is hard to believe,' Mr Dee said, 'that a beautiful island can turn so ugly and so fast. But it *can*. It *has*.' He looked north-west, to where Tess and Arlo were going, to their other island. In the distance, the sea was so still and dark it could have been solid. But at the coast, the grey-brown water churned, lipped at the cliffs, tore at the land, grinding the country down.

Tess and Arlo got out of the car. Vera got out too. She handed over a carrier bag – clothes she'd retrieved from their flat while the workmen worked and the door was open. Tess took Vera in her arms and they held each other, drowning in the smell of cedarwood. Vera pinned her chin to Tess's shoulder. 'Lost,' she said.

Which applied to so many things.

They swayed on their heels in a slow, last dance. 'We're not lost, Vera. We're just not upstairs anymore.' Then Tess glanced back to where the *Pride* lumbered as if drunk in the water. 'And Albie?'

'In the freezer already, along with his grave goods.' She meant the catering-sized bags of chips and burgers and ready-battered cod. She'd had the call to say he was on board even before getting to work. 'You will let me know how Albie gets on at the other end?'

Yes, Tess would give her a ring straight away.

'And you will remember his flowers?'

How could Tess ever forget Albie's flowers? Every Midsummer's Day, she and Arlo would take a bunch of roses and re-enact the moment of their first meeting at his grave.

Then Vera told her about the text she'd had from Nomie. He hadn't done anything about the seven people due to sail today. She cast an arm at the empty ship. 'There's room for seven more on that ferry. And in England.' His text was all lower case, she said. He couldn't even be bothered with the shift key as he'd thumbed the message into his phone.

'It's not over yet. Their cases are still pending.'

'And how long will they pend? How long do they have to wait?'

Most likely, Tess thought, until they were tired of waiting. Until they gave up – that would be the Home Office plan. She said, 'I'll do what I can as soon as I get back.'

Vera brightened at that.

And she would. Tess would do whatever she could. Which probably wasn't much. What could you do about seven individuals not let into a country that didn't want them, that didn't want to know, which really couldn't care less about a few foreign people from a country they couldn't place on a map?

Then Nomie appeared at the top of the passenger walkway. He'd dressed nautically for the occasion: white chinos and a navy blue shirt. He was small, and even smaller up there, but his scarf flapped like a flag as if Nomie were an entire territory.

Vera nodded up to the ship. 'I am glad he listened in the end, that his conscience got the better of him – about *you* at least. I am happy I could do that for you.'

Tess took her hand. 'You did great things, Vera.' She wasn't going to tell her that Duke had swung it with Nomie, not her. That money had made the difference. Because Vera taking a stand against Nomie was how it should have been. Not Tess holding Duke to ransom by his inconvenient past and Duke paying whatever it took to get his records back so he could bin them.

Then thumping from the engine of the ferry. The *Pride* was fretting to go. From the speakers, a recorded message pledged to deliver excellence in the safest possible environment. Tess said, 'If Dr Kontos ever asks for help...'

'Kontos? As in your ex-boss, Duke?'

'If he ever asks for help...'

'You want to *help* Duke?'

'With any kind of paperwork...'

'You mean *my* kind of paperwork?'

The *Pride of the Strait*, the PA said, was fully equipped with state-of-the-art life-saving equipment. For the duration of the journey, passenger safety was their priority. 'And now please take a moment to identify your nearest exit.'

'Please say yes,' Tess said. 'Please help him.'

Because didn't everyone need a safe way out?

Tess and Arlo went on board. It was the first time Nomie had ever set eyes on Arlo and his eyes made a point of not settling. They brushed over him in a momentary flicker, as if Arlo were a mirage, a trick of the light. There were no greetings. Nomie strode ahead. Tess and Arlo fell into step with each other and out of step with him, their feet drumming chaos on the thin steel floor.

He stopped at the reception desk, where three crew members were waiting. 'Captain Edwards, Chief Mate Jones and Chief Steward Barker. I know how busy you are. I won't keep you long.'

Tess thought: *You're all so English, so pale and pappy.* They were like buns lined up in the window of Gregg's. Actually, she loved Gregg's. When she got to England, she'd stuff her face from Gregg's. And that made her stomach ache. She hadn't eaten since the chocolate she'd had for breakfast.

Nomie thanked the captain and his crew for overseeing the final leg of the APRIL journey. He wished them a safe and speedy passage. 'I am extremely proud,' Nomie said, 'to have headed up Project APRIL. It has been a major humanitarian effort requiring patience, cooperation, flexibility and concession.' Over his shoulder, old copies of the *The Sun*, *Mail* and *Mirror* and clocks that said it was 10am in Dover and 11am in Calais. His voice was raised over the churn of the engine, the creak of metal, the undoing of moorings. 'I am happy to say that my role in the project is now complete.'

Except Nomie didn't look happy. He looked owed and hard done by. Today, he'd be much better off thanks to Duke. But maybe this wasn't the outcome he'd banked on. He'd wanted to send an empty ship back, for the headlines to be: *Migrant boat that doesn't need stopping because there are no migrants on it.* The project would have been a triumph but for Tess. She was the one fly in the ointment. True, one immigrant was only half as bad as two. But still, she was an immigrant. The UK was accepting a foreign body and it would have to go through the motions.

The ferry throbbed away from the dock, kicking the water white, casting out lace and frills. Tess and Arlo went onto the deck. Vera stood on the dockside waving a white hankie as if surrendering to loss. Mr Dee flashed his headlights. Was that code for something? But no, that was just a finger on a lever, registering the flutter of a heart. They watched the places that they knew merge, the island shrink, the Blue Mountains turn grey, the country sink into the sea.

And then it was just wind and water in every direction, vast and unmarked, and it took a while to wonder which way they were going. 'Didn't you know?' Chief Steward Barker said. 'Lampedusa's off.' This morning, London had been in touch. They'd overruled Mr Langberg. Whoever it was had told the captain: 'Bring them all the way. Let them face the music.' Tess and Arlo would get off the *Pride* in Dover. 'They need some news, apparently. It's Christmas, gone quiet. They want reality TV, some proper drama.' Then he showed them to sofas in the Club Lounge and said to make themselves at home. They'd be here for the next ten days. He threw them blankets, said they could wash in the toilets, the daily hot meal was at one. There were vending machines all over the shop if they got hungry. 'I take it you've got sterling.'

They lived on St Mira; they didn't carry pounds around.

So Arlo withdrew cash from the ATM and the chief steward turned it into coins so they could feed themselves confectionery as they made their way along the north coast of Africa.

Arlo spent the journey becoming an expert on the *Pride*. After so many years teaching *Life*, he couldn't help memorising facts. He recited them to Tess: that when it was built in 1990, it was called *Highway to Europe*; that it had a passenger capacity of two thousand; that it was registered now in Durrës, and flying under an Albanian flag because Europe no longer applied.

Tess managed a distant smile when he told her things like that, listening and soon forgetting. She spent the journey picking up the news on the radio – first in Greek and Arabic, then as the days passed, in Italian and Spanish. And on the evening they sailed through the Straits of Gibraltar and turned the corner and headed north, Arlo burst into the lounge with a bagful of pound coins. He'd hit the jackpot in the gaming arcade. It was a lucky sign. He fed her Maltesers that he'd bought from a vending machine – sweet English things, he said. 'It means everything's going to be all right.'

Was it though?

She wondered about Tess Matthews. Where was she now? Not in Dover, or Elmer would have called to say so. Tess pictured her on the train from Euston to Birmingham then Birmingham to Smethwick. Several St Mirans had married Brown Sauce men and tried to make a life in the Midlands. Maybe she'd started off there.

Tess wondered about her job. Had Noam Langberg International really been approved by the Home Office? Did Nomie have a sponsor code? Could she trust that visa? She was worried about her seventy points and how loseable they were. She didn't want to be a foreigner in England. She didn't think that being Arlo's wife would make any difference. They'd changed the rules, hadn't they? *They'd* changed too, hadn't they – the English?

And then, on the tenth day, as the sun was starting to sink, over the PA: 'Attention all passengers. We will shortly be arriving in Dover. We hope you have enjoyed sailing with us and to see you onboard again soon.'

Tess and Arlo went onto the deck to watch the approach of England. The cliffs lay on the horizon like a line of crushed millennia. Arlo waved at them. He called hello. He seemed happier about England than she'd ever known him. Perhaps that was what happened when your presence wasn't questioned, when you weren't unwelcome: you liked a place, you felt warm towards it.

'That chalk,' Arlo said, 'runs under the Channel and comes out the other side as the other white cliffs, the French ones, the Côte d'Albâtre.' Not that anyone would know that – apart from the French.

Seagulls had joined them, hovering like balloons tethered to the ferry. Tess watched England loom larger. She could see the town now, radio masts on the top of the hill, the original Dover castle.

Arlo said, 'The Channel tunnel doesn't go in a straight line from one side to the other. It follows a layer of chalk.'

He knew that because of Elmer. Dear Elmer. He'd know what to do about England. He'd make sure it was going to be all right.

Tess said, 'Wait for me here. I just need to do something,' and she went inside and found a quiet corner. She called the Browns' number. It had barely started to ring and Elmer picked up.

'Hello, love. I was just thinking about you.'

Hearing his voice made her want to cry.

He said, 'The ferry's all over the news. They're saying a boatload of immigrants is heading towards Dover.'

'Who's saying?'

'On the news.'

Where was Elmer getting it from now?

'They're calling it a taxi service for illegals.'

'There's only Arlo and me on it.' And Albie. What was she going to do about Albie?

There'd been protests on the quay, Elmer said, and Joy had gone down there to set them straight. '"My own son is on that boat. You have *no idea* what brings people here. You have *no idea* what anyone on that boat has been through."' Then someone had punched her and Joy had landed one back. She was in Buckland Hospital now with a fractured jaw.

Tess listened to Elmer tell the story. She listened to the throttle of the engine. And in her head: *That the lowest boughs and the brushwood sheaf, Round the elm-tree bole are in tiny leaf...* How many Englands were there?

Then over the PA: 'Will car drivers please make their way to the car deck. Foot passengers assemble at your exit. Please remember all your belongings.'

All of Tess's belongings were in one bag.

Elmer said, 'I'll be there to meet you. We got a call this morning. We're next of kin. They're docking you round the back. Threat of another firebomb. Not sure they can contain the fray.'

'Thanks, Elmer.' Tess heard how exhausted she was. 'I can't wait to see you.'

'Are you all right, love?'

'Fine. I'm fine.' No she wasn't. She'd spent ten days cooped up on a ferry, having chips for lunch that had been stored next to Albie, playing out the future in her head, and worrying about getting into England.

'It must be very upsetting, uprooting yourselves like that. One minute you're there, next minute you're gone.'

'If I actually belonged somewhere, Elmer, I think I'd probably feel lost.' Would anywhere feel like a place she could settle? The white cliffs were up against the boat now. She could see wafer-thin strata of billions of creatures that had drifted here, and died, and turned the sea a milky blue, and over millennia, been pressed so hard their bones made rock.

The gangway off the ferry was steep, tipping them out of the *Pride* and onto land. Tess stepped into a purple dusk. The tarmac was soft, could almost have been carpet. It was quiet for a dock, for a return, for all the apparent fuss. In the distance, metal blundered into metal – three ringing blows, as if this were theatre and now please take your seats.

In front of them, a shingled, single-storey building, the windows papered with posters, the woodwork glossed over, a doormat worn through by smokers. Tess and Arlo were the only passengers in Arrivals and a single border guard ushered them in. She was bulky, stuffed into her uniform, her chest thick with kit. She had the kind of build that would have no trouble blocking your way into the country.

They waited in front of the passport booth, behind the yellow line. In the booth, a man watched them, his face grey and ruled like a ledger, half-moon spectacles lit by his desk-lamp. Over his shoulder, the Dos and Don'ts: *No phones. No photography. No smoking. Sanitise your hands.*

And then, 'If you'd like to come forward, sir!' It was a stagey invitation, as if Arlo had been pulled from the audience and into the glare of the show.

Arlo went up and handed over his documents. He took off his fisherman's cap, and there it was: his shock of off-white hair that had started the journey as a source of light, but was dulled and crumpled and looked now like a dandelion clock.

The man breezed through his passport – a glance at a few pages that he knew by heart. Arlo was a formality: a Briton coming home.

He slid the passport back with a 'Thank you, sir!' Then the exit doors opened, and Arlo went through. He turned to Tess. He pressed a hand to his heart. He made a heart with his hands. He mouthed: *Marry me.* And then the doors shut. Tess watched, and carried on watching, waiting for the curtain call, for Arlo to appear again, bowing and blowing kisses.

But he didn't.

Instead, 'Good evening, Miss. And how are we today?'

She turned, saw the nod, went up to the passport booth and put her documents on the counter. She was alone – that's how she was. And exhausted. And nauseous. The rest of her life depended on what happened next. 'I'm very well, thank you.'

'And where have we come from today?'

Today? The sun had risen somewhere off the coast of Brittany. 'The ferry journey started in St Mira.'

'St Where-a?' A glance at her over his half-moon spectacles.

Did he really not know? 'It's an island in the Mediterranean. Near Malta. Near Crete.'

'Been to Malta. Fond of Malta.' He unfolded Nomie's paperwork. 'Wouldn't mind trying Crete.' He pressed the creases out with a palm, ran a finger along the pages. 'So, you've come to the United Kingdom to live and work.'

She wasn't sure if she'd actually have to work for Nomie. She had no idea what was expected of her. But probably he'd be glad never to see her again. 'That's right.'

'As a what?'

'As a Senior Analyst of St Miran Affairs.'

'Starting when?'

'Immediately.'

'Salary?'

'£25,600.' It was the lowest salary Nomie could offer that scored her twenty points.

'Correct.'

Was this a quiz? She looked at him with a question, saw lips drawn as two lines, pencil-thin and lead-grey. They could have been an equals sign – though nothing here was equal.

He picked up her St Miran passport, turned it landscape, took his time with the engravings of the Blue Mountains, the ancient monasteries, the jagged coastline, perusing it like a travel brochure. Then he turned to her photo and read the personal details. 'So, this name of yours... *Tess*. Is it short for something?'

Yes, but only for those with the right to know.

He waited. He ran fingers along the spine of her passport, as if feeling for a point of weakness. 'Have you forgotten?'

Did this man have the right to know? Did he, in fact, know anyway? People like him had power, their reach was everywhere. Did he already know what only a handful knew: what Arlo and Stan knew, and Nomie and Duke?

'No.'

'Meaning?'

'No, it's not short for something.'

He placed the passport face down on his desk. 'Let's go with Tess, then. Is it a common name over there?'

'My mother was British.'

'So, the Petrou comes from your father?'

Tess nodded.

'So, *he's* St Miran.'

No, he was Greek. 'My mother's father was St Miran.' She meant Stan. Konstantinos Matzarakis. Stanley Matthews.

'So this connection with St Mira is some way off, then. Quite tenuous really.'

What did he mean by that? The light in his spectacles seemed to be waning. The moon was going out.

'Because, if I'm honest, you sound English to me. Perfectly, one hundred per cent English.'

Tess reached a hand to the counter as if to take her papers back, but his palm stayed on them. He beckoned to the border guard, who came over, swaggering like a pantomime dame: booted feet, eyebrows arched, hand wringing and rattling her jewellery: truncheon, walkie-talkie, handcuffs.

They conferred in whispers.

Tess thought: *It's behind you.* She turned and saw the door. A few meters between here and running. Should she run? Could she outrun the Home Office – that state-within-a-state with its own police and prisons? Which had the power to spy on you, raid your home, lock you up for as long as they liked, and deport you? Her eyes shifted to the window and the message frosted into the glass: *Welcome to the UK Border*. Not to the UK. Not to a country. You were welcome to this Borderland, this hall of lino, neon, melamine and plastic, where everything was artificial – even the laws, made up as they went along.

Then a hand made a grab for her – a swipe and an armlock – and the officer pulled Tess to her chest. 'Would you like to step this way, Miss?'

They walked to the back of Arrivals, Tess hanging from her arm like a ventriloquist's doll. In her head: *Don't say a word. Not a word.*

They stopped at an unmarked door. The guard reached for the handle. 'We won't detain you long.'

Detain?

Tess looked at her fingers: fatty, ringed, forceful. Would she soon be pressing her thumb to Tess's fingertips, taking the perfect prints?

The guard made a move to open the door – and then she stopped. 'But before we go through, one minor matter.'

Tess knew this moment. She'd seen it in dramas, that last-minute pause to pose the question on which the story turned.

'You're Tess *who*, exactly?

And there it was.

Who – exactly – was she?

1.

What is your FULL name?

TESS PETROU.

Have you ever used any other name?

No.

What is your name? Questions like that should be so easy to answer, but in times like these, what do you do? Nothing is clear cut, no truth simple, no life unweighed against another.

Tess listened to footsteps coming down the corridor, the tread heavy, ponderous, bored. She knew who it was, what she'd say, the look she'd give her. Henry. Or the woman she'd come to call Henry. It was the sheer breadth of her, and the red hair, and the Border Force badge that shone on her chest like a livery collar.

The footsteps stopped outside her door, then the drawn-out pause, the play of keys and the rough slice of metal as the lock disengaged.

'How far have we got, then?' She chewed on her jowls. 'Any chance we're done yet?' though she was turning away already.

Tess checked the pages, made sure nothing was blank. She remembered that from exams: always put something. Anything. Anything might score you points. 'Yes,' Tess said. 'I'm done.'

That caught Henry off-balance. She swung her weight back into the room. 'Shall I sample the oeuvre?'

Tess handed the form over and watched her small, black eyes land like full-stops on each page. It took her ages. But then, everything here took ages. Minutes were hours and hours were days. Tess didn't know how long she'd been in this room with the flat-pack bed and desk and chair, and the grey walls with the skirt of pink. Pink was meant to be a calming colour – she'd heard that somewhere – which was why they used it in prisons. Though this wasn't a prison. It was an STHC, a Short Term Holding Centre. A short term that was already so long that time had lost its markers. There was no rhythm, no beat. The heart of the day had stopped.

But every so often in this eternity, Henry had come by and asked about the form. And every time, Tess had thought: *A Bomb Scenario Clearly Helps Patriots.* She'd thought about Henry's wives, and what had happened to them, and how uncertain their world had become by marrying him. She'd pictured her own wedding with Arlo, and how the opposite would be true: that their world was already uncertain and marriage would be a bond that made them safer.

'Thorough,' Henry said. 'Though we still need a signature.' She pointed to where. 'And a date.'

'What day is it?'

'The twenty-fourth.' A glance at her watch – chunky and cheap. Was she doing overtime and keen to knock off? 'Home in time for Christmas.' Henry cleared her throat. 'So we're happy, are we, Ms Petrou, that this form is complete and correct to the best of our knowledge.'

'Yes.'

'And we're aware, are we, of the legal implications of knowingly providing inaccurate or incomplete information, as set out in the Notes?'

Tess hadn't read them.

Henry handcuffed herself to Tess. Close up, she smelt of spearmint, which was the chewing gum she kept in her cheek. 'So if you'd care to follow me.' They stepped into the corridor. Henry moved with the sideways shunt of a body unbalanced by its own weight. They walked in awkward tandem through locked-up air and the stench of sour bodies and sweet canteen food. Outside, blank walls topped with barbed wire and the pivot of birds on the wind. They followed a maze through key-swipe doors and into parts of the building Tess had no idea existed.

And then, there it was: the first sign to *Release*.

They went into a windowless room that was lined with lockboxes labelled in Border Force code. There was something of a cemetery about it: one box per inmate. Henry undid the cuffs. She took Tess's prints, took her photograph, and sent them off on her phone. Then she unlocked a box and reached inside. 'Your passport.' She placed it on the table. 'Your employment contract. Visa. Keys. Phone.' She lined them up in front of Tess like a royal flush: Ten, Jack, Queen, King, Ace. 'If you'd care to check everything's in order?'

Tess scanned the documents and they were as she remembered them. Those were the keys to her life in Exodus Square. She tried her phone, found the battery flat.

Then Henry got a text – confirmation of what they both knew: the prints and photo were a positive match. Tess had stayed Tess all the time she'd been kept here; no miracles; no turning into somebody else.

Henry's hand went back into the lockbox. 'And then there's this.' There was a flourish to the way she moved, a finality to it, like a referee with a red card.

It was a passport.

A British one.

'What's that?' Not the Joker?

'It's yours.'

Tess knew what it was and she didn't want to take it.

'She was stopped at the airport,' Henry said. 'We knew Agnesa was on the plane.'

The name 'Agnesa' rang like a misplaced echo. It belonged to a person who didn't exist anymore, a name left behind on St Mira. Tess looked at the floor, saw Henry's shoes: outsized, thick-soled, government issue. How far had Tess Matthews got? Not Dover. Not Smethwick. Maybe not even into the country. Had she been detained in this No-Man's Land too? Tess said, 'Where is she now?'

'Sahara.' A slap of her chewing gum. She'd relished saying that. 'No... *not* the desert.' Henry meant the women's unit at Colnbrook, the Immigration Removal Centre next to Heathrow.

'She mustn't be deported.'

A key went back in the lockbox. Henry wasn't interested. 'Not my department.'

Tess said, 'You know she can claim asylum.'

'She can't claim asylum.' The key turned in the lock.

'She'll be in danger if she's sent to St Mira.'

'So let her claim asylum then. Fat chance she'll get it.'

And that was true.

St Mira didn't count as dangerous. And even if it did, would anyone care?

Henry slid her thumbs through the loops on her waistband. She addressed the blank space between her and Tess. 'Your room with be cleared of any personal effects and they will be sent, Royal Mail, recorded delivery, to an address given in section five of your form.' She'd said it so often the words blurred. 'The room will be inventorised and inspected for damage.'

That wouldn't take long: it was bed, desk, chair.

'Any replacements or repairs will be charged at standard rates. If you wish to lodge an objection, please do so in writing, with supporting evidence, within two weeks of receipt of the invoice.' Henry presented a checklist and a biro. Tess confirmed that she'd understood the release procedure, that she'd received the itemised items. She signed *Tess Petrou*.

'You can drop that now you know.'

Yes, she knew. But she'd never be Tess Matthews again. She'd given that person away and Agnesa had been forced to give her up. She'd twice been surrendered and now she was spent.

Then Henry handed Tess a leaflet. It told her the buses from here to the centre of Dover, the address of Citizens Advice, the location of an emergency hostel, connections to London, the number for the police and ambulance services. *Welcome to the United Kingdom*, it said.

'All done.' It sounded like the end of a check-up, not the end of five days' detention. She moved towards the door. Then, as if an afterthought, 'There's a man waiting in reception.' Henry nodded in that direction. 'A Mr Brown?' said as a question, as if the name might be unfamiliar.

Then: *Best of luck! Happy Christmas!*

That was what Tess heard in her head. Actually, Henry left without a word, didn't look back, just let the door slam shut.

Arlo stood by the *EXIT* sign, shimmering under a neon light. He was wearing clothes she'd never seen before. He must have been shopping. They made him look like somebody else, someone neat and English. Arlo was smaller than she remembered him too, and slight and fretful. But he was still in his fisherman's cap, which marked him out as not really from here, and meant his sky might be about to fall in. He waved wide, as if Tess might not have seen him, might not recognise him now.

Tess waved back – a comic little wave like the ones she gave him right at the start when he ran the projector at StUKCO and said 'hello' as if he meant 'goodbye'. Slowly she approached him. She wanted to remember this moment, this meeting, this exit that was also an entry, this homecoming. She pinched the corners of her eyes, felt the wet. She thought she caught a trace of citronella, of Karelias cigarettes, but it was a trick of the mind, a trick of the heart.

And then, here in front of her, stood a blurred vision of the man she'd always known.

Arlo was holding a flower.

It was a rose.

A red one.

He held it like a microphone. Was he about to make an announcement, to ask her something important?

*

Tess said, 'Bombs are falling all the time somewhere in the world. But that one was different because that bomb fell on us.' It was one year exactly from events at Amyna, when a five-hundred-pound burst of TNT cracked open the midsummer sky; one year on from a brief dawn at dusk that meant Tess and Arlo were leaving.

And now they'd arrived, and here they were sitting against the castle wall above the white cliffs of Dover. Tess cast an arm in the direction of St Mira. Their other island was 1,500 miles away, south-east, across an ocean channel and a continent and a sea. 'And lost now to darkness.'

St Mira was two hours ahead and the sun had already set.

That morning, soon after sunrise, they'd taken the train to London and laid roses on Albie's grave. His remains, such as they were, had been cremated and buried in a cemetery not far from the Thames with a view across the river to where he'd grown up. *Albert Vertete*, his plaque said:

Born sadly Newham London 1945
Blown on stormy seas to his destiny
Died contentedly Mirapolis 2002
Reinterred Greenwich 2023

'Nothing that we do is done in vain.'

Tess and Arlo had taken photos and sent them straight over, and as soon as Vera got them, she'd rung. She sounded glad and grateful, and weary and a long way off. She stayed on the phone as if it were a lifeline and talked about St Mira. She didn't know what was going to happen, she said. She didn't really know what was happening right now. She didn't even know what had already happened: it took time to make sense of things, and by then events had overtaken you; you were always at a loss.

Vera didn't know anything about Agnesa. Neither did Tess. Sahara wouldn't answer enquiries if you weren't related or a legal brief. She'd been swallowed by a system of retribution – could be here, could be there – and now she was gone, probably for ever.

Vera didn't know what had happened to the seven pending cases who weren't given space on the *Pride*. She'd tried to find out from Mr Langberg, but he never returned her calls. Tess had heard from Nomie, though. Word must have reached him that she didn't need his visa anymore because soon after Christmas, a letter had arrived terminating her employment with NLI.

Vera didn't know what had happened to Rron and Rrock, how they could have changed so much. She barely saw them now. None of the neighbours talked to her – not Mr and Mrs

Moros, nor Rron and Rrock, nor the St Miran couple who'd moved in upstairs with their three children. 'Everyone in this block is unhappy. And that makes them happy. Or satisfied, or justified, or something.'

'And how are *you*, Vera?' Though Tess knew the answer. Vera was alone. She missed Tess and Arlo.

'Unwanted.' Tess listened to Vera's sipped-at breathing and the smothered roar of the A205. 'No-one likes foreigners and no-one likes me because I won't go along with it. But then, having someone to dislike makes them feel better.'

Tess reached for Arlo's hand. 'You have to leave, Vera.'

'Yes.'

'Can you?'

'No.'

'What about Mr Dee?'

Once or twice, Vera had seen his cab, a ghostly streak of beige creeping down a side street. But not for a while now – she didn't know what had happened.

'Or Jeannie?'

Vera didn't know where Jeannie was – probably still at the Holiday Inn. But the networks were being picked apart, the routes out failing.

'But I do know the truth about Duke,' Vera said.

There was a pause. Tess glanced into the distance: Victorian headstones were tilted by time and stripped by the weather; the bare-knuckle fingers of the O2 arena; across the river, the naked glare of Canary Wharf. Then down the line, 'Please tell me happy things,' Vera said.

And there were happy things to tell her.

Tess said that they were happy here in England. Or happi*er*. Or safe, anyway. That England was OK in many ways. Or in some ways, if you chose your time and place and people. She said that they were happy to be married, and that tonight they'd be at Dover Castle to raise a toast, as they always had.

And now, here they were, at the end of the longest day, the English Channel at their feet, flat and black and busy. Lorries at the dock had got into line, their roofs laid out like a long game of patience. Every now and then, the echo of metal and the grate of gears. Heat rose, bringing the smell of salt and diesel. And above it all, gulls soared and tilted, the last sun lighting up their undersides.

Arlo raised his glass. 'Happy us,' he said.

Tess took a sip. It was Kit's Coty, grown in Kent, and tasted like the wine Vera used to give them from the woman in Euphoria Valley. 'To mark your wedding,' she'd always said when she presented them with the bottle. And now Tess and Arlo were officially married, and a legal document witnessed by Elmer and Joy, was lodged in the General Register Office. Because Tess and Arlo had always known and finally made it fact that they were settled together in this unsettled world – for better for worse, for richer for poorer, in sickness and in health, as long as they both shall live.

'To you, Arlo.'

'To you, Tess Petrou. To you, Tess Brown.'

Above them, the darkness began to shine. There was the moon, and close by Venus. And then in the east, the night's first stars – light years apart and bonded in patterns since people chose to name them. That was the Summer Triangle: Vega, Deneb, Altair.

On the water, the lights of little boats made their own brief constellations. Some of the lights, they knew, would grow bigger and closer and then touch land. And some would rock and sway, nameless and overburdened. And then they would go out.

Notes on source material

The questions at the start of each section are adapted from Home Office and UK Visa and Immigration forms, all accessible on the internet.

Chapter 3

'he ran the Life in the UK course, which followed the bestselling *Life in the UK Test Handbook*': All quotes from the handbook are taken from the *Life in the UK Test Handbook*, Dillon, H. & Smith A. (eds.), Red Squirrel Publishing (2022).

Chapter 4

'Ladies and gentlemen, I am deeply moved. Thank you all for coming. What a *momentous* show of support.': Details are taken from notes I made at a rally of the far-right Alternative for Germany (AfD) in Zeulenroda, 25 October 2019, addressed by Björn Höcke.

'Parts of St Mira are unrecognisable': Nigel Farage claimed in 2014 that parts of Britain were 'unrecognisable' and 'like a foreign land'. He had also claimed he felt 'awkward' when he heard people speaking other languages on the train. From www.hopenothate.org.uk (accessed 03.06.2020)

Chapter 5

'a swarm of people coming across the Mediterranean': The then British Prime Minister, David Cameron, talked about 'a swarm of people coming across the Mediterranean,' in July 2015. See for instance: www.theguardian.com/uk-news/2015/jul/30/david-cameron-migrant-swarm-language-condemned

'mugs that said *Controls on Immigration*': In 2015, the British Labour Party issued mugs printed with 'Controls on Immigration.'

'The Foreign Minister was rousing herself with her own oratory': Her remarks are taken from the speech 'Defence in Global Britain,' delivered by the then British Defence Secretary, Gavin Williamson, to the Royal United Services Institute in Whitehall on 11 February 2019. The full transcript of his speech is at: https://www.gov.uk/government/speeches/defence-in-global-britain

'Two-thirds of Exodus Square was on its feet, scoring the air with rattles and releasing red balloons': Details are taken from notes I made at the end-of-campaign election rally of the Alternative for Germany (AfD) in Erfurt, 31 August 2024. In this case, the balloons were in the shape of aeroplanes intended for the 'remigration' of criminal foreigners.

Chapter 6

'As we finally have our great country back': The note in Tess and Arlo's hallway is taken from a sign entitled 'Happy Brexit Day' posted in a block of flats in Norwich shortly after the EU referendum. The original contains typographical and grammatical errors in a sentence about language. See for instance: www.theguardian.com/politics/2020/feb/01/police-called-in-after-poster-tells-residents-of-flats-to-speak-english

'The freeborn people of St Mira': This line is adapted from Boris Johnson's comment during the 2020 Covid lockdown on the 'ancient, inalienable right of free-born people of the United Kingdom to go to the pub.' See for instance: https://www.reuters.com/article/us-health-coronavirus-britain-pubs-idUSKBN21732F

Chapter 7

'*GO HOME OR FACE ARREST*': This was a 2013 slogan that appeared on vans touring six London boroughs. The pilot programme was codenamed Operation Vaken and was part of the Home Office's hostile environment policy. *Hostile Environment*, Maya Goodfellow, Verso Books (2019) p.6

Chapter 8

'DEPRIVATION OF ST MIRAN CITIZENSHIP': The wording of Arlo's letter is taken from Home Office UK Border Agency Deprivation of British Citizenship notices, accessible online.

'It's only water, do you not bathe?': This interaction taken from *Hostile Environment*, Maya Goodfellow, Verso Books (2019) p.22

'I'm not here to be helpful.': This is adapted from an article in the *Guardian*, 3 May 2018. See www.theguardian.com/uk-news/2018/may/03/home-office-official-tells-man-facing-deportation-my-job-is-to-piss-you-off

'No phones.': At immigration reporting centres, phone use is proscribed. 'Because they know that if you use your phone you can record something. If you use your phone, they'll kick you out.' *Hostile Environment*, Maya Goodfellow, Verso Books (2019) p.22

Chapter 9

'I'd don khaki': In 2017, Nigel Farage claimed he would 'don khaki, pick up a rifle and head for the front lines' if Theresa May failed to deliver Brexit properly. See for instance: https://hopenothate.org.uk/chapter/who-is-nigel-farage/

'We are policy experts. We are delivery practitioners.': The statement from Noam Langberg International is taken from the website of the Tony Blair Institute for Global Change. See https://www.institute.global/what-we-do/approach

Chapter 11

'Weren't they going to repatriate them and sink the rescue boats?': Italy's Prime Minister, Giorgia Meloni, leader of the Brothers of Italy party, has said that Rome should 'repatriate migrants and sink the boats that rescued them'. See for instance: www.theguardian.com/world/2022/nov/15/writer-roberto-saviano-to-go-on-trial-for-comments-about-italy-pm-giorgia-meloni

'Twenty-five thousand people have gone missing in the Mediterranean': That was the figure at the time the story is set, but the number continues to rise. Between 2014, when the UN's Missing Migrants Project began, and late 2024 (when this novel went to print), more than thirty thousand migrants were dead or missing in the Mediterranean. See https://missingmigrants.iom.int/region/mediterranean

'where most boats went: Morocco to Gibraltar, or Libya to Italy, or Turkey to Greece':
From www.missingmigrants.iom.int/region/mediterranean

'It's a processing centre, not a detention centre – though even if it were, it wouldn't be a first.': Until the 1990s, the UK didn't have any permanent detention centres; people were put in prisons or held in a converted car ferry called the Earl William. *Hostile Environment*, Maya Goodfellow, Verso Books (2019) p.25

'I've got doctors – specialist paediatricians – who can tell how old a child is just by X-raying their teeth.': Non-EU spouses and family members have long been treated with suspicion, and children's teeth and wrists are X-rayed to try to ascertain their age. *Hostile Environment*, Maya Goodfellow, Verso Books (2019) pp.16-17

Chapter 12

'I'll be just another suicide.': Between 2000 and 2023, 40 people have died by suicide while in immigration detention in England and Wales. Between the end of July 2020 and December 2020, when the Home Office was operating a programme of 'compressed' charter flights, one-third of the detainees at Brook House immigration removal centre near Gatwick were placed on constant suicide watch. See: https://www.inquest.org.uk/deaths-of-immigration-detainees and https://www.theguardian.com/uk-news/2021/may/21/uk-asylum-seekers-at-unprecedented-risk-of-suicide-amid-deportation-threat

Chapter 14

'they'd check the Safe Country of Origin list': What counts as a Safe Country of Origin varies from country to country. For information on the UK, see: https://asylumineurope.org/reports/country/united-kingdom/asylum-procedure/the-safe-country-concepts/safe-country-origin/

Chapter 16

'What is St Mira, Atlas?': The exchange between Atlas
and Mrs Pappas is taken from the Patriotic Alternative
publications *Be Proud of Your People* and *The People of
England*.

'Can we all count to four?': The four criteria in the 'Definition
of Ethnicity' is from the Patriotic Alternative. See: https://
www.patrioticalternative.org.uk/khan_hirsch_and_lammy
(accessed 29.08.2024)

'abstractions such as "humanity"': This part of Varela's Our
Own speech is taken from the Britain First document
'Globalism or Nationalism'. See: www.britainfirst.org/
globalism_or_nationalism (accessed 25.03.2021)

'For morality to function': This discussion of morality –
including the reference to every ant in the grass – is taken
from *Flying Free*, Nigel Farage, Biteback Publishing (2011)
pp.287-288

Chapter 19

'They're calling it a taxi service for illegals.': Nigel Farage
accused the Royal National Lifeboat Institution of running a
migrant taxi service and facilitating illegal immigration. See
for instance: https://www.bbc.com/news/uk-65893789

'Threat of another firebomb.': Firebombs were launched at a
migrant detention centre in Dover on 30 October 2022, just a
few weeks before Tess and Arlo arrive at the port.
See for instance: www.theguardian.com/uk-news/2022/nov
/05/dover-firebomb-attack-motivated-by-terrorist-ideology-
police-say

'that state-within-a-state': The description of the Home Office comes from Danny Trilling, author of *Lights in the Distance: Exile and Refuge at the Borders of Europe* (2018). For this specific quote, see: https://www.theguardian.com/politics/2021/may/13/cruel-paranoid-failing-priti-patel-inside-the-home-office

Chapter 20

'Nothing that we do is done in vain.': The quote on Albert Vertete's plaque comes from *A Tale of Two Cities* by Charles Dickens.

Acknowledgements

I would like to acknowledge all the writers and the books that the world will never read because the market calculates they're not worth supporting. This novel was only possible thanks to Kevin and Hetha Duffy and the team of courageous and imaginative people at Bluemoose Books. I make special mention of Lin Webb, editor and magician, who knows more than it's possible to know and sees further than any eye can see.

I drew on several non-fiction books to write *The Accidental Immigrants*, and as novels have no bibliography, I'd like to thank Maya Goodfellow for *Hostile Environment*, Danny Trilling for *Lights in the Distance* and *Bloody Nasty People*, and Dina Nayeri for *The Ungrateful Refugee*.

My thanks to dear Andrew Wille, who for over a decade has pointed the way for me and taken 'the utmost care and kindness in all things'. Herzlichen Dank to Bianca for sitting in German graveyards, and listening and laughing, and helping keep this English soul alive.

I thank Töffe for his on-going support of the arts, and Is – a true believer – for being ready when all else fails. I want to remember Dave Armour who died while I was writing this book. It was he and his wife, Pauline, who, fifty years ago first showed me the way into other people's lives.

And the other life that I hold most dear is my beloved Guy, also an accidental immigrant, who stood beside me and said all the things that matter, and who gives me courage in the face of what might come.